Also by Frances Quinn

The Smallest Man

THAT BONESETTER WOMAN

Frances Quinn

SIMON &
SCHUSTER

London · New York · Sydney · Toronto · New Delhi

First published in Great Britain by Simon & Schuster UK Ltd, 2022
This paperback edition first published 2023

1 3 5 7 9 10 8 6 4 2

Simon & Schuster UK Ltd
1st Floor
222 Gray's Inn Road
London WC1X 8HB

Simon & Schuster Australia,
Sydney

Simon & Schuster India,
New Delhi

www.simonandschuster.co.uk
www.simonandschuster.com.au
www.simonandschuster.co.in

A CIP catalogue record for this book is available from the British Library

Paperback ISBN: 978-1-4711-9347-7
eBook ISBN: 978-1-4711-9346-0
Audio ISBN: 978-1-3985-1446-1

Typeset in the UK by Palimpsest Book Production Ltd,
Falkirk, Stirlingshire
Printed and Bound in the UK using
100% Renewable Electricity at CPI Group (UK) Ltd

MIX
Paper | Supporting
responsible forestry
FSC
www.fsc.org
FSC® C171272

To my husband, Mike Jeffree, and my furry marketing
assistants, Nalle, Siggi and Freya

Chapter 1

It's usual, they say, for a young person coming to London for the first time to arrive with a head full of dreams. Well, Endurance Proudfoot did not. When she stepped off the coach from Sussex, on a warm and sticky afternoon in the summer of 1757, it never occurred to her that the city would be the place where she'd make her fortune; she was just very annoyed to be arriving there at all.

'We're here, Durie. We're in London!' said her sister Lucinda, blue eyes sparkling (though London couldn't take credit for that; barring the times when they filled with tears, real or otherwise, Lucinda's eyes always sparkled). 'Aren't you even a bit excited?'

'No,' said Durie, and pointed out their bags to the coachman handing down the baggage from the roof. It had been a long day. Eight hours of bumping and jolting in the coach, six spent listening to a dumpling-faced woman who'd boarded with her husband at Uckfield, and spent the journey pointing out things they could plainly see for themselves – 'That's a big oak tree', 'Here comes another coach', 'Lots of folk in Tunbridge today', 'That woman's got a pink bonnet on' – until Durie began to think the people with cheap tickets, perched up behind the coachman, had the best of the situation. The husband answered each remark with a smile and a nod – did he really not find her annoying at all? – and entertained himself by watching the effect of the rutted roads on Lucinda's bosoms.

The mystery of his tolerance was solved when, at last, they pulled up in the cobbled courtyard of the inn that was the coach's final destination, and his wife asked him whether he thought it might rain. On getting the usual nod and smile, she'd slapped his arm and said, 'You fool, you've sat with your deaf ear towards me again!' Lucinda caught Durie's eye and winked, hoping to share a laugh at their expense, but Durie wasn't going to be got round that easily. It was Lucinda's fault they were there, when Durie had good reason to wish they weren't, and if Lucinda thought she was going to 'think of it as an adventure', like she'd said as they waited for the coach that morning, she could go and scratch.

Durie had wondered if her sister's looks might be quite everyday in London, but of course they weren't: with the biggest, bluest eyes you'd ever see, skin like fresh cream and thick curls that could have been actual gold spun into hair, she stood out even there. She was like a doll, and not any old doll but one the doll maker had slaved over to make perfect, throwing away two or three versions before he got it just right. Even before their baggage was piled on the cobbles, she'd attracted admiring glances from two soldiers and a costermonger with a basket of apples on his head, who weren't to know that slender waist wouldn't be slender much longer. And now look at her, twinkling at a foppish-looking youth in a canary-yellow coat, who could have been just about anyone. A good job Durie was here, even if she didn't want to be, because otherwise, who knew what kind of trouble Lucinda might stroll into? She might, at nineteen, be two years older than Durie, but she didn't have the sense she was born with, and that couldn't have been a lot.

A porter appeared.

'Carry your bags, girls?'

'No, thank you, I can take them,' said Durie. 'But could you direct us to South Audley Street?'

He looked at their baggage, and in particular the trunk their stepmother had packed with everything Lucinda would need in the coming months, and laughed.

'That's a good long walk. Call it sixpence, and I'll carry all this and show you the way.'

'There's no need,' said Durie, hefting up the trunk and balancing it against her shoulder, then picking up the bag with her free hand. The porter's mouth dropped open.

'Blimey. Was your father a packhorse?'

'Can you give us directions,' she said, 'or shall I ask someone with a civil tongue in their head?'

He scowled but told them the way and he was right, it was a good long walk. Which would have been fine at home, but the London streets were so busy! They made Lewes, even on market day, look like a little village. You couldn't move for hawkers and costermongers, yelling out their wares – in the first hundred yards alone, they had to dodge a rabbit seller with six furry carcases strung from a pole, a knife grinder's cart, and a woman carrying a basket piled high with silver salmon, bellowing that they were straight out of the river and waving one about for potential buyers to sniff. Not much room to get out of anyone's way either, with carriages and carts trundling by, their wheels churning up clouds of dust and dirt from the dry streets, and releasing the stench of horse muck to join the coal smoke hanging in the air.

After a while the streets got wider and smarter-looking, with great long stretches of shops, the sun glinting off their windows. What could they all find to sell? People dawdled about like idiots, looking in the windows and pointing things out to each other. What with them and the hawkers – selling flowers and fripperies now, but just as numerous – and the carriages and carts, it was impossible to walk at any kind of a pace. Lucinda stopping to buy a posy of violets didn't help – she couldn't just pay for the stupid things, she had to chitchat to the girl – and the last half a mile took as long as two.

By the time they arrived at their aunt's street, what with trying not to knock people into the road with the trunk (not entirely successfully), watching out for the pickpockets their father had warned were everywhere, and looking for street names to make sure they weren't lost, Durie was hot, sweaty and thoroughly fed up. Lucinda, strolling along in her wake, now and then peering into a shop window, looked as though she'd just taken a dip in rosewater.

South Audley Street was blessedly quiet and empty after the streets full of shops. Houses on either side; not large, but very smart-looking, with white-painted fronts, railings separating them from the street, well-scrubbed steps down to basements and up to their shiny black doors, and troughs of scarlet geraniums on the windowsills. A couple of ragged-looking boys were sweeping the cobbles, and every window gleamed.

'Nice,' said Lucinda. 'Our long-lost aunt must be doing well for herself.' She looked at Durie, sighed and took out a handkerchief. 'Here, clean your face, you look like you've been digging a ditch. And cheer up – it'll be fun, being here, you'll see.'

Before Durie could answer, the door was opened by a maid, and behind her appeared an older woman who had to be their aunt. She had their father's eyes, grey-blue and serious, the same sharp nose, and iron-grey hair that made her look older than she could feasibly be, in a forbiddingly tidy bun.

'So you're here,' she said, looking them up and down, her eyes pausing for a second at Durie's feet. 'Well, you'd better come in.'

Durie put down the trunk and bag on the black-and-white tiles. What a relief, to have a free arm to wipe her sweaty neck.

'It's very kind of you to have us, Aunt Ellen,' said Lucinda, giving their aunt the full force of her dimples, and handing over the flowers. 'These are for you. I hope we won't be too much trouble.'

'I hope so too,' said Aunt Ellen, without giving the posy a glance. 'And kindness didn't come into it; your father said there was nowhere else for you to go. Now, take your things upstairs – your room's on the right.'

She walked off down the hallway, light footsteps clicking on the tiles. Lucinda and Durie exchanged glances.

'Welcome to my home,' muttered Lucinda.

'Then come down and we'll have some tea,' Aunt Ellen called over her shoulder. 'And I'll tell you how things are going to be while you're here.'

'Old cow,' said Lucinda when they got upstairs. 'You'd think she'd be glad of the company, living on her own.'

'Perhaps she likes living on her own,' said Durie, dropping the bags and flopping down on the bed. 'I wouldn't mind it.'

'What, be a sad old maid, with people feeling sorry for you? No thank you.'

Durie couldn't see much to feel sorry for. The bedchamber might be smaller than their room at home, the window looking out onto a little yard behind instead of a garden, but probably houses had to be that way in London, with so many people to cram in, and the quality of the furnishings and the smartness of the street told their own story. Their aunt kept a shop, their father had said, her own business entirely, and if that had paid for a house like this, with no husband on hand, it was quite impressive.

Lucinda peered into the dressing-table mirror, tweaking one golden curl so it sat perfectly, and smiled at herself.

'Did you see how that gentleman in the carriage looked at me as he passed?' she said. 'I think I'm going to enjoy London.'

'Oh, well good for you,' said Durie, who hadn't seen the gentleman in question, but didn't need to. 'I'm going to miss all the summer carriage accidents, you know that, don't you? It'll be autumn before we go back.'

'Who says I'm going back?' said Lucinda. 'When this is

all done with, I might find myself a husband in London. A rich one.'

'I think you'll find they've already got someone in mind for the Prince of Wales.'

Lucinda shrugged.

'Plenty of dukes left.'

'Oh, honestly, Lucinda! You think dukes marry the likes of us?'

'Not the likes of you, obviously. But someone like me could do very well here in the city. It might all turn out for the best, after all.'

Durie was saved the bother of a tart reply when Aunt Ellen called up the stairs:

'Come and get this tea before it's cold and wasted.'

Downstairs, Aunt Ellen was sitting in the parlour, a gleaming silver teapot on the polished wood table beside her and a large black cat dozing on her lap. It was the sort of room Durie thought she'd like to have herself, if she did ever happen to live alone: entirely free of the knick-knacks that cluttered the parlour at home, but with a full bookcase, a comfortable-looking chair by the fire and, over the marble fireplace, a painting of the seafront in Brighton on a sunny day. She stroked the cat as she passed but it pulled down its spine, as though it found her touch offensive.

'I hope you've brought some slippers for indoors,' said Aunt Ellen, looking up at her. 'You've a very heavy foot.'

Lucinda giggled, and Aunt Ellen gave her a sharp look.

'You'll be heavy yourself before long. Your mother was the

same build exactly, and she swelled up like a sow when her time came.'

Durie and Lucinda looked at each other; a fortnight ago they hadn't even known this aunt existed.

'I was there when both of you were born,' said Aunt Ellen, 'and longer for you, Durie, for all you don't remember me now.'

She was there. She saw it all.

A clump of shame knotted Durie's stomach as Aunt Ellen went on, 'I took care of you until you were nearly a year old. The wet nurse your father found could barely see straight, you'd have been sozzled on gin four times a day, and he'd no idea what to do with Lucinda. I found someone reliable to come in and nurse you, and stayed to take care of everything else myself, despite it being far from convenient. Then he announces he's found himself a new wife, and my services are no longer required. And not a word from him for sixteen years, until suddenly I'm useful again.'

With her birth being the subject no one talked about, Durie had never questioned who looked after her as a baby. She was still digesting the fact that it was this unknown aunt, when the subject was briskly changed.

'But never mind. As it happens, it's a busy time in the shop, and I've just lost my best counter girl to a Frenchman with a double front on Grosvenor Street. So two extra pairs of hands will be welcome. Now, there'll be some rules while you're here. I keep a maid and a cook, so you've no need to help in the kitchen, but you'll do your share in keeping the place tidy and clean. And since I spend all week being pleasant to customers at the shop, I like my own company on a Sunday, so you can take yourselves out for the day then.'

She turned to Lucinda.

'And there'll be no callers of the male variety. What you got up to at home brings no shame on my household, since I didn't have the managing of you. But here you'll behave as a decent girl should.'

Lucinda lowered her eyes, for all the world as though she was actually embarrassed.

'Of course, Aunt Ellen.' She looked up again, her head on one side. Wait for it . . . yes, there it was, one single tear, rolling prettily down her cheek. She'd taught herself to cry at will when she was ten – it had got them both out of trouble more than once, and got Durie into it even more often – and it was always impressive to watch.

'I hope Father explained,' said Lucinda. 'I was . . .' Little intake of breath, like a stifled sob. 'Taken advantage of, by the son of my employer. He promised—'

'None of my concern,' said Aunt Ellen. 'If you were daft enough to believe the words that come out of a man's mouth when he's trying to get under your skirts, well, the good Lord clearly didn't take as much time over the inside of your head as the outside. But there's nothing to be done about that now.'

As she was speaking, the cat lifted its head and blinked big green eyes at Durie. She reached to stroke it; it hissed and swiped, catching her fingers with needle-sharp claws.

'Naughty boy,' said Aunt Ellen fondly. 'He doesn't like anyone but me to stroke him, do you, Lucifer?'

As Durie sucked her finger – he'd drawn blood – Aunt

Ellen said to Lucinda, 'Anyway, you'll do nicely behind the counter, at least until you get too big. A pretty face sells a lot of cakes.'

Lucinda smiled sweetly.

'I'll do my very best for you, Aunt Ellen.'

It was going to be a very long summer.

Chapter 2

Durie couldn't remember when she first knew that their mother had died when she was born. It had always just been there as a fact, like the fact that they lived in the High Street and their father was a bonesetter, and their stepmother Margie was a dressmaker, and their brother Richie was really their half-brother, though they didn't think of him that way and only pretended to when he was being annoying.

But the day she discovered *how* their mother had died? That, she remembered exactly. A Thursday morning, market day in Lewes, when she was eight and Lucinda ten. The marketplace full of people, Margie buying apples, and she and Lucinda bickering nearby. Lucinda had torn her dress and wanted Durie to take the blame.

'Go on,' she said. 'You won't get into trouble, because you're younger.'

'No.'

She'd only get the lie wrong, and then she'd be told off for fibbing, as well as Lucinda for the dress. Where was the sense in that?

'You're so selfish,' said Lucinda.

'But I—'

Lucinda held up a hand.

'Don't talk to me.'

As they stood facing away from each other like two book-ends, a farmer was telling two other men how he'd just lost his best cow.

'Heart gave out, did it?' said one.

'It did, in the end,' said the farmer. 'The calf was just too big. It took too long to come, and wore her out, poor thing.'

Lucinda turned, her eyes wide.

'That's what you did.' She looked Durie up and down. 'You were too big, and you wore our mother out.'

Margie called them then, and Lucinda skipped away, smiling up at Margie. Durie stood there, thinking, until Margie called over her shoulder, 'Come on, Durie love, I've lots to do at home.'

She had to run to catch them up.

All day, Lucinda's words kept coming back. Durie had seen next door's cat give birth, so it was no mystery why a big baby would be a problem. And she must have been big, mustn't she? She couldn't recall a time when she wasn't taller, and broader, than Lucinda; her sister's dresses were too small for Durie long before Lucinda outgrew them, and there was no question of her great big feet ever fitting into Lucinda's shoes.

That night, she lay in the dark, still thinking, as Lucinda snored beside her. What Lucinda said was so terrible, and yet it had to be true, didn't it? Because it explained her name. No one ever called her anything but Durie, but she'd seen her proper name written in the family Bible: Endurance. That meant being brave about something horrible, something that went on and on. They must have called her that because of what her mother endured, giving birth to her. Because she was too big and she wore her mother out.

Before that day, she was proud to be bigger than her sister. Children always want to grow, don't they? So when Mrs Flint from next door commented to Margie that Durie was 'a strapping lass', Durie didn't understand why Margie made a face behind her back, and she didn't understand either why their father frowned when she beat Richie at arm wrestling. But after that day at the market, she started noticing things: the clomp of her feet on the stairs, and the skittery tip-tap of Lucinda's; the mess her big, clumsy hands made of the daisy chains that Lucinda and Margie could thread so beautifully; and the way, when the Whitsun festivities came, all the other girls skipped in and out of the maypole ribbons like kittens, when Durie knew, without even trying, that she'd trip over her own feet and likely bring the whole thing down on them all. And every time she noticed those things, she'd remember that it was her being such a lump of a thing that killed their mother.

Margie was always saying that everyone was good at something – she had a lot of cheery but unhelpful sayings – but over the years since then, Durie had proved her wrong. Both girls had been helping her since they were old enough to stand and pass her pins, but while Lucinda's dainty fingers soon sewed as neatly as Margie's, Durie's fumbled and fiddled, dropping the needle and knotting the thread. Her stitching was invariably bumpy and uneven, so she was only allowed to work on bits that didn't show, and even then, Margie would often sigh and unpick a particularly awful seam when she thought Durie wasn't looking.

She wasn't good with the customers who came to the house either. Margie and Lucinda could flannel away all day long. 'It matches your eyes so beautifully,' Lucinda would say, when anyone could see the dress was the colour of a fresh oak leaf, and the eyes just the normal muddy green eyes generally are. But the customer would twist and turn in front of the mirror, making big eyes at herself, and say, 'Why yes, it does, doesn't it?'

It didn't make sense: why would you want to go about thinking you looked better than you did, when it's other people who are looking at you and they can plainly see what you really look like? Durie found the whole thing impossible to fathom, so she tried to say nothing at all, but when Mrs Bailey the magistrate's wife asked if she thought the neckline of her new frock suited her, she couldn't not answer.

'It suits you very well,' she said.

Mrs Bailey smiled at herself in the mirror.

'Thank you.'

'You being quite flat-chested, you're wise to cover the area up with that lace.'

If Mrs Bailey's face hadn't told Durie that she'd said the wrong thing, Margie's would have. But the woman *was* flat-chested; she wasn't telling her anything she didn't know, surely? In fact she was complimenting her on her good sense. Still, Mrs Bailey left in a huff, and after that Margie said it would be best if she and Lucinda did the fittings.

From time to time, Margie tried to find her work elsewhere, but after a week at the pie shop, they said she had too heavy a hand with the pastry, and when Margie asked at the Pelham Arms, the landlord said he had no need of anyone just then. Margie didn't hear what he muttered to the men standing at the bar as they walked out, but Durie did:

'I'd take the sister on happily, but that one'd only be good for getting rid of the stragglers at the end of the night, and we've got the dog for that.'

Though she held her head high and pretended not to hear the comment, nor the laughter that followed it, she couldn't say it didn't sting. But it came as no surprise. The evidence of her own eyes when she happened to pass a mirror was enough to tell her she hadn't been blessed with a face or a figure that gave her much to thank the Lord for. And if it hadn't been, a lifetime of hearing people say 'You'd never think they were sisters' or 'But the older one's so pretty' would certainly do it.

In short, the message life had for Durie was that she was neither use nor decoration. By the October morning, not long after her fifteenth birthday, when she walked with her father to the town pump to fetch water for laundry day, she was starting to wonder what was to become of her.

'One trip should do it,' said her father, his empty buckets clanking. 'You all right to carry those two back again?'

'Of course,' said Durie, swinging hers high.

She could manage them easily, to Richie's irritation; he could only lift one and had to keep stopping to put it down for a rest. All the same, it was usually his job, but that morning he'd been sent on an errand and she'd welcomed the chance to escape the house. The sorting of bedlinen and undergarments before each month's laundry day invariably unearthed bits and pieces needing mending, and anything was better than extra sewing.

They'd barely gone ten yards when the landlady of the White Hart, at the far end of town, ran up, red in the face, shouting that her husband had hurt his shoulder.

'Can you come quick? He's in terrible pain.'

Her father turned to follow the woman, saying over his shoulder, 'Go indoors and get my bag – catch us up quick as you can.'

Chapter 3

Durie's long legs made her a fast if inelegant runner, and her father had only just reached the inn when she arrived with the bag. They hadn't opened up yet: the stale smell of ale and yesterday's stew hung in the air, the counter was covered with unwashed tankards and the floor was half cleaned, the mop and bucket standing abandoned. The landlord was sitting at a table, his left arm cradling his right, his face grey and his brow speckled with sweat. He'd been swinging a barrel of ale up from the cellar, his wife was explaining, and slipped. Though he looked a big, strong man, he kept biting his lip, like a little boy trying not to cry.

'The pain is terrible,' he said. 'Thought I was going to pass out.'

'Let's have a look,' said Durie's father.

Durie hadn't ever seen him work and seeing the state of the man, she was suddenly curious. As her father gently felt around the shoulder, the wife clucked and fussed.

'Is it broken?' she said. 'I heard it pop, horrible noise! I bet it's broken, and that's all we need because—'

'Could you boil some water?' said Durie's father. 'Couple of pints?'

17

The woman hurried off.

'It's out of joint,' he said to the man. 'Just needs putting back in. Are you ready?'

The man nodded, fresh beads of sweat seeping from his forehead. He yelped in pain as her father helped him lie on the floor. Then her father sat down himself and took off his left boot. What on earth was he going to do?

'Now,' he said, 'count backwards, slowly, from a hundred.'

As the counting began, her father straightened the landlord's arm and held it. When the counting got to fifty, he lifted his leg and put his foot into the man's armpit. The poor man shut his eyes and groaned out the next few numbers, and every muscle in Durie's body clenched in sympathy with him. His face screwed up in agony as her father pulled and slowly turned the arm, the effort bringing him out in a sweat too. Surely you could die of pain like that?

He screamed; he was, he was going to die, right in front of her eyes! Then there was a soft clunk, his face relaxed and he breathed out a long, relieved sigh.

The woman came running in with a steaming bowl of water.

'All done,' said Durie's father. 'Didn't need that in the end.'

He took a wide strip of muslin from his bag, and made a sling. Already, the colour was coming back into the man's face.

Durie looked at her father, repacking his bag as though nothing out of the ordinary had happened. How had she not known what he could do? Pulling someone out of such terrible pain with just the knowledge in his head and the strength in his arm. Imagine being able to do that.

The man wiped his brow with his free hand.

'Worst pain I've ever had, and now it's gone,' he said. 'Get this man a mug of ale, Jess.'

'Thanks, but I need to get along,' said Durie's father. 'Keep that sling on for a couple of weeks – and get your potboy to bring up the casks.'

Outside, he said, 'I promised to see a customer out on the Brighton Road this morning – since I've got my bag, I may as well go from here.'

Well, now she really wanted to know what he was going to do there.

'Can I come with you?'

'What do you want to do that for?'

'It's interesting. I'll fetch the water when we get back, both lots, I promise.'

He shrugged.

'Come on then. But you're to be quiet, and not speak out of turn.'

As they walked, Durie said, 'I didn't know you could do that. It was like magic.'

'There's no magic in it, it's skill.'

'How do you know what to do?'

'You know how, I learned from your grandfather, and he learned from his father. It's the knack, it's in our blood.'

'But someone must have worked it out first. How did they do that?'

'I suppose they looked, and felt with their fingers, and got to know how everything fits together, and when a joint feels right and when it doesn't. And they tried out different things and learned what works.'

'Do you listen as well? Because she said his shoulder made a noise when it came out, and then I heard one when you got it back in.'

'That's right. Bones tell you a lot, if you listen.'

'Why did you make him count backwards though?'

'Distracts them. Stops them tensing up too much. When a joint pops out, the muscles get as tight as a dog sucking a bone, and you've got to have the strength to work against them. That's why people come to me instead of a doctor who's never lifted anything heavier than a pen.'

'What was the boiling water for?'

'To get rid of the woman. She was getting on my nerves.'

They walked to a cottage in the last row before the town's buildings petered out. The woman there, who looked vaguely familiar, had a sore knee; she showed them into a fearsomely tidy little parlour and rolled down her stocking as Durie's father set out a jar of balm and a roll of muslin bandage. As he rubbed in the balm, the room filled with the scent of rosemary. Durie was watching so intently that at first she didn't realise the woman had spoken to her.

'I said, weren't you at the school with my Susan?'

Of course. Same beady eyes.

'Yes,' she said.

Susan Hopkiss. Always sucking up to Lucinda, though to be fair, everyone wanted to be Lucinda's friend. Durie had only ever had one friend at the school: Peter Gleeson, the night-soil man's son. The day he started, no one would sit next to him; they were all wafting their hands in front of their faces, saying he smelt, and Susan Hopkiss pretended to faint. So stupid!

'Why are you being such idiots?' Durie said to them. 'The stuff his father collects came out of your backsides in the first place!'

That got her a black mark for vulgarity from Old Ma Haines who kept the school, and an hour standing in the corner. When she sat down again, Peter quietly passed her his apple. They'd got along well after that, until one day, as they were walking home, Susan and a little knot of girls came up behind, giggling.

Susan said, 'Look at those two, holding hands! They're going to get married and have babies that look like her and smell like him!'

They weren't holding hands – why would they have been holding hands? – but Peter sprang away, a stricken look on his face, and walked off home. After that he stopped talking to Durie and sat by himself.

'Susan's working over in Brighton now,' Mrs Hopkiss went on. 'Got a place in a big house there – she could put a word in for you.'

Durie opened her mouth to say she'd had experience of Susan's words and didn't wish for any more, but her father threw her a glance, and instead she said, 'I don't think I'd be any good at that sort of work.'

'Well, not everyone has my Susan's lovely manner.'

Durie's father strapped the knee up tight with the muslin bandage, and Mrs Hopkiss stood and thanked him.

'That feels better. Been agony, this week.'

'Like I said before, take it gently, but keep it moving. That strapping should keep the pain at bay for a while.'

* * *

As the door closed behind them, Durie's father asked, 'Her girl wasn't a pal of yours, then?'

Where had he got the idea that she'd ever had pals?

'No.'

'Thought not, from the look on your face. But you kept your tongue. Shows you can, if you want to. Now, I've another customer a bit further on this way, I may as well go now as later. Can you be trusted to keep quiet or should I send you home to Margie?'

'You can trust me.'

On the way, she asked him what was wrong with Mrs Hopkiss' knee.

'Her kneecap's worn, bone's grinding on bone and like she said, it's agony. I can't fix it, but the strapping stops it sliding about so much, and the balm helps with the pain. I've sometimes wondered if the good Lord was concentrating on the sixth day, because there's a lot of people like that, with knees that wear out before the rest of them does. Hips as well. I wish I could do more for them, but at least I can ease their pain.'

Strange, hearing him speak like that. Her father and Margie were like Jack Sprat and his wife when it came to words; she could spin out the story of a trip to the fishmonger's till it was longer than the Bible, whereas he usually used words so sparingly you'd think they'd put a tax on talking. He must like his work, to be so easy at talking about it; she'd probably just heard the most words he'd ever used in one conversation.

'Which do you like best?' she asked. 'The ones you can fix, like the man at the inn? Or the ones like Mrs Hopkiss? Because she'd be in pain every day, wouldn't she, if you didn't help her?'

He chuckled.

'You ask some strange questions, you do. I'll tell you though: what I like best is a cruncher.'

'What's that?'

'Well, sometimes people get an injury, and it's not fixed right at the time. For months – can even be years – they're hobbling with a crutch or they can't straighten up, and they're in horrible pain, but if you catch it just right, you can get the bone back in and fix them. We don't get a lot of crunchers round here, because people have always known to come straight to your grandfather and then me, but I've had a few from Brighton way. Best job there is, a cruncher.'

They stopped at a ramshackle cottage, out on its own, with a few scraggy chickens pecking about outside. A wizened little woman was leaning on a broom as a makeshift crutch when she answered the door. Her swollen foot was lumpy like a mangel-wurzel and as Durie's father felt around it, bones crunched.

'It's broken, I'm afraid,' he said. 'I wish you'd called me sooner, the pain must be bad.'

The woman nodded.

'Thought it was just a sprain, but it's got worse and worse.'

'Don't worry, I'll set it for you, but I'll need another pair of hands. Is there a neighbour I can fetch?'

'Nearest is Jed Barrell, but he'll be out in the fields, I should think.'

'I'll do it,' said Durie.

Her father glanced at her, his eyes flicking to her hands.

'All right, but you're to do exactly as I say.'

'I will.'

This was turning out to be a lot better than doing laundry.

Once the old lady was lying on the kitchen table, Durie's father gave her a leather strap to bite on.

'It's going to hurt, but I'll be as quick as I can,' he said.

Durie's heart thumped as she followed his instructions, holding the woman's knee as he took her foot in both hands.

'I need to get the two ends of the bone back together,' he said. 'So when I pull the foot, you hold firm. The more still you can keep it, the quicker I can work.'

As he pulled the leg, the bones grated and crunched. It must have been agony for the poor woman, but she was a brave old stick, biting down on the leather and gripping the sides of the table. Durie concentrated with all her might on holding the knee still, and then, at last, her father gave a hard tug and she half heard, half felt a crunch that was different from the rest. He looked up and said, 'There. That went back in very nicely. It should heal good and straight.' He looked at Durie. 'Good job I had you with me, as it happens, you did well there.'

As he splinted the foot, the woman said, 'Soon as I'm back on my feet, I'll pop half a dozen eggs down to Margie.'

'Only if you can spare them,' said Durie's father. 'I was coming this way anyway.'

They set off back into town, dust rising from the road as carts and coaches passed, heading for Brighton in one direction and London in the other.

'Lucky we were nearby,' he said. 'If I'd realised her foot was broken, I'd have gone sooner. She didn't want to ask, because she couldn't pay, but your grandfather always said, the knack is a gift, and it doesn't hurt us to give it away now and then when someone needs it.'

'What if everyone said they couldn't pay?'

'I'll worry about that when it happens.' He hefted his bag higher on his shoulder. 'Now come on, let's get home.'

Durie was quiet all the way home. She had a lot to think about.

That night, in bed, she grasped her shoulder, circling it round, feeling the bones slide against each other.

'What are you doing?' mumbled Lucinda. 'Lie still, can't you?'

'I'm trying to understand something.'

'What?'

'How a shoulder works.'

Lucinda sighed, pulling the coverlet close so Durie got a cold patch of it.

'Sometimes,' she muttered, 'I wonder what goes on in your head.'

'Sometimes I wonder if anything goes on in yours,' said Durie, yanking it back.

Lucinda settled down to sleep, but Durie couldn't. Everything she'd seen that day kept playing again in her head. She'd known her father must be good at his work, because they had a comfortable-sized house, with always at least one maid to do the heavy work and most of the cooking. Two, sometimes, if Margie was especially busy making dresses for people. There'd been enough money to send all three of them to the dame school too – Richie still went there – and it wasn't every family that did that. But she'd had no idea just how astonishing it was, what her father did. The man at the inn, in such terrible pain she'd been sure he was about to die, then right as rain, just like that. Mrs Hopkiss had said her knee was agony without his help, and what would that poor old lady have suffered, if he hadn't fixed her?

And the thing was, it had been nice, him saying she'd done a good job, helping him when he'd set the woman's ankle, but she hadn't needed to hear it. She'd felt it: her big hands, usually so clumsy, knew what to do, and her strong arms were made for the job. When the bones slid back into place, it felt as though everything was right with the world and she'd played a part in making it that way. And it was the best feeling she could possibly imagine.

It's the knack, it's in our blood.

Could it be in hers too?

Chapter 4

All the next day, as she battled a hem that insisted on puckering under her needle, Durie kept thinking about it. Imagine, getting to fix people every day, instead of stitching. Being useful, instead of getting in the way.

That evening, when her father went into the garden to smoke his pipe, she followed him out. It was warm still, even though you could feel autumn in the air, and the smell of tobacco mixed with the spicy scent of the roses by the door. She sat on the bench beside him, shielding her eyes from the low sun, and said, 'Can I ask you something?'

'Go on then.'

'Could you teach me to do what you do? Could I be a bonesetter?'

He rolled his eyes.

'What nonsense are you talking now?'

'I know I'm clumsy but I think, if I was doing that, I could learn not to be. And I'm strong enough.'

He laughed, shaking his head.

'Don't be daft, bonesetting's not a job for a girl.'

'Why not?'

'Because it's passed from father to son.'

'You mean you'll teach Richie?'

'When the time comes. He'll have another year or so of schooling first.'

'But you could teach me now. I'm only getting in the way, working with Margie, but I could help you.'

'I don't need anyone to help yet, and when I do it'll be your brother. So you just try and make yourself more useful to Margie, and we'll all be happy. Now, can I smoke my pipe in peace?'

Of course, she could see why most women couldn't do bone-setting – Lucinda could no more set a shoulder than fly through the air, she couldn't even lift a sack of potatoes, and nor could Margie. But Durie wasn't like other women, and that had always seemed like a bad thing, but what if it wasn't? What if she was meant to be a bonesetter, and that was why she was the way she was?

The knack was passed from father to son, he'd said. Well, in this case, that was ridiculous; now she'd seen what bone-setting entailed, it was impossible to imagine her brother doing it. Because Richie was squeamish; the slightest thing could turn his stomach. Once, they'd seen next door's cat playing with a mouse, the poor little thing covered with blood and squealing fit to bust, the cat patting it around and tossing it up in the air. Durie grabbed the mouse and killed it quick and clean with a big stone, then gave it back to the cat to eat, and when she turned round, Richie was bringing up his breakfast. Said it was the sound of the stone breaking the mouse's skull that did it. So how was he going to cope with the clunk of a shoulder sliding back into place, or the grinding and grating of Mrs Hopkiss' knee? Let alone move the ends of a broken bone back together.

Wasn't it much more likely that the knack was in her blood than his? The more she thought about it, the more certain she was: this was the thing her strong arms and her big hands were made for. No point in arguing with her father, that never worked. But a year or so, he'd said, before he started teaching Richie. Well, what if by then she could learn some of it by herself? That would show him she was serious, and then when he saw how hopelessly unsuited Richie was, he'd realise. How she was going to learn was yet to be figured out – he certainly wasn't going to agree to take her out with him and show her – but there had to be a way, and she was going to find it.

Chapter 5

People had often told Margie what a good person she was, taking on another woman's children and bringing them up like her own. It was nice of them, but truth be told, she'd happily have taken on ten of them, if it meant she could marry Dan. In the dancing light of the candle on her nightstand she pretended to read her novella, but really she was watching him undress. His dark curls might have turned to gunmetal but he was still a fine-looking man, tall and muscular with broad shoulders and strong arms. He pulled on his nightcap and slipped into bed beside her; even though he'd done the same every night for nearly fourteen years, she still couldn't believe her luck. It just went to prove what she always said: good things come to those who wait.

He'd broken her heart when he married Elizabeth, but it had all worked out in the end, hadn't it? Not that she'd wished Elizabeth dead, of course she hadn't, but she did die and some things were just meant to be. So she hadn't thought twice about taking on the girls, not when three-year-old Lucinda was such a sweet little thing, and Durie was just a baby; she wouldn't even remember being held in Elizabeth's arms, and she couldn't have got much affection from that bossy sister of Dan's. Margie would have liked them to call her Mother, really, but Lucinda already knew her as Margie, so as Dan said, it wasn't surprising she'd carried on. Durie said 'Mama' when she started talking but Margie hadn't missed the flash of sadness in Dan's eyes, so it seemed to be for the best when her sharp ears picked up what her sister said and she copied that.

She'd been right about Lucinda, she was an easy child to love. It was barely three months before she stopped crying for her mother and soon they were as close as could be. It helped, of course, that they were so alike: you could see that in the way Lucinda had taken to dressmaking. She had an eye for style, and even as a little girl, such a sweet manner. Now and then, there'd been incidents of untruthfulness, but you only had to remind her that good girls didn't tell lies, and she'd say sorry with such a sad little face that you couldn't be cross with her for long. Whereas Durie . . . oh, what a child. As an infant, she'd been like a little hedgehog, impossible to soothe in your arms, and prone to fix you with a look that said, who are you, and what business do you have with me? And then when she learned to talk! Margie sometimes felt she'd spent every day of the last fourteen years being asked questions she couldn't answer. Boys had the same number of fingers as girls, so why didn't Richie have to do sewing? Why did Margie tell the rector's wife her new son-in-law seemed a fine chap and then say to Mrs Flint from next door that he looked like a wet Tuesday? And then later, how could it be wrong to lie but also wrong to confirm Mrs Brown's suspicions that pink satin made her look fat? Yet in all that time, she'd never asked about her mother; odd, but also a relief, because Margie hated seeing the look on Dan's face when someone mentioned Elizabeth.

And now this latest strange idea! Dan had laughed when he told her, as they locked up before bed.

'You won't believe what Durie asked me today. She wants to be a bonesetter.'

'That child! What goes on in her head?'

'She says she's strong enough, which to be fair is true. Takes her half as long to fetch water as Richie.'

'Richie's quite a bit younger though—'

'I know, I didn't mean it that way. Anyway, I told her, she's to concentrate on being useful to you.'

'Ah, well, she tries her best.'

She did too; you couldn't accuse Durie of being lazy. But though she'd never have said it to Dan, Margie didn't have hopes of her ever being able to do more than the plainest of stitching, and that not too well. But it was hard to imagine her fitting in anywhere else either. That very straightforward manner she had was a lovely quality, in many ways – there wasn't a dishonest bone in her body, and if she did something wrong, she'd admit to it straight out – but if you didn't know her, it could come across as rudeness. And then there was the cackhandedness and clumsiness and though Margie would never have said this to another soul, the way poor Durie looked, with that height, and the big feet and hands, and let's face it, the child was behind the door when the pretty faces were handed out. Margie had once tried to suggest a different way to dress her hair, that might soften the whole effect – what girl didn't want to make the best of herself?

But Durie had batted her away, saying she didn't care how her hair looked as long as it kept her head warm. Hard to believe now, what a tiny little scrap she'd been when she was born, and how they'd all doubted she'd survive.

'Well,' said Dan, as he turned over to go to sleep, 'thank goodness Richie was a boy.'

Margie smiled to herself, blew out the candle and burrowed under the covers, resting her cold feet against his warm ones. She might not have been the love of his life, but she'd given him a son to carry on his name and his trade. Elizabeth hadn't done that.

Chapter 6

The first thing to do, Durie decided, was to learn about bones and joints; how they worked and how they fitted together. So at the market, or when she was out running errands, or on the occasional Sunday when Margie decided they should all go to church, she watched people walk and sit and turn and bend, lift things up and put them down, and then back at home, she drew what she'd seen and made notes. Shoulders and arms were straightforward, but when she got to legs and feet, it was useless looking at women because their skirts concealed so much, so she was forced to concentrate on men.

'What are you doing?' hissed Lucinda one Sunday, as Durie leaned forward in their pew to see exactly how Mr Allen the apothecary's thighs bent as he sat in front, and whether he bent his knees at the same time.

'Never you mind,' Durie whispered, as Margie shushed them with a finger. But of course, Lucinda got it out of her later, when they were getting ready for bed.

'You want to do what?'

'Be a bonesetter, like Father.'

Lucinda rolled her eyes.

'Why do you have to be so peculiar, always?'

'It's not peculiar. You should see it – that time I went with him, the man was screaming and I honestly thought he might die of the pain, but Father instantly knew what to do. Imagine being able to fix someone like that.'

'And what's that got to do with peering at Mr Allen's backside?'

'I'm learning how joints work.'

'Well, you want to be less obvious about it, or Mrs Allen'll be after you for giving him the eye.'

She struck a pose, wagging a finger and catching exactly Mrs Allen's habitual expression, that of a woman who's become conscious of an unpleasant smell and is casting around for the culprit.

'Durie Proudfoot, avert your wanton gaze from my husband's posterior! The beauty of his form is for my eyes alone, to be enjoyed in the privacy of our bedchamber.'

The thought of Mr and Mrs Allen, who were at least forty, enjoying anything at all in the privacy of their bedchamber made both of them laugh so hard that the candle on the nightstand blew out. As they wiped their eyes in the darkness, Lucinda said, 'Seriously though, you don't want to be going about peering at people. They'll think you're odd – which you are, but we don't need the whole town knowing it.'

Durie tried to be more discreet after that, but in any case, just looking at people wasn't going to be enough.

I suppose they looked, and felt with their fingers, and got to know how everything fits together.

Somehow, she was going to have to do that too.

* * *

Of course, it had to be Margie who found the rat. Durie had gone downstairs to look for something when she heard the scream that told her there was going to be trouble. Lucinda got upstairs ahead of her, and she shrieked when she saw it too.

'It was already dead,' Durie shouted up the stairs. 'I found it in the street.'

Margie stood in the doorway of their room, hands at her mouth. Lucinda turned to Durie.

'What have you done with it? It looks . . .' She stepped closer and peered at the rat lying on the chest of drawers, its pointy little face staring accusingly up at the ceiling and its mouth open, showing sharp yellow teeth. 'Ugh . . . you've cut it up.'

Margie gave a little wail and wafted her hand in front of her face, as though the rat smelt, which it didn't. It was already dried out when Durie found it; that's why it was difficult to cut. She tucked Margie's second-best scissors behind her back.

'Are you feeding Mrs Flint's cat again?' said Margie.

Durie had planned to give the remains to him, so it wasn't a lie.

'His teeth aren't very good now,' she said. 'He can't catch rats himself.'

'What kind of a girl cuts up rats?' said Margie. 'What kind of a girl even has anything to do with rats? I don't know what your father's going to say.'

Her father didn't guess what she was doing; he'd obviously forgotten all about her wanting to be a bonesetter, which was actually quite annoying, even if it was for the best at the time. She had to scrub the bedroom floor and clean the rug with old tea leaves, even though the rat hadn't bled at all, but it was worth it, for what she learned. Of course, it wouldn't be quite the same as in a person, but she'd seen how the leg bones fitted together, then broken them in several places and had a practice at setting them and strapping them up with a scrap of ribbon filched from Margie's workroom. It was fiddly though, so she was keeping an eye out for something bigger – a dead fox maybe, or a dog, people sometimes threw them in the ditch at the end of town – when a much better opportunity presented itself. Margie had made a dress for the doctor's wife, and when she returned from the fitting, she announced it was time Durie's father had a place to see customers at home, like the doctor did.

'You shouldn't be traipsing from place to place, like a common labourer. Dr Fernley only goes out to see the better class of person. The rest come to him, Mrs Fernley says, and that means he can see twice as many in a day.'

'I can't ask someone who's broken their ankle to walk here,' he said.

'No, but if you saw twice as many of the run-of-the-mill kind, you could hire a horse to visit the others, instead of walking.'

'I like walking.'

'That's not the point. The point is, I'm not having Mrs Fernley, who let's not forget was just the baker's daughter three years ago, looking down her nose at us, when you do the same job as the doctor, more or less.'

'I don't do the same job as the doctor.'

'Well no, that's right, because nobody ever died of what you do, and that's more than can be said of Dr Fernley, because did I tell you, Mrs Harper said . . .'

There was a lot more in that vein, and though Durie's father nodded and said 'I see' now and then, he wasn't listening. Probably thought he was safe, because it wasn't as though they had a room he could use. But Margie had a plan; keen to attract customers from what she called 'the fashionable set' of Lewes, she'd come to an arrangement to share the premises of a milliner in the High Street, where she'd be more visible. That left the workroom available and, when Durie's father realised there was no point resisting, it was agreed he would make it known that customers could come at particular hours each day, though he put his foot down about still visiting people who had trouble getting into town.

At the beginning of this new regime, Durie trooped off to the milliner's shop every morning with Lucinda and Margie, but it was an awful place. Everywhere you turned, there was a hat perched or a half-made dress hanging, and though Lucinda, Margie and Mrs Carroll the milliner flitted about quite easily, Durie had only to walk from the door to the counter to send bonnets flying and leave a wake of bodices and skirts cascading to the floor. After an unfortunate incident when she swerved to avoid dislodging a dress and knocked a customer off her feet, Margie suggested – quite kindly – that she might be happier doing her stitching at home.

It was after they'd been working that way for a while that Durie saw her opportunity. The workroom – now named the 'consulting room' by Margie and kitted out with a sturdy table for customers to sit or lie on, and shelves for her father's pots of balm and baskets of splints and bandages – had a tall cupboard, built into an alcove. The wall inside was damp, so the only things kept there were a couple of worn-out brooms that for some reason hadn't been thrown away, and a long stick with feathers tied to the top, used mostly in the autumn when cobwebs appeared in the corners of every room. Margie had asked Durie to fetch the stick, and as she took it out, a thought struck. She stepped inside and pulled the door almost closed. Through the gap, she had a perfect view.

Durie learned a lot from inside that cupboard. Her father, fortunately, was very regular in his habits, and once Margie and Lucinda left for the shop, he'd head for the outhouse, and be gone at least twenty minutes. Why it took him so long to do what the rest of the family accomplished in a fraction of the time was a mystery, but it meant she could hide in the cupboard before he came back and the first customer arrived.

It was uncomfortable: the damp wall was cold against her back and arms, and her legs got stiff from standing still for so long. But it was worth it. She saw him put back several dislocated elbows, a hip, a knee and two more shoulders. She watched him set two broken arms and a wrist, and she peered through the crack in the door as he rubbed and pummelled stiff backs, strapped up crunching knees, and pulled and twisted shoulders and hips. She listened to the questions he asked, and the answers, and put her ear to the crack to hear the noises the joints made.

Bones tell you a lot, if you listen.

She could only do it twice a week, so as not to get behind with her stitching, but she stayed there, in the cold, musty-smelling cupboard, watching, listening and learning, for the whole morning. Then while he was showing the last person out at the front door, she'd escape and be stitching at the parlour table by the time he came in. Later, she'd write down everything she'd seen, to make sure she'd remember it. She got away with it for almost ten months. And then the rector had to go and take his breeches off.

Chapter 7

It had been a useful morning: a sprained thumb, purple with bruising, and a swollen knee that her father rubbed with a salve that gave off a sweet smell. She watched where on the shelf he put the jar back; she'd return later, read the label and add it to her secret notes.

The rector arrived, a tall, thin man with a permanently creased brow that made him look as though he'd prepared himself to disapprove of most things, and nothing had changed his mind yet. As he explained his problem, Durie's face grew hot.

'Right,' said her father, 'let's have a look.'

She'd been taken aback to see that when her father needed to get at any part of a person other than their ankles, knees or wrists, they stripped to their underclothes. It was quite strange to see him working on Mrs Gant from the bakery's shoulder as she stood there in her shift, but he was very matter-of-fact about it, and displayed no more interest in the other bits of her than if she'd been a sow or a ewe.

But the thing with the rector was, his trouble was in his hip, and the pain, he told her father, was right round the top of his leg. When he unfastened his breeches, she squeezed her eyes tight shut. But curiosity got the better of her and as she squinted through the gap, he dropped his drawers, revealing what Durie, having never seen what was inside a man's breeches before, took to be some sort of horrible growth. She must have gasped; her hand flew to her mouth, and that dislodged one of the brooms. It fell forward like an executioner's axe and the door swung open with a creak. Durie looked at the rector, standing there with his goods on display, and her father frozen still, with his hands ready to start poking about, and they looked back at her, wedged in the cupboard. There was a moment of horrified silence on both sides, and then her father started shouting at her, and the rector shouted at her father, and all in all, the morning didn't end well.

Durie wasn't good at lying, so she rarely tried it, but if he found out the truth now, it would ruin everything. So when her father asked, after he'd calmed the rector down and seen him off the premises, what she thought she was doing, she mumbled about looking for something in the cupboard.

'And then the door shut behind me and got stuck, and I thought it'd be best to stay there and not disturb you when you were working.'

He opened his mouth to say something, but at that moment, Margie came home, rabbiting on about what she'd heard from the baker's wife about Mrs Flint next door's cousin. He gave Durie a hard look, but didn't say any more, and after a second, she realised why: he didn't want Margie to know about it. Her tongue had a life of its own, and she wouldn't have been able to stop herself mentioning it to someone else, sending the story right round the town and embarrassing the rector, who it had taken her father quite a while to placate.

So she got off lightly, but her real punishment was that she couldn't learn any more. Hiding in the cupboard again was too risky, so she was back to stitching, stitching, stitching, all day, every day. And to make things worse, that same week Lucinda came home from delivering some dresses, and announced she'd got herself a place as a laundry maid at the big house on School Hill, home of one of Margie's fashionable new customers.

'I knew it!' said Margie, clapping her hands. 'I saw, at that last fitting, she was taken with you. I said to your father, I think our Lucinda impressed there, I shouldn't be surprised if they offer her a place. Didn't I say that to you?'

'You did,' said her father.

'They didn't ask you for a character?' asked Margie.

'No, Mrs Beresford said she knew you well, and that was enough.'

'She said that? She knows me well? Did you hear that, Dan?'

'I did.'

'What do you want to be a laundry maid for?' asked Durie. 'You hate doing laundry.'

'It's not like doing it here, silly. I'll be pressing fine lace, not boiling up father's shirts and your tatty stockings. Anyway, I don't intend to stay a laundry maid for long.'

'I haven't said you can take the position yet,' said their father. 'How's Margie expected to manage?'

'Oh, don't worry about that,' said Margie, flapping her hands. 'It'll be useful to have Lucinda up there, seeing all the latest fashions. And Durie's coming on now with her stitching. We'll be fine, won't we, Durie?'

So Lucinda skipped off to her new life, and Durie had to go back to working in the shop, after Margie promised she'd stay in the back room and not, as Mrs Carroll put it, 'go barging her customers to the floor'. Poor Margie, she was so patient, showing Durie time and time again how to do the more delicate work Lucinda used to help her with, describing how this silk was best for one type of dress, and that for another, and explaining why pink was the thing this season and lilac for some reason wasn't. And Durie tried to be helpful, because Margie must miss having Lucinda there to talk about fabrics and fashions with, and she was no substitute, but Margie never showed it, and when Mrs Carroll commented one day that it was a shame Durie wasn't more like her sister, Margie snapped back that Durie had many fine qualities, and what a boring world it would be if we were all the same.

Durie missed Lucinda too. If working in the shop was tedious before, it was worse without her making up comical songs about the customers, and winking behind their backs as she buttered them up with outrageously inaccurate compliments. But Durie told herself it wouldn't be for much longer. From the back room, she could see out of the front window, and, so as not to forget what she'd learned, she looked out for her father's customers walking by on their way to see him, trying to work out from how they walked what their problem was, and what she'd seen him do to fix it. Every night, she read through five pages of the notes she'd made, then tested herself on how much she could remember. It wouldn't be long before Richie finished school; she had to be ready to persuade her father to train her, and not her brother.

Chapter 8

Durie wasn't at all surprised when Lucinda fulfilled her own prediction; she was a laundry maid for less than two months. When the lady's maid was sick one day, she jumped in and offered to dress the mistress's hair, and if there was one thing Lucinda was expert at, it was fiddling around with hair. Before long, the mistress was asking for her instead, the lady's maid went off in a huff and found a place elsewhere, and Lucinda stepped her dainty little feet into her shoes. And with her being so pretty, the mistress made a pet of her, giving her bits of lace she had no use for, and half-used pots of face cream when she'd found one she liked better.

When Lucinda came home, on the last Sunday of each month, she talked of nothing but the gowns Mrs Beresford wore: this one trimmed with lace from Paris, and that one with matching shoes in the exact same shade of Venetian green, whatever that was. And one Sunday, she brought home a dress of dark blue silk.

'She's got too big for it,' she said, holding the gown against her and whirling round the parlour. 'She said I had to have it, because it matched my eyes so well.'

'That'll fetch a good price,' said Margie. 'It's lovely silk.'

'I'm not selling it, I'm keeping it.'

'Don't be daft,' said their father. 'Where could you ever wear that?'

Lucinda smiled.

'We'll see.'

Their father rolled his eyes, and the talk turned to something else. But there'd been something about the way Lucinda said 'We'll see', like she had a secret she was itching to tell. So when it was time for her to go, Durie said she'd walk part of the way with her.

Sure enough, as they strolled down the Sunday-quiet High Street, Lucinda's dainty heels clicking, she couldn't contain herself. She'd caught the eye of the son of the family, she said, and she wouldn't be a servant for much longer.

'He says I'm the prettiest girl he's ever seen. Prettier than any of the girls in London. And my lips taste like honey.'

'You haven't let him kiss you?'

Lucinda giggled.

'I've let him do a bit more than that.'

'Are you mad?'

Surely she knew about sons of houses and their dalliances with the servants? Every ballad singer you ever heard had a tragic refrain about a lusty lord and a maid disgraced, inevitably ending with the maid either face down in a pond or starving in a hovel with a child who had his father's nose but not his name.

'Oh, I won't allow him the full liberties until I've got a promise of marriage,' Lucinda said. 'Just a tickle and a tease, enough to make him desperate for the rest.'

'A promise of marriage isn't hard to make,' said Durie. 'It isn't hard to deny either.'

'I might have known you'd be jealous. I'm not just doing this for myself, you know. It could raise the whole family up.'

'Oh, my stars, Lucinda, you are so stupid! It's not going to raise anyone up, because he's not going to marry you! When have you ever heard of anyone marrying their maid?'

'Just because no one else has done it, doesn't mean I can't. And you might be happy to settle for a boring little life, but I'm not.'

'Nor am I!'

Lucinda snorted.

'You'll never make anything of yourself, you've no imagination.'

'Well, that's all you know. I'm going to be a bonesetter.'

'You're not still wanting to do that? I thought you were just being contrary.'

'Well, I've got to persuade Father first. You could always wind him round your little finger, can't you tell me how to do it?'

Lucinda laughed.

'There's about as much point telling you how I'd do that as telling you how to dance the gavotte.'

Durie had never seen anyone dance the gavotte and she wasn't convinced Lucinda had either, but she knew what her sister meant. Winsome smiles and pretty tears were going to be as much use to her as a fishing rod to a cat.

'Well, just tell me how to say it to him. I'm only going to get one chance, and honestly, Lucinda, I've never wanted anything as much as this.'

'You are so peculiar. But all right: what you need to do is pretend you don't want to do it. That's what works with men.'

'But that's stupid. He knows I want to do it.'

'Well, then, can you make him think it's his idea? That sometimes works.'

'Not when it's me that's asked for it, and him that's said no.'

'Well, if you're just going to be sarcastic, I've nothing else to offer you. Except don't do what you usually do, and blunder in like a bull at a gate. That'll get you nowhere.'

Durie meant to take that advice, she really did. But when she got home, the situation had already moved on. There'd been another bonesetter, in one of the villages between Lewes and Uckfield, called Fred Callett – not a proper one who knew all about bones and joints, like their father, but one like they had in a lot of small places, who was really the local farrier, and just set bones and dealt with dislocations when needed. Their father had just heard, from a neighbour, that he'd died. He and Margie were sitting in their usual chairs, on either side of the crackling fire, talking about it.

'Next nearest bonesetter is Uckfield,' he said. 'Anyone this side'll call on me instead now – I'll be working all hours.'

'I think it's time then,' said Margie. 'If you don't get Richie started now, you'll get too busy to teach him.'

Lucinda's advice was still in Durie's ears, but if she didn't get in quickly, the decision would be made. She took a deep breath.

'It should be me you teach,' she said. 'Not Richie.'

Margie laughed.

'The things you say!'

'I'm serious.' She turned to her father. 'I'd be good at it. Honestly, I would. I think I was meant to do it.'

Her father shook his head.

'It's not work for a girl, Durie. I told you that before.'

'Why not? I'm strong enough. You know I am.'

'That's not the point,' said Margie. 'It's not a proper thing for a girl to be doing. You can't go touching men, it's not right.'

'Father touches women.'

'That's not the same.'

'What's the difference?'

'The difference is, you're a girl,' said her father, 'and girls don't do bonesetting.'

'Just because no one else has done it, doesn't mean I can't.'

It sounded better when Lucinda said it. Their father's face reddened, but she couldn't stop now.

'Explain to me why, then. If you can give me a good reason why it shouldn't be me, I'll shut up about it.'

'The reason is this: bonesetting is passed from father to son, always has been, always will be.'

'Just let me try, let me show you—'

'Durie, you are trying my patience now,' he said. 'You can sit here with us and talk about something else, or you can go up to your room.'

As she stomped up the stairs, he said to Margie, 'I'll speak to Richie tomorrow.'

Chapter 9

At breakfast the next day, when her father gave Richie the news, Durie had to stuff a big chunk of bread into her mouth to stop herself telling him he was being an idiot. But it wouldn't be long before Richie's weak stomach showed itself, and then their father would have to think again, surely? So she was delighted when, a few days later, he was called to an accident where it looked as though someone had broken his leg.

'Richie will hate it,' she said to Margie as the door slammed behind them. 'You wait till he hears the bones crunching.'

'Must you talk like that, Durie? Anyway, your brother will do fine, you'll see.'

Margie was wrong there. When they arrived back, their father's face was like thunder. Richie's was white, and sour-smelling vomit speckled his shirt. He sat and rested his head in his hands.

'What happened?' said Margie.

'Very bad break,' said their father. 'Don't see the fellow surviving, to be honest. That sort of wound, it'll be stinking to high heaven by Wednesday.'

Richie lurched for the door, just making it outside before vomit spattered the flagstones.

'Wouldn't have taken him if I'd known how bad it was, not his first time,' said their father. 'Puked before I'd even touched the boy, all over the parlour floor.'

'He'll get used to it,' said Margie.

'He won't, you know,' said Durie.

'That's enough from you,' said their father. 'It was a bad one, that's all. He'll be all right, in time.'

That evening, Durie walked with Richie to the pump. As he worked the handle, she asked him about the accident.

'It was horrible,' he said. 'The bone was sticking out through his skin.'

'I wish I'd seen it. What did Father do? How did he get the bone right again?'

He shuddered.

'I don't want to talk about it.'

'Why don't you just tell him you don't want to do it?'

'I can't, can I? It's like he says, it passes from father to son.'

'He could teach me instead.'

He laughed.

'What, and I'll go and stitch dresses with Mother?'

'They could find you other work, same as they'd have to if they had two sons.'

'Are you being serious?'

'I could do it.' She swung the full bucket aside and replaced it with the empty one. 'I'm as strong as you are.'

'Yes, and that's embarrassing enough, without you trying

to do a man's job as well. You know they call you Lenny Loudfoot at school?'

She did know that.

'I had to punch Rob Turner for asking me why my brother wore a dress.'

She hadn't known that.

'They'd have a good old laugh if I couldn't do the work and Father gave it to you, that's for sure. Anyway, he wouldn't. It passes to the son, and I'm the son.'

Every day, she had to watch Richie going into the consulting room with their father, or the pair of them hurrying off if someone called, while she trailed up the High Street with Margie to spend the day stitching and getting in the way. It was miserable, but she was biding her time: eventually, her father would see Richie was useless, he had to.

One afternoon, as her father and brother came home from seeing a customer over towards Brighton, she heard Richie say, 'I do try, but there's a lot to remember. I thought it was rosemary for swelling.'

'It's willow bark,' said Durie.

'There,' said their father. 'She only came out with me once, and she can remember it.'

'Good for her,' said Richie, and stomped up the stairs.

In the middle of dinner, Durie's father said, quite casually as he helped himself to more ham pie, 'I've been thinking about who I should train as my assistant.'

Richie, who'd been sitting in a sulky silence, looked up.

'What do you mean? You're training me.'

'I'm trying to train you. But you can't keep the simplest things in your head. So I'm wondering now, if there's some sense in what Durie says. Perhaps she should be my assistant.'

Durie dropped her fork with a clang on the flagstones.

'Do you mean it? You'll teach me instead?'

'That's not fair!' said Richie, and Margie started on about how he'd hardly had a chance and people would talk.

Their father put up a hand.

'We'll give it three months. You'll both work with me, turn and turn about. Durie, on your days you'll make up your work for Margie in the evenings.'

That didn't seem fair when Richie didn't have to do extra, but she didn't argue; what did it matter if at the end of it she was the one fixing people?

'At the end of the three months, I'll decide – whoever suits best will be my assistant.'

She couldn't sleep for excitement that night. She'd be able to show him how much she'd learned already, and he'd see how ridiculous it was to choose Richie. She was going to be a bonesetter. She was going to fix people.

Chapter 10

Awake before dawn, Durie was dressed and at the breakfast table before anyone else, and when her father came back from the outhouse, she'd already set out splints, strapping and the balms he used most often. It was a busy morning: a lad from the smithy who'd hurt his wrist, a little boy whose arm she could see immediately was broken, and Mrs Wright from the High Street, who came regularly with her sore knee. Durie had seen her treatment from inside the cupboard, but it was so much better to be able to watch close to and ask questions.

She studied every movement he made, trying to work out how it eased the pain or freed up the joint. Thanks to her time in the cupboard, she knew which salve he'd want before he even asked, so she was quick and neat at handing them to him, and she had bandages or splints ready just at the right time. The Durie who knocked hats down and knotted up thread was gone, and in her place was someone useful.

The morning flew. In the afternoon, he was called to a cottage outside the town, where a man had taken a tumble while fixing his roof. It sounded bad: possibly a broken ankle.

In her excitement as they got ready to set off, she forgot the buckle on one of her shoes was loose, and it came away in her hand. Her others were at the cobbler's; they wore through at the soles twice as quickly as Lucinda's. She'd have walked barefoot rather than not go, but by the door, an old pair of Richie's caught her eye. Low boots with wide soles and laces up the front. She put them on and stood up. So that was why men could walk so much faster and further than women.

They set off at a brisk pace, but she easily matched her father's long strides and, as they left the town behind, he said, 'You're a good walker. Your sister'd be whinging by now.'

Then he noticed the boots.

'What have you got on your feet?'

'They're Richie's. My shoe broke. But they're good, they make it easy to walk fast.'

He shook his head.

'Don't let Margie know you came out in them, or I'll be for it.'

The man, an elderly widower whose cottage was stuffed with knick-knacks that hadn't seen a duster in a while, hadn't broken his ankle, just sprained it – a disappointment because she already knew how to treat sprains – but he'd also broken his finger in the fall, so at least there was that. She'd brought paper and pen, so she could make a note of anything new to her, and she did a drawing, with arrows to show how her father splinted the finger. He laughed when he saw that.

'You don't need to write things down, you daft ha'p'orth.'

'I like to. It helps me remember.'

'Women,' said the old man. 'Always got to complicate things.'

'Well, I'm learning to be a bonesetter,' said Durie. 'It's quite a complicated business.'

The man laughed, as if she'd made a joke.

Durie opened her mouth to explain that she hadn't, but her father shot her a warning look.

'She's just helping me out,' he said. 'Very busy today, so she's sorting out the bandages and that sort of thing.'

'Why did you say that?' she asked, as they walked home. 'About me just helping you out?'

'I don't want to put customers off,' he said. 'We don't know yet what people will make of you being a girl.'

It spoiled the first day a bit, him saying that, because she'd thought he'd be pleased with her. But it didn't matter: she had three months to prove herself, and as soon as he let her do proper work, he'd see she had the knack, and then the choice would be simple.

Margie hadn't liked the idea of a competition between Durie and Richie. The job was Richie's by birth, he was the son, and it was demeaning to him, making it look as though Dan was considering Durie instead. And unfair to Durie too, because even though the idea was obviously crazy, the poor girl was taking it seriously, fairly bubbling with excitement on the days where it was her turn to work with him.

'Does it have to be three months?' Margie asked him, a fortnight into the taking of turns. They were sitting by the fire, all cosy and content, after Durie and Richie had gone to bed. 'Wouldn't a month do?'

'No, he's picking things up quicker now he thinks he could lose to Durie, but I need to be sure he'll stick at it.'

'Of course he will. He would have picked it up anyway, if you'd given him more time. I don't suppose you knew how to do things right from the start.'

She hadn't meant to sound so huffy, but honestly, couldn't he put a bit more faith in Richie?

'You do mean what you said?' she went on. 'This is just to get Richie up to the mark? You wouldn't really take Durie?'

'Don't be daft, of course it is. And it'll work, you'll see.'

Over the following weeks, Durie did everything she could to show she was the right one to pick, without giving away how much she'd learned from inside the cupboard. But every time she asked to do more than just getting the salves ready, or setting out the strapping, her father said she wasn't ready yet. In the meantime, Richie had managed to conquer his problem with the noises by humming to himself, and only spewed once more, when someone had jumped off a moving cart and caught their ankle in the wheel.

One evening she overheard them talking.

'You see what I mean now?' said their father. 'The bones tell you what you need to know.'

'I knew it was a sprain, soon as I felt it,' said Richie.

Durie's stomach clenched. Did Richie have the knack as well? But even if he did, it shouldn't be him. He didn't lie awake at night, thinking about whether there might be a better way to splint an ankle, or wondering why Mrs Gant's shoulder was more painful when the weather was damp and what they could do to ease that. He hadn't cut up a rat to see how its bones worked. He just thought he ought to do it, because he was the son, and people would laugh at him if she did it instead.

She couldn't lose. She couldn't go back to being clumsy and getting in the way and not being any use for anything. It would be worse than before, because she'd seen the life she was supposed to have. So when a chance came to show her father why he should choose her, what was there to do but take it?

Chapter 11

It was one of Richie's days with her father, and they'd been called out. Durie was only still at home because Margie had gone to do a fitting, and she was dragging her feet about going to the shop to spend the morning under Mrs Carroll's critical eye.

'I'm looking for the bonesetter,' the woman at the door said. 'My husband's put his shoulder out.'

Durie didn't recognise her; probably one of Fred Callett's old customers.

'He's not here,' she said. 'But I'm his assistant. I'll come.'

'You do bonesetting?'

'Yes.'

The woman looked doubtful.

'I don't know what he'll think about a girl—'

'Well, you can wait for my father to get back if you like. But he could be an hour or more.'

'All right,' the woman said. 'You'd better come.'

It was an hour's walk and, all the way, the woman wittered on about how unusual it was to see a woman bonesetter, and how she wasn't sure her husband was going to like the idea. Durie didn't answer. Was this mad? Should she say she couldn't do it after all? But she'd seen her father put back shoulders three times, hadn't she? She just had to copy what he'd done: lie the man down, make him count to a hundred, set her foot in his armpit, pull and twist. Surely she could do that?

The man was sitting on the ground outside a substantial thatched cottage, the ladder that must have caused his accident lying on the ground. Enormous, with arms like hams, he roared at the woman, 'Where's the bloody bonesetter?'

'I couldn't get him,' she said. 'She's his assistant.'

What followed was a stream of very bad language, the clear message being that he had no intention of letting Durie anywhere near him. And if he didn't, that would be it. Her father would be furious she'd come at all; her only chance was to do the job and do it right.

'You'd better go back and get your father,' the woman said, wringing her hands.

'Look,' said Durie to the man. 'It's taken us an hour to walk here, it'll take two hours to fetch my father. I know how to fix that shoulder, and I can do it now, or you can wait in pain till he gets here.'

He didn't say yes, but he didn't say no.

'Right,' she said, 'lie back, and count backwards, slowly, from a hundred.'

'What? Are you some sort of idiot?'

'Do you want me to fix you or not?'

'Fred Callett just got on with it!'

'Well, Fred Callett's in his grave, so he's no use to you. I

61

am and the sooner you start counting, the sooner I can fix you.'

He muttered something rude, but started to count. Durie sat and got into position, with her foot in his armpit. He yelped as she pulled his arm. It was tight, a lot tighter than she'd expected. She pulled harder, but it didn't budge. What if she was wrong? What if she couldn't do it?

She took a tighter grip and prayed harder than she'd ever prayed for anything. When she pulled again, there was movement. Slowly, slowly, she began to twist his arm, and he yelped.

'Keep counting!' said Durie.

By sixty she was sweating; by thirty, she was struggling to hold on. He stopped counting and screamed.

The woman said, 'I'm going for your father—'

Durie took a deep breath, kept twisting. And the shoulder slipped back in, as sweetly as anything.

She almost laughed with the relief of it. And more than just relief: in that moment, in the soft click of a shoulder slipping back into place, Durie Proudfoot felt again as though everything in the world was exactly as it should be. And this time it was her and her alone who'd put it that way.

As she stood, he looked up at her.

'Damn me,' he said. 'Your father taught you well, didn't he?'

She walked home slowly, carrying the memory of that moment when the shoulder slipped back in, like an egg she had to be careful not to drop and break. It had been hard work, but she'd fixed him. Her hands had known what to do, and her arms had been strong enough to do it.

It's in my blood.

Her father must have been watching for her; he yanked open the door, brandishing the note she'd scribbled before leaving.

'This had better be a joke.'

'I wanted to show you I could do it. And I can. I fixed the man's shoulder.'

'What do you mean, you fixed it?'

'I remembered what you did, that time at the White Hart.'

'Tell me the place. I'll deal with you when I get back.'

As soon as he slammed the door behind him, the feeling she'd carried home slipped away like water through her fingers. What if she hadn't done it right? What if his shoulder had popped out again, and he was screaming in agony when her father arrived?

Two hours passed. They sat down to dinner, Durie's favourite, baked ham studded with cloves, but she ate without tasting anything.

'Never seen him as cross as that,' said Richie, taking a second helping of potatoes and adding a knob of butter. 'Thought his eyes would pop out of his head.'

'What were you thinking of?' asked Margie.

'I wanted to show him it's me who should be his assistant. That's all.'

'Did you really fix the man's shoulder?' asked Richie.

'Yes. It was right out of joint, but—'

Her father walked in.

'Well?' said Margie.

He sat, without speaking, and took off his boots.

'But it clunked,' said Durie. 'And I felt it sit right.'

Her father reached over, cut himself a thick slice of ham, and ate it with a hunk of bread. It took for ever. Then, leaning back in his chair, he knotted his hands together over his stomach, looked at Durie, then at Richie. All the while, she was imagining that poor man being in agony with his shoulder popped out again.

Finally, he looked back at Durie.

'You did a good job,' he said. 'I've never heard of the knack passing to a girl before.'

'Perhaps no one ever looked for it before,' said Durie.

'But we've still two months to go, haven't we?' said Richie. 'Before you choose?'

'That's right,' said their father. 'Two months more, and then we'll see.'

The very next day, he let Durie do all the splinting; not just putting the splints on, but deciding which size and type were right. It was progress, but when he came out of the consulting room with Richie the day after, she heard him say, 'Well done, son, you're really picking it up now.'

It was her turn the day after that, and they walked to a little house a long way down the London Road, where the customer was an old lady who'd hurt her wrist. She was tiny, like a bird, but tough, sitting bolt upright, not making so much as a squeal as Durie's father examined it.

'This your girl?' she said.

'That's right,' said Durie's father.

'You're the one who fixed my nephew's shoulder then. He reckons you did it twice as quick as old Fred Callett, and half as painful.'

Fred Callett obviously hadn't known about the counting down from a hundred.

'She's not been learning for long, but she's coming along,' said her father. 'Now, I need to get this wrist into the right position before I splint it. Are you ready?'

The old lady's milky blue eyes looked from him to Durie. 'Let her do it,' she said.

Durie couldn't have said who was more astonished, her or her father. The old lady nodded at Durie.

'Now be quick about it, before I change my mind.'

They walked home in silence. He'd started telling her how to do it, but stopped when he saw she knew. The splinting was as neat as any she'd seen him do, and he didn't even test if it was tight. The old lady winked at her and said, 'She's good, this one. Got good hands.'

He was quiet all the way, but when they got to the door, he said, 'She was right. You have got good hands. I just wish you'd been born a bloody boy.'

After that people started asking for her. First time, it was Richie's turn to go, but the woman at the door said, 'My father said to ask you to bring the girl.'

Turned out they were neighbours of the old lady. This time, when her father finished checking that the woman's father had only sprained his ankle and not broken it, he said, 'My girl will splint it for you,' and let her get on with it.

That happened twice more, both times with old customers of Fred Callett. Then Mrs Martin, who'd been coming with her stiff shoulder for years, asked if Durie could work on it, saying she'd heard she had a way with shoulders. And after she'd watched her father deal with a few more breaks, he'd trusted her to fix a little boy's broken arm, when the child unaccountably took a shine to her but screamed the place down if her father tried to touch him.

By the time they were halfway into the third month, she'd set two more broken bones. Richie, in the meantime, had mastered strapping and splinting, but still hadn't touched a break. He was much better than when he started, and she had to concede he must have the knack too, but all the same, her father couldn't possibly choose him over her.

Then Lucinda came home, and everything fell to pieces.

Chapter 12

Durie had been out, fetching bread from the bakery. Nibbling at a piece of the loaf's warm crust, she walked in to see Lucinda sitting at the table, silvery tears running down her cheeks. Their father was shouting, his face red; Margie stood beside him, her hands clenched together. Obvious what had happened. How could she have been such an idiot?

'What were you thinking of?' yelled their father. 'We brought you up better than this.'

'He loves me!' said Lucinda. 'He promised to marry me, and he would too, if that witch of a mother would let him.'

She laid her head on her arms and sobbed piteously. Hard to tell whether they were real tears or not, when you knew how convincing Lucinda's fake ones could be, and certainly Durie didn't think Lucinda cared a button for the young man. But perhaps she really had believed she was going to marry him and become a lady. Either way, the sobs worked on Margie, who sat and laid an arm round Lucinda's shoulder.

'There's no sense in shouting at her. What's done is done.'

Lucinda lifted her tear-stained face, and pressed home her advantage.

'I thought it would raise us all up. I thought I'd be able to buy you a house, and . . .' She thought for a second – clearly the plans for raising them up hadn't been detailed ones. ' . . . and a horse. And now I've got nothing.'

'They've thrown you out?' asked Durie.

She nodded mournfully.

'I should have listened to you—'

Margie gasped, and their father turned his glare on Durie. 'You knew this was going on?'

'Yes, but I told her he wouldn't marry her. She wouldn't listen.'

'You could have told us,' said Margie. 'We could have taken her away from there.'

'I'm disappointed in you,' said their father.

'I'm not the one who's got myself in a predicament, she is!'

Lucinda renewed her sobs and Margie patted her back.

'You're not the first to be caught like this,' she said, 'and you won't be the last. We'll sort something out, don't worry.'

'What a business,' said Dan as he set the candle by the bed. 'If I could get my hands on that Beresford boy . . .'

'If you could get your hands on him, you'd find yourself up before the magistrate, and what good would that do?' said Margie. 'The only thing to do now is write to Ellen, eat some humble pie and hope she'll take Lucinda until the child's born.'

'I'll write in the morning.'

He went to blow out the candle.

'Wait,' she said. 'I was thinking . . . we should send Durie with Lucinda.'

'Why?'

She hesitated for a moment. But no, it had to be said.

'This idea she's got about working with you. It's not right, you know it's not.'

Dan sighed.

'I know you don't like the idea, and I didn't either, at the start. But she's good – really good. She's not just got the hands, she's got the mind for it too. And mostly, when people see she can do it, they don't mind her being a girl.'

That was what Margie had been afraid of.

'You said Richie had the knack.'

'He has. And he's good too, now he's thrown himself into it.'

'Is he good enough?'

'Yes. But she's better. And there's only enough work for one of them.'

She took a deep breath.

'Dan, I've never asked you for much, have I? I know you loved Elizabeth more than you'll ever love me—'

'Don't be daft.'

'It's true, but it's fine, you love me in your own way. And I've brought up your girls, and you know, I love them as if they were mine. But Richie's my son.'

He didn't answer.

'You said yourself, he's good enough. And he'll get better, like you must have done. So I'm asking you, for me, to take him, not Durie.'

'Does it really mean that much to you?'

It means you love my son as much as her daughters.

'It does.'

He sighed.

'All right. I'll tell her tomorrow, and be done with it.'

'No, don't – there'll only be an almighty row, and I don't want poor Lucinda upset any more than she already is. You've no need to tell Durie at all – that's why I'm saying, let's send her to London with Lucinda. She'll probably have forgotten all about it by the time they come back.'

Durie threw the last of her things into her bag, then flopped down on the bed. Downstairs, Margie and Lucinda were fussing about, looking for something Lucinda had forgotten to pack; she wouldn't go down till she had to.

It wasn't fair. Her father had decided Lucinda was to be packed off to an aunt in London, who'd never even been mentioned before, to have the baby secretly. A place there, the Foundling Hospital they called it, took in infants whose mothers couldn't keep them, and brought them up and educated them. Which was all fine and dandy, but then they'd said Durie had to go too.

'But why?' she'd asked.

'Because it's not safe or proper for her to travel alone,' said her father.

'And because she's your sister, and she'll need your support in her time of trouble,' Margie put in.

When she asked what was going to happen about the competition between her and Richie, he said he'd decide when they came home. But that meant Richie would have months to get better, while she had no chance to practise at all. She'd tried to argue, but they wouldn't listen. So there was nothing to do but hope that, just as competition had spurred Richie on, the lack of it might lead him to slacken off.

'Durie, come on, you'll miss the coach,' yelled her father.

Her one act of rebellion was, at the last minute, to leave her shoes under the bed and walk out in Richie's old boots. Margie was so busy fussing over Lucinda, she didn't notice. She had the feeling her father did, but he said nothing.

Chapter 13

The girls' first impression on arriving at Aunt Ellen's house proved to be right; their aunt had done well for herself. Her shop, a confectioner's, was on Brook Street, a very smart road nearby, lined with shops whose big windows were polished every morning to show off displays of very expensive gloves or hats or canes and catch the eye of people who had nothing better to do. Hers sold delicate little cakes, jellies and sweets, all made in the basement kitchen by Aunt Ellen and her two pastry cooks. The shop itself was on the ground floor, with spotless glass shelves in the window to display pyramids of sweets and cakes, a long marble counter, and a roped-off area with spindly gold chairs and tables, where ladies who even Durie could see were fashionably dressed and hatted looked each other up and down, drank tea or hot chocolate and chitchatted about nothing in particular.

Durie and Lucinda started work there on the Monday after they arrived, and from the moment Aunt Ellen opened the doors that morning, the shop was busy, with a parade of carriages stopping outside and, inside, a constant hum of chatter and the tinkling of tiny forks on porcelain. The customers' gowns sent Lucinda nearly cross-eyed with delight. 'Look at the lace – that'll be from Italy', she would whisper to Durie, or 'They call that colour Paris pink, isn't it pretty?', even though she knew perfectly well the dresses could have been made of potato peelings for all the interest Durie had in them.

As if it wasn't bad enough being there at all, when she should have been getting on with fixing people, Durie felt like a carthorse among the dainty cake stands and glass dishes full of sweets, the fiddly little tongs and the curly ribbons to tie round the boxes, not to mention the silver pots of chocolate that had to be carried across the shiny floor and poured into the teeny tiny cups without scalding anyone. It was even worse than the milliner's shop, and at the end of the second day, after she'd sent a tray crashing to the floor with her elbow and managed to spatter the skirts of six customers with tea and raspberry jelly, Aunt Ellen said she'd be better employed down in the kitchen.

After her experience in the pie shop at home, Durie didn't hold out much hope of being a good fit there either, and she was swiftly proved right. So after producing cakes you could crack a tooth on and sweets that looked like old men's ears, she was confined to washing up, running errands and carrying sacks from the storeroom and trays of cakes up and down the stairs.

Lucinda, of course, fitted right in upstairs, dimpling and twinkling for all she was worth. She had even the women customers smiling and saying yes, why not, to a cake that was a bit more expensive than the one they'd asked for, while the men invariably walked out with a spring in their step and at least two prettily ribboned boxes of things they hadn't intended to buy.

'You're a natural,' Aunt Ellen said, as she locked up at the end of their first week. She pointed at Lucinda's still-flat belly. 'When this business is done with, we might think about you staying on.'

Lucinda smiled prettily, but as soon as Aunt Ellen disappeared down to the kitchen, she said, 'She can forget that idea, my feet are killing me. I want to be on that side of the counter, not this one.'

It was hard work, and they were both so tired by the time the shop closed that first Saturday that, next morning, they were still dozing when Aunt Ellen came into the room, whisked open the curtains and said, 'Wake up, you girls!'

Durie sat up, squinting against the morning sun, while beside her Lucinda groaned and burrowed under the covers.

'As I've told you, I like my Sundays to myself,' said Aunt Ellen. 'And besides, you two have seen nothing of London yet.'

To Durie's surprise, before they left, she handed them wages for their work in the shop. Margie hadn't ever done that.

'I expect a proper day's work from you both, family or not, so I'll pay you a proper day's wage,' she said. 'And it's good for a girl to earn her own money, and know what her work's worth.'

Lucinda wanted to go to St James's Park; she'd heard customers talking about it.

'It's where all the smart people go to be seen on a Sunday morning. Lords and Ladies as well.'

Well, queen or no queen, Durie wasn't wasting a day looking at people and listening to Lucinda telling her what colour their clothes were, so they agreed to part and meet later. Durie had a fancy to see the Tower, and a chair man who'd just dropped off a passenger outside the park gave her directions. It was a long walk, from the west of the city to the east, but pleasant, with the streets quieter and church bells ringing out from every direction. By the time the turrets of the Tower loomed up though, the hot buttered rolls at breakfast seemed a long time ago. A wan-looking girl was selling rabbit pies – 'Lovely pastry, plenty of meat' – and Durie stopped to buy one. As she handed over her money, there came a loud roar from the direction of the Tower.

'What's that?' asked Durie.

The girl looked at her as though she was a bit simple.

'It's the lions, innit?'

'They've got lions in there?'

'Got all sorts. Wild hellcats, birds as big as sheep.'

'Can people go in and see them?'

'Course they can. You can get in free, if you've a dead cat to feed them with.' She looked Durie up and down, as though she might have a recently deceased pet concealed somewhere. 'Otherwise, it's sixpence – gate's round the corner.'

Durie asked the man at the gate the way to the lions. He jerked a thumb.

'That way and follow your nose.'

The Lion Tower was a large semicircular building on the

other side of the moat, and a pungent blend of very strong wee and old meat hit her as she crossed the little bridge. The walls enclosed a large courtyard, with brick dens set into the walls, their open fronts barred with thick iron struts. The four lion cages were in the centre of the semicircle, but there was a crowd there and at first she couldn't see through.

'Look at that one,' a man in front said to his wife. 'Them teeth are as big as my finger.'

'Rip your hand off in a second,' said another man.

As if to confirm the statement, one of the lions gave a great roar. People at the front jerked back and Durie took the chance to elbow her way through. There he was, staring out at the crowd as if to say, how dare you look at me? As tall as a pony, with a rough mane and a long tail swishing backwards and forwards. He threw back his head and gave another roar, showing enormous yellow teeth and releasing a blast of exceptionally fetid breath. He was the most beautiful thing she'd ever seen.

She stood there a long time before she went to see the others: two lionesses, with sleek fur the colour of wheat, and a smaller male with a shaggy mane that looked as though he hadn't quite grown into it yet. The crowd around the cages thinned, as people went to see the jewels. Durie had planned to do that too, but that was before she saw the lions: why would you walk away from them for a load of old gold and silver?

She saw the other animals too: wildcats with tufty ears and angry eyes, pacing up and down as though they had an important decision to make; a sad-looking tiger, huddled at the back of its den; three enormous, sharp-beaked eagles and a snow-white owl; a strange kind of wild dog that made a noise like a mad person laughing. But she kept going back to the lions, and stayed so long, she had to hurry to meet Lucinda.

They'd agreed to meet at the park gates, but Lucinda wasn't there.

Don't say she's got lost.

The park was full of people strolling gravel paths between immaculate lawns, with children and frisky little dogs running ahead: she squinted into the distance, to right and left, for a flash of blue that might be Lucinda's dress, but she was nowhere to be seen. Didn't she understand, this wasn't Lewes?

It was a good five minutes of waiting and worrying before Durie spotted her – with a man. Thirty, at least, poet-looking and dressed like the men who came into the shop: fancy coat, very tight breeches, fine stockings and silver-buckled shoes that looked as though they were pinching his feet. Lucinda was giggling as they strolled up. He swept off his hat and bowed.

'The younger Miss Proudfoot, I presume?'

'This is Mr Connelly,' said Lucinda, looking up at him from under her lashes. 'He very kindly stood me dinner in the park.'

'Since when did you go about having dinner with strange men?'

'Durie, don't be so rude!' She turned to him. 'I apologise for my sister, Mr Connelly.'

Before Durie could answer, he swept another bow and said, 'Not at all. A pleasure to meet you both. And one I hope to repeat.'

He gave Lucinda a wink and walked off across the park.

'What are you thinking of?' said Durie. 'You can't go eating dinner with any old person.'

'He's not any old person.' She clutched Durie's arms. 'He's in the theatre! And listen to this – he thinks I could be an actress!'

She babbled on about Mr Connelly all the way home, how he'd said she was prettier than someone called Peg Woffington, and her speaking voice was more melodic than Susannah Cibber's, whoever that was. She didn't even ask where Durie had been. Then, as soon as they walked through the door, she started telling Aunt Ellen how they'd spent the day in the park.

'We saw so many fine people in their carriages! I heard someone say one was the Duchess of Bedford, she had on such a pretty hat, trimmed with green feathers. Then we bought pork pies and saved some crumbs to feed the ducks – Durie got attacked by a swan! – and took chairs near the bandstand to listen to the music.'

Had Lucinda actually done all those things with Mr Connelly or were they conjured up entirely in her head? Either way, she was so convincing that by the end of the tale Durie could almost feel a bruise coming up on her arm from that swan, so it wasn't surprising Aunt Ellen swallowed the story whole. Which was annoying, because Durie wanted to talk about the lions, and now she couldn't.

It wasn't until they went to bed that Lucinda finally asked. 'Where did you go, anyway?'

Durie told her about the lions, about the great big male

who looked like he was king of the place, and the bars in front were just an inconvenience he hadn't got round to dealing with yet. About the beautiful lionesses, so sleek and haughty, and the smaller male shaking his mane as though he was testing whether it would stay on.

'He was so funny – he looked as though it had grown overnight, and taken him by surprise.'

But Lucinda was already asleep, her hands folded beneath her cheek, no doubt dreaming of her career on the stage. So gullible: thinking she knew how the world worked, and then falling, a second time, for promises a man didn't mean. At least it looked as though Mr Connelly's goal had only been the company of a pretty girl for an afternoon, but Lucinda didn't deserve to have her feelings played with like that. Durie would have liked the chance to give him a piece of her mind, but they wouldn't be seeing him again, that was for sure.

Chapter 14

He called at the shop the very next day. Durie wouldn't have recognised him – the fashionable men all looked the same to her – but the blush on Lucinda's cheeks caught her eye as she came up the spiral staircase with a tray of almond dainties, and then came his smarmy voice.

'May I say how very pretty Miss Proudfoot is looking today?'

He caught sight of Durie and, smooth as you like, said, 'And of course the younger Miss Proudfoot is looking very well too.'

Did he think she was an idiot? Did he imagine she missed the half-wink he aimed at Lucinda?

'Good of you to say so,' she said, 'but since we have a mirror at home, I'm not in need of opinions on the matter.'

He gave a little bow, a smirk playing around his lips. As Lucinda handed over his parcel with a dimpled smile, he said, 'Noon on Sunday then. I look forward to it.'

He gave a little wave through the window as he walked away.

'What was that about?' asked Durie.

'I don't know that I should tell you, when you've been so rude to him.'

'Don't then,' said Durie.

Of course, Lucinda was dying to. Durie wasn't more than a few steps down before she scuttled to the top of the stairs and said in a loud whisper, 'He's giving me an audition. For the stage!'

He'd got her pegged for a fool, hadn't he? There'd be some reason why they couldn't do the 'audition' at the theatre, but wouldn't you know it, his house would be round the corner, and Durie didn't want to think what might happen there. So, later that morning, when Aunt Ellen sent her to the market for eggs, she took a detour; if she could prove the man was a fake, Lucinda would have to listen.

She found the theatre in a street near the Strand, a most unprepossessing building, hemmed in by shabby alleyways. The front doors were closed, but down the side, a woman whose face looked as though it could do with a good scrub was sitting in a doorway eating an apple, her feet hitched up against a door, propping it open and showing most of her legs in the process.

'If it's tickets,' she said as Durie approached, 'you'll have to come back later.'

'I have an enquiry,' said Durie.

'Well, if it's an unpaid bill, I can't help you. You'll have to speak to the manager, he'll be back in a while.'

'Can you tell me his name?'

'Jack Connelly.'

'Are you sure?'

'Well, let's see . . . I saw him this morning, and that was his name then. I can't swear to you he hasn't changed it since, but I think it's unlikely.' She nibbled away the last of her apple and tossed the core over her shoulder. 'So come on then, what's he done now?'

'He told my sister he could make her an actress.'

'Did he now?' She looked Durie up and down. 'Well, I know he's looking for some new comic turns, but I shouldn't think—'

'We're not alike.'

The woman nodded past Durie as crisp footsteps approached.

'Well, here he is. Ask him yourself.'

'If it isn't the younger Miss Proudfoot,' he said, sweeping another insincere bow. 'Miss Proudfoot made the excellent almond dainties we enjoyed this morning, Eleanor.'

'I don't bake the cakes,' said Durie. 'I just scrub the trays.'

He opened his mouth, then closed it and opened his hands, as if to admit even he couldn't come up with an oily little compliment about that.

'Who's this new actress then?' said the woman.

'I hope to audition the elder Miss Proudfoot on Sunday. But I fear the younger Miss Proudfoot isn't keen on the idea.'

'You're right.'

'Come with her then. You can meet some of the company, and check for cloven hooves.'

The woman smirked.

'Now, if you'll forgive me,' he said, 'rehearsals call. Come on, Eleanor.'

So he was who he said he was. Didn't mean he wasn't out

to use Lucinda, just like the father of her child, did it? If he seriously intended to make her an actress, then Durie was the Queen of Sheba. She couldn't stop Lucinda going on Sunday, but she wasn't going alone.

She was ready for an argument, but to her surprise, Lucinda asked her to come.

'He said I've got to make my voice carry all the way to the last row,' she said, as they got ready for bed that night. 'If you sit near the back, I can pretend I'm just talking to you.'

'It's not like you to be nervous.'

'I'm not nervous,' Lucinda snapped, then sighed. 'All right, yes. I am. My knees knock at the thought of it. Because this could change everything. If I impress Mr Connelly, I'll never have to be anyone's servant ever again. Look at this.'

She handed Durie a copy of the *Weekly Miscellany*, one of the newspapers that Aunt Ellen bought for customers to read, then took home to see who was new to town, so she could send a free box of comfits and entice them into the shop. There were a ridiculous number of London papers; at home, titbits of news filtered down over days or even weeks, from the papers taken at the big house and the rector and the magistrate, but in London, Aunt Ellen said, people wanted fresh news every day and if they couldn't afford their own newspaper, they read, or listened to someone else reading, in coffee houses, taverns and tea shops. Yet it seemed to Durie that most of what was in the papers was nonsense that no one needed to know, and the story Lucinda was pointing to, about an actress called Susannah Cibber going to buy a hat, was a perfect example.

'There was such a crowd outside, she couldn't come out of the shop for an hour,' said Lucinda. 'Imagine, being as famous as that!'

Durie couldn't imagine anything worse. But it showed how seriously Lucinda had taken Mr Connelly's promises. She wasn't just flattered by the idea that she was pretty enough to be an actress, she really believed it was going to happen.

'But what about when he finds out you're expecting?' said Durie.

'He doesn't need to, not for ages. By then, I'll have proved myself. And once the child's born, I can go back.'

What an odd place London was. Fancy standing waiting outside a shop, just to get a glimpse of an actress. It wasn't even as though she was going to burst into song when she walked out with her hat, was it? But Londoners were obsessed with looking at each other, one way or another. Durie didn't often bother to read the newspapers, but when she did, half the stories in them were about someone being seen in such and such a place, or noticed wearing such and such an outfit, or observed out with this or that person. It was as though the newspapers were spare pairs of eyes that went about the place seeing all the things their readers couldn't be there to see, and reporting back.

And yet, the thing that Durie noticed everywhere, the thing that was considerably stranger and more interesting than anything in the papers, was something no one else seemed to see at all: so many people with bad backs and stiff knees, hips and ankles, especially around the smart streets of Mayfair. You could tell from the way they walked, favouring one leg over the other, bending where they should have been straight or, sometimes, just from their faces, where pain always shows.

'Don't people go to bonesetters in London?' she asked Aunt Ellen one day.

'Not these days. People think bonesetting's old-fashioned, something only country people do. And we have all the best physicians here, so they see them instead.'

Ridiculous. How could the person you chose to get you out of pain be a matter of fashion? No one at home would go to Dr Fernley with a backache, any more than they'd go to Durie's father with a sore throat. But that was London people for you: very peculiar altogether. And now her stupid sister wanted to become one of them.

Chapter 15

Durie usually woke first in the mornings, but when she opened her eyes that Sunday, Lucinda was already sitting in front of the glass, doing something with her hair. Of course: the audition.

'At last,' said Lucinda. 'I need you to help, I can't reach the back.'

Her instructions were very complicated and when Durie finally got the last bit twisted up and jammed the pins in place, Lucinda shook her head and the whole thing fell down again.

'Leave it alone, you're hopeless,' she snapped. 'Perhaps I should ask Aunt Ellen . . .'

'Why not? I'm sure she won't think it remotely odd you doing yourself up like the Empress of Russia for a stroll in the park.'

'Then hold these pins and give them to me when I tell you.'

Turning sideways to the mirror, Lucinda twisted up a lock of hair. The movement pulled her shift tight across her belly, showing a roundness Durie hadn't noticed before. Their eyes met in the mirror.

'It seemed to happen overnight,' said Lucinda. 'I thought it wouldn't show for ages yet.'

They both looked at her reflection for a long moment.

'I'll wear my green,' said Lucinda. 'It's nice and full. Now, pass me that hairpin.'

They didn't have a theatre in Lewes, so Durie had never seen inside one, and after the drab exterior, it was a surprise. No windows, and only the lanterns at each side of the stage were lit, but even in the dim light all the gold paint glimmered: the high ceiling and two tiers of boxes that ran along each of the sides were crusted with it, and the stage was framed in gold too. It reminded Durie of one of Aunt Ellen's more elaborate cakes.

There were more lanterns above each box, and four big chandeliers hung from the ceiling. When they were lit, the players would get as good a view of the audience as the audience of them. Who on earth would want to stand there and see all those faces looking at them?

Durie ignored Mr Connelly beckoning them from the front, and took a seat at the back. He gave a smarmy bow in her direction, and exchanged a few words with Lucinda, then gestured for her to climb the steps beside the stage. She walked to the centre, her hands knotted in front of her, her face pale.

'Begin,' said Mr Connelly. 'You remember the line?'

Lucinda nodded. Even from the back, you could see her hands were trembling, and when she spoke her voice quivered.

'"Here am I, a poor maiden yet honest . . ."'

'Take a deep breath,' said Mr Connelly. 'Nothing to be nervous about.'

She started again, but stumbled over the line.

'Don't worry, just carry on,' said Mr Connelly, but when Lucinda did, Durie could only just make out the words. Lucinda said 'I'm sorry' and turned to walk off. Well, that was a relief. She'd be upset for a bit, but Lucinda always bounced back.

Mr Connelly bounded up the steps, took Lucinda's hands and whispered in her ear, then ran down again. Durie never did find out what he said – some old flannel, no doubt – but whatever it was, it worked, because when she spoke again, her voice was clear and sweet, and every word carried right to the back. By the time she'd got to a bit about her lover being thrown into prison, she wasn't Lucinda, she was a poor girl who was all alone in the world, and Durie believed every word that came out of her mouth.

The curtain at one side twitched; a little knot of people stood there listening. When she finished, pausing, perfectly poised, before delivering the last line, they clapped.

'Bravo,' said Mr Connelly. 'I knew it. A natural talent.'

Lucinda smiled.

'Sal,' called Mr Connelly, and a woman stepped out from the side of the stage. 'Try her in Eleanor's costume.'

The woman beckoned to Lucinda. 'Come with me.'

'So,' said Mr Connelly, 'what did the younger Miss Proudfoot make of that?'

Durie walked to the front, to give herself a moment to think. He was right, Lucinda did have a talent. Where had that come from? But then when you thought about it, it had always been there, hadn't it? In the tears she could summon at will, in the way she made Margie's customers believe the most improbable compliments – even in that story she'd told about how they spent their Sunday.

'She was very good,' she said.

'She was. She is. The talent's raw, but in time, she could do very well. And it just so happens, we have a gap in the company – young Eleanor who plays doxies, maids and assorted women of the town is off to try her luck with a touring company in Ireland.'

The woman he'd called Sal appeared on the stage again.

'Bit of a snag with this one, Con,' she said. 'Got a bun in the oven.'

Durie followed them up the steps to the stage and off to one side. In a room at the end of a dark corridor, Lucinda was standing in front of a mirror that had been squeezed between racks of costumes, wearing a blue dress that gaped open a good four inches.

'Never going to get that done up,' said Sal.

Mr Connelly sighed.

'How far gone are you?'

'Four months,' said Lucinda. 'But I'll get my figure back as soon as it's born—'

He shook his head.

'Can't wait that long. Eleanor's impatient to be gone and it's showing in her performance. I'm sorry, my dear, you've wasted my time and I've wasted yours.'

'You said I had a natural talent.'

'You have. But you're not the only one. And I need someone now.'

'Can I come back after the child's born?'

'I can't promise anything, but by all means, come and see us.' He looked her reflection up and down. 'Once you're back in shape.'

Poor Lucinda. She had such big dreams, and even though they were dreams Durie wouldn't have given tuppence for, it must sting to have two of them shattered in quick succession. But this last was a lucky escape, surely? On the way home, she said so, but Lucinda, of course, couldn't see it.

'Oh, you think so, do you?' she said. 'Well, I'm not giving up. You heard what he said, I've got a natural talent. And you might be going back to a sad little life in Sussex when this baby's born, but I won't.'

Chapter 16

Every day, as Durie scrubbed trays in the basement kitchen, she looked up at the shallow window that let in light from the street, watched the parade of feet passing by and tested herself. That one had a stiff ankle, what would you do for that? This man here, favouring his left foot: a badly set hip, for certain; could it be a cruncher? It kept her knowledge solid, but it wasn't the same as doing the work, feeling bones and joints under your hands and listening to what they told you. What if Richie was really getting good now? She wished Lucinda's poor little baby would hurry up and come, and then go, so she could get back and fight for her chance.

The only good thing about being in London was the menagerie at the Tower. When they got their wages from Aunt Ellen, Lucinda, predictably, spent hers on fripperies: a hat trimmed with cherries, a set of pompoms for her shoes. But Durie saved hers so she could go back to the Tower every Sunday.

'Why go there every week?' Aunt Ellen asked. 'There's so much else to see.'

She couldn't explain it, really. She just liked watching the animals – though mostly the lions – and trying to understand why they did what they did. What made the big male suddenly wake from a doze and prowl up to the bars to roar? Why did one lioness spend her time sleeping, while the other paced relentlessly? What did they think about the people gawking at them? And of course, she looked at how they moved, so easy and graceful; that long, slow way they stretched, front legs out and spines curled up backwards. How much better off people would be if they had backbones like that, instead of ones that stiffened so easily and clearly weren't built to last.

In the beginning there were crowds around the cages, but as the weather turned, fewer people came. A cold snap at the beginning of November brought a biting wind that made it feel like February, and that Sunday, the handful of people round the cages soon scurried off to the jewel house, leaving Durie the only visitor. She had a routine by then: lions first, a walk round to see the other animals, then back to the lions, to watch them till it was time to go. By the time she came back to the lions that day, the wind was nipping her face and making her nose run. The lionesses and the smaller male were curled up at the back of their cages, tails wrapped round to keep out the cold, but the big male padded across.

He looked around, as if wondering where everyone else was, then sat, staring off into the distance with his golden eyes. Because it was just the two of them, Durie started to talk to him, telling him how fed up she was, stuck in London while Richie was at home doing the work she should be doing.

'It's the only thing I've ever been good at. The only thing! And if he won't let me do it, what am I—'

A clank behind her made her jump. She turned; a man,

perhaps two or three years older than her, stood there, with a broom and bucket, a woolly hat pulled down over his ears against the cold. He was smiling and she waited for the joke at her expense, but he just said, 'Don't mind me, I talk to them all the time.'

He had the build of someone whose work kept them active, and spoke with an accent she didn't recognise; from somewhere in the north, perhaps?

'Crowley here's a good listener,' he went on. 'The girls are easily bored, and young Edward just wants to play. But this one's a wise old boy, I tell him all my troubles.'

Was he laughing at her? He didn't seem to be; his smile was open and friendly. He had kind-looking eyes as well, brown ones, but not dark, more the colour of hazelnuts. All the same, she was about to walk away, but then he took a bunch of keys from his pocket and unlocked the gate at the side.

'I usually clean this lot out early on, before the visitors come,' he said, 'but I didn't think there'd be anyone today.'

Inside, the big lion padded up to him and offered his enormous head to be petted, like a cat.

'Good boy,' he said. 'Let's get your house cleaned up, shall we?'

He swept the straw into a big heap, talking quietly to the lion as he worked. After a few minutes, he took off his hat and shoved it into a pocket; it left his dark hair standing on end, like a cat's fur when it's brushed the wrong way. When he carried the pile of straw to the front, the smell made Durie's eyes water, but he didn't seem to notice it at all. As he dumped it near the gate, he said, 'You come every week, don't you?'

He probably thought she had nothing better to do.

'There's no law against that, is there?' she said.

He held up his hands.

'No need to be prickly, I've just noticed how quietly you watch them, that's all. Most people try and attract their attention, shouting and yelling, but you're always respectful.'

'Do you think they mind people shouting at them?'

'Wouldn't you? Everyone here thinks I'm cracked, when I say the animals have got feelings like we have. But I think they must do.'

He swept the last scraps of straw into the pile, then slooshed the floor with water and scrubbed it with the broom. The lion sniffed the ground.

'Don't lie there now, boy, it's wet,' he said to it. 'I'll fetch you fresh straw presently.'

Locking the gate behind him, he said, 'You look frozen.' He nodded at a low building by the gate. 'There'll be a hot cup of tea in there, if you'd like to thaw out a bit. We're not supposed to let visitors in, but there's only old John who looks after the hyenas in today, and he won't care.'

She hesitated, but the cold was biting, and he seemed harmless. Nice, even. And she shouldn't have been so snappy, when he was just making conversation.

It was cosy inside, and the steam rising from a kettle hanging over the fire was a welcome sight. A man was huddled into a chair in the corner, apparently asleep; he looked about a hundred and four, though he was wrapped in so much woolly scarving, topped off with a hat pulled down to his eyes, it was hard to say.

'Tea, John?' said the younger man.

The old one's eyes opened, and his head rose out of the mess of scarves, like a snail emerging from its shell. He peered at Durie with surprised eyes.

'This your missus, George?'

She waited for the look, the one that was on Peter Gleeson's face when Susan Hopkiss teased him about marrying her. But this George didn't turn a hair.

'No, this is our one and only visitor,' he said. 'I thought she deserved a cup of tea for turning up in this cold.'

'Didn't think that could be your missus,' said John, sinking his head back into the woolly layers and re-closing his eyes.

George handed her a steaming cup.

'You know my name now,' he said. 'What's yours?'

'Durie. Durie Proudfoot.'

'Never heard that name before. Is it short for something?'

'Endurance.'

'That's a nice name. Interesting. Why don't you use it?'

Durie had never discussed the story behind her name with anyone, and she wasn't going to start now.

'It's just a bit of a mouthful. Tell me about the lions – how is it they don't attack when you go inside the cages?'

'They've been around people all their lives. That's not to say they wouldn't turn wild if they got out, but they know anyone who comes into the den is likely bringing food.' He smiled. 'If they eat me for dinner, there'll be no breakfast.'

He told her how the young male, Edward, liked to play with a peacock feather, like a kitten, and how the lionesses would growl and flick their tails if a pigeon was pecking around in front of their cages.

'And Crowley, I swear sometimes he has a sympathetic

look on his face, even though I know he's probably just sitting there thinking about meat.'

'Where do they come from?'

'Barbary, way across the sea. Hundreds of them there, living free in the mountains. The Sultan of Morocco himself sent Crowley to King George – got himself a sapphire the size of a hen's egg in return.'

'Sounds like King George got the best of the bargain. Who'd want an old jewel instead of a lion?'

'I reckon most women would choose the sapphire.'

'Well, perhaps I'm just odd then.'

That came out more sharply than she'd intended, but he just smiled and said, 'I wouldn't say odd, I'd say unusual.'

'What's the difference?'

'It's good to be unusual,' he said. 'I think so, anyway. Makes life more interesting.'

Just then old John gave a great yawn, his head rising out of his scarves in the process. As the yawn tailed off, he glanced at the little window in the door of the hut, and said, 'Be getting dark soon.'

'I'm sorry,' she said to George, 'I've kept you from your work.'

He smiled.

'Not at all. Good listeners are all very well, but it's nice to talk to someone who talks back, for a change. Now go home, Durie Proudfoot, and get yourself out of this cold.'

A sleety rain fell as she plodded down Tower Hill, thinking over the conversation. Nice, being called unusual. Better than odd. George was quite unusual too, certainly if she compared him to the lads at home, who'd no more strike up a pleasant conversation with her than dance down the High Street in their nightshirts. And certainly none of them would go into a den with a lion.

It was a surprise that he was married, so young, but then again, having a steady job and no apprenticeship to finish would make a difference. What would his wife be like? The marriage rule was generally quite straightforward: wives about a third better-looking than their husbands, unless the husbands were rich, in which case the rule went awry and a perfect toad might win himself a beauty. George clearly wasn't rich, but he was nice-looking. So she'd be pretty: dark perhaps, like him, with laughing eyes, but small and dainty, where he was tall.

Didn't think that could be your missus.

Well, who would?

She wrapped her cloak tight around her, put her head down to stop her eyes from watering in the wind, and headed for home.

Chapter 17

The following day, a letter arrived from home. After telling them everyone was well, and he hoped they weren't being a trouble to Aunt Ellen, their father wrote:

> *We were called out to the London Road last week, a carriage overturned – two lots of broken ribs and a cracked wrist. Richie fixed up the wrist by himself and made a fine job of it.*

Oh, did he? At this rate, her father would forget all about the work she'd done. Well, she wasn't having that. She took pen and paper and wrote back straight away.

> *Dear Father,*
>
> *I hope you and Margie and Richie are keeping well. We are well here.*
>
> *I was at the Tower menagerie yesterday – you remember I told you about the lions there? I was watching one of them stretch, and it gave me an idea for how we could help some of the people that come with bad backs – the ones you said come from bending over their work. Could we teach them*

to stretch like the lions do, curving their spines up and back?
Once a day perhaps? I've done a drawing on the other side,
to show you.
    Your loving daughter,
    Durie
    PS: Did the comfrey salve work on Mrs Gant's shoulder?

The drawing wasn't very good, but it got the idea across. It would show him she had ideas, good ones, for making their treatments better. He wouldn't get that sort of thing from Richie.

Margie always wrote once a month, and when her next letter arrived, Durie unfolded it with excited fingers, expecting to find a letter from her father tucked inside. What would he make of her idea? Might he even ask her to come back? But there was just the one sheet, in Margie's beautifully neat handwriting. Blathering on about the weather, and some nonsense about a problem next door had with their maid. Then at the end:

Your father said to thank you for your letter. He and Richie
had to go out to Arrowlea Farm yesterday, a young lad
kicked by a horse. Very messy, your father said, but Richie
stood by through the whole thing and made himself useful.

Not a mention of her idea, and he'd completely ignored her question about Mrs Gant. It put her in a bad mood for the entire week. And it was a horrible week anyway: she dropped a tray of glass dishes on the stairs on Monday, making all the customers jump and some of the sillier ladies shriek; on

Thursday, she sent a cake, piled high with sugared rose petals and rosettes of cream, spinning to the floor just by walking past the counter; and on Saturday, she was pointing out to the pastry cook where she'd put the sugar, and her arm brushed a tray of fruit tarts, flipping the edge and catapulting the tarts to the floor. And of course, they landed upside down, spilling fruit and custard everywhere. Each time seemed like a reminder that she just didn't fit in the world like other people did. Except when she was doing the one thing she wasn't clumsy and cack-handed at, and what was she going to do if she wasn't allowed to do that?

Sunday came at last. The cold snap had passed, and the crowds were back at the menagerie. Durie waited for them to get bored and head for the jewel house, then went up to Crowley's cage. He'd been asleep at the back, but once the crowds wandered off, he came up and gave the same great stretch she'd seen before, his front paws out, his head down and his bottom in the air. Well, a fat lot of use it had been her seeing that.

A voice behind her said, 'Good morning, Durie Proudfoot. Not so cold today.'

It was George, holding a bucket full of what looked like sheep's heads.

'I saw you as I was passing,' he said. 'Sorry if I startled you.'

Well, of course she'd wondered if she might see him again, but she wasn't expecting to just then and she blurted out the first words that came into her head.

'I was just thinking about Crowley's backbone.'

He laughed.

'His backbone?'

'I'm interested in backs, I'm a bonesetter. Well, I want to be.'

'You mean, fixing broken legs and things? At home the farrier did that.'

'They do in a lot of places, if there's not a proper bonesetter. But my father does that and a lot of other things. Any problem with a bone or a joint, he can fix it.'

'It's unusual work for a woman, isn't it?' He grinned and wagged a finger. 'Unusual, mind. Not odd.'

'It is unusual, yes. But I'm very good at it.'

'Ah, and your father doesn't want you to do it – that's what you were telling Crowley last week.' He held up his hands. 'I wasn't eavesdropping, I promise. But I heard that bit. You sounded upset. I don't want to poke my nose in, but as it happens, I'm quite a good listener too.'

So she told him the story: how she'd tried to learn all she could, and prove herself, and yet her father still seemed to prefer Richie, just because he was a boy. She even told him about the rat.

'Did you think maybe to do the same with a dead cat, or a dog?' he said. 'I'd say you could learn more from bigger bones.'

'I did, but what I could see from the rat was, being on four legs, it all works a different way from how it is in a person. So it wasn't much use, really. A monkey would have been better, they can stand upright, but—'

'They're a bit thin on the ground in Sussex?'

'Exactly. And I don't want to think what my stepmother would have said if she'd found one of them in the bedroom.'

She told him about setting the man's shoulder, and how it had looked as though her father was finally taking her seriously, and then Lucinda's trouble came along and gave Richie such an unfair advantage that he might win after all.

'The thing is, I'm no use at anything else. And I'm really good at this. I know it sounds silly but I think I was born to do it.'

'Doesn't sound silly to me. You smile when you're talking about it. Not many people do that when they're talking about their work.'

'You do though, when you talk about the lions.'

'Well, I'm lucky. I could have ended up breaking my back unloading ships down at the docks, or scraping a living blacking shoes for pennies, but instead I'm here' – he nodded at Crowley – 'with four lions, and I didn't even have to give away a sapphire to get them. You could say I'm better off than the King.'

'How did you come to be here? You're not from London, are you?'

'No, I came down from Yorkshire, but that's a dull old story, one for another day,' he said, picking up his bucket. 'I'd best give young Edward his dinner. It was nice seeing you again, Durie.'

Two of them watched him as he walked away, Durie and Crowley. And what surprised her was the twitch of envy she felt, knowing the lion would see him again before she did.

Chapter 18

To Durie's surprise, Lucinda turned out not to be one of those women who gets a big belly in pregnancy but otherwise looks just the same, like a pea on a stick. She swelled all over, and as her waist thickened, the delicate features of her face took on a moony look. Even her legs and arms got fatter, though how much was due to her condition and how much to the sudden love she'd developed for iced fancies was a matter of conjecture. She tired easily, was prone to cry for no reason, and her dainty gait disappeared; she reminded Durie of a donkey overladen with hay.

Aunt Ellen bought her a cheap brass ring to wear, so her billowing skirts wouldn't provoke talk in the shop; if asked, she was to say her husband was in the navy, but no one asked. And by her eighth month, the number of tight-breeched gentlemen visiting the shop was noticeably lower.

'Well, I think we always knew it wasn't your wit that brought them,' said Aunt Ellen as she counted the takings one evening. 'Time for you to retire from the stage, I think.'

She wasn't to know what effect that word would have on

Lucinda, who burst into tears and fled downstairs. Aunt Ellen rolled her eyes.

'I swear, a baby in the belly makes women go soft in the head. I'm glad I was spared that particular gift from the Lord.'

'Did you never want to marry and have a child?' asked Durie.

'Never for a second.'

Aunt Ellen looked up from the piles of coins.

'Surprised, are you? Not every woman wants that, you know. No one's at all surprised when a man gets satisfaction from his work, but we're supposed to be happy pushing out a brat a year, which any cat can do. I always knew I wouldn't be.'

Durie knew there were women who no one wanted to marry – Susan Hopkiss had seen to that – but she'd never heard of one who'd chosen to be a spinster.

'How did you get started?' she asked. 'With the shop, I mean?'

'I was in service, a big house in Brighton – kitchen maid, to start with. Worked my way up, and the mistress noticed I was good with sweetmeats. They entertained every week, and we'd plan a new surprise each time – ices in flavours you'd never heard of, big bouquets of marzipan flowers you'd have sworn were real.'

There was a light in her eyes that Durie hadn't seen before.

'It sounds like you were happy there.'

'I was.'

For a moment, Aunt Ellen looked far away.

'Then when they came to London for the season, she

insisted I came as well. What a summer that was! One week, we made a dessert table that was an exact replica of their garden – flower beds of coloured sugar, gravel walks made from dragées, sugar-paste trees. It took me the entire week to do, and three newspapers wrote about it. She always had such clever ideas, she'd have done very well at this business herself.'

She picked up another handful of coins to count and, not looking at Durie now, went on.

'But their London chef wasn't happy about me getting so much attention, and he did a bit of stirring with the master of the house. I lost my place, but she lent me the money to start the shop. Took it out of her dressmaking allowance, so the husband wouldn't know.'

She looked around at the shop.

'That's the thing, you see. You marry, and the law says your husband owns everything you have, and every penny you make. Well, no man gave me this, and no man's going to take it away from me.'

She nodded towards the stairs.

'Your sister, she'll always be at a man's beck and call. She thinks she's in charge because she can make their day with a smile. And even if she was aiming too high last time, I'd say, once she's put this current trouble behind her, she'll be able to take her pick of the young men in Lewes and prob- ably marry a bit above herself.'

Best not to mention that Lucinda had other plans.

'But who's in charge then?' Aunt Ellen went on. 'Oh, if she gets a decent one, she'll be able to wheedle and persuade when she wants something, that's what most wives do. But when it comes down to it, he holds the purse strings, and her hands are tied with them.'

'I hadn't thought about it that way.'

'No, well, most women don't give it a lot of thought. Most women would tell you they feel sorry for someone like me, with no husband. But I feel sorry for them. Now, let's get these trays downstairs and washed up, so we can all go home.'

She was a lot more interesting than she'd seemed, Aunt Ellen.

For quite a while, when Durie set off for the Tower each Sunday, she pretended to herself that it was still the lions she was going to see. She stuck to her routine of saying hello to them first, then having a look at the other animals, and finally coming back to the dens and spending the rest of the time watching Crowley, or Edward, or the lionesses, Miss Lucy and Miss Kate. Around midday, George would wander up with a bucket of sheep's heads, and they'd chat for a while. They talked about anything and everything, from his worries about whether the lions were happy, to her ideas about different ways to fix backs; he understood immediately when she explained about teaching people to stretch like the lions did. And yes, sometimes she thought about those conversations during the week, but what of that? Not much else to think about when you were scrubbing trays or fetching flour. And it was true that on a Sunday morning she woke up smiling, but it was a day out of the shop, and she liked the lions, that was all.

One Sunday, the bells of All Hallows rang one o'clock, and he still hadn't appeared. Well, that didn't matter, did it?

She strolled over to Miss Lucy's cage and stood behind the little knot of people watching the lioness lick herself clean, like a cat. He'd probably forgotten, which he was quite entitled to do, because after all, he was really just passing the time of day, and what was it to her anyway when she had the lions to look at?

She was about to edge through a gap to get closer to the front when he came running up. When people said 'my heart leapt', it always sounded so stupid, because how could it? But there it was, the feeling they must mean: like a happy little skip inside your chest. Well, she was pleased to see him, what of it?

'I'm sorry,' he said. 'Got into an argument with the Keeper of the Lions.' He stopped and caught his breath. 'I was worried I might have missed you.'

Another little skip, quite out of her control. Probably indigestion; the porridge at breakfast had been very stodgy.

'No,' she said, unnecessarily, 'I'm here.'

Did her voice sound odd? If it did, he didn't seem to notice.

'Well, thank goodness for that,' he said, 'because nothing else has gone right today.'

'Who's this Keeper of the Lions? I thought that was you.'

He shook his head.

'It's just a title, in the gift of the King. He's in charge of the whole place, gives out his orders but doesn't know the first thing about looking after the animals. He wants to block up the back of the dens, so the lions can't hide in there when it's cold.'

'But that's cruel.'

'That's what I told him. And he reminded me there were

plenty of other men who'd like my job and wouldn't be constantly giving him trouble.' He ran his fingers through his hair, leaving it standing on end. 'Old John says I should keep my head down, but this lot can't speak for themselves, can they?'

Back home in Lewes, Lucinda used to list the qualities she required in a husband.

'Rich, of course. Very good-looking. An excellent dancer. And blue-eyed.'

Durie had never made a list like that, but if she were to have made one right at that minute, it would say, 'The kind of man who stands up for his lions. With eyes the colour of hazelnuts.' And that was not a good thing, because what definitely wouldn't be on the list was, 'Belongs to someone else.'

What an idiot you're being.

'Is something wrong?' he said. 'You haven't had bad news from home, have you? About the contest with your brother?'

'No, it's just, I said I'd get home early today, and help my aunt with the shop's accounts. I'm sorry about your row with the Keeper, but I was just going.'

'Well, I'll see you next Sunday, then.'

Durie didn't answer.

She wouldn't go back. Behave like the lovelorn girls in the novellas Margie and Lucinda borrowed from the circulating library, weeping and wailing about what she couldn't have? No. He had a wife, and let's face it, he wouldn't be interested in her in that way even if he didn't. There was already one thing she loved and, right then, couldn't have, and she didn't need another to make her miserable.

The next Sunday, she went to the new museum in Bloomsbury, looked at statues and stuffed animals, and annoyed the guide by asking a question he couldn't answer about who all the things belonged to before. The Sunday after, she walked down to the docks, where a dead whale had been hacked apart; interesting but very smelly, and not a patch on the lions.

On the third, she woke later than usual. Lucinda's belly was like a pumpkin by then, and her fidgeting to get comfortable had kept Durie awake. As she surfaced from a hazy dream, church bells were ringing. She smiled, because it was Sunday and she was going to the Tower, before she woke properly and, with a sinking heart (another silly phrase she now understood), remembered.

'I thought I'd go to the park today,' she said to Lucinda. 'Why don't you come with me, for a walk?'

Lucinda narrowed her eyes.

'All right, what's happened?'

'What do you mean?'

'Aunt Ellen might be fooled by all this nonsense about the lions, but I'm not. You go there every Sunday, and come back with a silly smile on your face, then you stop and you're as miserable as a monk. There's a fellow involved, and I suppose you've had a falling out. You might as well tell me, I might be able to help.'

That seemed a forlorn hope, but she'd only keep badgering if Durie didn't say.

'Oh, honestly,' Lucinda said, when Durie got to the end of the story. 'Trust you to take it all so seriously. You're having a little flirtation, that's all. And look.' She gestured at her belly. 'We won't be here much longer – what harm can it do to flirt with him for a few more weeks? You could do with the practice.'

How many of us, when we want to do a thing, but know it's best not to, would continue to resist when someone says, so breezily, no, don't worry, it'll be fine? By the time she got down to Piccadilly, Durie had convinced herself Lucinda was right. She liked George's company, he appeared not to mind hers, and really, it wasn't even a flirtation, because she didn't have the first clue about how to flirt anyway. Even if she had, it was plain he had no intentions in that direction. And what harm could a few more weeks do? So she left behind the crowds flocking towards the park gates like so many brightly plumed birds and took the familiar route to the Tower.

She was later than usual, and George was coming out of Edward's cage, his bucket empty. Her stomach did an annoying flip when his face broke into a smile.

'Durie! How are you? I was worried when you didn't come the last few weeks, thought maybe you were ill.'

'No, I just . . . I had some things to do for Aunt Ellen.'

'Well, wait there, I've got something for you.'

He ran off towards the hut, bucket clanking, and came back with a small hessian sack.

'It's a bit of a strange present . . .'

At first she couldn't make out what was inside, but then she saw. Bones.

'It's – well, it was – a monkey,' he said. 'Someone brought it last week– you know how they do with cats and dogs, so they don't have to pay? I remembered what you said, about their bones being more like ours. You said you were worried about getting rusty, so I thought you could use it for practice.'

She took out a bone; it was clean and smooth.

'How did you get it like this?'

'I boiled the bones up in the hut.' He grinned. 'John wasn't happy, it stank the place out. I didn't realise the skeleton would fall apart, but you'll be able to figure out how to put it back together, won't you?'

'Yes,' she said. 'Thank you. It's the best present I've ever had.'

When Lucinda saw the bag of bones, she laughed.

'They're from your little flirtation?'

'He knew I wanted a monkey to practise on,' said Durie. 'He remembered me saying it.'

'He's supposed to give you flowers – what kind of man gives a girl a load of old bones?'

The kind who understands me better than anyone else in the world.

Chapter 19

Lucinda's baby was born in February, a cold, dark night that Durie would remember as the most frightening of her life. She'd tried not to think about what was coming, but how could she not remember that day at the market?

You were too big, and you wore our mother out.

Lucinda was like their mother, Aunt Ellen had said. The same build exactly. Durie suspected that anyway: years earlier, she'd found the key to a little wooden box their father kept in the wardrobe, and inside was a lock of hair as golden as Lucinda's and a bracelet of beads that barely went halfway round Durie's wrist. What if Lucinda's baby was like Durie, a big lump of a thing? Would she die too?

The pains started in the early hours, and on Aunt Ellen's instructions, Durie stayed at home with Lucinda. By midday, her sister was pacing their room, moaning and gripping her back. Durie fetched her water, and tea, and whenever Lucinda rested a while on the bed, she sponged her brow with cool water. It was frightening, the way each wave of pain gripped her, but at first she was surprisingly calm, breathing deeply in between, sometimes even singing to herself; she said it distracted her. But as the hours wore on, the singing stopped and when she took the deep breaths, she clutched Durie's hand so hard her nails left little horseshoe marks. Aunt Ellen was home by then and Lucinda asked her over and over again, 'When will it stop? It's been hours, when will it stop?'

Aunt Ellen just sighed and said, 'It'll be a while yet. First babies take their time.'

She seemed calm, but was that just to try and keep Lucinda calm too? Durie kept checking Aunt Ellen's face for signs that she was seeing what she'd seen on the night Durie was born. Was this how it had been? Had her mother begged for the pain to stop too?

At around nine, when the pains were coming faster and each wave seemed to hold Lucinda in a giant claw, Aunt Ellen sent for the midwife, a pinched-faced woman who made Lucinda get down on all fours on the rushes they'd laid on the floor. By then Lucinda was bathed in sweat, her hair hanging round her face in hanks, her nightshift all rucked up and showing her belly, so round and hard it looked as though it might burst. On her hands and knees, she swayed backwards and forwards, giving out low moans, like an animal, and when Durie knelt beside her and tried to lift her hair back off her face, she batted her away and swore. The pain had taken her somewhere else; Durie couldn't reach her there and that frightened her even more.

The next few hours became a blur. Afterwards Durie could remember seeing Lucinda on the floor, leaning against a mound of pillows covered with an old blanket, her legs wide apart and her sweaty face screwed up in pain. Hearing her grunt and growl and whimper, and the midwife telling her to push harder. Feeling Lucinda's nails digging into her arm as the pain swept over her again and again. Then a scream, and the midwife saying the head was there. Blood dripping onto the rushes, and it was all Durie could do to stay by her side and not run away. Because if the baby was a baby like her, it was going to kill her sister.

It went on and on, the screaming and the pushing. Lucinda gripped her arm each time, and Durie wished she could take the pain for her, because she was too small for it, and she was tired now, like their mother had been tired. She looked at the midwife and Aunt Ellen. What was wrong with them? Couldn't they see what was happening? This baby was taking too long, it was wearing her out.

Lucinda groaned loud and long; she seemed to be pushing with her whole body now, her poor, tired little body, just like their mother must have done, for all those hours, to birth a child she would never get to love.

And then the midwife said, 'You have a son.'

When the midwife had left, and they'd cleaned up, Durie sat on the bed beside Lucinda as she held the baby. It turned out that, terrifying as it had looked, the birth was quite a normal one; the midwife even said, rather huffily, that Lucinda had been lucky, first babies could take a lot longer. So what had their mother gone through? How could it have been worse than that? And yet it must have been.

The baby was ugly, with a wizened face and very little hair, but they always were. Why women cooed over them like they did had always been a mystery to Durie.

'He doesn't look a bit like his father,' said Lucinda. 'I thought perhaps if he did . . .'

Poor Lucinda, still clinging to her dream. As if it could possibly make any difference: the baby could have been the spitting image of his father, they still weren't going to welcome him into the family.

'Here,' said Lucinda, holding out the bundle to Durie. 'You take him, I need to sleep.'

He fitted into the crook of her arm as though it was made for him. In all her worry about the birth, there'd been no room for the thought that at the end of it all there'd be an actual person in the world who hadn't been there before. And that he was her flesh and blood, as well as Lucinda's.

As Lucinda lay back against the pillows and dozed, Durie looked down at her nephew, reaching out with tiny curled fists. Had her mother had a chance to hold her and look at her face like this? Or to feel any love for her at all? And had there been a moment, that night, when her father looked at what he'd lost and what he'd gained and wished she'd never been born?

The baby yawned, showing pearly pink gums. Poor little boy. He was going to grow up never knowing whether his mother or his father loved him. Would he wonder what he'd done wrong, to be left at the Foundling Hospital like an unwanted parcel? He'd certainly realise, in time, that his birth, like hers, hadn't been a cause for celebration.

Glancing across to make sure Lucinda was asleep, she lifted him up and whispered into his tiny ear.

'It wasn't your fault. Remember that.'

Chapter 20

On Sunday, when George joined her by Crowley's cage, she told him the news.

'And he's healthy?' he asked.

'Well, his lungs certainly work. I had no idea someone so little could make so much noise.'

'Ah, it comes as a shock, that.'

'You've got children?'

'No,' he said, quite sharply.

He must have seen her surprise at his tone.

'I didn't mean to snap. We had a little girl. But she died.'

'I'm sorry, I didn't realise.'

'No reason you should have.'

'Is that what you talk to Crowley about?'

He told Crowley all his troubles, he'd said, and she'd wondered, then, what troubles such a cheerful-seeming person could have.

'Sometimes, yes.' He looked away, watching Crowley pace backwards and forwards. 'I like talking about her, it brings her back. But people get embarrassed, or they say, you'll have another one soon, like she was a pair of boots you could just replace. So I talk to Crowley instead.'

'I wouldn't get embarrassed,' said Durie. 'You can talk about her to me, as much as you like. What was her name?'

'Polly. My wife wanted Jane, but she looked like a Polly to me, from the first moment.'

'What does a Polly look like?'

'I can't explain it, it was just the right name for her. She was fair, with big brown eyes, and right from the start, she looked like a happy child. Even the midwife said so.'

He told Durie how Polly chuckled when he sang to her, and how she'd reach up her arms when he came home each day.

'You'd have thought I was the best thing she'd ever seen. And then when she started to find her feet, even though she wobbled like a drunken sailor, she'd hold my finger and look up at me, as if she could walk to the ends of the earth as long as she was holding my hand.'

She'd been sickly from the beginning, he said, so they'd known they might not have her for long.

'We hoped she'd get stronger, but it wasn't to be. And I tell you, Durie, a child's coffin is the saddest sight you'll ever see.'

All the time he was speaking, he kept his eyes on Crowley, as if he was still talking to the lion, but then he turned, and said, 'Sorry, I've talked your ear off. Can't stop once I start, as Crowley well knows.'

'I don't mind. I liked hearing about her.'

He smiled.

'You're an unusual person, Durie Proudfoot. Your nephew's lucky to have you for his aunt.'

Lucinda would have had a pretty answer to that, but Durie didn't, so she didn't say anything. But as she walked home that afternoon, those words kept out the cold.

Chapter 21

Having been too young to remember their brother being born, Durie had no idea how much a tiny baby disrupts a household. In his first weeks, Lucinda's son cried for hours on end, and the only thing that soothed him was to be held with his head resting on your shoulder as you walked around. But Lucinda seemed not to want to pick him up.

'You take him, Durie,' she would say. 'He won't quiet for me, I think he likes a big shoulder to rest on.'

He did settle more easily when Durie held him. Aunt Ellen jiggled him too much, while Lucinda would only walk with him for a few minutes, and as soon as she stopped, he would take up his crying again. Durie picked him up and comforted him then, walking with him round the house for as long as it took.

'Your mother can't help it,' she whispered in his ear. 'She's trying not to get too attached to you because she knows you have to leave us, that's all it is. It's not that she doesn't love you.'

And yet, when Aunt Ellen asked Lucinda when she wanted to take him to the Foundling Hospital, she avoided the question, saying there was no hurry. A little voice in Durie's head said she needed to get back to Lewes. At that time of year, with icy roads and slippery cobbles, Richie would be getting plenty of practice, while she was just getting rusty; with the baby to take care of, she hadn't even had time to put the monkey bones together and practise with them. But someone had to make sure the poor little boy knew he was loved, if his mother couldn't, and it wouldn't be for long.

When he was a month old, Durie asked Lucinda why she didn't give him a name. It didn't seem right to keep calling him 'the baby'.

'They name them there, don't they?' said Lucinda. 'At the foundling place?'

'But you could give him a name for now.'

She shrugged.

'You think of one if you like.'

Durie looked into his serious blue eyes. Even if he wouldn't keep the name, he should have one that made him part of their family. The name of their grandfather, Thomas Proudfoot, who she didn't remember, but who taught their father the work that he'd taught her.

'Tom,' she said. 'We should call him Tom.'

Perhaps that was her mistake. Perhaps she should have kept her distance from him too, and it would have been easier if he hadn't had a name. But as the weeks went on, she found herself lingering over saying goodbye to him in the mornings, and looking forward to getting home in the evening and picking him up, feeling the soft weight of him in her arms and bending her head to take in his warm, milky smell. It was ridiculous: he was still ugly, and all he did was cry, expel surprisingly copious quantities from his little backside, and puke up curdy, half-digested milk (she thought of writing to Richie, saying 'It's in the blood'). But the idea of taking him to the Foundling Hospital and leaving him with strangers was getting harder and harder to bear.

She thought it must be worse for Lucinda, yet her sister was uncharacteristically calm about the whole thing. And when Tom was about eight weeks old, Durie discovered that Lucinda had her own reasons for putting off the day when he had to go. Durie was going down with a cold, sniffing and sneezing all afternoon, and Aunt Ellen sent her home early. Hearing Tom crying, she ran upstairs. Lucinda was standing in front of the dressing table in her petticoat, weeping; she jumped as Durie came in.

'What are you doing?' Durie said. 'You can't just leave him to cry, look how upset he is.'

Poor little Tom was bawling in his crib, fists waving, his face like a tomato about to burst. Durie held him against her shoulder, rubbing his back to soothe him.

Lucinda sat down heavily on the bed, rubbing her eyes.

'What's the matter?' said Durie. 'Why aren't you dressed?'

'Look at me,' said Lucinda, throwing out her hands. 'I thought once it was over, I'd look like myself again. But I'm as fat as ever.'

Not quite true, but not wildly inaccurate either. Giving birth had shrunk her stomach, but the weight on her face and limbs was holding fast. And it wasn't flattering. A lot of women looked quite bonny with a bit of extra poundage, but Lucinda's delicate features just got lost. And looking in the mirror and not liking what she saw must feel to her like losing a leg or an arm would to Durie.

'It's not been long,' said Durie. 'It's bound to take a while.'

'But if I don't lose it soon, Mr Connelly will have forgotten all about me. And I'll lose my chance.'

'What?'

'The dresser at the theatre said letting him suckle would get the weight off. But . . . ' She picked up a letter from the bed and waved it at Durie. 'Margie wrote this morning, asking why we hadn't taken him yet.'

'That's why you're keeping him here?'

'She said it was the quickest way.'

She couldn't mean it. That couldn't be the reason. Lucinda pouted.

'Don't look at me like that.'

'He's your child, Lucinda. Don't you care about him at all?'

'What would be the point of me caring about him? I'd just be making myself unhappy, I wouldn't be doing him any good.'

'He should know his mother loves him.'

'Oh, don't be ridiculous, he's too little to remember any of this.'

Tom snuffled his face against Durie's shoulder, his cries subsiding. As though he knew he was safe with her.

'How long do you plan to keep him?' she asked.

Lucinda shrugged.

'I can't see me getting into a costume without a couple more months of nursing him. But I suppose you're going to tell, and then they'll make me take him.'

'No,' said Durie. 'I won't.'

* * *

After supper that evening, as they sat by the fire, Lucinda said, 'I was wondering, Aunt Ellen . . . would you consider taking me back at the shop, once the baby goes?'

Durie looked up. What was she talking about? She had no intention of working in the shop.

'Lewes would seem so small now, after London,' Lucinda went on. 'And I think I'm quite well suited to the work, don't you?'

'If your father agrees, it's fine by me,' said Aunt Ellen. 'I'd have to take another girl on anyway, once the season starts, and you've got a nice way with the customers.'

'Oh, good,' said Lucinda. 'I suppose it might be best though, if I carry on nursing him for a while, so I can lose the weight more quickly. I want to look nice behind the counter.'

Aunt Ellen agreed, quite readily, as Lucinda must have known she would, and there it was: Lucinda's problem solved. She winked at Durie behind Aunt Ellen's back, but Durie pretended not to see.

Chapter 22

Once Tom was three months old, and the weather turned warmer, Durie took him with her to the menagerie.

'So this is the lad himself,' said George, reaching out to wag Tom's fist. 'I've heard a lot about you, young man.'

Tom wrapped his fingers around one of George's and gazed up at him, but just then, Crowley gave a great roar. It startled him and he whimpered, his little lip trembling as though he might be building up to a cry.

'Why don't we take him to see the owl?' said George. 'She's nice and quiet.'

As they walked across, Durie shifted Tom up and held him against her shoulder.

'Is he heavy?' said George. 'Here – let me carry him.'

He tucked Tom against his shoulder, and pointed out the different animals as they passed.

'I thought I'd do this with Polly, but I never got the chance. She was born in the autumn, and by the time it was warm enough to bring her out, she was too sickly.'

'How long did you have with her?'

'Just a year and a half. But babies make you love them

very quickly.' He looked at her. 'But I think you know that already, don't you?'

'If you'd told me three months ago, I'd never have believed it,' said Durie. 'I thought all babies were the same, but I could pick him out in a thousand of them.'

She didn't mean to say what she said next, but it came out anyway, all in a rush.

'I know it sounds silly because he's not even mine, but I wish we didn't have to give him up.'

'I was thinking that might be how it was, hearing you talk about him these last few months,' he said. 'And it doesn't sound silly to me. You might not be his mother, but you love him, anyone can see that.'

'I just keep wishing there was a way we could keep him.'

'It wouldn't be easy for him if you did.'

He hesitated, then said, 'My mother had me out of wedlock. Nobody in our village ever let her forget it, nor me neither.'

'That's why you never talk about your father, then.'

'She'd never say who he was, but I believe he was someone who had a wife already. And someone in our village, because she never went anywhere else. So he must have seen me all the time, but he didn't want anything to do with me.'

'But surely you don't wish your mother had given you up?'

'No, she gave me enough love for a mother and a father. But she couldn't stop people turning their noses up when I went looking for work, or expecting me to take half the pay of another lad, because I was desperate. That's how we came to be down here, me and my wife. My mother saved up, to give us a fresh start.'

He looked down at Tom, lying in the crook of his elbow.

'Does your sister want to keep him?'

'No.'

Durie explained what she'd learned, why Lucinda was putting off taking him to the Foundling Hospital.

'That can't really be the reason, surely?'

'I didn't want to think so either, but it's what she said.'

'When will he have to go?'

'In a couple of months, I think. And then he'll be lost to us, and he'll grow up thinking no one loved him.'

'Well, you're doing your best for him until he does, and that's all you can do. And even though he's only little, I think he can tell someone loves him, and that must make a mark on him, even if he doesn't remember this time with you.'

The snowy-white owl blinked at them with yellow eyes. George turned Tom to see.

'Look at this, Tom. This is an owl, from the frozen north.'

After that Durie took Tom every Sunday, so he'd have some happy experiences before he left them. Some wisp of memory might stick, to tell him he'd been loved by his family. George carried him around, showing him the animals, and sometimes talking about Polly.

Durie asked him once if he and his wife talked about her much at home. He looked down at his feet, and said, 'We don't talk about her, or very much else. You might as well know – we married because she was expecting. We were very young and I was flattered she liked me, when the other girls turned up their noses because of my mother's situation. By the time we realised we're as different as chalk and cheese, it was too late. If we'd had more children, or if we were still up in Yorkshire with our families round us, I daresay we'd notice it less, but as it is . . . '

He looked up, and gave a grim little smile.

'But as my mother said at the time, you make your bed, and you have to lie in it. We're no worse off than plenty of others, and I'm better off than most, having work I like to come to every day. And a good friend to talk to.'

'I should think Crowley listens better than a lot of people do.'

'I didn't mean him,' he said. 'I meant you.'

She turned away so he wouldn't see the blush creeping up her face, and luckily Crowley was having a good scratch and George said something about that, and she answered, and the moment passed.

Walking home with Tom in her arms that day, she wasn't proud to realise she was pleased George wasn't happy with his wife. Which was ridiculous, because what difference could it ever make to her?

Chapter 23

Ellen watched as Durie unwrapped the baby on the rug, after yet another trip to the Tower, tickling his tummy and making him chuckle. She should never have let this go on so long. She'd been concerned, at first, when Lucinda put off taking the child, fearing hysterics once he did go, but it soon became clear there was no strong attachment there – look at her now, she'd barely looked up from that daft novella when Durie came in with the child, much less asked how he'd been all day.

Then of course the truth had come out: she fancied a few months off her feet at home. Ellen didn't approve of laziness, but in this case, she was willing to overlook it. She hadn't been entirely happy at the idea of sending Tom off when he was tiny; it must be good for him, surely, to spend his first few months nourished by his own mother's milk before he had to be handed over to a wet nurse. She shuddered to remember the parade of slovens she'd had to interview before she found one to nurse Durie. And from her own point of view, Lucinda's presence in the shop had had an extremely pleasing effect on the takings, and it was welcome news that she wanted to come back. If giving her time at home, nursing the baby to get her weight off, was the price of that, well, it wasn't a bad investment.

'There,' said Durie, taking off the child's bonnet and smiling at him. 'That's better, it was squashing your ears, wasn't it?'

It had been such a busy time in the shop these last few months, what with that damn Frenchman opening a second place just two streets away. People were so easily seduced by anything new, and she'd had to work twice as hard to entice the regulars back. Coming home tired every night, she hadn't seen what was happening. Which was unforgivable, because hadn't she been in just that position herself, all those years ago? With a little baby that wasn't hers, but had smuggled itself into her heart without her realising, until it was too late, and she was surplus to requirements, expected to hand it over to someone else without a thought. And the longer it went on, the worse it would be.

'Girls,' she said. 'I think it's time for Tom to go to the Foundling Hospital. We'll take him next week.'

Durie didn't protest; there was no point. As she laid Tom in his crib that night, she told herself it was for the best. He snuffled as she tucked the covers around him, gently rubbing his back until the slow, even breaths of sleep came. It was for the best, and there was no way round it. The Foundling Hospital would give him a good start in life; he wouldn't be the boy who had to scrap around for work at half-pay, like George had been. But the thought that he'd be gone so soon was hard to bear.

There was one last thing she could do for him, so the people there would know he was a child someone loved.

'You know you have to leave a token with him?' she asked Lucinda, as they got ready for bed. 'Something they can identify him by, if you want to claim him back.'

'I won't be claiming him back.'

'Well, you have to leave one anyway. So let me make it for him.'

Lucinda shrugged.

'Please yourself.'

Inside Aunt Ellen's mending box, Durie found a scrap of yellow fabric, and on the way to the shop next morning, she called at the haberdasher's and bought a pair of shiny green beads, and a skein of brown wool. It took all evening: the thread tied itself in knots, the wool wouldn't lie right, and she couldn't get the beads level with each other, but finally, there it was. A small, highly inaccurate replica of Crowley, with a wonky eye, a patchy mane and flecks of blood from where she'd stabbed her finger with the needle.

Chapter 24

The days passed far too quickly. Durie tried to print memories of Tom on her mind: his gummy smile, the way he sounded when he slept; the smell of the back of his neck. And when she was alone with him, she whispered in his ear, 'Your family loved you, and none of this was your fault.'

Later that week, as they sat in the parlour after supper, Lucinda set aside the mending she was doing, and gave a dramatic sigh.

'You two can take the baby to the foundling place next week. I don't want to come.'

'You've got to come,' said Durie. People always wanted to please Lucinda: she'd been counting on them treating Tom better if they'd met her. 'It's his mother that has to give him up.'

'No, it isn't. It said in the newspaper, there's a basket, outside, for people who want to leave a child anonymously.'

'We're not leaving him in a basket, like we're ashamed of him!'

'Well, I can't face saying goodbye to him there.'

Lucinda made a noise that was obviously meant to be a stifled sob, though it wasn't up to her usual standards.

Durie looked at Aunt Ellen. Surely she wasn't taken in?

'Aunt Ellen, make her come,' she said. 'They've got to know he came from a respectable family.'

'I think you owe the child this,' said Aunt Ellen. 'You'll come with us, and that's an end to it.'

When Lucinda had flounced upstairs, muttering that no one understood what she'd suffered, Aunt Ellen put down her book and turned to Durie.

'I know this is hard for you,' she said. 'I should never have let Lucinda keep him this long. Your father and Margie wanted him to go quickly, but it didn't seem right, and when I saw Lucinda was keeping her distance from him I thought we could wait longer, get him strong and healthy, with no damage done. It never occurred to me you'd be the one to suffer.'

'I just hate the thought of him being with strangers. He should be with his family.'

'Durie, you are not stupid. So you know perfectly well it's not possible. Your father and stepmother would never agree, and even if they did, what kind of life would he have? The Foundling Hospital will give him a clean slate, with no blame attached to his birth. They'll educate him, and make sure he gets a good start in life. You can't do that for him, however much you want to.'

Durie wiped a stream of dribble from Tom's mouth, so she didn't have to answer. Aunt Ellen reached across and patted her knee; she flinched in surprise.

'You think I don't understand. Old, cold Aunt Ellen never loved a child, she doesn't know what it's like.'

That, to be fair, was exactly what Durie was thinking.

'I told you I never wanted a child of my own, and it's

true,' said Aunt Ellen. 'But after you were born, I took care of you, and your sister, for nearly a year. Do you think I didn't become fond of you in that time? When it was me you cried for if you woke in the night, and me you smiled your first smile at?'

'I don't remember that.'

'Of course you don't, you were too little.'

'So why didn't you ever come back?'

'I fell out with your father. I was very fond of your mother, and I thought it was disrespectful of him to take up with Margie so quickly. He said it was because you needed a mother, which told me I was surplus to requirements. He was right, but at the time, I didn't take it well.'

She sighed.

'So I made myself harden my heart about you. It wasn't easy, but it can be done. And you'll do it too.'

George hadn't hardened his heart about Polly. Durie wouldn't about Tom, either.

'I won't,' she said. 'I don't want to forget about him, and I'm not going to pretend he was never here.'

Wednesday was to be the day they'd take him. When Aunt Ellen locked the shop door on Tuesday evening, she called Durie upstairs and said, 'Don't wait for me, I've the accounts to do. You get off home.'

It was still light, and warm; there'd be time to take him out and have a last couple of hours together.

She called a hello to Lucinda as she came in, then went upstairs.

The crib was empty.

Chapter 25

Lucinda was standing in the hall.

'I took him today,' she said. 'I've got an audition tomorrow, with Mr Connelly. It came up at short notice, they need someone quickly, and I couldn't miss the chance. I know you'll be angry, but it's done now.'

Durie stood there, looking at her, and all she could think to say was, 'Did you give them the lion?'

'Yes. Durie, I wish you'd try to understand. I couldn't let him ruin another chance for me. And it's just a few days, what difference does it make? He won't remember—'

She was still babbling when Durie closed the front door behind her.

She didn't have anywhere in mind to go, she just couldn't stand to be near Lucinda. But she found herself walking east, until the turrets of the Tower loomed up. The gates were closed by then, of course, and she was standing there like an idiot, not wanting to go home and not knowing where else to go, when a smaller door in the gate opened and George stepped through it.

'Durie!' He smiled, but then he must have seen the look on her face. 'What's happened?'

She told him.

'I'm sorry,' he said. 'That's very hard on you.'

'I know he had to go anyway. But I wanted to give him one last happy evening.'

'You gave him lots of happy times. You did your best for him.'

Just then, the bells of All Hallows struck seven.

'Sorry,' said Durie, 'you'll be wanting to get home.'

'Would you like to walk for a while? I don't need to go straight home, and I don't think you want to, do you?'

So they walked, through a warren of narrow streets where the houses still leaned in towards each other in the old-fashioned way and the late evening sun disappeared. She told him how Aunt Ellen had said she had to harden her heart. He shook his head.

'I'm sure your aunt's a wise woman, but I don't think that's the way to go. We're none of us better for having harder hearts, whatever we've lost.'

A narrow lane brought them into a street full of booksellers, busy with people browsing the stalls outside, and then into the churchyard of the great cathedral, St Paul's. They sat on the steps, side by side. A woman walked past, holding a little boy by the hand as he chattered away.

I'll never hear Tom talk.

'He won't even remember me, will he?' she said.

'Maybe not in the way you mean, but all the love you gave him, that must stick. He'll feel the benefit of it, even if he doesn't know why or how.'

'I can't believe she just took him! There were things I wanted to tell them, like about what to do when he's restless. The only thing that gets him to sleep is rubbing his back, but she won't have told them that.'

'Well, perhaps it's not too late. You could go there, couldn't you, and tell them?'

'Do you think they'd take any notice?'

'They might. And at least you'd know you'd tried.'

Next morning, she raced through her errands, so there'd be time to get to the Foundling Hospital and back without Aunt Ellen noticing. It was on the edge of the city, and by the time she reached the grand houses of Great Ormond Street, the air was noticeably fresher. Behind them, the streets came to an abrupt end, and the hospital was surrounded by fields, with the hills of Hampstead and Highgate green in the distance. Bigger than she'd expected, with three stone archways in front, a long drive leading up to what looked like a chapel, and on each side of that, two substantial red-brick wings, three floors high.

She told the porter at the gatehouse she'd come to reclaim a child; it seemed more likely to get her in than the truth. Judging by the way his eyebrows shot up, that didn't happen very often, but he waved her through. The woman who opened the big main door showed her into an office and gestured to a chair in front of a large desk.

'Wait here, and Mrs Waring will come and see you.'

The place was surprisingly grand, with tall windows, paintings on the walls and gleaming wooden floors, which explained the smell of polish in the air. The smell of food cooking hung about too – boiled mutton, at a guess – but the thing there was no trace of was children. She strained her ears, foolishly thinking that if Tom was crying somewhere, out of sight, she'd hear him, but it was deathly quiet; so quiet that footsteps clicked along the corridor long before a tall woman with spectacles on came in, introduced herself and sat down on the other side of the desk.

'I understand you wish to reclaim a child,' she said, picking up a quill.

Suddenly it felt silly to say what she'd come to say, but poor Tom had no one else to tell them.

The woman raised her eyebrows when she said she'd lied, but she listened as Durie explained what she'd really come for.

'I wanted to make sure the people who look after him know. That's all. Will you tell them?'

'The babies go to wet nurses, in the countryside, where they spend their first four years,' Mrs Waring said. 'We choose them very carefully. Your nephew's nurse will know how to soothe him, I promise.'

There'd never really been any point in asking. But to give the woman her due, she could have lied, and said yes, we'll tell them, and at least she hadn't done that.

'Where will he go?' Durie asked. 'Because we live in Sussex, and if it was out that way, we could visit him. Just to see he's settled.'

'I'm afraid that's not possible. Your sister will have been made aware that once a child comes into our care, the family relinquish all contact. It's to give the children a fresh start.'

'And once he's four, what happens then?'

'He'll come back here, and we'll begin educating him for a useful occupation. He'll be well cared for, and when he's grown, he'll get a good start in life.'

'Is it possible for me to find out, from time to time, if he's well?'

'I'm sorry, we can only give information to the mother. If your sister were to enquire . . .'

'She won't.'

As Durie stood to leave, Mrs Waring said, 'I don't know if this would help . . . Some of the mothers write letters to the children. We keep them, and when the children are grown, and settled, if they ask about their families, we give them the letters then. I think it would be all right for an aunt to write, if you wanted to.'

'So he could find me then, when he's grown-up?'

Mrs Waring gave an apologetic smile.

'I'm afraid not. We give the mothers a fresh start, as well as the children. So you couldn't give your full name, because that would expose your sister. But we'd keep the letters and he'd know—'

'That someone loved him.'

'Yes. He'd know that.'

They always gave the shop kitchen an extra-thorough clean on Wednesdays, making it Durie's least favourite day, but that afternoon she willingly set to, scouring the great copper pans with sand until they gleamed and plunging glass dishes into the scalding water that got them sparkling. Hoping it would take her mind off the thought of Tom, lying in a strange crib, looking round with frightened eyes, not knowing where he was and why he'd been left there. But it didn't.

Lucinda had got herself let off early, telling Aunt Ellen she needed to buy some hair ribbons. When they got home, there she was, strolling towards them from the opposite direction. And the bounce in her step said it all. She'd got what she wanted.

She didn't say so though, she just told Aunt Ellen some rubbish about the Mount Street haberdasher not having the right colour so she'd had to walk all the way to Oxford Street. Aunt Ellen, having very little interest in the colour of ribbons, and being quite hungry for her supper by then, readily accepted the story.

Indoors, Lucinda skipped upstairs; Durie took as long as she could about following, but it couldn't be put off for ever. Lucinda was perched on the edge of the bed, hugging her knees, smiling all over her face.

'I did it, Durie. I'm going to be an actress. Only small roles at first, Mr Connelly says I need to learn stagecraft, but he thinks I could have a lead role by the end of the year.'

'Good for you.'

'You might be a bit pleased for me. After all I've been through.'

'All you've been through? What about Tom? You left him like a parcel and you don't even care.'

'For goodness' sake, Durie, how would it help him if I was weeping about it? You've done more damage, fussing over him. It'd have been better for him if he hadn't got attached to anyone. So think about that before you start judging me.'

She flounced downstairs, and Durie watched her go. If Aunt Ellen was right about hardening your heart being the best thing to do, Lucinda was clearly going to be fine.

20 October 1758

Dear Tom,

I know that's not your name now, but it's the only one I have for you. I am your aunt. Until you went to the Foundling Hospital, you lived with us — me, your mother, and our aunt. Your mother had to give you up, but every day you spent with us, you were loved. I think it's important you know that.

I used to take you to the menagerie, at the Tower, every Sunday. My friend, George, looks after the lions there, and he used to carry you around and tell you about the animals. You liked the lions best. Well, I think you did. You never cried, even when they roared.

I'll write every year so you'll know your family didn't forget you.

Yours,

Aunt Durie

Chapter 26

Lucinda didn't say a word to Aunt Ellen about Mr Connelly's offer. But three days later, he came to the shop, presented himself to Aunt Ellen, and said he'd happened to meet Lucinda in the park and thought she had the 'bearing' to make a fine actress. Now a place had come up in the company, but she'd said he had to talk to Aunt Ellen first. Durie was down in the kitchen, but when she heard about it later, she had to admire his technique.

'He said he understood your father and stepmother would need to be consulted as well, but he thought, being a businesswoman, I might like to inspect the contract,' Aunt Ellen told her, as they cleared up after closing. 'So as to be able to reassure them everything's above board.'

He wasn't as clever as he thought, though. Seeing the expression on Durie's face, Aunt Ellen laughed and said, 'Don't worry, I know flannel when I see it. And I'll be giving that contract a proper going-through. But, though I'm loath to lose her from the shop, this could be a good chance for your sister.'

'Prancing about on the stage for people to gawp at?'

'People are always going to gawp at Lucinda. At least this

way, she can put what God gave her to good use, and make her own money. That's the best protection for any woman, believe me.'

So Aunt Ellen read the contract, and wrote to their father and Margie, saying it seemed fair but they should come and meet Mr Connelly for themselves. The reply from their father was brief, but it said:

> . . . *and we can bring Durie home with us. She's been very much missed here.*

Much missed? Well, it was obvious what that meant! The customers must be asking for her, mustn't they? And at last, he'd seen sense. She'd beaten Richie, she could go home and do the work she was born to do. And that would be the way to drive two faces out of her head: a baby one, with wispy hair like a just-fledged sparrow, and a grown-up one, with eyes the colour of hazelnuts.

She'd hoped the menagerie might be uncrowded that Sunday, so she could say goodbye to George in peace and quiet, but bright blue skies had brought people out and the crowd around the lions' dens was five or six deep, among them half a dozen screechy children. Crowley had curled up in a corner with his back to them, and the children were trying to attract his attention with yells and whoops.

She stood at the back, waiting for George to walk up, wanting to keep a picture of him in her head. And there he was, striding towards her, smiling.

'Busy today,' he said, putting down his bucket. 'No wonder poor Crowley's tucked himself away.'

She'd already told him about the business with Mr Connelly; as she explained what her father's letter said, she had to raise her voice over the yabbering of the children.

' . . . so I'll be going home next week.'

Did his face fall? Or was she seeing what she wanted to see?

'I didn't realise it would be so soon,' he said. 'But it's good news that you won the contest, I know how much you wanted that.'

He looked across at Crowley, and said something, but at that moment one of the children yelled and she missed his words.

'What did you say?'

'I said, he'll miss you. Crowley, I mean.'

He bit his lip, then said, 'And so will I. Durie, I shouldn't say this, and if you weren't going, I wouldn't—'

'Here, mate,' said the father of the children, pointing at George's bucket, 'can I take one of those and throw it to that lion? If the young'uns don't get to see him move—'

'No,' snapped George.

'All right,' said the man, backing away with his hands in front of him. 'Only asking.'

'Idiots,' said George. 'Wish I could sling one of their heads in there.'

He turned to Durie.

'I'm just going to say this because . . . well, I don't know why, but I'm going to say it. You know I'm not in a happy marriage. I promise you, I'm not the type of man to seek comfort elsewhere, and I never have, but these last few months, I've found myself thinking about you a lot. Saving up things to tell you, during the week. Waking up on a Sunday smiling, because I'll be seeing your face. For a long time I told myself that was just because we were friends. But it's not.'

He took a deep breath.

'The thing is, Endurance Proudfoot, I love you. And I know nothing can come of it but I wanted to tell you in case you felt the same.'

'It's the same for me,' said Durie. 'It has been for quite a long time.'

They looked at each other for a long moment. He had such kind eyes. How could his wife not be happy, waking up next to him every day?

He reached out and took her hand, stroked it very gently with one finger, and then let it go again. It made her shiver, but in a good way.

'If things had been different, we could have been so happy, you and me,' he said. 'But we met at the wrong time, didn't we?'

'I'm not sorry we met,' she said. 'Are you?'

'No, and I never will be. But things being what they are, it's for the best that you're leaving – otherwise, we'd only make each other unhappy, sooner or later. So let's say goodbye today, and be happy that we met, and had this time at least.'

She didn't watch him walking away. She kept her face turned towards Crowley, still curled up at the back of the den, his twitching tail the only sign that he was aware of the screeching children. It had been one thing, saying goodbye to George when she was sure all the feelings were on her side, but now, when he'd said he felt the same . . . And yet what difference did it make, when nothing could come of it anyway?

Back at home, she went upstairs, and took out the monkey bones. There's someone for everyone, Margie used to say, and Durie had never believed it but perhaps it was true. She picked up a long leg bone, and stroked it, remembering him laughing about how he'd boiled them to get them clean and driven Old John mad with the stink. She'd put them back together, when she got home to Lewes, and they'd be her secret way to remember George.

She'd been lucky to find her someone, even if it was only for a little while. So she wouldn't be sad about saying goodbye to him, she'd be happy that she met him, and that he thought she was his someone too, even if nothing could ever come of it. She'd hope that he got another child with his wife, and that made them happier. That last bit was going to be tricky, but she'd try her best, because he deserved to be happy and quite possibly his wife did too. Even if she patently didn't realise how lucky she was to have George, so was probably quite stupid.

And Durie would miss him – she'd miss him so much – but she was going to go home, and get back to her work, and that would have to be enough.

Chapter 27

Mr Connelly's flannel might not have worked on Aunt Ellen, but it did on their father and Margie. They arrived on the Thursday, and he sent theatre tickets for the Friday, with a note saying he'd be pleased to give them a tour backstage beforehand. He showed them the dressing rooms, the racks of costumes and the painted panels that moved in and out, so one minute the stage was a castle on a cliff, the next a country meadow, as if he was giving a private tour to the King and Queen. Ladling out the compliments: what a beautiful dress Mrs Proudfoot had on, hadn't he seen one like it on the Countess of Coventry? Mr Proudfoot, he was sure, had spotted how the mechanism for moving the scenery worked before it was explained. He even told Durie she was looking very lovely, which you'd have thought would be a clue he was just a flanneller, but they hung on to his every word. And Lucinda, well, of course she was loving it, twinkling and dimpling as he told them she had a natural gift and was sure to go far.

The play was a load of nonsense about a poor maiden kidnapped by pirates, and the audience made as much noise as anything that came from the stage: talking among themselves, shouting across to acquaintances in the box opposite, yelling their approval or otherwise of developments in the story, and all the while shovelling food into their mouths: fat red cherries, pies dripping with gravy, greasy-looking fritters, vinegary cockles picked from brown paper cones. The maiden's capture provoked howls of anger that drowned out the pirate chief's triumphant song, and the actor playing him had to stand back to avoid a hail of orange peel and cherry stones.

After an interlude of country dancing that added nothing to the proceedings, the maiden was rescued by a lord who, naturally, fell instantly in love with her. As she delivered the epilogue from the front of the stage, the audience bellowed their approval, stamping their feet and kicking against the fronts of the boxes, and then at last it was over. A waste of an evening, in Durie's view, but at least it was done with; on Monday, she'd be on her way home.

With Friday being taken up with talking about going to the theatre, going to the theatre and talking about having been to the theatre, she didn't have a chance to speak to her father properly until Saturday morning. He and Margie were eating hot rolls and drinking tea at the parlour table when she came downstairs.

'Well, Durie,' he said, 'it seems we're to have a famous actress in the family.'

'We'll miss her,' said Margie. 'But what a stroke of luck! It wouldn't have been easy finding her another place in Lewes, when Mrs Beresford wouldn't give her a character. And we'll be glad to have you home.'

'I'm looking forward to getting back to work with Father,' said Durie, sitting down and reaching for the teapot. 'I'm probably a bit rusty, being away all this time.'

Her father looked down at his plate, picked a shard of crust apart, then glanced at Margie. She made a funny shape with her mouth.

'Not that rusty though,' said Durie hurriedly. 'It'll soon come back.'

'I hoped you'd given up on that idea,' said her father. 'I was going to tell you when we got home, but since it's come up . . . I've taken Richie as my assistant.'

The words came like a splash of cold water; for a second she wasn't sure she could breathe.

'But you promised you'd wait. You said you wouldn't decide until I got home.'

'I didn't really promise—'

'You did!'

He sighed.

'Durie, you were good at the work, I won't deny it. But Richie is too, and by rights it passes to the son. I can't pass him over, it wouldn't be fair.'

'But you're passing me over, even though I'm better than him. You know I am! And what am I supposed to do then? Go back to stitching? How can it make sense for me to do that instead of the thing I'm good at?'

'Durie, don't take it that way,' said Margie. 'Your father just thinks—'

'No, he doesn't. He isn't thinking at all, because this is stupid.'

'That's enough,' said her father. 'It's decided, and that's that.'

Aunt Ellen came in then; she must have heard their raised voices.

'What's going on?'

'Ask them,' said Durie, and stomped upstairs.

She sat on the bed. So many reasons why her father was wrong, and none of them made any difference. He wanted Richie because Richie was a boy, and there was no sense to that, so sense wouldn't shift him from it.

She looked down at her hands. That feeling, when her hands took away someone's pain, when it seemed as though everything was right with the world and she'd put it that way . . . she'd never have that again. All the ideas she'd had, for better ways to fix people, none of them could happen. She'd never walk through the town with her father, getting respectful nods like he did. And worse, she was going to have to watch Richie get better and better while she felt the knack slipping away.

Even scrubbing trays was better than that.

In the kitchen, Aunt Ellen was instructing the cook on the beef rolls and apple turnovers to be prepared for the journey back to Lewes the next day.

'Aunt Ellen,' said Durie. 'Can I stay here too?'

Durie stood and watched the coach join the throng of carts and gigs and coaches trundling down Cheapside, carrying Margie and her father back to Lewes. A relief to see them go: she'd barely spoken to either of them since the day before, she was so angry and sad.

They'd been surprised when Aunt Ellen said she'd asked her to stay – 'It'll be better if it comes from me' – but relieved too, it was obvious.

'Durie'll work hard for you, have no doubt of that,' her father said.

'I don't,' said Aunt Ellen. 'I wouldn't have asked her otherwise.'

'Well, there you are,' said Margie. 'It's all worked out for the best.'

How could they think that? The only reason to stay was that anything was better than going home and having to watch Richie do the work she was meant to do. But not much better. Though she was grateful to Aunt Ellen, the thought of going back to the shop the next day, and the day after that, and who knew, perhaps for the rest of her life . . .

'Oy, you, out of the way,' a chair man shouted. 'Standing there like a tit in a trance!'

She stepped back to let the chair pass, only to bump into a couple walking behind; the woman tutted and the man told her to watch where she was going. They walked off up Cheapside and turned right into Queen Street, the route she always took to the Tower. It was all she could do not to follow them. She could walk there in twenty minutes, and tell the one person who'd understand that she was never going to get to fix people, she was just going to be useless and get in the way for the rest of her life.

It's for the best that you're leaving – otherwise, we'd only make each other unhappy, sooner or later.

He was right. So it was best, now, that he knew no different. Even if it was going to make staying worse, knowing she wouldn't even have Sundays to look forward to. She walked out of the courtyard and turned west, towards home.

Chapter 28

What do you do when life doesn't go the way you want it to, and there's nothing at all you can do about it? Durie did the only thing she could do: she got up, went to work in the shop, came home and went to bed, then did it again the next day, and the next. She didn't look up at the parade of feet passing the window any more. It was just a reminder of what she couldn't have, and if she did glimpse someone who swung one foot a little more awkwardly than the other, or had that heaviness to their step that meant they were in pain, she could swear her fingers itched.

On Sundays, to prevent questions about why she didn't visit the menagerie any more, she went for long walks, and sometimes she'd let herself pretend George was strolling beside her, carrying Tom, and some unspecified miracle had happened so they could all be together. But after a while that just made her sad, so she walked faster and further and tried not to think about anything at all. She saw a lot of London on those walks, and she didn't notice any of it.

It didn't help that Lucinda was beside herself with excitement as she prepared for her debut at the theatre. She talked of nothing but rehearsals and costume fittings, and spent hours in their room pulling ridiculous faces at herself in the mirror.

On the day, though, she was more nervous than Durie had ever seen her; she must have visited the outhouse four times in an hour. The weather had turned exceptionally wet, so the roads were too bad for their father and Margie to come, and a letter from them wishing her luck sent her into a temper.

'Everybody knows it's bad luck to wish an actress good luck!' she said, tearing the letter into shreds and throwing it into the fire.

'I didn't,' said Durie. 'What are you supposed to say then?'

'You're supposed to say break a leg.'

Well, if that didn't tell you how peculiar theatre people were, what would?

The audience was even more rowdy than last time, and when the heroine's dastardly landlord cast her out into the snow, the actor playing him was almost hit in the eye by an orange, hurled from three rows back. So when Lucinda walked on, playing the heroine's maid, Durie's stomach clenched for her. She was beautiful, in a simple pale green gown that made the heroine's purple one look overdone, but the hand that held out a letter to her mistress was trembling. Then she spoke: the trembling stopped, and though she wasn't shouting or even, it seemed, raising her voice, every word was as clear as if she'd been standing next to you. A few lines in, the heroine threw herself to the ground in distress at the news in the letter. But she might as well not have bothered, because for those few minutes, no one was looking anywhere else but at Lucinda.

It was a small part, but it got her noticed. A week later, after the Tuesday matinee performance, she came home brandishing a copy of the *Gazette*.

'Look at this,' she said.

There was a review of the play and she pointed to the end of it.

The production also features a new face, Lucinda Ellwood, in the role of Molly McFee. A face which we have no doubt will light up the stage in bigger roles before long.

'But that's your part,' said Aunt Ellen. 'Who's this other girl then?'

'Oh, didn't I say?' said Lucinda. 'Conn said Proudfoot was too clumsy a name, it didn't look right on the billing. So I'm to be known as Lucinda Ellwood. But look what it says – "light up the stage"! You should have seen Lizzie's face, sour as a quince.'

'Who's Lizzie?' asked Durie.

Lucinda had developed an annoying habit of sprinkling her conversations with names that she clearly felt Durie and Aunt Ellen ought to know.

'Elizabeth Woolf, of course. Conn's favourite, she gets all the best roles.' She smiled. 'For now.'

12 February 1759

Dear Tom,

    You are a year old today. It's been five months since you left us; you've probably forgotten me already, but I miss you every day. I don't know where you are, except that you're in the countryside somewhere, and with a family. I hope they're kind to you.

    I wonder if you miss going to the Tower and seeing the lions. I haven't been for a long time, and I miss them a lot. I read in the Mercury *that the Sultan of Morocco has sent two more, little cubs called Hercules and Cassius. They'll be keeping our friend George busy, so he probably doesn't miss us at all.*

    Your mother is well and happy. Very happy.

    Yours,

    Aunt Durie

Chapter 29

Aunt Ellen liked to read quietly in the evenings, with Lucifer the cat on her lap, and didn't encourage chat; Lucinda used to complain it was like living in a monastery, but after a busy day in the shop, Durie found it quite pleasant. But one evening, after Lucinda had left for the theatre, Aunt Ellen closed her book and said, 'It's not easy for you, is it, watching your sister get what she wants, when you haven't?'

'Well, it'd be easier if she wasn't so annoying about it. Lizzie this, Conn that, look at me lighting up the stage.'

Aunt Ellen laughed.

'She is quite full of herself at the moment, I'll grant you. But give her some credit. She could have moped about, wailing about how unlucky she was after that scoundrel in Lewes left her holding the baby. But she didn't. She gave that child the best start she could, and then she found herself a chance and grabbed it. You're more alike than you realise, you two.'

'What do you mean?'

'You, with the bonesetting. Your father was against it from

the start, but you didn't let that stop you. You found a way to learn it, and you showed him you could do it.'

'And it didn't work.'

'No, it didn't. But that's down to your father's foolish stubbornness, not want of effort on your part. And there are other chances you can seize, if you want to.'

'If there are, I can't see them.'

'Well, what would you say to learning the confectionery business?'

'I'm useless at making the sweets, you know that.'

'Durie, stop being petulant, it's not like you. That's not what I mean. You've impressed me, you know, since you came. You're a hard worker, you never shirk, no matter how dirty or boring the job. And you've a quick mind. I could train you to help me with the business side of things – the accounts, and keeping up with the competition, and so forth. I know it's not the thing you want to do, but we can't always have exactly what we want in life. Let the bonesetting go, and make up your mind to be successful at something else instead.'

When she went to bed, Durie got out the bag of monkey bones again. She picked up the big shoulder bone, and fitted the long arm bone into the socket. They slid against each other so perfectly. She stroked the long leg bone – he'd got it so clean and smooth – and laid out the bones of the hand, flat on the quilt. Aunt Ellen was right: no sense in thinking about bonesetting any more, and it was kind of her to offer another opportunity. Durie didn't want it, but she would try to make the best of it.

No point in trying to put the bones back together now

either, but she couldn't bring herself to throw them away. She put them back in the bag and pushed them to the side of the wardrobe, so she wouldn't have to see them and remember what she'd lost.

The lessons began the next day.

'Come and look at these,' said Aunt Ellen, as Tessa the pastry cook set a tray of iced cakes on the big wooden table in the middle of the kitchen. 'Know what they are?'

Durie shook her head.

'They're what Monsieur Laurent's seducing my customers with, that's what. Honey and lavender cakes – everybody's talking about them.' She took a bite of one, thought for a minute, and said, 'Good work, Tess – better than his. Let's see the recipe.'

Tessa handed her a piece of paper. Each of the ingredients had a figure written beside it, and there was a total at the bottom.

'Fourteen pence a dozen, and we'd sell them at tuppence each . . . So if we cut the sugar in the icing by a third – you'll need to give it longer to set, mind . . . ' She crossed out a figure and wrote in a new one. 'And if we use the cheaper honey . . . no one will notice, not in a sponge . . . '

Another figure crossed out, she totted up the list.

'We can make a dozen for tenpence.'

Eager to show she was paying attention, Durie said, 'So then we can sell them for less, and more people will buy them.'

Aunt Ellen looked at her as though she'd suggested taking the entire stock and throwing it in the river.

'The first rule of shopkeeping is people want what they can't afford, and long for what they can't have,' she said. 'You give people six buns for tuppence, they'll think the buns are rubbish. Charge tuppence for one, and it's a special treat. Charge tuppence for one and say there's only two dozen available, and they'll form a queue.'

'I'd never have thought of that.'

'Well, you've a lot to learn then.'

Durie didn't have it in her to get excited about a new recipe for sponge cakes, but over the months, the more she learned, the more she admired her aunt. The shop was always busy, but Aunt Ellen never stopped thinking how to bring in more customers, how to get the ones who already came to spend more, and most of all, how to get one over on her rivals, especially Monsieur Laurent. Once a week, she'd head off to a different area of the city to see what was new and popular in the confectionery and tea shops there, then work out how to better it. And she could see in a flash how to use a little less of this, or a different type of that, so it cost less to make but still tasted good enough to justify the price she wanted to charge.

Durie learned to do the accounts, and order in the supplies, and after a few months, if the shop was especially busy, she was trusted with the job of heading off to Covent Garden or Cheapside or Ludgate Hill to peer into shop windows and see what was new. She tried her best for Aunt Ellen, because she was grateful for the chance. But she was still hoping that her father might change his mind, that one day, a letter would come from home saying Richie hadn't come up to the mark after all. Month after month, just the usual one from Margie came, and then, in the August, there was one from her father tucked in with it. Her fingers fumbled as she opened it; he'd realised, he must have done!

It was short; some stuff about the weather, and how he hoped it was better in London, a joke he'd heard from someone at the inn. And then two sentences jumped out.

Richie set a very messy break yesterday, made a fine job of it. It's all worked out for the best, with you two so well settled in London.

15 January 1760

Dear Tom,

I can hardly believe you'll soon reach your second birthday – it seems so long ago that you left us. I still miss you, and often wonder what you're doing.

I hope you're happy out there in the countryside. Sometimes I wish I could go back to Sussex – that's where our family comes from, by the way. Lewes, to be exact, quite a nice town. London is very grey in the winter, and to be honest with you, Tom, my life is quite miserable at the moment, what with one thing and another. Of course, you won't read this for years and years, if you ever do, so don't worry, I might be quite happy by the time you read this. Probably not, but you never know.

Yours,
Aunt Durie

Chapter 30

Sometimes, as she scrubbed trays in the kitchen or hauled sacks of flour and sugar from the storeroom, Durie looked at her hands and wondered if they still knew what they used to know. Was the knack something that slipped away, if you didn't use it? You could say it didn't matter, since she was never going to get the chance to use it again, but it did. It mattered like being able to bend your knee or say your name. Or breathe. Sometimes, when the itch was impossible to ignore, she took out the monkey bones from the back of the wardrobe and played with them, and then of course she couldn't help but think of George, which didn't help matters at all.

Walking to the flour mills at Lambeth, she'd see coaches taking advantage of the quieter road outside the city to go a bit too fast, and think, if that overturns and the passengers are thrown out, I'm here, I'm ready. A horrible thing to think, and she didn't like herself for it. But short of that, how were her hands ever going to do what they were meant to do again?

The answer came in the person of Gregory Philimore,

whose acquaintance she made one morning in the spring of 1760, not long after her twentieth birthday. She would look back later and wonder at how normal that morning seemed, when so much came out of it, both good and bad.

As she arrived back from an errand, a carriage pulled up: four footmen in green velvet and gold braid, a crest on the door. One opened the carriage door, but before he could unfold the steps, a boy of eight or nine jumped out, raising his arms in triumph at landing upright on the cobbles. Good job he was young; older bones wouldn't stand for that.

'Gregory, must you always jump?' came a voice from inside the coach. 'Wait for Mama.'

The boy's mother descended, all lavender satin and frothy lace, with feathery bits and pieces nodding from her hat.

'Come, Greggy,' she called. 'You can choose a cake to have with your milk.'

The kitchen was busy that morning, and Durie didn't give them another thought until she happened to open the area door as the carriage was moving away. The boy was at the carriage window; he reached out and fiddled with the latch, the door came open and he tumbled to the ground. Durie was already running up the steps by the time Mrs Philimore screamed and the carriage clattered to a halt. The boy was lying in the road, his arm hanging crookedly by his side, white-faced and howling in pain. Two footmen knelt beside him, flapping about ineffectually, and customers from the shop who'd seen what happened spilled out onto the pavement.

'Someone run for Dr Wilson,' Mrs Philimore was shrieking. 'Wigmore Street, quickly.'

Durie had dashed up the stairs without thinking, but would she even know what to do, after so long? Well, there was only one way to find out. Shoving one of the footmen aside, she knelt beside Gregory and felt around the boy's elbow, letting her fingers find their own way, trusting them to know. And they did. The elbow was out of joint, the mother must have grabbed him as he fell.

'What are you doing?' said Mrs Philimore. 'He needs a doctor!'

'I'm a bonesetter,' said Durie. 'It'll take your doctor half an hour to get here, if he's even at home, and your son is in pain. I'm going to stop that, whether you like it or not. You can help by standing back and shutting up. All your squawking is just frightening him.'

She turned Gregory's face towards her.

'You look like an intelligent boy, so I'm going to talk to you as if you were a grown man. Your elbow has got out of place. I can put it back. But you're to stop screaming and be brave, or I won't do it. Can you do that?'

He stopped mid-wail, stared at her for a moment, and nodded.

'Right. Take three deep breaths. Really deep ones.'

As he let out the last breath, she said, 'Now count to a hundred and sixty, slowly. You can count, can't you?'

He nodded as she began to manoeuvre his elbow. He was a surprisingly tough little boy and he kept counting even as tears sprang into his eyes. But it was an easy one: he'd barely reached the fifties when it popped back in.

He looked at her, wide-eyed.

'Come on,' she said. 'Up you get, you're fixed now.'

'Wait,' said Mrs Philimore. 'It might be dangerous for him to walk.'

'He hurt his elbow, not his legs. Walking presents no danger at all.'

Mrs Philimore turned to one of the footmen.

'You didn't latch the door properly! He could have been killed!'

'Madam, I did,' said the footman. The Irish accent was a surprise; you didn't get many of them in livery. 'I always make sure it's properly closed.'

'You couldn't have done, he only leaned on it. When Mr Philimore finds out—'

'Your son opened it,' said Durie. 'I saw him. He leaned out and turned the handle.'

'Of course he didn't!'

Durie turned to Gregory.

'I've seen you're brave,' she said. 'Now I want to see if you're honest. If you don't tell the truth, this man will get into trouble. So tell your mother what happened.'

Gregory looked at his shoes, his cheeks reddening.

'I opened the door. I wanted to see if I could.'

'Oh,' said his mother. 'Well.'

Durie was about to ask if she was going to apologise to the footman when Aunt Ellen rushed up with a beribboned box and a profusion of apologies. Both the box and the apologies were accepted by Mrs Philimore with an air of benevolent entitlement, as though it was the shop's fault the street was paved with cobbles and not cushions but she was deigning not to make a fuss.

The coachman mouthed a thank you at Durie. She'd heard

that ladies like Mrs Philimore chose their footmen primarily for their decorative qualities, and you could certainly believe it of this one: very good-looking, with that combination of dark hair and blue eyes you often see in the Irish, and broad shoulders that said he hadn't always spent his time standing beside the dinner table and looking pretty. She nodded, and turned to go down to the kitchen. Back to scrubbing trays, and no doubt a telling-off for upsetting a good customer, but it would take more than that to ruin her day now. Because it was still there, wasn't it? She still had the knack.

When Aunt Ellen came tip-tapping down the stairs, Durie turned, ready to get her defence in, but her aunt wasn't cross.

'Well, that was a surprise. I knew you helped your father out, but I didn't realise you could do that kind of thing. You were so calm, and so quick.'

'You have to be quick when a joint jumps out. The pain's terrible. He was lucky I didn't listen to his stupid mother.'

Aunt Ellen rolled her eyes.

'I know.' Durie sighed. 'I shouldn't have spoken to a good customer like that.'

'It wasn't ideal, but still, you did the right thing. And Gregory's doting mama will realise that when she calms down.'

The next morning Durie was down in the kitchen when the Philimore carriage pulled up outside the window again. A man stepped out, holding a silver-topped cane. He leaned on it as he walked to the door, favouring his right ankle and wincing when he put his weight on the left.

Durie was wiping her hands after greasing a baking tray when Aunt Ellen came down the stairs, smiling.

'Mr Philimore's here. Gregory's father. He wants to thank you.'

'He's got more sense than his wife then.'

Durie turned to walk up the stairs, but Aunt Ellen grabbed her arm.

'Come here.' She dusted a smudge off Durie's cheek, and sighed.

'Try and be nice. He's an important man, and they're very good customers.'

He was a perfect example of the marriage rule: older than his wife, and considerably less good-looking. But he had a friendly smile and less of the do-you-know-who-I-am than she did. He held out his hand.

'Miss Proudfoot. I wanted to thank you for helping my son.'

As they shook hands, his smile looked less easy, and when he took his hand away he held it a little to his side, so it didn't touch his coat. She probably should have been a bit more thorough about wiping hers.

'My wife sends her thanks as well. She was rather shocked by the whole thing, and is resting today, as is Gregory.'

'Well, he's got no need to. If it's fixed quickly, an elbow doesn't usually give any trouble later. That's why I said to your wife—'

'Can I offer you a treat to take home for Gregory?' said Aunt Ellen hurriedly. 'He's very fond of our apple puffs. A gift, of course.'

'That's very kind,' said Mr Philimore. He turned back to

Durie. 'Your aunt tells me you learned bonesetting from your father. Unusual for a woman, never heard of it before.'

'You've got to be strong, that's why,' said Durie. 'See, the muscles grip tight as a dog sucking a bone, and you have to pull till you hear a pop—'

'Here we are,' said Aunt Ellen, shooting Durie a look as she handed the box across the counter.

As Mr Philimore leaned forward to take it, pain flickered across his face.

'What's wrong with your ankle?' asked Durie.

'Twisted it dismounting my horse. Months ago. Stiffened up, and never been right since.'

'Can I have a look?'

'You must excuse my niece,' said Aunt Ellen. 'She's not long up from the country.'

'Why not?' said Mr Philimore. 'No one else has been able to do anything with it.'

'You'll have to sit down and take your shoe and stocking off,' said Durie.

'Durie, this isn't really the place,' said Aunt Ellen, but Mr Philimore waved a hand.

'I'm sure there's no one here who hasn't seen a foot before.'

As he sat at the nearest table and unbuckled his shoe, conversations dried up, and by the time he'd unbuttoned the knee band of his breeches and rolled off his stocking, the tinkle of pastry forks on china had died away completely.

She felt the joint; no question about it.

'Farmer's ankle,' she said. 'You didn't rest it after the sprain, did you?'

Her father called it that because a farmer said to him once

it was all very well telling him to rest, but who was going to tell the cows?

'I suppose I didn't,' he said. 'I thought walking would be good for it.'

'Well, it's not.'

Durie had seen her father fix farmer's ankle twice: a good strong twist in the right place was all it took, but it hurt like the devil. The farmers had both sworn loud and long, and by now all the ladies were watching. Should she warn Mr Philimore? But if she did, he'd tense up and make it worse. So she asked him to tell her exactly how he did it, and while he was talking, she took hold, felt around the joint for the right place – yes, there it was – and twisted. He didn't swear but he yelped like he'd stuck his hand into a fire; people gasped and a teacup shattered against the tiled floor.

'That should be right now,' said Durie. 'Try standing up.'

Holding on to the table for support, he stood. A smile spread over his face, as he bent his knees and flexed the ankle.

'I haven't been able to move it like that for months.'

'It'll swell up and be painful for a day or two, but that'll settle. Once you've sprained an ankle though, it's prone to spraining again. If it does, keep off it for a week at least. It's not as though you've got pigs to feed, is it?'

Someone sniggered, but Mr Philimore smiled at Durie with a twinkle in his eye.

'Well,' he said. 'I came here to thank you for one thing, and now I have to thank you for another. And no, I have no pigs at all, so I will certainly follow your advice.' He gave a little bow. 'Thank you, Miss Proudfoot.'

* * *

The shop got very busy once he left. People ordered more tea so they could chitchat about what they'd seen, which meant Durie could escape to the kitchen before Aunt Ellen could tell her off about not flannelling him enough. Though how you could flannel someone about a sprained ankle, she didn't know, especially when they'd been daft enough to think walking on it would help.

She was expecting the telling-off to come later, but instead, as they walked home that evening, Aunt Ellen said, 'You know, I never saw your grandfather at work, but when he talked about it, it sounded gruesome. But you make it look so natural. Almost elegant.'

Durie laughed.

'That's the first time anyone's used that word about me.'

'Perhaps elegant's not quite the right word, but you're not . . .'

'Clumsy like I am at everything else? I know. I feel it, myself. My hands know what to do. That's why it's so ridiculous that Father wouldn't let me do it.'

As they walked, Aunt Ellen asked questions. How did you tell if an ankle was broken or sprained? What could be done for a stiff neck? Had Durie ever set a broken bone? Durie happily answered. There was nothing she liked talking about better, and she hadn't had a chance since the last time she saw George.

'And you learned all that in three months working with your father?'

'Not exactly . . .'

Durie explained about the cupboard, which meant she had to tell about the rector dropping his breeches, and by the end of it, Aunt Ellen was laughing so much she had to take her spectacles off and wipe her eyes, and even though Durie hadn't meant to make her laugh, it was nice to see. She wasn't much given to laughing but when she did she looked like a young girl again.

'What I'd give to have seen your father's face,' she said. 'But I didn't realise you wanted to do it that badly.'

'I wanted it more than anything,' said Durie.

'Well, it sounds to me like your father got second-best,' she said. 'More fool him.'

A fortnight later, Durie was coming up from the kitchen with a tray of jellies when she caught her name. She stopped on the stairs to listen.

' . . . very well established in Sussex,' Aunt Ellen was saying. 'But she has such a good head for business, she's invaluable to me here. So she's not in that line of work any more, the other day was just an emergency, and then Mr Philimore happened to pop in and thank her, so she took a look at his ankle.'

The customer mumbled an answer.

'I can't promise anything,' said Aunt Ellen, 'but I'll ask.'

As the door closed, Durie hurried up the last few stairs. 'Ask me what?'

'He wanted to know if you were any good with knees.'

'Of course I am. Why did you fob him off?'

Aunt Ellen pointed at the cakes and sweets in the window. 'Which of those sells the best?'

'The jam tarts.'

'Why?'

'Because we make one tray a day, and when they're gone, they're gone. Lesson one of shopkeeping – people want what they can't have.'

'Exactly. So they'll want your services all the more if they think they have to ask nicely to get them.'

'My services?'

'He's the fourth person to ask about you since Gregory's accident.'

'Why didn't you say? I'd have—'

'You'd have jumped in and said yes. But we need to make you exclusive if this is going to work.'

'If what's going to work?'

'Establishing you. Here, in London. As a bonesetter.'

Chapter 31

The shop got busy and Durie didn't get a chance to ask more, but she thought about it all day. Aunt Ellen couldn't be serious, surely? Durie's father had taken over from his father, and her grandfather from his; that was how it went with bonesetting. How could she get herself established as a bonesetter, all on her own, here in London, where no one even knew her father, let alone her?

It wasn't until they'd closed the shop and set off for home, through an unseasonably chilly drizzle, that she was able to ask the question.

'Oh, it's more possible here than anywhere,' said Aunt Ellen, pulling her cloak tight to keep out the wet. 'You've seen the people who come into the shop – they want what's new and what's different, and when they get it, everyone else wants it.'

'I see how that works with cakes, but—'

'It works with everything. Hats, carriages, drawing-room curtains . . . Look at that.' She pointed to a grumpy-looking pug that a footman in scarlet livery was attempting to drag along the wet pavements on a lead. 'Last year, it was all poodles, but Lady Saltby gets one of those, and now no one wants anything else. We just need to show them *you're* new and different.'

Now Durie was thoroughly confused.

'You said London people thought bonesetting was old-fashioned.'

'You're a female bonesetter. Who's heard of that before? So that's what we'll use.'

'Do you really think it can work?'

'Well, nothing's ever certain, but you know I like a challenge.'

At the corner of South Audley Street, a young lad was sitting on an upturned pail, yelling, 'Black your boots, gents! Good as new for a farthing.'

No one was stopping. It had been raining on and off all day and the streets were awash with mud and dirt; cleaned boots wouldn't last ten minutes.

'Do you know how lucky a person is to find work they love?' asked Aunt Ellen. 'Most people are like that boy there, doing whatever they can to get a living. If money fell from the heavens tomorrow, he'd throw his brushes over his shoulder and never lift a finger again. But I wouldn't stop working, and once you're doing what you were meant to do, I don't think you would either.'

'I'd happily do it even if I wasn't paid.'

'Well, I won't encourage that, but I thought as much. And then you've got the women who come into the shop – they'll never have to do a hand's turn, but they're bored to distraction. I'll grant you some of them don't have the brains of a chicken, but they can't all be stupid, yet they're not allowed to do anything but waste their days on gossip and shopping. So that's why I say we're lucky, you and me, and Lucinda too, come to that.'

She turned to Durie as they reached the front door.

'It's my belief that if there's work a woman's got a talent for, she ought to do it. I'd have liked to hand my business on to you, in time. But I saw how you were, with Gregory Philimore that day, and with his father. And I've heard how much you know, and how hard you worked to learn it all. That's the work you were meant to do, and I'm going to do my best to get you doing it.'

Over a supper of hot buttered toast and herring roes, they thawed out by the fire and Aunt Ellen outlined her plans. Durie usually found roes unpleasantly fishy but what her aunt had to say meant she barely tasted them.

'Stay on at the shop for now, but we'll start letting you see people of the right kind, now and then. I've someone in mind for your first customer. Mrs Edwards – married to a wool merchant, lives in one of those big houses on Brook Street, knows everyone. She was complaining about a painful back, just yesterday, she'd be ideal. You know Mrs Boyd, the milliner on Mount Street?'

'Aunt Ellen, when have you known me to take an interest in hats?'

'Well, Mrs Edwards bought one from her when Mrs Boyd had a tiny shop in King Street, and wore it to the opening night at Marylebone Gardens. By the end of the season, Mrs Boyd was the most fashionable milliner in town. So if Mrs Edwards recommends you, you'll be on your way.'

Aunt Ellen finished off the last bite of toast, wiping it round the plate to soak up the fishy juices.

'You'll charge a pound a time, to start off with,' she said.

Durie laughed.

'I'm serious.'

'You can't be. Father never charges more than four shillings for a stiff back. He wouldn't ask a pound for anything less than a broken leg.'

Aunt Ellen sighed.

'Have I taught you nothing, Durie? If you put a low price on something, people think any old person could have it, and then they don't want it. A pound is just right, you'll see.'

'What about people who can't afford that, though?'

'You won't be treating people who can't afford it. Like I said, we need to keep you exclusive, or it won't work.'

Durie wasn't sure about that last bit. The knack was a gift, like her father said; it wasn't right to keep it from people just because they couldn't afford a pound a time. But it would be ungrateful to Aunt Ellen to say so, and if it made her decide not to bother after all, there would go Durie's chance, snatched away again. In any case, there was no need to worry about it, because who was going to pay a pound a time anyway?

Chapter 32

A week later, she had her first appointment. Mrs Edwards had heard all about Mr Philimore's foot and Gregory's accident, and when Aunt Ellen mentioned that Durie was very experienced with backs too, she was invited to visit the house on Brook Street.

The night before, she couldn't sleep. Making a good impression on Mrs Edwards might be the most important thing she'd ever done. Fixing her back wouldn't be difficult – Mrs Edwards had described the problem to Aunt Ellen, and it was unlikely to give Durie any trouble. But she kept remembering her time in the shop with Margie, and how hopeless she was at dealing with the customers.

She got out of bed and reached into the back of the wardrobe for the bag of monkey bones; perhaps feeling them under her fingers might be calming. She tipped the bones from the bag, and laid them out on the bed. There were lots of little ones she couldn't identify, but the leg bones and the hips were easy. She sat there for a little while, nestling the top of the leg bone into the hip socket, and feeling it move just the way it should.

I can do this. I've got the knack.

But this time, she had to say the right thing, as well as do it. When had she ever had the knack for that?

By the time Aunt Ellen had finished brushing smudges of flour from Durie's skirt, making her repin her hair, and sighing over her boots, Durie had the distinct impression she was expecting her to be turned away at the door, and it was doing nothing for her nerves. When the inspection was over, she ran upstairs, took out the monkey bones and tucked one under the ribbon of her hat, to give her courage.

She was glad of it when the footman who opened the door – all gold braid and sneer – looked her up and down as though he wasn't quite sure what she was, and said, 'Yes?'

'I've come to see Mrs Edwards,' said Durie. 'I'm Miss Proudfoot. The bonesetter.'

After a moment's hesitation, and an extra glance at her boots, he waved her into a hallway half as big as Aunt Ellen's shop, with a chandelier so large she hesitated to stand under it, and a wide marble stairway spiralling up out of sight. A maid was coming down. Durie didn't miss the smirk he gave, and the maid returned, when he said, 'Show Miss Proudfoot up to Mrs Edwards' chamber.'

There was a giggle in the girl's voice as she announced Durie, and although in other circumstances Durie wouldn't have cared a button for her opinion or that of the gold-braided lackey downstairs, it didn't help the churning in her stomach.

Mrs Edwards looked to be in her forties, pink and plump, and the room echoed her: a big bed was piled with pillows and hung with rose-coloured fabric, elaborately draped curtains billowed to the floor and the wool rug was so thick Durie's boots made prints in it. Mrs Edwards was reclining on a pink velvet chaise, in a loose, flowing wrapper, a cup of chocolate on a low table beside her. Wincing as she sat up, she said, 'I'm so glad you've come, the Philimores speak very highly of your skills. This back of mine has been plaguing me for weeks, and nothing Dr Bell recommends has made the slightest difference.'

Durie had decided her best chance of making a good impression was to open her mouth as little as possible, so she nodded and asked Mrs Edwards to stand so she could look at her back. Just as she'd expected; nothing out of place, just stiff as a board. A good hard going over, with rosemary balm to ease the tightness, would help that no end.

To Durie's dismay, Mrs Edwards turned out to be a talker, even face down on the bed, yammering on about her back, then throwing out a stream of questions.

'You're from Lewes, I hear?'

'Yes.'

'Do you find London very different?'

'Yes.'

'You have very strong hands for a woman. Is it true you fixed Mr Philimore's ankle with a single twist?'

'That's right.'

'And your aunt said you've even set broken bones?'

'I have, yes.'

'I've never heard of a woman doing that. Isn't it rather unpleasant?'

'No.'

She must have run out of questions after that, because she

stopped talking, and it was a great relief to Durie to be able to concentrate on rubbing out the knots instead of guarding her tongue.

She gave one last hard rub either side of the backbone, stood back and cleaned her hands on her skirt, remembering too late that Aunt Ellen had said not to. Oh well. At least she'd managed not to say anything bad.

'There,' she said. 'It should feel a bit looser now.'

Mrs Edwards sat up and twisted from side to side.

'It does. I feel I could walk a mile!'

'Two would be better. That's why it got so tight.' Durie gestured at the chaise. 'Too much lying down.'

'But Dr Bell was insistent I rest as much as possible.'

'Well, that shows how much he knows.'

'He's one of the best doctors in London, I should think he—'

'You said yourself, nothing he's recommended has made any difference. Best thing you could do is walk two miles a day. At least.'

'I don't think so. My back is much too delicate.'

Well, that was just nonsense.

'Backs are meant to work,' said Durie. 'They don't like sitting. You don't see a farmer's back get all tight like that, nor a miller's. You see it in clerks, and people who don't have much to do.'

'Indeed?' Mrs Edwards' face took on a pinched look. 'Well, I can assure you I don't belong in that category, Miss Proudfoot. I lead a very busy life, and in fact I have a great deal to attend to today. So I'll wish you good morning.'

* * *

Durie trudged back to the shop. Why couldn't she ever mind her tongue? What she'd said was right – her father had seen it over the years, people who had to get around on their own two feet always got better quicker than ones who rode in carriages. But if she'd flannelled a bit more, Mrs Edwards might have been more likely to listen. Now she'd gone and ruined her chance. Her father had had customers like Mrs Edwards, who'd ignore his advice to keep moving, in favour of drinking some potion the apothecary had recommended, or smearing on the ointment their granny swore by, and then be annoyed with him when they didn't get better. Mrs Edwards would carry on listening to this Dr Bell's advice, and her back would stiffen right up again. She wouldn't be calling Durie back, she definitely wouldn't be recommending her to anyone else, and Aunt Ellen might not bother trying again.

No. She couldn't leave it at that. She couldn't lose this chance.

The footman rolled his eyes when she said there was something she'd forgotten to tell Mrs Edwards, but he showed her back up to the pink room. Mrs Edwards sat up as she came in.

'I'm sorry,' said Durie. 'I'm sometimes blunt with my speech, and I can't flannel people to save my life. But what I said about walking, it'll work, if you give it a chance. Think about it: I'm not trying to sell you a potion or a device, I'm just telling you what I know your back wants. That's all. Goodbye.'

The footman was sniggering openly as he showed her out. As the door closed, she caught his words to the maid.

'Did you see the hat?'

She reached up: the monkey bone had slipped its mooring under the ribbon and was standing against the brim of her hat, like a feather. Well, so what. Let them laugh. A ridiculous-looking hat was the least of her troubles.

Chapter 33

That week, the baking trays seemed crustier than ever before, the trips up and down the spiral stairs with cakes and pastries more tiresome, and the wait at the mill for flour almost endless. How could she have been so stupid? She'd had a chance to escape all that, and fix people instead. All she had to do was flannel the woman a bit, and she'd seen it done enough times, for goodness' sake! Lucinda would have had her eating out of her hand in a minute flat.

She'd told Aunt Ellen the truth about how it had gone, in case Mrs Edwards complained. Aunt Ellen shook her head as Durie related the sorry story.

'You can't go saying the first thing that comes into your head with people like Mrs Edwards. They're used to being flattered, and having people bow and scrape to them. You don't have to do that – let's face it, you couldn't if you tried – but you do have to remember, they're paying the bill.'

'I know. I've let you down. I'm sorry.'

'Well, you've learned a lesson, anyway. I'll send round a box of comfits to Mrs Edwards – you can write a note saying you hope her back's feeling better.'

'But it won't be, not if she hasn't—'

'Just do it. And make sure it's not covered in ink blots.'

To Durie's astonishment, a week later, a message came from Mrs Edwards, asking her to call again.

'There,' said Aunt Ellen. 'Now this time, watch that tongue. Don't go telling Mrs Edwards she's lazy, and don't criticise her doctor either.'

'But her doctor gave her the wrong advice.'

'And she'll find that out for herself when she follows yours. But you don't want word getting round that you're going up against the medical men. They won't take kindly to it, and there's no sense in stirring up trouble for yourself.'

Before she left, Durie tucked the monkey bone into the ribbon of her hat again, leaving it sticking up this time. Perhaps it had worked as a lucky charm after all, and besides, it'd show that snooty footman and the stupid maid she didn't care tuppence for their opinion.

Mrs Edwards was sitting up this time.

'My back's not quite right, but it's not seizing up like it did before,' she said. 'That idea we had, of going for a walk every day, it seems to have helped.'

We had?

Bite your tongue, Durie.

'Good,' she said. 'Well, let's see if I can loosen it up a bit more today.'

Striding back to the shop, Durie was lost in thought. Mrs Edwards had been very complimentary about the improvement in her back, and asked her to come again the following week. Perhaps she'd add some wintergreen to the salve next time, to warm the muscles. She jumped when an Irish accent called, 'Hello there!'

The Philimores' carriage was waiting outside a draper's shop, the Irish footman on the box. He jumped down and ran across.

'It's Miss Proudfoot, isn't it?' he said. 'I'm Malachy O'Neill, I don't know if you remember me from when Gregory had his accident?'

There were very few women who wouldn't remember that face, not to mention the rest of him, and no doubt he knew that. Still, nice that he was polite.

'I do remember, yes.'

'I just wanted to thank you for what you said to Mrs Philimore.'

'It was nothing. I'd seen him open the door, so . . .'

'All the same, it's not everyone who'd bother to speak up for a stranger. And I'd have been dismissed on the spot if Mr Philimore thought it was my fault their little prince hurt himself.'

He had a twinkle in his eye when he said 'their little prince' and she couldn't help smiling.

'Does he do that kind of thing often?'

'All the time. And the little devil always blames the servants. You're the only person I've ever seen persuade him to tell the truth.'

'Well, I'm glad I did then.'

She was about to walk on, when he said, 'I'm curious, how did you know what to do? And for Mr Philimore's ankle as well? He hasn't stopped talking about that, every guest at their dinner table hears the story.'

'My father's a bonesetter.' She hesitated. Would he laugh? 'And I'm going to be one too. I'm just getting started.'

There, she'd said it. And he didn't laugh; in fact, quite gratifyingly, he looked interested.

'Are you now? We had bonesetters back in Ireland, but never a lady one.'

The door of the draper's shop opened and the feathers on Mrs Philimore's hat emerged, followed by Mrs Philimore.

'Well, I must be away,' he said. 'It was nice talking to you, and I wish you luck with your endeavours.'

'Thank you. And I wish you luck with Gregory.'

As she strode away, for the first time in her life, Durie wished she had a bit of a wiggle in her walk.

Malachy watched her head off down the street. Not an ounce of grace to her step, shoulders as wide as a docker's and sweet Jesus, weren't they men's boots she was wearing? He'd seen some sights since he came to London, but that was a new one.

He held out his hand to help Mrs Philimore into the carriage, releasing hers once she was in with just the suggestion of a squeeze. She liked that, the silly cow; now and then he purposely didn't do it, and he could tell she was disappointed. It tickled him to think she probably pictured his face, and maybe a bit more too, when she had that old chinless wonder on top of her. Made it easier to put up with having to bow and scrape to him too.

So the Proudfoot woman was setting up as a bonesetter. She had the arms for it, that was for sure, and she didn't have the face for much else. Well, good for her, if she could do it. She was an honest creature; you didn't get many of those in London. And Malachy was all for seizing your chances; wasn't that why he'd come to the city himself?

Chapter 34

Six more times Durie went back to the Edwards' house, and each time Mrs Edwards' back got looser under her fingers. She showed her how to stretch like the lions did – her father might choose to ignore the idea, but she was sure it helped – and even though Mrs Edwards was quite an irritating woman, it was a pleasure to see how much more easily she moved each time. How had Durie's father spent all his days seeing people get better like that, and then come home just as quiet and straight-faced as if he'd been mending shoes or milling corn?

After each appointment, she tucked another monkey bone into the ribbon on her hat, just to show Mrs Edwards' footman that she could look as mad as she liked, and still be made welcome because she was good at what she did. So by the time Mrs Edwards pronounced that she was 'quite cured and feeling like a young woman again', and told Durie to send round her bill, her bonnet sported a crown of bones. The footman was still smirking as he closed the door behind her for the last time.

Smirk away, it'd take you a year to earn eight pounds.

* * *

Aunt Ellen was – of course – right about Mrs Edwards' influence. The very next week, a message came from one of her neighbours, asking Durie to call at her earliest convenience. The week after, a summons to an even grander house than Mrs Edwards' on Brook Street, and another on Berkeley Square. All of them had stiff backs too, and all of them spent too much time sitting, or in one case reclining on a yellow silk chaise for fully half of every day; Durie could practically hear the woman's back screaming, 'Move, for goodness' sake!' But she bit her lip on that message and set to work with the rosemary balm, pummelling out the knots and then politely advising that a daily walk would be a good idea, 'As Mrs Edwards will tell you.'

Before long, she had at least one appointment every day from Monday to Saturday, sometimes two. But Aunt Ellen was strict about following the jam tart principle, to make her services more desirable, and had no hesitation in telling the less fashionable types that 'Miss Proudfoot is so very much in demand, she simply can't take on another customer at the moment', while the very much in demand Miss Proudfoot was downstairs scraping burnt caramel off a saucepan. But the first rule of shopkeeping was one thing; Durie almost dropped a mixing bowl on her foot when she overheard Aunt Ellen telling a customer one morning that female bonesetters were considered 'quite the thing' in Paris.

'They say the Queen of France sees one regularly,' she told the woman. 'For a problem with her knee.'

'How do you know the Queen of France sees a female bonesetter?' asked Durie, when Aunt Ellen next came down to the kitchen.

'I don't.'

'But you said—'

'I said, they say the Queen of France sees a female bone-setter. They say a lot of things about the Queen of France. How am I to know whether they're true or not?'

'But who says it?'

'Oh, Durie, no one says it! Or they didn't until this morning. Now Mrs Hollingworth's got hold of it, I daresay it'll be known from here to Marylebone by Friday.' She shrugged. 'I had one or two people asking if it wasn't a bit odd, you being a bonesetter and female. They won't be asking that once Mrs Hollingworth's gone to work.'

It didn't seem right to tell people things that weren't true, but Aunt Ellen said she wasn't telling people things that weren't true, she was telling them things that no one could be sure about one way or the other.

'And what you have to remember is that we're not selling them a pup – you're good at what you do. We're just helping people towards something that could be of benefit to them.'

'I know, but Father never told . . . I know they're not lies, exactly, but he never told people things like that. Things that weren't exactly true.'

'He didn't need to. Lewes is a small town – everyone knew about him, didn't they? In London, you have to carve out a place for yourself. And that's what we're doing.'

So Durie ignored the uneasy feeling she got when she heard Aunt Ellen telling people that 'a certain baronet's wife, she couldn't say who' was considering using her services, and 'a very well-connected military man' had taken a note of her name. If that was the way it was done in London, well, who was she to argue with someone who'd built up her own business there the way Aunt Ellen had?

Durie wasn't the only one making progress that season. One chilly Thursday night, she and Aunt Ellen took their seats to see Lucinda in her first starring role. The part had originally been given to the company's leading lady, Elizabeth Woolf, but on the day the play was due to begin, Miss Woolf tripped in the darkness backstage, over a stool that was where it shouldn't have been, gave herself a black eye and knocked out her front teeth. Wouldn't you know it, Lucinda had been practising her part – 'Just to improve my stagecraft', she'd told Durie and Aunt Ellen, with big, innocent eyes – and was able to step straight into the role.

'Conn said it was just until he could find someone, but the audience loved me – you should have seen them, stamping and shouting. So he said we'd give it a week and see, but when the review in the *Gazette* came, do you know what he said?'

'No,' said Durie. 'But I expect you're going to tell us.'

'He said I was radiant in the part, and he couldn't think why he hadn't given it to me before.'

Well, you could see what he meant. Lucinda walked on in a satin gown the colour of amber, to a hail of cheers. Her hair was like spun gold in the candlelight from the lanterns above the stage, and the dress was cut to show off shoulders so perfectly white that she reminded Durie of the marble statues in the museum. And when she sang, her voice was pure and clear.

'Look at that, not a tremble,' said Aunt Ellen. 'You'd think she'd been doing this all her life.'

Whether or not her sister had been backstage when that stool was moved, Durie didn't like to think, but one thing was clear: poor Elizabeth Woolf wouldn't be getting that role back.

Chapter 35

Ellen noticed the young man even before he'd pushed open the shop door. He'd been loitering outside, peering through the windows, before he came in and stood behind Lady Adney, who as usual was dithering over her purchases as though the fate of the nation might depend on whether she chose a pound of violet creams, or half violet and half rose. He wasn't shabby, but certainly a working man: shoes well-worn, and the hat he was turning round and round in his fingers had seen better days, and not recently. He wasn't even wearing a wig, and his dark hair stood up on end where he'd taken off his hat. Perhaps he'd just come in to ask the way to somewhere, though that didn't explain the loitering, and couldn't he have asked someone on the street?

'I'll take half a pound of each,' said Lady Adney, at last. 'And two apple puffs.'

The young man stood patiently as Ellen tied a box with ribbon, but his eyes kept straying to the stairs down to the kitchen. Was he looking for work? They did need someone to help with the heavy jobs, now Durie was so often out, but he ought to know to go to the area door, not stroll into the shop like a customer. As Lady Adney left, he pulled a note from his pocket.

'Pardon me,' he said. 'But would you be Durie Proudfoot's aunt?'

'I am, yes.'

'I was wondering if you could send this letter to her, in Sussex? I'm . . . well, I was, a friend of Durie's. I haven't seen her in a while, and I wasn't sure how else to get in touch with her. I have the money for the postage.'

Well, she hadn't been expecting that. And if he was a friend, why did he think she was back in Sussex?

He fumbled in a worn leather pouch, and pulled out a few coins.

'That won't be necessary,' said Ellen, holding out her hand for the letter. 'I'm sending her a parcel, I'll put the letter in with it.'

He smiled.

'Thank you, that's kind of you. Is she well?'

'She's very well.' She tucked the letter in the pocket of her apron, and said, 'If that's everything . . . '

He seemed about to ask something else, but apparently thought better of it.

'Yes, it is. Thank you for your help.'

He gave a friendly wave as he passed the window and walked off smiling.

Ellen took out the letter. Not even sealed with proper wax, just a blob from a melted candle; easy to refix. She flicked it off with her thumbnail and unfolded the paper.

Dear Durie,

I hope this letter finds you well. I thought of coming to see you in Sussex but it's been more than two years, and for all I know you are happy with someone else by now. I would never want to cause you embarrassment, so I decided it would be better to write.

Jenny died last winter, of the wasting sickness. I tried my best to be happy with her after you left, and to make her happy with me, but I never stopped thinking about you. I'm not good with fancy words, Durie, and I don't think you would want them anyway, so all I have to say is that I still care for you, and if you still care for me, we could be together now without hurting her. I hope with all my heart it's not too late.

Yours,

George Layton

Now that, she really hadn't been expecting. Of Lucinda, yes: her head was easily turned and she'd already shown a reckless streak. But Durie, entangled with a man who was, it seemed, married? How had it even happened? More than two years ago . . . well, no wonder Durie kept going back to the Tower every Sunday, she must have been meeting this George Layton there. It made sense, now, why she'd suddenly stopped; no doubt he'd kept quiet about his wife in the beginning, and then somehow Durie had found out, and done the sensible thing, telling the fellow she was going back to Sussex. It didn't sound as though they'd been lovers, either, thank goodness – there'd hardly have been the opportunity, and anyway, Durie was a level-headed girl. Ellen would lay money on her still being as innocent in that respect as the day she was born. But something had happened between them and now this George Layton wanted to rake it all up again.

Well, she wasn't going to let that happen. Let him come along out of the blue, just when things were going so well for Durie, and distract her from the work she loved so much, and had worked so hard to get? And for what? If things continued as they were, she'd be able to make a good living for herself, considerably better, by the looks of it, than he was. She could be independent, she didn't need to marry and let a man rule her life, and if she ever wanted to, it should be to someone who was her equal, not someone who couldn't even afford sealing wax.

The way he'd offered the money for the postage though . . . So unassuming, when most people left it to the person receiving the letter to pay. And that might be a day's wages for a man like that, yet he was willing to spend it on contacting Durie, when he didn't even know if he stood a chance.

No. She wouldn't do it. He seemed a pleasant enough chap, quite good-looking, and he'd managed to find himself one wife already, so he could find another one somewhere else. She went downstairs to the stove, and turned the letter to ashes.

Chapter 36

Durie's prediction about poor Elizabeth Woolf proved correct; Lucinda not only played her part for the entire run, but was given the starring role in the next play as well. With the increase in her wages, she decided to take rooms near the theatre, so she could walk home after the show.

'It's so difficult to hail a chair at that time of night,' she told Aunt Ellen, 'and I'm exhausted after the performance.'

Aunt Ellen might or might not have swallowed that, but Durie didn't.

'You sleep half the morning anyway,' she said to Lucinda later, 'so why do you need to get to bed early?'

'What I need,' said Lucinda, 'is to be able to have some fun. You ought to try it sometime.'

It made Durie think of George, when Lucinda said that, but what was the use of letting her thoughts go there? She had her work, and if she was sometimes lonely when Aunt Ellen nodded off over her book in the evening, well, no one had everything they wanted in life, did they? The requests from new customers were still coming and, as well as backs, she'd started getting people with sore knees, and stiff shoulders, and achy hips as well. She woke most mornings with a smile on her face. And that autumn, she got her first cruncher.

Mr Bennett was another one complaining of back pain, a tea trader with a big house on Berkeley Square. When she was shown into his drawing room, Durie didn't know his face, but as he walked across the fine silk carpet to shake her hand, she recognised him straight away.

'You walk along Brook Street every weekday morning, around ten, don't you?'

'I do, on the way to my office. How do you know that?'

She was about to say that she'd seen his feet walking past the basement window many a time, spotted his problem and itched to put it right. But she remembered just in time Aunt Ellen's warning not to tell customers that, when she wasn't fixing people, she was still scrubbing pots.

'I'm often at my aunt's shop around that time. I must have seen you then.'

'Well, I understand you're very good with backs.'

'I am, but it's your hip that needs fixing.'

'My hip?'

'You favour your right leg when you walk. Did you injure your left hip?'

'Indeed I did, in a fall from a horse, some years ago. But there's nothing to be done about that now.'

'Did a physician treat you after the fall?'

'Yes . . .'

'Poultices and bleeding?'

'Yes, but—'

'There you are then. You put your hip out, and you should have got a bonesetter to put it back in – physicians don't know bones like we do. It's left you with one leg sitting higher than the other, and walking like that's put a strain on your back. But don't worry, I can fix it.'

She delved in her bag, and pulled out a pair of loose cotton breeches with a drawstring at the waist. 'I'll need you to go and put these on.'

The tailor on Bond Street had laughed when she'd said what she wanted them for, but they were the perfect solution for customers whose trouble was anywhere higher than the knee or lower than the back: light and loose enough to feel the muscles and bones through, while rendering it unnecessary to bare all like the rector in Lewes had done.

When he came back, she examined the joint, remembering her father's advice about crunchers.

Take your time, get hold of it in just the right place. Then do it quick – don't mess about.

'Right,' she said. 'This is going to hurt.'

Later that week, Aunt Ellen was leafing through a copy of the *Weekly Miscellany* that she'd brought home from the shop. Suddenly she stopped and handed the paper to Durie.

'Look at this.'

Durie scanned the review of Lucinda's latest play; her second playing the lead role.

'Sounds like nonsense, but they always are. We should go though, she'll be hurt if we don't.'

'No,' said Aunt Ellen, pointing to a story on the opposite page. 'Not that, this.'

We hear of a remarkable cure exercised on Mr Bennett, a merchant residing in Berkeley Square. The gentleman in question has long suffered a lopsided gait, the result of a hip injury some years ago that caused a discrepancy in the length of his legs. On being attended by one Miss Proudfoot, a bonesetter, the discrepancy was reduced to all but nothing, with the result that Mr Bennett has regained the energy and vigour of his youth. Miss Proudfoot is lately come from Sussex and is the niece of Ellen Proudfoot the confectioner, of Brook Street.

Durie read the words three times before she was sure they said what she thought they said. She looked up at Aunt Ellen.

'How did that get in there?'

'Probably from Mr Bennett. Was he single?'

'A widower.'

'That'll be it then, putting himself back on the market. This is excellent, and quite likely other papers will pick it up too; they all copy from each other.'

Miss Proudfoot, a bonesetter.

That very first day when she'd seen her father at work, he'd said 'It's in our blood', and she'd wondered if it could be in hers. No doubt about it now, was there?

I am a bonesetter. And nobody is going to take my work away from me.

Chapter 37

Even Lucinda was impressed when she came round on Sunday afternoon.

'I couldn't believe it,' she said, helping herself to a second slice of lemon cake. 'Who'd have thought you'd end up in the papers?'

'I don't think anyone would have expected you to end up in the papers either, when you arrived here,' said Aunt Ellen. 'You've both done well.'

Lucinda took a sip of her tea, then said to Durie, in the casual tone that meant she wanted something, 'You won't let anyone know we're sisters, will you?'

'Why not?'

'Because you're going round to all sorts of people's houses now, and you know what you're like, you'll end up spilling all the beans about why we came here in the first place. Conn says ingénues are my forte, so I need to have an unblemished past.'

'Aren't you supposed to be acting?' said Aunt Ellen.

'He says audiences want to believe what they see is true.'

Considering that audiences had already swallowed the idea

that Lucinda had fought off a rampaging pirate with nothing more than a winsome glance and a rhyming couplet, it seemed ridiculous, but Durie agreed anyway. She'd had quite enough of hearing 'but the older one's so pretty' at home; she had no desire to hear it again in London, not now she'd finally managed to achieve something on her own account.

'I've told Durie the same as I told you, she should put aside half her earnings, for the future,' said Aunt Ellen. 'I hope your success will last a long time, both of you, but nothing's certain, and a woman who has savings has choices.'

The way Lucinda rolled her eyes told Durie that advice had fallen on deaf ears.

'But,' Aunt Ellen said to Durie, 'you should buy yourself something nice, to celebrate this. Some new shoes, perhaps?'

'I like my old boots,' said Durie. 'They're good for walking.'

Lucinda and Aunt Ellen exchanged glances.

'If I'm not bothered about how they look, I don't know why anyone else needs to be,' said Durie. 'Anyway, I know what I want to buy.'

The next time Aunt Ellen sent her to fetch fruit from Covent Garden Market, Durie made a detour down to the Strand, and persuaded a watchmaker to sell her one of his drills, and some metal wire. Then she spent a Sunday in the big museum, staring at the stuffed monkeys they had there, and drawing them from different angles.

'Not exactly Gainsborough, is she?' said a man as he passed by with his wife, but what did he know? The drawings were fine for her purposes.

Putting the monkey bones back together was tricky. The

tail definitely didn't look right, and he only had one back leg because she wanted to keep the rest of the leg bones on her hat. But despite that, and even though it wasn't the same as a person's skeleton, it worked a lot more like one than a rat's did. She could get an idea of what was on the inside of a person when she was working on the outside, and it was going to be an excellent way of figuring out better ways to do things.

She put the skeleton in the wardrobe, so as not to frighten Betsy, Aunt Ellen's maid, or have to explain to Aunt Ellen where the bones had come from; being as Aunt Ellen had no wish to look closely at the ones in her hat, it had been easy to convince her that she'd saved them from the rat. But every morning when she caught sight of the skeleton, she remembered George's proud smile when he'd given her the bones, and his grin when he told her how he'd stunk out the hut, boiling them up to get them clean. He'd believed in her, and even if she couldn't have him, she had that.

30 March 1761

Dear Tom,

Three years old — where has the time gone? You'll be a proper little boy now, and I often wonder what you look like. You were ugly as a baby, but most babies are, and your mother is very beautiful, so I expect you look better now.

I wrote you a gloomy letter last year, when I was very unhappy. But things have changed for the better. I'm doing the work I was born to do, I'm fixing people, and taking away their pain, and I don't even care if people snigger at my hat or my boots or, come to that, my face, because I'm useful now, and it's not everyone who can say that.

I don't know where you'll be in life when you read this letter, but if it happens to be a time when you're not very happy, I want you to remember good things might be just around the corner.

Yours,

Aunt Durie

Chapter 38

Ellen hadn't had the slightest of qualms about not passing on George Layton's letter to Durie; it was for her niece's own sake, and she was entirely certain it was for the best. But it played on her mind that, now Durie was getting mentioned in the newspapers, there was a chance he'd pick one up in a coffee house or a tavern and discover she wasn't in Sussex at all. She didn't want him coming back to the shop; that would be awkward now, and it was better for Durie never to know he'd been there at all. No, he needed to be told that there was no chance for him, and no reason to contact Durie again.

She couldn't recall the precise address on the letter, but the name of the street – Slaughterhouse Lane – had stuck in her mind because it sounded so unpleasant. Sure enough, when she made her way there one evening, it was a poky little byway, to the east of the Tower. A scruffy child of indeterminate sex told her which one of the row of small, rundown cottages Mr Layton lived in.

To her surprise, inside the place was clean and tidy, with a cheap-looking but serviceable table and two chairs, and a rug on the floor, made from rags, but colourful and clean. The work of his unfortunate wife, presumably.

'You didn't have to come all this way, I could have collected the letter,' he said. 'But it's very kind of you. Can I offer you some tea?'

'No, thank you. I'm afraid you misunderstand me. Durie hasn't written back, she just asked me to deliver her message.'

He wasn't stupid; his face told her he knew that wasn't good news. She wished she didn't keep remembering how he'd saved his money to send that letter to Durie.

'I'm afraid I wasn't entirely frank with you when you called at the shop,' she said. 'Durie didn't return to Sussex, she stayed here in London with me. She's working as a bonesetter.'

His whole face broke into a smile.

'Really? She must be cock-a-hoop! She wanted that more than anything, I know.'

'Yes, she's doing very well. And the other thing is, the reason she asked me to come, is that she's just become engaged. So she felt it wouldn't be proper to meet you herself, or enter into correspondence.'

'I see.'

She fixed her eyes on a cheap print of rolling green hills on the wall behind him, so she didn't have to look at his face.

'She asked me to thank you for your friendship when she first came to London, and to wish you well.'

'This fellow she's marrying,' he said. 'Is she happy with him?'

'Yes, he's got very good prospects and—'

'I didn't ask about his prospects, Miss Proudfoot. I asked if she's happy with him.'

'I believe she is, yes.'

'Well, then please tell her I'm happy for her.'

She'd done the right thing. Durie couldn't live in a place like that and then expect a good class of people to invite her into their homes. And while she wasn't entirely comfortable going behind her back, it was for the best: for all her I-don't-care-what-people-think bluster, Durie had a soft heart, and she'd have found it hard to tell the fellow there was no hope for him. So she'd done them both a favour really, letting him know he had no future with her. She just wished he hadn't been so decent about it.

Malachy was always pleased when Mr Philimore left a news-paper in the coach. The other footmen were happy to stand about, eyeing up women and smoking a quick pipe while they waited outside his club, but Malachy liked to catch up with the news. The hedge schools at home might not be fancy like the one the Philimore boy was being sent to, but Irish parents, even poor ones, believed in education, and Malachy had paid attention, like his father told him to, and come out a pretty good reader. A decent hand at writing too, which was more than you could say for a lot of Londoners. He'd worked on both since he arrived as well; when he went back home to Tipperary, he intended it to be as a rich man, and though he wasn't certain yet how that was to be achieved, a bit of polishing certainly wouldn't hurt.

Not much of interest in the paper today though: someone wanting information on the theft of a white gelding; a complaint about the price of Worthing mackerel at Billingsgate Market; advice against bathing too near weeds.

He lingered over a report of a countess running off with her dancing master – stupid, she'd have no money of her own – and read a review of the play he'd taken the new parlourmaid, a pretty little blonde with a glint in her eye, to see on their day off. He hadn't thought much to the show, but they'd had a kiss and a fumble in a quiet alleyway on the way home, so it wasn't entirely a wasted evening.

The review compared the leading lady to 'a goddess of old – Diana incarnate'. Bit fanciful, but that Lucinda Ellwood was a good-looking piece; half the men in the audience had their tongues hanging out when she did that thing of glancing back over her pearly white shoulder as she exited the stage.

As he turned the page, a familiar name caught his eye. Well, look at that, the Proudfoot woman had made a go of the bonesetting. Berkeley Square! If all her customers were that sort, she'd be doing very well for herself. Malachy had seen physicians' bills on Mr Philimore's desk, and if she was charging anything like what they did, she must be raking it in. And quite likely she was: that aunt of hers understood business, you only had to look at the types that went in there and paid silly prices for her tiny cups of tea to know that, and she'd be well aware the daft nobs in their big houses happily paid through the nose for everything else as well.

Was it worth a punt? She was a terrible-looking thing, but then that meant he wouldn't be fighting off competition, and she'd hardly be choosy, would she? Until recently his attentions had been focused on the widow of a moderately successful tavern-keeper on Bishopsgate, but she'd turned out to have a nephew who was set on taking over the business, so he'd had to abandon that enterprise. This one wasn't exactly a racing certainty, she'd obviously only just got started, but perhaps worth keeping an eye on.

'On his way,' the doorman of the club called.

Malachy threw the newspaper back inside the coach, and unfolded the steps for Mr Philimore. As the coach pulled away, he was whistling a merry tune.

Chapter 39

Aunt Ellen had asked Durie, once, why she hadn't told her father about the bonesetting; it had been months now, and as far as he and Margie knew, she was still learning the confectionery trade. She'd said it was because she was still cross with him for choosing Richie, and it was partly that. But the real truth was, she'd been afraid it wouldn't last, that one day, the messages would dry up, and it would all be snatched away from her again. Telling her father had seemed like tempting fate: imagine writing to say she was a bonesetter, a proper one, paid to fix people, and then in the next letter having to say, actually, I'm not any more, it was just a passing fad and I'll be spending the rest of my days scrubbing pots and fetching flour.

But it was there in black and white now. She cut out the piece from the newspaper and tucked it inside a letter telling them all that had happened. Difficult to resist adding 'I told you I could do it' but Mr Bennett's story could say that for her.

Allowing three days for the letter to reach them, and three days back, she wasn't expecting a reply for at least a week, but a fortnight passed. Surely he wasn't still clinging to the stupid idea that she shouldn't be a bonesetter just because she didn't wear breeches?

She and Aunt Ellen were eating breakfast when Betsy the maid brought in a letter, addressed to her and Lucinda. That wasn't unusual – no sense in paying for the same news twice – but it wasn't in Margie's handwriting or her father's, it was in Richie's untidy scrawl.

My dear sisters,

I am writing with bad news. Three days ago, our father passed away. We bury him this morning.

Both he and Mother were very ill with the influenza, which has been terrible here this year – half the town has been sick. We were sure he'd recover, but it went to his lungs and the end came very suddenly. Mother is recovering now but still weak and, of course, laid low with grief. You know how devoted she was to him.

Durie, your letter came just before they fell ill, and caused great excitement in the house. Father wrote a reply straight away, but with all that happened, it wasn't sent. I am enclosing it for you now.

Your brother,

Richie

'What is it?' asked Aunt Ellen.

Durie handed her the letter. Aunt Ellen's hand flew to her mouth.

'I can't believe it,' said Durie. 'Father's never ill.'

'My tough little brother,' said Aunt Ellen. 'When he was

very young, he used to say he was never going to die. Your grandfather used to laugh and say, everyone dies, Dan, and he'd say . . .' Her voice cracked, and sudden tears glistened in her eyes. 'He'd say, not me, I'm strong.'

Durie picked up the letter again, and looked at the date. Three days before would have been last Tuesday. There'd been an order to collect from the flour mill, she'd had to wait a long time for it, then she'd gone to see an acquaintance of Mrs Edwards', another stiff back. She'd had to run there from the shop because of the wait for the flour. And all that day, while life seemed just as usual, her father lay dying, and by the end of it, was gone.

'Poor Margie,' said Aunt Ellen. 'We must write to her, but first, I think we'd better tell your sister.'

Aunt Ellen sent a messenger and Lucinda arrived, quite annoyed, saying it had better be important because she had an appointment with a dressmaker. But on being told the news, she dissolved into uncharacteristically ugly tears.

'We should have been there to say goodbye,' she said. 'Why didn't Richie tell us?'

'It sounds as though there wasn't time,' said Aunt Ellen gently. 'It's no one's fault.'

Durie didn't cry; she still couldn't believe it was true. It felt like watching a play, from seats right at the back.

They drank a lot of tea, and once Lucinda's tears had subsided, they talked about him. Aunt Ellen made them laugh with stories of their father as a little boy; Lucinda mimicked him coming home, kicking off his boots and saying 'I'll just close my eyes for a minute', only to be snoring within seconds. Durie told them about the very first time she saw him work, how she thought the man at the inn would die of the pain, but her father knew exactly what to do and it looked like magic. It was only then she remembered the other letter, the one just for her. But it wasn't fair to read it then, not when it was a kind of goodbye and Lucinda didn't have one.

She waited until Lucinda had gone home and Aunt Ellen was locking up downstairs, before she unfolded the letter and read it.

> *Dear Durie,*
>
> *Well, my girl, you've surprised us all. I will admit, over these past months, we hoped you'd given up on the idea of bonesetting, and settled to working with your aunt, but you always were stubborn, and this time, it's paid off.*
>
> *Who would have thought the knack would pass down to you as well as Richie? But it's clear that it has, and what's more, you've put it to good use. Your mother would have been very proud of you, and so am I.*
>
> *Your loving father*
>
> *PS: That idea you had, about a way to stretch the spine, I'll give it a try on Mrs Woods this week.*

Her father had never, ever voluntarily mentioned their mother like that before; she'd come to understand now what she hadn't as a child, that it hurt him to think about her and it had become easier not to. So it meant a lot, that he'd said it. She'd hoped he'd be proud of her, but to read that he believed her mother would have been too . . . she hadn't even thought to hope for that. And even if he had wished, all those years ago, that she'd never been born, she'd made him proud in the end.

Chapter 40

She looked at her father's letter often over the next few months, wishing, very much, that she could tell him what had happened since then. But as Margie said when she was well enough to write, it helped to imagine that he was looking down on her now, and seeing it all. Because Aunt Ellen was right; other newspapers had repeated the story from the *Weekly Miscellany*, and enquiries began to come from beyond Mayfair, taking her across the city and even out to the villages of Chelsea, Fulham and Marylebone. Before long, she'd scrubbed her last tray in the basement kitchen and was seeing her own customers every day.

So when a letter came from Richie, asking her to come back to Lewes 'and be my assistant', she had a good mind to tell him to go and boil his head. If he'd asked her to work alongside him, she might have done it for her father's sake, knowing he wouldn't have wanted to lose work to anyone else. But be his assistant? Roll bandages for him, and have him tell her what to do, after she'd been attending the finest people in London, all on her own account? No, she wasn't going to do that.

Dear Richie,

Thank you for the offer, but I'm doing very well in London, and I like it here. Also I know as much about bonesetting as you, if not more, so your idea of asking me to be your assistant is ridiculous.

I hope Margie is well, I send my love to her and so does Lucinda.

Your sister,
Durie

With all the enquiries coming in, Aunt Ellen raised Durie's price to a guinea, saying the kind of customer she was attracting wouldn't turn a hair, and they didn't. Durie didn't need her lectures on setting aside a proportion of her earnings for the future, because in truth, she had no idea what to do with it all. After taking out a sensible amount for balms, bandages and splints there was nothing she wanted to buy, so the strongbox she'd bought and tucked under the bed was soon filling up with golden guineas.

It worried her a bit, the money. She kept remembering her father's words, especially now, about the knack being a gift. If he was looking down, he wouldn't approve, would he? But when she said to Aunt Ellen that perhaps she should find a way to make it known that people who couldn't pay could still use her services, Aunt Ellen looked at her as if she'd just suggested running through Hyde Park with a teapot on her head.

'Do you think people of fashion are going to want you touching them if you've just had your hands on a chimney sweep or a shrimp seller? You'll lose all your customers, it'll all have been for nothing, and though I'd happily have you back in the shop, it's not what you want, is it? Trust me on this, Durie. I've been right so far, haven't I?'

Durie couldn't deny that, and since no one was actually asking her to treat them without payment, it was easy to push the matter out of her mind.

The only time she resisted Aunt Ellen's advice was on the matter of appearance. Winter's icy streets brought her lots of sprained ankles and twisted knees, and by the end of a week in which she'd seen four such injuries, she'd come to the conclusion that strength wasn't the only reason there weren't more female bonesetters. Men didn't have to truss themselves up in stays that made it hard to stoop and see how a kneecap sat, or feel around an ankle when the person had their weight on it. After a fruitless morning searching the shops of Cheapside and being told there was 'no call for that kind of thing here', she walked out to the market gardens in Chelsea, where a woman tending rows of cabbages was surprised but very pleased to be offered a pound for the jumps she was wearing instead of stays.

'You can't go out in those,' said Aunt Ellen when Durie showed her the quilted cotton bodice, blissfully free of boning, with lacing up the front that she could loosen if need be. 'The boots are bad enough, and you know what I think about the hat, but whoever heard of a woman leaving the house without stays?'

'In Sussex women wear jumps when they're working in the fields,' said Durie. 'That's what gave me the idea. I've got to be able to move when I'm working on customers.'

'But what will people think?'

'They can think what they like. They're not paying me to be decorative, they're paying me to fix them.'

She wasn't daft: in London the style of your bodice and the tilt of your hat were matters of life and death, so of course they'd smirk behind their hands at her. But they kept coming back, and recommending her to their friends, so what did it matter? And not only that, but the newspapers kept writing about her too, if she fixed someone especially rich or notable. And each time it happened, she'd get even more customers. As the *Gazette* put it, 'Despite her eccentric appearance, Miss Proudfoot is welcomed into the finest addresses in London.'

Spending her days fixing people, and her evenings thinking about ways she could do it even better, Durie was happier than she'd ever been. When Aunt Ellen nodded off over a book after supper, she wrote notes on that day's customers. Her father had laughed when she'd suggested that, back at home; he said bonesetters kept all they needed to know in their heads. But it was useful: she could compare people with similar problems and try to work out why one got better quicker than another. And anyway, he'd still have been working alongside her grandfather when he was her age, but she had only her notebook to discuss things with. Though sometimes when she went upstairs to try something out on the monkey skeleton, she found herself talking to it, saying, 'Will this work, do you think?' as she tested a different way of positioning a twisted ankle for strapping, or, 'No, the angle's all wrong, isn't it?' when she'd fashioned a new shape of splint for a broken wrist. She always thought of George then, having to tell his troubles to Crowley again, who could no more answer back than the skeleton could.

Once or twice she'd been called to customers who lived near the Tower, and each time she'd been tempted, so tempted, to stroll the hundred yards or so to Tower Hill, pay her sixpence and go in, just for the pleasure of seeing his face again. It was starting to fade in her memory: she could still see the kind eyes, and the ready smile, but she couldn't bring the rest into focus. But tempting as it was, each time, she turned and walked in the opposite direction. Nothing to be gained by it, for him or for her.

The first time she saw a figurine of Lucinda, on the mantel-piece of a silk merchant's house in Clerkenwell, it gave her such a surprise that she dropped a pot of wintergreen balm all over his Chinese carpet. Her sister was playing her fourth lead role by then, a lovelorn milkmaid called Tilly Tipworth, and the play was so popular, the *Mercury* wondered if there was a person in London who hadn't seen it. And suddenly, her name and her face were everywhere. It was becoming a rare week that the papers didn't have a story about her, whether it was a new hat she'd worn to walk in the park, or a rumour about which fashionable gentleman had taken her to dinner after the show. Durie had seen playing cards with her picture on the backs, and fans that opened up to show her face, but spotting the little china figure on the merchant's mantelpiece was really quite peculiar. Lucinda laughed when she heard.

'You'd better get used to it,' she said. 'I hear they've made hundreds of them.'

It snowed for much of December, so they stayed in London

and celebrated Christmas with Aunt Ellen. Lucinda arrived on Christmas morning, looking like a Russian princess in a fur-trimmed hat and cloak, and handed Durie a copy of the *Gazette*. 'Look,' she said, 'you and me, on the same page.'

The stories were side by side: one calling Lucinda 'the darling of the stage' and describing in rapturous terms a dress 'straight from Paris' that she'd worn out to supper at a restaurant on the Strand; the other reporting that Durie had 'performed yet another remarkable cure' on a Mrs Howard, whose left shoulder had been 'treated by no less than four of the city's best physicians, to no avail' but was now entirely free from pain, allowing her to dance at her daughter's wedding.

'It was her right shoulder,' said Durie. 'And I don't think she'd seen four physicians, I think it was two.'

Lucinda rolled her eyes.

'My dress wasn't from Paris either. But they're talking about us, that's what counts. Do you remember, that day we came? I told you it would be fun then, didn't I? And look at us now.'

Chapter 41

After Christmas the weather turned even colder. The papers reported that not only was the Thames frozen over, but ships were stuck in ice two miles off the Essex coast, and the slippery streets meant Durie was busier than ever.

One morning, as she left the house for an appointment in Clerkenwell, someone called her name. She looked across the road and there was Malachy O'Neill, the Philimores' Irish footman, in his green and gold livery, waving. She'd bumped into Mr Philimore the previous week and he'd mentioned a niggling pain in his back; the footman must have a message for her. As he strolled across, she couldn't help noticing the easy way he moved, despite the frost on the ground. No back pain there, no crunchy knees when he got older either.

'Does Mr Philimore want me to call?' she said.

'No, I was just passing, on an errand, and saw you. How are you? The bonesetting must be going well, I keep seeing your name in the papers.'

'It's going very well, thank you.'

Durie thought she'd got better at making inconsequential conversation over the past months – a lot of the women customers liked to chatter inanely and she'd learned to nod and smile and say 'Yes indeed' now and then – but the surprise of him remembering her at all, let alone the conversation they'd had, made her blurt out what was in her head.

'You walk very well. You must have a strong back.'

He grinned and said, 'Thank you. That's not a compliment I've heard before.'

'I just meant . . . a lot of people here sit too much. That's why they get bad backs. But you look like you walk a lot.'

Shut up, Durie, you're making it worse.

'Where are you heading?' he asked.

'Clerkenwell.'

'I'm going east too, will I walk along with you a way?'

He didn't wait for an answer, so there was nothing to do but carry on along the street, beside him. His long legs matched hers stride for stride, and he chatted away easily, telling her about the boy Gregory's latest escapade, an attempt to climb up inside the drawing room chimney. He had a very entertaining way with him, capturing Mrs Philimore's flapping about when Gregory emerged, covered in soot, so well that by the time they reached Holborn, Durie had forgotten her embarrassment and was laughing along with him.

'Well, here's where we part,' he said. 'But I was wondering, it's my day off on Sunday, and there's a frost fair setting up on the river. Would you fancy coming to have a look at it?'

'With you?'

'Well, yes. They say it's quite a sight. So will you come? Or is it an altogether terrible idea?'

'Yes,' said Durie.

'It's a terrible idea?'

'No. I mean, yes. Yes, I would like to.'

He waved as he walked away. Could he have been joking, having a laugh at her expense? But why bother, when there was no one else to hear? And he didn't seem the type, he seemed nice.

Well, we'll see. We'll see on Sunday.

There was no reason at all for Durie not to tell Aunt Ellen about Malachy O'Neill's invitation, and when Aunt Ellen said she was going to see a friend on Sunday, that would have been the moment: to say, quite casually, oh, so am I. But she didn't. He probably wouldn't come anyway. Having thought it over, quite a lot, the most likely explanation was that he'd happened to spot her across the road and come over to say hello – he was clearly a friendly type, and he'd been grateful about her getting him out of trouble with Mrs Philimore, so that made sense – and then he'd said that about the frost fair in the same way customers in the shop said 'We must have you round for dinner' to acquaintances they'd bumped into, when you could tell by both their faces that no such event would ever take place. She'd get a message, probably Saturday afternoon, saying that unfortunately he couldn't come after all, and then a lecture from Aunt Ellen on how men weren't to be trusted. So it was altogether best to say nothing.

But the message didn't come on Saturday. It didn't come even when a dusting of snow fell on Sunday morning, which surely he realised would have been the ideal excuse? He'd said he'd call at two, and by half past one, she was pacing the parlour, pretending to herself that she wasn't watching for him through the window. Wasn't it far too cold for a walk anyway? Best if he didn't turn up and she could stay in and work on the new splint she was thinking about.

At two on the dot, he came strolling up the street, wrapped up warm against the cold. She hadn't seen him out of livery before; his russet-coloured coat suited that Irish colouring even better than the green. Before Betsy could amble up from the kitchen, she grabbed her cloak – why hadn't she mended that rip in the hem, it had been there for months – and stepped outside. He smiled, raised his hat and, to her astonishment, held out his arm.

Seeing her hesitation, he said, 'The pavements are dreadful slippery.'

Durie opened her mouth to say her trusty boots had managed worse, but it seemed ungrateful, so she swallowed the words and took his arm anyway.

Not that tight, he'll think you're marching him off to the magistrate!

But how exactly was your hand supposed to go? She loosened her fingers and tried, very awkwardly, not to rest her arm too heavily on his. But he didn't seem to notice, and as they walked towards the river, he chatted about the weather, and how Ireland wasn't as cold as England but had much more rain.

'That must be terrible for people's knees,' she said. 'Cold weather's bad enough, but when it's wet, bad knees crunch and grate like the devil.'

'Is that so?'

She explained her father's theory that something in the

air changed when rain was coming, and made people's knees swell on the inside.

'That's very interesting,' he said, as they turned down one of the little side streets that led to the river. 'Now, isn't this a sight?'

At the bottom of the street, where the river ought to be, stood rows of tents and booths, their reds and yellows bright against the ice; behind, people were playing ninepins, for all the world as though they were on dry land. As they got closer, the smell of roasting meat drifted up, along with the strains of a fiddle band and shouts of 'Hot wine and ale', 'Lovely gingerbread, fresh from the oven' and 'Gin to warm your cockles'.

Half of London looked to be out enjoying themselves: families strolling about, the children running ahead; giggling girls walking arm in arm and pretending not to look at the young men skating. And lots of couples, walking arm in arm like they were. Would people think they were a couple? As they joined the crowds on the ice, she glanced at him to see if he minded, but he didn't seem bothered at all.

Outside one of the tents, an ox was hanging on a spit over a fire; a man was slicing hunks of meat off with a big knife. The smell made Durie's mouth water.

'Doesn't that look tasty?' said Malachy. 'Let's have some.'

He found them stools at the rickety table set up behind the tent, wiping hers with his sleeve before she sat down. As he strolled over to the counter, the two women serving broke off their chat; one adjusted her cap, teasing out a few auburn curls. He pointed at the ox and said something that made them both giggle. The auburn one strolled over to it, hips swinging in a quite unnecessary fashion, and piled a plate with meat. The other leaned on the counter, bosoms spilling over her blouse; her face fell as Malachy turned and walked back to their table.

'That looks like good meat,' said Malachy, as they watched the redhead stuffing the thick slices into buttered rolls and spooning over the juices from the plate. 'Reminds me of home – there's nothing like Irish beef.'

'Why did you leave?'

'Same reason as most – to find work. Didn't want to be eking out a living on the land, like my father did, always beholden to the landlord. Here, a man can do well for himself, if he works hard. You hear about it all the time. Even Mr Philimore, his father was just a Norfolk carpenter, but now who's first in line when they want someone to build another grand square? He's made his own money, and plenty of it, and I intend to do the same. I just need a start, and then I'll work and work till I'm the one with a coach, and someone else rides behind it, tricked out with gold braid like a monkey.'

The redhead came over with their food, setting tin plates down in front of them.

'This looks good,' he said. 'Sorry, I get a bit carried away when I'm talking about my plans. You know yourself, of course, that you can do well here if you work hard. You must have customers all over the city now.'

'I do,' said Durie. 'It's peculiar, at home everyone went to my father for their aches and pains, but here, all the fashionable people had been going to physicians, apparently. So there's a lot of people with injuries that never got fixed right, and aches and pains that have never been treated properly.'

'Good job I got in early then.' He grinned. 'Before you get too rich and successful to come out with the likes of me.'

'I won't,' she said. 'I mean, I'm already quite successful. But I'd still come out with you.'

She should have asked Lucinda what sort of things you were supposed to say to a man in this situation. Because that just sounded idiotic, and he might not want to go out with her again and then it would be embarrassing.

But he just smiled and said, 'Well, that's good to know.'

When they'd finished eating, he stood and offered his arm again, this time gently positioning her hand so that it tucked into his elbow. So that was how it was supposed to go. It had been a bit of a strain, trying not to rest too heavily on him, but this was really very pleasant. It crossed her mind, just for a moment, to wonder what it would be like to walk arm in arm with George but she pushed the thought aside.

You can't have that, don't spoil this.

They strolled past the booths selling keepsakes, the ale tents filled with laughing drinkers, and the puppet theatre entertaining a rapt little group of children. In places, they had to jostle their way through the crowds.

'I never thought so many people could live in one place till I came here,' said Malachy. 'Was it strange to you too?'

Durie nodded.

'I thought Lewes was a big town, but I couldn't believe how crowded the streets were when we arrived here.'

'Ah, me neither. But I like it now. I like how you can meet all kinds of people, and they've all got their own stories, especially the ones who've come here from somewhere else, and made a life for themselves.' He squeezed her hand with his elbow. 'Like us.'

Her stomach fluttered at the way he said 'us'.

Don't be ridiculous; it's a perfectly normal word and he meant nothing by it.

The conversation flowed so easily that when he asked why she'd come to London in the first place, she spoke without thinking.

'Lucinda – my sister – had a baby. We came so she could take him to the Foundling Hospital.'

After the words came out, she remembered Lucinda's instructions. But she couldn't just not answer, could she?

'And then you stayed on because you started the bonesetting here?'

She was about to say it was Lucinda who'd decided to stay first, but he didn't need to know that. If he didn't know Lucinda was Lucinda Ellwood, if she let him think she'd gone back to Lewes, it didn't matter that he knew about Tom. And Durie had no inclination to see the look on his face if he'd heard of Lucinda and made the comparison between them.

'It didn't happen straight away,' she said. 'I worked in my aunt's shop for a while. She's taught me a lot.'

'I bet she has, she's got a good business there. No offence, but I never thought I'd see people paying tuppence for a jam tart.'

'Ah, well there's a reason for that . . .'

She explained about the first rule of shopkeeping, and the second, and then, when a chill wind began to blow, they stopped for hot chocolate by a blazing fire, and he told her about his family at home, five brothers all younger than him. By the time they left she'd got quite used to having her hand tucked into his elbow, and they were chatting away like old friends. So when they turned into South Audley Street, and he asked if she'd like to meet again on his next day off, in a month's time, she wasn't even surprised.

Perhaps I'll get myself a new cloak before then, instead of just fixing the tear in the old one. So I look nicer for him.

Aunt Ellen was by the fire when she came in, a copy of the *London Courier* open on her lap. As Durie took off her cloak, she said, 'I didn't know you were going out. Did you go to see Lucinda?'

'No, just for a walk.'

The afternoon had been so unexpectedly nice, she wanted to hug it to herself for a bit before she exposed it to Aunt Ellen's beady eye.

'Well, there's something here you need to see.'

She handed Durie the paper, and it was only then that Durie noticed the grim look on her face.

Chapter 42

On page six, between an appeal for information about a lost poodle, and a warning about falling icicles, was a letter from a Dr Candleford.

It is much to be regretted that so many people in this city put their faith in the promises of quacks and charlatans. The more outrageous the claims, the more willingly the gullible hand over their money, and no better example have we seen than that bonesetter woman — by the name of Proudfoot — who touts her so-called cures around the town. While it may be allowed that Miss Proudfoot has, through some peculiar quirk of nature, the brute strength to set a broken leg, this sets her no higher than a country farrier. Examples of her dangerous incompetence are many, and to believe her claims of curing long-suffered deformities or offering methods of pain relief superior to those of qualified medical men is to prove the old adage: a fool and his money are soon parted.

'What does he mean, dangerous incompetence?' said Durie. 'And what claims? I don't make any claims, I just fix people.'

'It was bound to happen. You're competition, and they don't like it. And one way or another, you've upset this one.'

Candleford, Candleford. She'd couldn't have met him, she'd never met any physicians in London, but the name was vaguely familiar. Yes . . . Mrs Howard, the woman the *Gazette* had written about, whose shoulder Durie had fixed in time for her to dance at her daughter's wedding, hadn't she mentioned a Dr Candleford? He'd recommended strapping her arm tightly to her side to rest the shoulder, and Durie had told her that would do more harm than good. He'd sold her a jar of 'balm' too, but it was just goose grease, you could tell by the smell.

'Oh, Durie,' said Aunt Ellen, when she'd heard the story. 'I warned you about this, ages ago. You don't want to make enemies in business.'

Durie read the words again. *Examples of her dangerous incompetence are many.* Well, she'd like him to name them. She couldn't always fix people; sometimes a joint had got too stiff, or an old break had been set too badly. But then she said so, like her father did. She'd never told anyone she could fix something unless she was certain she could, and to the best of her knowledge, she'd never made anyone worse.

'How did he get the newspaper to print all that, when it's not true?'

'They print what they like, surely you knew that?'

'But that's ridiculous. People might just as well get their news from any old person in the street, who might or might not know what they're talking about, and save themselves tuppence.'

'That may well be but, Durie, you need to be more careful.'

'I don't see how this is my fault. I'm not the one telling lies to a newspaper.'

'Fault's neither here nor there. When it comes to business, men don't like women on their patch. You go around saying this doctor's given bad advice, or that one's treatments don't work, and they'll bite back. You're already stirring them up with what you do. Don't make it worse by what you say.'

That night, when Durie went up to bed, she tried to push Dr Candleford's words out of her head, and think about Malachy instead. Quite astonishing, how well the afternoon had gone. Especially the part where he'd chosen to walk back to her instead of flirting with the serving women. The look on the busty one's face! She definitely would get a new cloak in time for next month. He'd suggested a jaunt out to Islington, and that was a good hour and a half's walk each way, so it must mean he'd liked being with her, mustn't it?

All the same, the words in Dr Candleford's letter took the shine off the day a bit. Aunt Ellen had said not to worry about it, just to be careful not to say anything bad about physicians to her customers. Well, she'd try, but she wasn't going to lie to people, and if Dr Candleford didn't like that, he could just go and scratch.

Chapter 43

All that week, and the next and the next, Durie looked through every paper Aunt Ellen brought home – the *Gazette*, the *London Courier*, the *Crier*, the *Weekly News*, and a dozen more – just in case Dr Candleford's nonsense had been picked up elsewhere. If she'd always assumed what was in the papers was true, mightn't other people do the same? The customers she had already would know it was rubbish, but what if other people read it? They'd take their sprained ankles and their ricked necks somewhere else, her work would dribble away and if she couldn't carry on fixing people, what was she going to do?

To her relief, there was nothing about her, but in the third week, a report in the *Weekly News* caught her eye.

Sunday services at the Foundling Hospital chapel continue to draw London's finest. The Duchess of Bolton was among those gathered there last Sunday, an elegant figure in dove grey with a hat of emerald green trimmed with ostrich feathers. She was heard to say that the young foundlings sang like angels, and is believed to be making a substantial contribution to the hospital's funds.

How strange, to let people who didn't know them go and gawk at the children, as if it were like visiting the menagerie. But Tom would be four soon, he'd be back there then; if she went, she could check he was well. Didn't sound like they opened the doors to just anyone, but if a donation was what got you in, she could do that. And she'd ask Lucinda to come. Whatever she'd said at the time, surely it would be a comfort to her, too, to see he was all right? She'd go and see her that afternoon. Perhaps she could even ask her advice about a new cloak.

The thaw had come and gone, and it was a bright day, if still chilly. When she arrived at Lucinda's rooms near Soho Square, her sister was sitting in the front parlour, her feet up on the sill of one of the tall windows overlooking the street, her face to the sun and her hair glowing bright gold.

'Thank goodness that grey weather's over,' she said, turning her chair back round to face Durie, and smiling. 'Seen this?'

She handed Durie a copy of the *Weekly Miscellany*. Not another missive from Dr Candleford that she'd missed? But no: the story was about Lucinda.

We hear that the radiant Miss Lucinda Ellwood has caught the eye of a certain member of the Yorkshire aristocracy, currently in town without his lady wife. The two were seen dining very cosily on veal chops and Burgundy wine at Morrin's on Floral Street, after last Saturday's performance of The Milkmaid's Lament, *where Miss Ellwood enraptured the audience with her performance as Tilly Tipworth, the lovelorn milkmaid of the title.*

'That's not true, is it?' asked Durie.

'More or less. We didn't have veal chops, we had lobster. Morrin's have probably got some veal chops they want rid of. This little titbit must have come from them.' Lucinda's eyes sparkled. 'Told you I'd catch a duke, didn't I? He owns half of Yorkshire.'

'You haven't exactly caught him, he's got a wife. What's she going to say when she reads this?'

Lucinda rolled her eyes.

'How are you still so naïve after four years in London? All the nobs have mistresses, at least the ones who don't spend their evenings at the molly houses. It's expected. Their wives either don't care, or they're at it themselves while his lordship's away. And that kind of thing' – she flicked a finger at the newspaper – 'will sell a lot of tickets. Not just tickets either – I've had two artists already ask if they can paint me as Tilly Tipworth and sell prints of it, with twenty per cent of the price to me. Elizabeth Woolf's sold in their hundreds, and I'm already more popular than she was.'

'Aren't you worried about falling for a child again?'

'No, I've learned my lesson there, don't worry. I won't be giving him what he wants until I'm sure of what he'll do for me.'

'As it happens,' said Durie, 'it's Tom I've come about.'

She told Lucinda about the services at the Foundling Hospital chapel.

'I thought we could go, one Sunday. Just to see he's well.'

'Are you serious? I've told you before, I can't have anyone finding out about him.'

'They wouldn't, all sorts of people go there. I can't think

why they want to gawk at children they don't know, but they do. So no one would know why we were there.'

'No. I've left all that behind. And I'm not having you making moony faces at me again because you don't think I loved him enough, when there was never any point in me loving him.'

'You don't even want to find out if he's well and happy?'

'I hope he is. But if he's not, there's nothing I can do about it, is there? So no, thank you, I won't be going to listen to the little angels singing.'

Chapter 44

The Foundling Hospital chapel was obviously the place to be on a Sunday morning. As Durie crunched up the long gravel drive, a stream of carriages and gigs was dropping off well-dressed passengers outside the door, then circling back down to wait outside. The throng heading into the building were twittering at each other: 'Such a good cause' . . . 'I like to help where I can' . . . 'They do so well by the poor children'.

A man standing by the chapel door, some kind of official, looked her up and down as she approached. No one else seemed to be handing over money, but she pulled out the bag of guineas she'd brought anyway.

'I have a donation,' she said.

The man looked down his nose, a smirk playing around his lips.

'Our benefactors usually take out a subscription if they want to come to services,' he said, as though everyone and their dog would be aware of the arrangement.

Behind her, someone sniggered.

Durie's face flushed hot.

'Well, I didn't know that,' she said. 'So do you want my money or not?'

'We certainly do,' said a voice, and behind the official appeared the woman she'd seen after Lucinda left Tom there. Mrs Daring? No, Waring, that was it. No sign that she recognised Durie though.

'Donations are welcome in any form,' she said, as Durie handed over the money. She glanced at Durie's hat. 'It's Miss Proudfoot, isn't it? Thank you, this is very kind.' She turned to the official. 'Miss Proudfoot will be our guest today.'

Stick that in your snooty-nosed pipe and smoke it.

The chapel was as big as the church in Lewes, with six rows of pews facing each other across an aisle, galleries along each side, and a central one at one end, an organ at the front of it. She asked an attendant where the children sat.

'Up there,' he said, pointing to the organ. 'Best view's from the gallery seats.'

Durie took a seat near the front. He'd be able to see her from there. Was there a chance he might recognise her face? No, of course not, silly to hope for that. But she'd see him and that would be something.

When everyone was seated, the children trooped in, directed by an attendant. They filled the gallery from the front, smallest first, and girls on one side, boys on the other, all well-scrubbed and identically tidy in their little uniforms: the boys like toy soldiers in brown jackets and breeches with red neckerchiefs, the girls in brown dresses with spotless white aprons on top. The ones in front must be the four-year-olds, just back from their wet nurses. So tiny, perched like little sparrows on the benches; their feet couldn't even be touching the floor. Some looked as though they were seeing the chapel for the first time, staring out at the congregation with wide and frightened eyes. What must they be thinking? Did they wonder why they'd been taken away from the only families they'd ever known, and brought here to be gawped at by people in big hats and showy wigs? A child could easily think it was their fault, that they'd done something wrong and the families didn't want them any more. Did anyone explain to them that they hadn't? Looking at the stern-faced attendants, it didn't seem likely.

She stared at the front two rows of boys, looking for . . . what? She'd last seen a baby, with tufty blond hair, bright little button eyes, fat cheeks and just two tiny teeth. They might be tiny still, but these were boys, not babies, and not a single one was familiar.

The organ boomed out the notes of the first hymn, and everyone stood. The woman beside Durie had on a stupid hat, festooned with feathers, that blocked her view, and she tutted as Durie tried to look round it. There had to be something, some feature she could recognise, but it was impossible to see with all the feathers dancing about.

When the congregation sat again, she leaned forward – another tut from the hat woman – and peered at each face, one by one. That one was too ruddy and freckly; Tom had Lucinda's peachy skin. Another had very large ears, strangely shaped; he must have had those from birth. A couple were easily ruled out by their dark skin. By the time the minister started his sermon, she'd narrowed it down to three. One boy with fair curls, the colour very like Lucinda's. Another who had a dreamy look, as though in his head he was somewhere else; Lucinda had that sometimes. His hair was dark, but Richie's had changed in just the same way. And then in the row behind, another fair-haired lad, who, she couldn't really say why, just looked familiar.

Absorbed in watching the three of them, she wasn't listening to the service, and then suddenly the minister said the final words, the gallery attendant raised a hand and the children began filing out. Had she seen Tom, or not? She'd come to find out if he was well and happy, and the children did look well enough, even if the older ones were pale and pasty, without the rosy cheeks of the four-year-olds just back from the countryside. But happy? No, she couldn't say they looked happy, lined up there like little soldiers. All wondering, surely, why they were there and why their mothers and fathers didn't want them. She'd been so lucky to have Margie, who wasn't her mother, but who'd tucked her in every night when she was little, and picked her up when she fell and grazed her knee. If, even with Margie's love, she still felt a hole where her mother should have been, what must it be like for them, living like so many boxes in a warehouse, not one of them special to anyone? She should have done better by him. He was her flesh and blood and he deserved better than this.

As she was leaving, Mrs Waring came up to her.

'Do you think you'll take out a subscription, Miss Proudfoot? It's such a good cause.'

'You don't remember me, do you?' said Durie. 'I came to see you, nearly four years ago, after my sister left my nephew here.'

'Ah, I did think you looked familiar. I'm sorry, I see so many people—'

'Could I give some money for him? To be given to him when he's grown?'

'It isn't necessary, we make sure the children can support themselves. Our benefactors' subscriptions help us to do that.'

'I know, but I'd like to help him, because he's my family. I earn more than I need and this would be something useful I could do with it.'

'A subscription would help us to look after all the children here, that would be our preference.'

She was dogged, Durie had to give her that.

'All right – what if I take out a subscription, but at the same time, I'll save money for Tom, and when he's twenty-one, I'll give it to you and you give it to him? He needn't know where it came from, I just want him to have it.'

'I'd have to check . . .'

'Well, you do that then. And let me know.'

28 February 1762

Dear Tom,

I'm writing this not long after your fourth birthday, and I don't know if you'll remember this when you come to read these letters, but this is the year you came back to the Foundling Hospital.

I wish I could say this to you now, when you might need to hear it, but I can't, so all I can do is write it here instead for you to read when you're grown-up. I am so sorry we had to give you up. I believe the people at the Foundling Hospital mean well, and that they'll give you a good start in life. But it's not a home and it's not a family. You need to know though that your family loved you, and it was not your fault we couldn't keep you. And I'm sure the family who looked after you for the past four years loved you too, and they didn't want to give you up either.

I came this morning to the chapel, but I'm afraid I couldn't tell which boy was you. I won't come again; it'll make no difference to you, anyway.

Yours,

Aunt Durie

243

Chapter 45

Durie didn't go back, but the faces of the little boys at the Foundling Hospital wouldn't leave her alone. The first time she'd visited the place, when she'd gone to tell them about how to get Tom to sleep, hundreds of children must have been there, yet the place had been deathly quiet, with only the smell of boiled mutton in the air to say that anyone lived there at all. Until now, she could hope Tom was having a happy time in the countryside, with plenty of fresh air and a kind foster family, but now, he was stuck in that stiff, cold, gloomy place until he was old enough to go out and earn a living, just because his mother had been stupid and his father had been a liar. And yet by the sound of it, if Lucinda managed to hook her duke, she could have his children and keep them in style, wife notwithstanding, and no one would turn a hair. It didn't make sense.

The letter from Mrs Waring came: though it was 'highly unusual', if Durie took out a subscription, they would make the necessary arrangements for 'the gift she wished to bestow'. So there was that at least. She bought a new strongbox and tipped half the contents of the original one into it. She'd add to it each time a customer paid her bill; by the time Tom was twenty-one, there'd be enough to give him a really good start in life, and let him choose the work he wanted to do. It wasn't as good as a family, but it was the best she could do.

When Sunday came, Durie told Aunt Ellen she was planning to walk out to Islington, as the day was sunny, but she still didn't mention Malachy, and she didn't let Aunt Ellen see her give her hat a good brush, and put on her new cloak. In the shop, she'd dithered over one in blue, but when she looked in the mirror all she saw was how much better it would have looked on Lucinda, who suited blue so well the colour might have been invented for her. But the brown she chose was in a finer wool than her old one. It wouldn't be as hard-wearing, but if Malachy's hand happened to brush against it, it would feel soft.

Just as she was about to go downstairs and slip out, there was a rap on the door.

Didn't we agree to meet on the corner?

By the time she was halfway down the stairs, Betsy had already opened the door: to Lucinda.

She looked Durie up and down.

'You look more presentable than usual.'

'Sshhh,' said Durie. 'I'm going out.'

'You can't! You know she's going to give me a lecture about not relying on a man and making my own money and all that nonsense.'

'Well, she'll do that whether I'm here or not.'

'Where are you going?' Lucinda narrowed her eyes. 'And more to the point, who with? It's not the lion man, surely?'

'No. His name's Malachy. Malachy O'Neill.'

'Irish? Really?' Lucinda wrinkled her nose. 'Where did you find him?'

Durie reached for her hat.

'I'll tell you another time. He'll be waiting for me on the corner.'

Lucinda stopped in the middle of taking off her cloak, her eyes wide.

'Wait a minute . . . Dark hair, blue eyes, russet-coloured coat?'

'Is he there already? I should go—'

Lucinda gave a low whistle.

'Is that you, Lucinda?' Aunt Ellen called. 'I want to talk to you.'

Durie jammed on her hat and left.

As she strode up, he smiled and it hit her once more how handsome he was, and how unlikely it was that someone who could have his pick of London's pretty shopgirls and parlourmaids would choose to spend his time with her. Lucinda's reaction had confirmed it. But he was here, wasn't he?

'There you are,' he said. 'I thought maybe you'd changed your mind.'

'No, my sister called round unexpectedly.'

'Your sister?'

You let him think she went back to Lewes, you idiot. This is why you shouldn't even try to tell lies.

'She's in town unexpectedly. We didn't know she was coming.'

It didn't sound convincing, even to her, but he just smiled, and held out his arm, and this time, she didn't feel so awkward, because if she'd done it wrong last time, he wouldn't have offered it again, would he?

As they passed the elegant white houses on Grosvenor Square, he said, 'You wanting to meet on the corner, is that because you haven't told your aunt about me? I suppose she wouldn't think a mere footman is good enough for you?'

'No, it's just—'

'Don't worry, I agree with her. But I've told you, haven't I, that I don't intend to be a footman for ever? So here's what I think. We keep this just between ourselves, until I can present myself to your aunt as a man who's worthy of her niece. Then I don't have to worry that she might talk you out of having anything to do with an Irish ruffian like me.'

'What makes you think I'd let her talk me out of anything?'

He laughed.

'I hope you wouldn't. But all the same, shall we do that? I promise it won't be long – I'm looking into opportunities already, good ones.' He nudged her gently with his elbow. 'We'll meet on street corners, like star-crossed lovers running off to Gretna Green.'

Durie turned away so he wouldn't see the blush warming her cheeks. She was still catching up with the fact that he'd talked about presenting himself to Aunt Ellen, and being worthy of her, and now he was talking about them being lovers.

As they strolled along the wide pavements of Oxford Street, past the shops, he talked about Ireland, and the village where his family lived, and asked Durie about Lewes, and her family. He was so easy to talk to that she even found herself telling him about her mother dying.

'I don't even know if she ever got a chance to see me,' she said.

'Ah, that's very hard on a child.' He squeezed her hand. 'She'd be proud of you now though, wouldn't she?'

'I hope so. My father said she would.'

'And rightly so. You've done very well for yourself, and all from your own efforts. I think we're very alike, you and me.'

She felt herself walk a little taller, hearing that, and it seemed no time at all before they were striding along the road towards Islington, with fields on either side and only the occasional house. The bright weather meant plenty of people were heading the same way, and gigs and coaches trundled by, but still, it was quieter than the city and the air was fresher. The sky even seemed bluer, without the fug of coal smoke that hung about even the widest streets.

The last of the daffodils were still in flower at the edges of the fields; he picked a bunch, handing them to Durie with a bow.

'No one's ever given me flowers before,' she said.

'About time, then.'

The road climbed uphill and by the time they reached the outskirts of the village, it was steep enough to stop them talking.

'Let's stop here a minute, get our breath back,' he said,

steering her towards a stile. As they looked out over the fields to the rooftops of the city, he turned to her.

'I want to say something to you, and I hope I'm not out of order.'

To her surprise, he took her hand.

'I know we haven't known each other long, but these last few weeks, I've thought of you a lot.'

Barely a moment to take that in, before he moved closer, put his hand on her waist and said, 'To be precise, I've thought quite a bit about what it might be like to kiss you. And what I'm hoping is, that you might be wondering the same about me.'

She hadn't been wondering anything of the sort. She'd thought there'd be a lot more walking and talking, arm in arm, before it was reasonable to let her daydreams wander anywhere near that kind of territory. But anyway, he didn't wait for an answer, he just leaned in and kissed her. Durie almost fell over backwards with the surprise of it, but he caught her and held her close as though she was as light as a feather.

When he let her go, she stood there like an idiot; after what he'd said about wanting to know what it was like to kiss her, she was expecting a verdict. But he just smiled and said, 'So, will we stroll on up to the village and find ourselves some sustenance, after this long walk?'

The inn by the green was busy, but Malachy charmed a couple into letting them squeeze onto the end of a long table, and ordered steak and oyster pies. He was talking about the pies his mother cooked, and Durie nodded and smiled but all the time she was thinking, will he kiss me again? She wanted to be ready: the way he caught her around the waist last time was lovely, but it had only been a matter of lucky timing that she hadn't pulled him off balance and sent them both tumbling to the ground. When she'd finished her pie, she waited until he wasn't looking and gave her mouth a thorough wipe with the edge of her cloak. Highly unlikely that her lips tasted of honey, like Lucinda's, but she didn't want them tasting of gravy instead.

But all the way back, he chatted amiably about this and that, as though the kiss had never happened. What if, after all that wondering what it would be like to kiss her, his conclusion was that it wasn't up to much? He'd seemed to like it, as far as she could tell, but having never been kissed before, she didn't have a lot to go on.

When he asked how her work was going, she told him about the letter in the newspaper.

'I expect he's envious,' he said. 'I daresay you can charge as much as a doctor does, these days.'

'I don't know what they charge, but people pay me a guinea a time – more if it's something I have to go to straight away, like a break or a dislocation. It's quite mad, really, my father never charged more than a pound for a broken leg. But Aunt Ellen says rich people only appreciate things if they're expensive.'

'Well, she's right there. Clever woman, your aunt. I expect she's said to you as well to put a bit aside for a rainy day. My mother always said, it's not how much you earn that matters, it's how much you spend.'

'She has. But I hardly spend anything anyway, so your mother would be pleased with me.'

'She would indeed, you're a very sensible woman.'

Which was all very well, but who wants to be called sensible by a handsome man? No more kisses on the way home either; obviously the embrace had fallen short of his expectations. Well, it was no surprise, and she shouldn't have got her hopes up. What an idiot.

But when they reached the corner of South Audley Street, he said, 'I'd like to steal another kiss, but we'd best not give your neighbours anything to report to your aunt.'

He touched her cheek, very gently, with one finger, then kissed her on the forehead.

'That will have to do for now. Or they'll all be saying, who's that, come courting Miss Proudfoot the bonesetter?'

Durie wasn't given to fanciful ideas, but as she strolled away, she could have sworn she was walking on air.

Malachy watched as Durie galumphed off down the street in her big old boots. Well, wasn't she full of surprises? She'd seemed an open book, but she'd managed to hide that one well enough. He'd recognised Lucinda Ellwood straight away when she'd passed him on the corner, and he hadn't missed the glance back over her shoulder, either, nor the wiggle of that peachy backside. He'd nearly fallen over when she went up and knocked on Durie's door. But that was the sister's name, wasn't it?

Lucinda had a baby. We came so she could take him to the Foundling Hospital.

She'd confirmed it, with the blush as much as with the mention of her sister calling round, but he was already certain by then; what other business would Lucinda Ellwood have with her and the old biddy? So all in all, it had been quite a useful afternoon. Those two were both on the way up, and he had one wriggling on the hook, and a useful bit of information about the other. Not bad for the price of a steak and oyster pie.

Chapter 46

With her head full of Malachy, Durie had put the letter from Dr Candleford out of her mind. In the weeks after it, she'd tried to heed Aunt Ellen's advice, and not criticise a customer's physician. But when someone said they'd been told to lie flat for six weeks to cure a backache, or questioned her strapping up a sprained ankle because their doctor said to leave it open to the air, she couldn't just nod and say, yes, that sounds sensible, could she? How could doctors, whose job it was to fix people, take money for treatments they must have known wouldn't work, or at least had no good reason to trust? If someone presented her with a complaint she couldn't fix, she said so, and if it was something a physician could help with, she advised them to go there instead. But she'd never had anyone come to her on the advice of a physician; they preferred, it seemed, to see their patients in pain than to let someone else have a try at fixing them.

But Aunt Ellen turned out to be right again. This time, it was the *Mercury* that she brought home.

It has been widely reported that many have found great benefit from a certain female bonesetter's performance. This is to give notice that any persons afflicted with lameness will be welcome to see the state of my leg, which was sound before her ministrations. They may then judge to whom I owe my present unhappy confinement to my bed and chair, and decide for themselves whether her claims to skill are true or not.
Thomas Barber
Saffron Hill

'This is completely mad,' said Durie. 'I've never even met a Thomas Barber.'

'I thought as much. I warned you, didn't I?'

'You think Dr Candleford is behind this?'

'Him or one of the other doctors. This is why I said to you, don't make enemies of them.'

'I'm not the one who's done anything wrong. All I've ever done is fix people, and tell the truth, and I'm not having them telling lies about me. I'm going to find this Thomas Barber, and tell him to write to the paper and take it back.'

Ignoring Aunt Ellen's entreaties to calm down, Durie threw on her cloak, snatched up the paper, and marched all the way to Saffron Hill, a narrow street of watchmaker's shops. She enquired at every shop, but no one knew of a Thomas Barber. How could a doctor, an educated man, sit down and make up a story like that? Well, she couldn't let him get away with it. If she didn't put a stop to this now, people would start believing it.

Everyone knew where the physicians spent their days: Brown's Coffee House, on Cornhill. She'd even seen some advertise that they held consultations there. It wasn't far from Saffron Hill, so fury powered her all the way, but outside the door, she hesitated. She'd never been inside a coffee house, but she could guess what it was like: all men together, joshing and joking. Like the men sniggering at the bar with the landlord at the Pelham Arms back in Lewes.

That one'd only be good for getting rid of the stragglers at the end of the night, and we've got the dog for that.

Well, let them do their worst, they were still going to hear what she'd come to say. She pushed open the door into a fog of tobacco smoke and a wave of noise; there must have been fifty men in the low-ceilinged, wood-panelled room, seated at three long tables, smoking pipes and, by the sound of it, all talking at once. The only woman was a harassed-looking redhead behind the counter, where coffee pots stood warming on hooks above a fire.

And there were the physicians, seated round the table nearest the door. Easy to recognise: bigger wigs than anyone else, gilt-buttoned coats outlining well-fed bellies, and on the table, three small glass flasks of what must have been urine. One, with his back to her, was holding forth, pointing at one of the flasks. She took a deep breath.

You are not taking my work away.

As she walked to their table, the din of conversation died. Faces turned to stare and someone said ' . . . that bonesetter woman'. The man with his back to her turned, glanced at her hat, and smirked.

'If it isn't Miss Proudfoot, the bonesetter.'

'Since you know me, may I ask your name?' said Durie, though she had a pretty good idea.

'Dr Josiah Candleford. At your service. Is there a medical matter I can help you with?'

Behind her someone sniggered and said, 'This'll be good.'

'You can help me with this,' she said, laying the newspaper on the table.

He glanced at the words, not even pretending he didn't already know full well what they said.

'It seems you have a dissatisfied customer. That won't do your reputation any good at all, I'm afraid.'

'But I've never treated this man. He doesn't even exist.'

Dr Candleford raised a shaggy eyebrow and looked around at his companions.

'Are you sure? Because he seems very angry, for a man who doesn't exist.'

The others around the table smirked.

'I think one of you wrote this letter,' said Durie.

'Why would we do that? We're busy men, Miss Proudfoot.'

'Because you don't like competition. You don't like that sometimes I can treat things you can't. That's why you sent the other letter too.'

'What I said then, and I stick by,' he said, 'is that you, and the likes of you, are no better than charlatans. You have no university degree, no knowledge of anatomy. You take money under false pretences, and it's time people knew it.'

'I take money under false pretences? Who told Mrs Howard to strap her shoulder to her side? If a shoulder's been out, and it's not put back right, you've got to move it till it is. She could have been in pain for years if she'd listened to you. And that balm you sold her was nothing more than goose grease, useless for pain.'

'You must have a very large brain for a woman, Miss Proudfoot, to know all this. But then . . . ' He looked her up and down. 'You're not exactly typical of the fair sex, are you?'

Well, she'd expected that.

'Is that the best you've got in the way of insults, Dr Candleford? Because you're no work of art yourself, but I wouldn't say that's what makes you a bad doctor.'

The man opposite spluttered his coffee across the table, and guffaws and whoops rang round the room. Dr Candleford's cheeks reddened. They were laughing at him, but she wasn't daft enough to think that meant they were laughing with her.

'Watch out,' someone called from another table. 'Size of her, she can probably put a shoulder out as easily as put it in.'

'I daresay I could,' said Durie. 'But unlike some of you, I don't care to make people worse instead of better, and then take their money for it. Tell me, Dr Candleford – has Mrs Howard needed your help with her shoulder since I fixed it?'

'I don't discuss my customers with the likes of you.'

'Well, there's no need, since we both know the answer. So I'd be obliged if you'd stop spreading lies about me. You do what you do, and I'll do what I do, and then we needn't trouble ourselves to meet again.'

She forced herself to walk calmly to the door. As she opened it, he called out, 'You're no better than a charlatan, Miss Proudfoot, and you can count on me to make sure people know it.'

Aunt Ellen was right. She'd made things worse.

Chapter 47

In the weeks that followed, there were more letters, in different newspapers, from people she'd never heard of, saying she'd promised to cure them and failed.

'They've got you in their sights now,' said Aunt Ellen. 'This is what I was afraid of.'

'But it's ridiculous. They can't do what I do. Why on earth would you want to give someone a treatment that won't help them?'

'Because men like Dr Candleford – well, men in general – don't like to admit they don't know the answer. But that's up to them. What you need to worry about is how you're going to stop him and his cronies ruining your business.'

'You really think it's that serious?'

'Yes, if you don't nip it in the bud. You remember how quickly word got around after you helped Mr Philimore? A bad reputation can bubble up just as fast, and once people have lost faith in you, it's not easy to win them back.'

Durie stomped off to bed then, but she couldn't sleep. She didn't care about the money. She'd made enough to live on for quite a while anyway, being as her needs were small, and the fund for Tom was healthy too. But if she couldn't fix people any more, if nobody wanted her to, she might as well shrivel up and disappear.

She thumped the pillow to try and get it comfortable. That Dr Candleford sitting there all smug-faced, with his great big wig and his gold-topped cane, sniffing at bottles of urine, what right did he have to feel superior to her? She might not have studied at a university, but she'd seen a lot of bodies and felt a lot of injuries, and she'd learned what worked. And if she didn't always know why it worked, well, were they any different? They could tell you dark urine meant this and cloudy urine meant that, but they couldn't give you a good reason why, so they must be doing what she did – watching and learning and working things out. So how dare he call her a charlatan? If she'd been a man, she'd have pulled him out of his chair and punched him on his big red nose. That would show him.

Durie sat up. That was it. Show him. And not just him. No point telling people what she could do, if Candleford and his cronies just countered that with lies. But if she showed them, how could they argue with that?

The coffee house was just opening up when Durie arrived next morning, and the red-haired woman was sweeping outside. Durie asked after the owner and the woman jerked a thumb towards the door, yelling, 'Jake, someone here to see you.'

He was sitting at a table near the back, a dish of coffee beside him, poring over an accounts book. As Durie introduced herself, he interrupted her.

'I know who you are, that was good entertainment you gave us yesterday. But if you've come for another jibe at Dr Candleford, you're too early, the medical men come in later.'

'I haven't. I want to hold consultations here. Like the doctors do.'

Before she'd finished explaining, he was shaking his head.

'A coffee house isn't a place for a woman. The customers like to discuss ideas, and the higher things of life, without being interrupted by women's chatter.'

'I don't chatter. Let me see my customers – just men and boys – one afternoon a week, and I'll give you fifteen per cent of everything I take.'

He narrowed his eyes at her.

'I don't know . . . The medical men won't like it.'

The woman had come in by then, and was leaning on her broom, listening to the conversation.

'The lawyers would though,' she said. 'You know they hate the doctors. If word gets around she's got the docs riled up, we'll get more coming in, for the entertainment.'

'I can't afford to lose the doctors, Jeannie.'

'They won't go anywhere else, they don't like mixing with trade. I say give her a chance. Three weeks, say, and see how it goes.'

'All right. Three weeks it is.'

Chapter 48

Durie's stomach churned as she stepped into the fug of tobacco and noise again. The table on the far side – they must be the lawyers – gave a cheer, and one shouted, 'Here comes your competition, doctors – look to your pockets!'

The doctors carried on their conversation as though they hadn't seen her, but Durie wasn't having that: being seen was the point. As she passed their table, she said, 'Good afternoon, Dr Candleford.'

He turned and nodded.

'Miss Proudfoot. Looking lovely as ever.'

His colleagues smirked, but Durie held her head high and walked on. Which meant she didn't see when the one at the end of the table stuck out his leg in front of her. She hit the flagstone floor with a thump, banging her knee. Bandages, splints and jars of balm spilled from her bag and a whoop went up that didn't just come from the doctors.

'Oh dear,' said Dr Candleford, to a background of snorts and sniggers. 'I do hope you haven't broken anything. Apart from the floor.'

As she clambered to her feet, the woman, Jeannie, came

out from behind the counter, bent to brush down Durie's skirts and said, very quietly, 'Ignore them. They're just jealous. Can't stand to see a woman making her own money.'

She helped Durie pick up her things and then, raising her voice, said, 'You take a seat, Miss Proudfoot, and I'll bring you a dish of coffee. We've had a lot of people enquiring about you, so you'll have a busy afternoon.'

The owner, Jake, had been adamant she couldn't sit at one of the communal tables, so Jeannie suggested putting a smaller one in the corner farthest from the door. At the time, it seemed perfect, being visible from every seat in the place. Now, as Durie sat there, knee throbbing, face burning, pretending not to notice the grins and smirks and sudden outbreaks of laughter at the doctors' table, she wasn't so sure.

'Here you are,' said Jeannie, setting down a steaming dish of coffee.

'How many people have enquired about me?' asked Durie.

'None.' She winked. 'I only said that to stir them up.'

Durie had paid a lad to put up notices on busy streets, with her times and prices, so that was a bit surprising. But then again, she'd taken care to give all the necessary information, so perhaps there was no need to enquire and people would just turn up. She sipped her coffee and tried to look unconcerned.

An hour passed – it felt like three – and no one came. Then, at last, in walked Mr Alexander, a merchant she'd treated for a stiff hip the previous spring. Please, let it not be troubling him again – that could happen with hips, and Candleford would seize the chance to say she hadn't fixed it properly in the first place. But Mr Alexander was walking well, so, silently praying for something she could fix there and then and wipe the smug looks off their faces with, Durie stood and said, 'Good afternoon, Mr Alexander.'

The hum of chatter fell silent.

'Good afternoon, Miss Proudfoot,' he said, tipping his hat. 'You're seeing people here now, then. Very convenient.'

She gestured for him to come over. He shook his head.

'Oh no, I've not come to see you, my hip's fine now.'

He turned to the doctors' table, and the one who'd tripped her up – younger than Dr Candleford, with a face like a weasel's – said, 'This gentleman is here to see a proper doctor, Miss Proudfoot. But if you're bored, I daresay there are some horses in the street that need shoeing.'

The entire table laughed, and the lawyers joined in. Mr Alexander sat down in front of weasel face, and Durie watched out of the corner of her eye, her face flaming, as he pointed to his stomach. Of course he wouldn't have come to her for that, but they'd still count it a victory. Why had she been so stupid, and let them see she was desperate?

They made the most of it, of course. Even before Mr Alexander left, clutching a note for the apothecary, three more people had arrived to see one or another of the doctors, and each time, Dr Candleford enquired loudly whether they were sure they hadn't come to see Miss Proudfoot the bone-setter.

Aunt Ellen had made her promise not to rise to them.

'You'll be providing entertainment, if you do. Don't give them it.'

She kept reminding herself of that and pretending not to hear them, until the fourth customer came in. Dr Candleford asked yet again if the man wanted to see Miss Proudfoot, and when the man said no, he replied, loudly, 'She's already tried to steal one of Dr Marshall's customers. These quacks, they're no better than street hawkers.'

Durie walked to the doctors' table, forcing herself not to limp on her sore knee. Conversations on all sides dribbled to a stop.

'What did you call me?' she said.

Dr Candleford looked up, and smiled his smug smile.

'Quack was the word I used. Though charlatan would do just as well.'

'I'm not a charlatan. Or a quack. I do what I say I can do. And I don't need to steal your customers, I have plenty of my own.'

'Oh, really?' he said, looking round the room. 'Where are they then?'

He winked at the weasel-faced one, and she knew. No one was coming. She didn't know what they'd done, but they'd done something, and they were mighty pleased with themselves about it. She wasn't going to give them the satisfaction of accusing them though.

'Some days are busy, some not,' she said. 'I make a very comfortable living, all the same. Comfortable enough that I don't worry about competition from you gentlemen, though you seem very worried about competition from me.'

There was laughter from the lawyers' table, and shouts of 'Nicely put!' and 'She's got their measure!'

Dr Candleford opened his mouth to reply, but Durie put up a hand to stop him.

'I'm leaving now. But I'll be back, because I've as much

right to make people well as you have. And . . . ' She gestured to the flasks in front of them. 'I don't have to sniff people's piss to make my money.'

It was only as she reached the door that she noticed the man sitting on his own at the end of the lawyers' table. Writing down every word she'd said.

Chapter 49

Penny scribblers, they called them. She found that out later from Jeannie. What a way to make your living – sitting in coffee houses, eavesdropping on people's conversations, adding a few made-up bits of your own, then selling the whole load of nonsense to the newspapers. Two days later, there it was in the *Mercury*.

Reports reach us of a feud between the female bonesetter, Miss Proudfoot, and London's medical men. Miss Proudfoot, who has become known for her eccentric appearance and brusque manner, has recently begun to offer consultations at Brown's Coffee House on Cornhill. On being challenged by Dr Candleford as to her qualifications, she raged at the assembled doctors, shaking her fist and calling them piss-sniffers. The contretemps concluded with Miss Proudfoot vowing to show Dr Candleford the strength of her arm if she should come across him in the street, and exiting the coffee house in high dudgeon.

'It's nonsense,' she said to Aunt Ellen. 'I didn't rage at the doctors, or shake my fist. I didn't even raise my voice.'

'Did you call them piss-sniffers?'

'No . . . Well, yes. In a way. But not the way it says there. Why didn't he write what really happened?'

'I expect he thought it would be more entertaining this way.'

'He's got no business making it more entertaining.'

'That's exactly his business. That's what people read newspapers for. You were foolish enough to give him a handful of crumbs, and he's turned them into a loaf.'

What the paper didn't tell its readers was why none of her customers had turned up. Every one of the notices had been torn down; she walked the length of Oxford Street and there wasn't one left. Of course no one had come; no one knew she was there.

'I'm going to write to the *Mercury* and tell them,' said Durie.

Aunt Ellen shook her head.

'You'll add fuel to the fire. Just go back next week, and this time we'll make sure people know about it.'

Malachy had proposed a jaunt out to Marylebone on his next day off, and no sooner had they set out, than he asked about the coffee house; she'd hoped to avoid talking about it, but of course he'd seen the penny scribbler's nonsense.

'It sounds like you gave them what for, and rightly so,' he said. 'And you got plenty of customers, did you?'

She didn't want to tell him, and make him disappointed in her, but what was the point in lying?

'I didn't get any. They took down all my notices, no one knew I was there. It was horrible.'

'Well, that just proves they're afraid of the competition, doesn't it? You'll go back again next week though, like you planned?'

'Of course I will. I'm not letting them win.'

'That's my girl,' he said. They were walking arm in arm as before, and he gave her hand a little squeeze that made Durie feel warm inside.

As they reached Marylebone Lane, where the city came abruptly to an end and the roadway was bordered by market gardens full of fat green cabbages, he said, 'I've got some news. I wasn't going to tell you till it was completely settled, but I'm pretty sure it'll work out, so . . . I'm going to be leaving the Philimore house soon, I've found a better opportunity.'

'A bigger house?'

'Oh, no. My days as a lackey are over. I told you, I came here to make my fortune.'

He'd met a man, he explained, who was a corn factor.

'How it works is, instead of farmers bringing their corn all the way to London from Essex, or Kent, or Suffolk, and taking a chance on finding a buyer, they sell through him. He has a stand at the Corn Exchange on Mark Lane, the buyers come there. He tells them who's got what they want, and takes a cut. He says if you work hard and make yourself a good reputation, the money's there for the taking.'

'And he's offered you a position?'

'He has. But that's just the start. He's getting on a bit, this fellow, and his health isn't good. He's got a big house in Chelsea, and in a couple of years, he wants to get his money out and spend his time where the air's nice and fresh. The idea is, by then, I'll be able to buy him out, take on the stand myself. And then you'll see I'm not just an Irish chancer who's all talk.'

'I've never thought you were that.'

'Well, now you know. I'm on my way.'

They bought apple turnovers from a bakery and sat on a bench on the green to eat them, throwing crumbs of pastry to a couple of sparrows. When they'd finished, he said, 'I was thinking . . .'

He took Durie's hands in his, his face serious.

'I'm not in a position to put a ring on your finger just yet. But I've got prospects now, and if I could know that – just between ourselves – we were promised to each other, well, that'd spur me on better than anything else in the world.'

It took a moment for Durie to take the words in; she'd thought he was going to suggest where they might go on his next day off.

'But that's . . . you hardly know me.'

'Sorry, I've embarrassed you now. Forget I said anything. I shouldn't have tried to bind you to me when I've nothing to offer you yet. It's only that I thought, if I wait till I've made my fortune before I speak, you might have waltzed off with some other fellow by then.'

Was he joking with her? He didn't look like he was, his face was entirely serious, but he couldn't really think she had other fellows to waltz off with, could he?

When she didn't reply, he let go of her hand.

'Better that we part now then, if we're not going to—'

Part? Where had that come from? Had she done something wrong? She took a breath to keep her voice steady.

'What do you mean?'

'You don't want to tie yourself to me, when you can't be sure if I'll ever amount to anything.'

'I am sure you'll amount to something! And I do want to . . . tie myself to you.'

He smiled and put his arms round her, and this time when he kissed her, it didn't occur to Durie to worry about what her lips tasted like.

That night, she dreamt about George. She was in front of Crowley's cage at the Tower, but with Malachy. She was telling him how flexible the lions' spines were, and he stopped her talking by kissing her. When she opened her eyes from the kiss, George was standing there, watching.

She woke with a heavy feeling that she'd done something wrong, but that was stupid. George wouldn't want her to still be moping after him; he'd want her to be happy, just as she wanted that for him. In truth, she didn't feel as easy and comfortable with Malachy as she had, right from the very beginning, with George. It was more like being spun like a top, and she was dizzy with the speed of it. But wasn't that what love was supposed to feel like?

Chapter 50

Durie hadn't seen Lucinda for a couple of months, at least not in the flesh, though she'd spotted two more figurines and prints of her were everywhere. But that low whistle, when Lucinda realised she'd seen Malachy, had rankled. It meant 'What's he doing with you?', didn't it? So when she found herself near Lucinda's rooms on the way back from an appointment, how could she resist the chance to tell her they were as good as engaged?

When the maid showed her up to the parlour, Lucinda was surrounded by packing cases, wrapping a vase in paper.

'What's going on?' asked Durie.

'What does it look like? I'm moving. I was going to come round and tell you, but I've been so busy. William's letting me have the whole place redone, exactly as I want it, and you wouldn't believe how long it takes to choose curtains.'

'What place? And who's William?'

Lucinda put on a plummy voice, repeating the words Durie had seen in the paper.

'A certain member of the aristocracy . . .'

'The one who owns half of Yorkshire?'

Lucinda giggled.

'The very same. He's taken a house on Queen Street for me. Not very big, but it's a good address.'

'So you're . . .'

'I am his very good friend.'

'But why? You're earning enough to support yourself – why would you want to be dependent on a man?'

'You sound like Aunt Ellen.'

'Well, I think she's right.'

'You do, do you? Well, if you think that's a life, slaving away in the shop all day, obsessing about whether that Frenchman's sold more jam tarts than her, then coming home to a set of accounts and a cat, good luck to you, but I don't. I want an easy life, with plenty of sparkle in it, and William's money will buy me that.'

'You're not giving up the theatre?'

'Of course I am. He's not going to want other men gawping at me, is he?'

'I thought you loved it.'

'Well, of course I make it look like that.' Lucinda sighed. 'No, I do love it, sometimes. But it's hard work, Durie. Even when you're as popular as I am, you still get bad audiences, and you just try standing there singing while there's a couple in the front having a fight about last night's fish, and the second row are roaring drunk, and the dandies in the first box think it's fun to see who can get a peanut down the front of your dress. And I can't do it for ever, can I? No one's going to want a wrinkled Tilly Tipworth.'

'But what makes you think he'll keep you for ever?'

'I'll keep him happy. He's a simple soul, not the sort who has one mistress after another. He wanted his innocent milk-maid, and now he's got her.'

She picked up a glass dish and began wrapping it.

'Anyway, I want to know about this Irishman of yours. He's quite the pretty face, and the rest of him's not bad either.'

'That's what I came to tell you. We're promised to each other.'

Lucinda frowned.

'You're what?'

'He wants to marry me. But it's just between ourselves for now, until he gets himself established in business. So don't go telling Aunt Ellen, or Margie.'

'I see.'

'You don't seem very pleased for me.'

'I'm not sure I've reason to be. Has he asked you for money yet?'

'Of course he hasn't!'

'Has he asked you *about* money? Does he know how much you've got stashed away?'

'Not the exact amount, no, and anyway—'

'Durie, you've known him five minutes, he's as pretty as hell and you're . . . you. And he wants you to promise yourself to him but not tell anyone?'

'Not everyone's like you, obsessed with how people look – Malachy likes me for myself.'

'You won't believe me when I say this, but I hope that's true. But be careful, Durie. You think everyone's as straight and honest as you are, but they're not. And I don't want to see you taken advantage of.'

Durie stomped home. They were fine words coming from someone who was taking her chances on that old toad of a duke, Yorkshire or no Yorkshire. What did Lucinda know anyway?

Chapter 51

Before she went back to the coffee house, Durie had a stack of handbills printed, and paid six boys to give them out in different places; if anyone from Marylebone to Bow wanted her services that afternoon, they'd know where to find her.

And if they don't come, the doctors will make mincemeat of me.

She took a deep breath, and pushed open the door. Conversations stopped and through the fug of smoke every eye turned towards her; if the coffee house was busy before, it was nothing to the congregation gathered around the tables now.

She gave the doctors a nod as she passed, making sure to keep well clear of weasel face on the end. Jeannie came over with a dish of coffee.

'Had to borrow some extra seats from the Grecian in Bottle Street. That piece in the *Mercury*'s done wonders for business.'

Durie glanced across at the scribbler; he raised his dish with a grin. She'd been good for everyone's business so far, except her own.

The clock on the wall showed five minutes to two; the handbills had stated her hours as between two and four.

'Looking lonely over there, Miss Proudfoot,' called Dr Candleford. 'No customers again?'

'A little early yet,' said Durie as pleasantly as she could manage, and took a sip of her coffee.

They'd come, wouldn't they? It had rained all week and slippery cobbles were always good for business. All the same, by the time the hands ticked round to two, she was wishing very heartily that she was just about anywhere else, and by quarter past, after Dr Candleford had pointed out her lack of customers three more times, it was a struggle not to pick up her coffee, pour it over his head and then walk out and forget the whole idea.

She picked up a newspaper, keeping her eyes on the pages each time the door opened. So when Mr Philimore – father of Gregory – came in, it was only the sudden hush that made her look up. He was striding – she'd done good work on that ankle – towards her corner. He paused and raised his hat to the doctors.

'Good afternoon, gentlemen. How convenient to have you all and the marvellous Miss Proudfoot in the same place. A treatment for every ill.'

Dr Candleford snorted.

'She may call it treatment. I call it quackery. I'm surprised a gentleman such as yourself would have anything to do with it.'

'Miss Proudfoot is highly skilled, and both I and my son have a great deal to thank her for. Now, if you'll excuse me, I have a painful neck that needs her attention.'

Sitting down at Durie's table, he said quietly, 'Horrible man. Used to treat Mrs Philimore for headaches, charged me a fortune and never made a blind bit of difference. I saw there'd been some unpleasant letters in the *Mercury*, meant to write in and tell them what you did for Gregory, but I never got round to it. So when I read what happened here last week, I thought, I'll go and see Miss Proudfoot about my neck, and take the chance to tell them face to face.'

'Thank you. That's kind of you.'

'Not at all. Gregory's never forgotten it, you know – how frightened he was and how you took the pain away so quickly. And my ankle . . .' He stuck out his foot and flexed it. ' . . . gives me no pain at all now. So I won't see that lot telling lies about you.'

What a kind man he was. No wonder Malachy liked working there, despite Gregory's antics.

By the time she'd finished working on his neck, there were two more people waiting to see her, and Dr Candleford looked as though he'd lost a shilling and found a nail. In the end, she had to stay on till six, and saw five people in all, including a man almost bent double with a stiffness in his back, who walked out upright and thanked her profusely. The doctors pretended not to notice, but the lawyers cheered and clapped. When she left, the penny scribbler was writing nineteen to the dozen.

Aunt Ellen was smiling when she handed Durie that week's copy of the *Mercury*.

On Tuesday last, patrons at Brown's Coffee House on Cornhill witnessed a remarkable cure by Miss Proudfoot the female bonesetter, who set to rights a gentleman plagued with a stiffness of the spine. The gentleman was heard to say he had not walked upright for months, but after manipulation by Miss Proudfoot, exited the premises as straight as any youth. Miss Proudfoot's services were also provided to Mr Christopher Philimore, who recommended her to the assembled company.

The following week there were three people waiting to see her, and for the rest of the afternoon, as she finished with one person, there was another through the door. Some were customers she knew, who just happened to find it convenient to see her there, but the rest were new. Pleasing in itself, but even more so for the sour look on Dr Candleford's face each time the door opened and yet another customer walked to her corner. They'd exchanged a 'Good day' when she arrived – cheery on Durie's part, rather stiff on his – but otherwise the doctors behaved as though she wasn't there. The lawyers weren't going to be cheated of their fun though; each time a new customer arrived, they called out 'Another for the bonesetter!' and 'Look to your laurels, doctors!'

She was so busy that her coffee went cold before there was a chance to drink it. After the last customer left, Jeannie came over with a fresh pot.

'You must be worn out,' she said. 'That last one looked like hard work.'

'I'm used to it. But thank you for the coffee.'

'Thank you for the custom – we've never been busier.' She looked over at the doctors' table, and winked at Durie. 'And for the entertainment. I've never seen that lot look less pleased with life.'

'Serves them right.'

Jeannie laughed.

'It does. Anyway, what I came over to say was, Jake says never mind the three weeks' trial – if you want to carry on, you're very welcome. And could you have a look at his neck?'

Chapter 52

Durie wasn't sure how to tell Aunt Ellen about Lucinda's new domestic arrangements, but as it turned out, the *Mercury* got there first.

> *We hear that Lucinda Ellwood, darling of the stage, is lately moved to an elegant property in Queen Street, where she frequently enjoys the company of a certain member of the Yorkshire aristocracy. Miss Ellwood is currently delighting audiences as Julia in* Love Lost, Love Won, *but is said to be retiring from the stage in favour of quieter pursuits.*

'That's what they call it now, is it?' said Aunt Ellen. 'What a waste.'

All the same, she agreed to go with Durie to see Lucinda's last performance. Arriving a little late, the only seats they could find were at the back of the stalls, next to a couple slurping oysters noisily from the shells. There was a convoluted first scene involving a shipwreck, then the scenery switched from a seascape to a London street, and Lucinda walked on in a dress of rose pink, to a storm of applause and stamping feet. She gave a little bow, and began to sing, and once again, as her clear, bright voice rang out, it was as though everyone else disappeared.

The song was something about the scarcity of true love, and at the last verse, Lucinda turned to one of the boxes. The audience followed her gaze to a gentleman twice her age, with jowls like a bloodhound and an air of being very pleased with himself.

'She's like an angel,' said the woman beside Durie to her husband. 'Looks like an angel, sings like an angel.'

'I shouldn't think she's an angel with him,' he replied. 'You don't get a house on Queen Street for that.'

'Don't be smutty,' said the woman. 'She really loves him. Look at her face, you can tell.'

They spoke as if they knew her. What would they say if Durie told them Lucinda was her sister, and she'd seen how that face could make people believe anything she wanted them to, long before any of them clapped eyes on her?

'I daresay he loves her too, till the next one comes along,' said the man. He nudged his wife in the ribs. 'Think yourself lucky you only fell for a docker – we're a lot more faithful than the nobs are.'

'Only because you can't afford to keep a string of mistresses,' she said. 'I bet you would if you could.'

He laughed.

'What man wouldn't?'

I knew one that wouldn't.

I'm not the type of man to seek comfort elsewhere, that's what George had said. What would she have done if he had been? Was she really in any position to judge Lucinda? All the same, she didn't like the look of the duke. As Lucinda finished her song, he threw her a rose; she caught it, bobbed a curtsy and blew him a kiss, and the audience cheered. No one cared that he had a wife; they were as pleased for the pair of them as if they'd been two newlyweds coming out of church. But there was a sort of amused carelessness in the way he tossed that rose down to her, and her curtsy in response made Durie think of the puppets they used to see at the fair back in Sussex, dangling on strings.

'Stupid girl,' muttered Aunt Ellen. 'Come on, let's go home.'

Chapter 53

Durie didn't like keeping Aunt Ellen in the dark about Malachy. True, she wasn't looking forward to getting the same lecture Lucinda had had, which apparently went on for over an hour and covered in detail the general unreliability of men and the stupidity of giving up your independence for one. And she suspected that even the promise of a wedding ring wouldn't lessen Aunt Ellen's disappointment in her. But that would have to be faced at some point anyway, and she wanted to be able to talk about him, and not have to pretend, on the one Sunday a month that they were able to meet, that she was just going for a walk alone. And once Aunt Ellen met him, surely she'd be impressed with his determination to work hard and make his fortune.

'Well, I hope she will be,' he said when she suggested telling Aunt Ellen and getting it over with. 'But just now, all she's going to see is a footman with a lot of talk. So let's wait, till I can prove to her and the rest of your family that I'm making something of myself. I just wish it could be sooner.'

He'd agreed with the corn factor to join the business when the summer was over.

'He wanted me earlier, but the Philimores'll have guests over the next few months, and they're generous with the vails – the money they give to the staff when they leave. That'll help me out when I start, because the money won't be marvellous to begin with, and I need to start saving to buy into the business.'

Durie took a deep breath. She'd been trying not to think about Lucinda's warning, but it kept creeping into her head. And it wasn't that she wanted to test Malachy, but there was an easy way to prove Lucinda wrong, wasn't there?

'I could help,' she said. 'My savings are sitting in a strongbox, doing nothing.'

'No, it's kind of you to offer, but I'll not take a penny from you. I can make my own way, you'll see.' He laughed. 'And I don't want your family saying I'm after your money, do I?'

She felt herself flush and turned away, but he'd seen it.

'Someone's already said it, haven't they?'

'My sister. Well, she didn't say it, exactly, but . . .'

'I thought we were going to keep this between ourselves?'

'I've only told her. I know we said we wouldn't but she won't tell anyone else.'

'You don't see it, Durie, because you're not cynical that way, but people are very quick to assume the worst. And now your sister's made you doubt me.'

'She hasn't. I don't doubt you at all.'

'Well then, let's talk of it no more. And when the time comes I'll be very happy to show your sister she's wrong.'

So they continued to meet, one Sunday a month, at the corner of the street, and head out to Hampstead or Chelsea or East Ham, when there was time, or stroll in the park if he couldn't get away for long. At the same time, Durie's consultations at the coffee house were attracting so many new customers that she'd agreed to do two afternoons a week, to the obvious and very pleasing irritation of the doctors. She'd had to buy another strongbox to keep her money in, and the fund for Tom was growing nicely. She was mentioned again in the *Mercury*, and the *Gazette*, when the coffee house saw its first cruncher, a young man who'd dislocated his elbow as a boy, and couldn't straighten his arm. Jeannie handed her the *Mercury* at the end of her Thursday-afternoon consultations.

'This'll bring in even more people,' she said. 'Sometimes it's worth having the penny scribblers in.'

Durie was about to read the story, when one on the facing page caught her eye.

We were surprised to hear that Miss Lucinda Ellwood, who so convincingly portrayed the innocent milkmaid Tilly Tipworth, brought a certain trouble with her when she first came to London from Sussex. Miss Ellwood eased her predicament by a visit to the Foundling Hospital, concealing her youthful indiscretion from the public gaze, as well as from that of the very good friend who provided her with an address on Queen Street, and who may be shocked to learn that a milkmaid is not always a maid.

A sketch beside it showed Lucinda on stage as Tilly Tipworth, but with her belly big and round.

Durie's first thought was to go straight to Queen Street, but she quickly thought better of it. Lucinda was probably already talking herself out of trouble. And surely, this duke could hardly blame her for not being as pure as the driven snow, when he wasn't exactly an upstanding moral example himself. There'd be pretty tears, and sweet words, and she wouldn't thank Durie for walking in on that.

So she went home, but as she stepped inside, there were voices in the parlour. She hesitated, listening.

'Who else could have told them?' Lucinda was saying. 'No one outside the family knows.'

'Betsy would never do that,' said Aunt Ellen. 'And nor would my cook or, before you say it, anyone at the shop. I pay them well, and that buys loyalty. Mightn't it be someone at the theatre?'

'Only Conn and the dresser knew. He's married to her now, and neither of them would want it getting out. Not when the audiences loved Tilly Tipworth so much.'

A sob escaped her; it sounded like a real one.

Durie went in. Lucinda was on the couch, her head in her hands, Aunt Ellen beside her, patting her back ineffectually. Lucinda looked up; her face was red and the tears weren't pretty.

'Of course,' she said slowly. 'It was you. You never could keep that mouth shut. You told the Irishman, didn't you?'

'What Irishman?' said Aunt Ellen.

'It wasn't him,' said Durie. 'I told him about Tom, yes, it just slipped out, but he doesn't know who you are.'

'He saw me, you idiot! I walked past him on the corner, didn't I? He must have watched me all the way down the street.'

A flush warmed Durie's cheeks.

'He'd have told me if he'd recognised you. And why would he want to tell the papers anyway?'

'For money! The papers pay for stuff like this.' Lucinda threw up her hands. 'Do you realise what you've done? The rest will have it tomorrow, and all William's friends will be laughing at him.'

She buried her head in her hands again.

'It wasn't Malachy,' said Durie. 'But anyway, what difference does it make? It's not as though you're marrying him – he's keeping you as his mistress, for goodness' sake, so he's not exactly a saint himself, is he?'

'He doesn't have to be, he's a man! A man who owns half of Yorkshire! And I had him dangling on a string until you ruined it all.'

Durie thought of the puppets at the fair again. It hadn't looked to her like he was the one dangling.

'He can't just throw you away. You gave up your place at the theatre for him.'

'You got the agreement though?' said Aunt Ellen. 'You took my advice?'

'Of course, I'm not stupid. Ninety pounds a year at pleasure, forty at displeasure.'

'He'll quibble, with it being such a short time,' said Aunt Ellen. 'You'll probably have to settle for less, but at least it's something.'

Durie looked from one of them to the other.

'What does that mean?'

'It's the contract,' said Lucinda. 'He has to pay me a settlement if we part. Don't look at me like that, Durie, it's no different to what rich women get when they marry, they just describe it differently. And don't think it lets you off. I'm losing at least fifty pounds a year and a house on Queen Street, and it's all your fault.'

She wiped her eyes, and stood.

'Well, at least I know where it came from now. I suppose that's how you got him interested in the first place, telling him you were my sister. I'm surprised you didn't bring him to the stage door. At least you had some pride, though obviously not much.'

'I didn't tell him who you were! And it wasn't him!'

'You carry on believing that if you like. But while you're with him, don't come anywhere near me. I've got to repair my reputation now, and I don't want you and him feeding titbits to the scribblers.'

As the front door closed behind Lucinda, Aunt Ellen said, 'I think you'd better tell me about this Irishman.'

Chapter 54

After Lucinda's accusations, Durie wanted to make Aunt Ellen understand, make her think well of Malachy, and her words came out in a rush.

'He's the Philimores' footman. That's how I met him, when Gregory had his accident, but he's not going to stay a footman, he's got plans, and Lucinda's wrong, he likes me for myself, he doesn't even know she's my sister, and he wants to marry me.'

And there it was, all spilled out like a cup of tea splashed across the rug.

'I see. So you've been meeting him secretly? Was that his idea?'

'No, it was mine.' That was almost true. 'Because I knew you'd be like this about it.'

'Tell me about these plans of his.'

'He's going into business as a corn factor. They find out who needs corn and who's got corn—'

'I know what a corn factor does. And why is Lucinda so against him?'

'She thinks he wants money from me. But she's wrong, because I've offered it, and he turned me down.'

Aunt Ellen frowned.

'If you marry him, it'll be his anyway. That's the law.'

'I knew you'd say that! Well, he says he won't marry me until he's established himself, so he won't need my money, will he? And I don't know why you're so cross with me, when you were quite happy for Lucinda to hitch herself to that old toad without even the benefit of a wedding ring!'

'I most certainly wasn't happy about it. I tried to talk her out of it. But I could see she wouldn't be stopped, so I made sure she wouldn't be out on her ear without a penny if it went wrong. Luckily, as it turns out.'

'Well, this is nothing like that. Malachy's a good man, and he wants to marry me, and I want to marry him.'

'Then you can introduce him to me, can't you? Perhaps you'll put my mind at rest.'

Those girls, thought Ellen as she walked to the shop the next morning: if I'd known what trouble they'd be, I'd have told Dan he could find someone else to have them. But that wasn't true, really. She'd got fond of them both and it had surprised her how much she'd grown to like having them in the house, and how pleased she'd felt when they both wanted to stay in London.

Lucinda's gifts weren't ones she'd had a lot of respect for in the past, but there was a determination about the girl that she quite admired; she knew what she wanted and she'd gone out and got it. And that pretty head wasn't entirely full of fluff either. She'd known enough to ask for advice about negotiating a settlement on displeasure before she accepted the duke's offer, and thank goodness for that. She'd survive this and find someone else to pay the bills, even if the next one's blood might be a little less blue.

And now Durie . . . what was she to make of that? The idea that this Malachy was the one who'd taken Lucinda's story to the papers for money was worrying. As for those plans of his, a footman in a big house with plenty of visitors could do quite well for himself over time, but well enough to buy in with a corn factor? Durie was a clever girl, and usually not prone at all to having the wool pulled over her eyes, but anyone could fall for a handsome face and a good line in chat. Well, neither of those were going to work on Ellen, so she'd meet him and see what he had to say for himself.

Chapter 55

Malachy was beginning to wonder if it was all worth it. First the sister had stuck her oar in – though he'd got his own back for that very satisfyingly, and by the sound of it, Durie wouldn't be listening to any more warnings from her – and now he was up for inspection by the aunt. Durie had mentioned it quite tentatively the last time they met – he'd managed to fob her off with a walk in the park again, so he could meet that frisky little parlourmaid later – and he'd pretended he didn't mind, but avoided committing to when. That old biddy was sharp: she could ruin the whole thing.

He'd taken things too slowly with the Bishopsgate widow, wasting nearly a year before the nephew's claim was ever mentioned, and he wasn't going to get caught like that again. This one was on the hook – he'd practically smelt desperation when he'd suggested they part – but she wasn't stupid, and if the aunt was whispering warnings now, perhaps he'd left it too late here too, and he'd be best to cut his losses and move on.

The prize, though: a guinea a time, twenty or more customers a week, and she'd been doing it for a good while

292

now, hadn't she? And most of it just sitting there, because she clearly wasn't lying when she said she barely spent anything; he'd seen less shabby hats on a donkey. He couldn't earn that much in years and years of bowing and scraping to Mr and Mrs Philimore and that devil of a boy, and even half of it would send him back to Ireland a rich man.

The aunt was smart, but he'd never met a woman yet who didn't melt when you told them what they wanted to hear, and he'd heard enough about her from Durie to know exactly what that was. No, he wouldn't abandon this one – but it was time to move things on a bit.

Durie was delighted when Malachy suggested a visit to the pleasure grounds at Vauxhall; she'd always wanted to go, but Aunt Ellen wasn't interested. They took a boat from Westminster steps and sat at the front, his arm round her shoulder, watching the market gardens of Lambeth go by. He was telling her stories about his childhood in Ireland, funny stories, and he looked so handsome. If Aunt Ellen could just meet him, she'd see there was nothing to worry about.

'I was thinking,' she said, 'when you have your day off next month, you could come to tea.'

He pulled a face.

'Come and be inspected, you mean?'

'It's not like that—'

'Durie, it is, we both know it. You're a well-off young woman – all thanks to your own efforts – and as far as your aunt's concerned, I'm just a servant on the make. I might not be a rich man, not yet, but I'm a proud one. I'll do it, for you, but you can't expect me to feel happy about being examined by someone who thinks that of me.'

He hardly spoke for the rest of the journey, and then, as the boat passed the big glassworks and Vauxhall steps came into view, he said, 'I worry she'll turn you against me, that's all. That's why, really, it'd be best if I released you from your promise, and went off and made something of myself, and then if you still wanted me—'

'No! I don't want to be released from my promise.'

'Are you sure?'

'I'm certain.'

'Well, good.' He squeezed her hand. 'Because I don't want to release you.'

The pleasure grounds were pretty, with statues, grottoes and alleys of lime trees, and music drifting out from a band playing in a central rotunda. It was so crowded that wherever a path narrowed, people had to slow to a stop until there was space to fan out again, but even so, it should have been a pleasure to stroll there beside Malachy, her hand on his arm. But Durie kept remembering the conversation on the boat, and how unhappy he'd looked when he'd said it might be better for them to part. Why did Aunt Ellen have to be so suspicious? It wasn't fair to him at all, and what if it drove him away?

Just as it began to get dark, a loud whistle pierced the hubbub, and men with tapers scurried to the glass globes that lined the alleys on poles and hung from the trees. At a second whistle, hundreds of lamps lit up and people gasped as the light travelled along to the next and the next; a man behind Durie began a long explanation to his wife about how there were fuses made of cotton cord laid between all the lamps that the flame could travel along. Within moments, there were thousands of them glowing, a beautiful sight, and she should have been happy to be there with the man who wanted to marry her, but there was a clump in her stomach that wouldn't go away.

She wasn't really sorry when they left. It was chilly by then; on the boat, he put his arm around her and pulled her close.

'I'm sorry I was cross earlier, about your aunt. It's only that, I didn't tell you, because I wanted it to be a surprise, but I thought I'd be starting at the Corn Exchange next month. So I'd have been able to present myself to your aunt as a man with prospects. But I saw the fellow today, and there was a bit of bad news.'

'What bad news?'

'Well, like I said to you before, he wants someone to buy him out, and he's had an offer. If he sells now, there'll be no chance for me in a couple of years.'

'He's still offering you the position though?'

'He is, but there'd be no point taking it now. I won't make my fortune working for someone else.'

'Couldn't you get your own stand later? Once you've learned the trade?'

He shook his head.

'That's the rub. There's only fourteen stands, and they don't change hands often, not when there's a pile of money to be made. That's why this was such a good chance.'

It was ridiculous. All that money sitting in the strongbox

under her bed, when she could use it to help him, and bring closer the time when they could be together. But because of stupid Lucinda and Aunt Ellen, he wouldn't want to take it.

They watched a wherry go by, laden with barrels. He was still looking at it when he said, 'What I'm wondering is, perhaps I should make him an offer myself. It's a hell of a lot he wants, but I could get it from a moneylender.'

He'd told her the price already; if he could get the money at all, the interest would be so high, it would take years to pay off.

'You can't do that.' She took his hand. 'Look, let me give you the money. Please.'

'Oh, no. No, no, no. I shouldn't have said anything. Now you think I was asking you to help me and I wasn't.'

'I don't think that at all. But I've got money and no other use for it, and I want you to take it.'

'No. I want to prove myself to you, and I can't do that if it's your money giving me a start, can I? But you're right, the interest would be deadly. I'll have to let this one go, wait for another opportunity.'

He sighed.

'It's just frustrating, thinking how long it'll be before I can offer you the life you deserve.' He stroked a finger from the top of her shoulder right down her arm. 'Before we can be together properly.'

The touch and the words together made her shiver. If she wasn't lost before, she was then.

'If you won't take it as a gift, let me lend the money to you. And we won't tell Aunt Ellen, she can think you borrowed it somewhere else.'

He thought for a minute, looking up at the stars, then turned to her and smiled.

'You are a genius. Of course that's the way to do it. I'll pay you interest, mind, but if you could wait and take it all at once, when I pay the capital back, then I can start making money for us straight away.'

'I don't want interest. Honestly, I don't need it.'

'Well, we'll sort out the details later. But if you're sure, I'll gladly take you up on that offer.'

'I'm sure.'

He kissed her then, long and slow, and when the kiss ended, he pulled her close.

'If I act quickly, we can get it all agreed this week, and then I'll have something to say for myself when I meet your aunt. But I'd need the money by Tuesday. Would that be all right, do you think?'

'That would be fine,' she said.

Chapter 56

Ellen had not been looking forward to meeting Durie's Irishman. It was Betsy's day off, so Durie answered the door and brought him into the parlour. He was certainly easy on the eye; with that face and such an easy bearing, he'd have done well on the stage. In fact he was a good deal better-looking than the hero of Lucinda's last play. Which wasn't necessarily a recommendation.

'It's a pleasure to meet you, Miss Proudfoot,' he said, extending his hand. 'I've heard a lot about you.'

His handshake was firm; Ellen never trusted a man with a limp handshake, but it didn't always follow that the opposite applied.

'Well, I've heard very little about you,' she said. 'So let's put that right. Durie, go down and fetch some tea, and the caraway biscuits.'

She'd hidden the biscuits at the back of the pantry, so that would keep her out of the way for a bit.

'You're in service with the Philimores, I hear.'

'I am, yes.' He smiled. 'And I don't apologise for that, Miss Proudfoot. I came here from Ireland with nothing, and the position with the Philimores is a good one. I won it on my own account, with no connections, and I've worked hard for them for four years.'

So he knew how to speak up for himself. Before she could reply, he went on.

'But I'm working my notice now. Perhaps Durie told you, I've plans to—'

'Go into business as a corn factor, yes, she told me. But surely, this is a business you know nothing about?'

'It's a business I have no experience in yet, that's true. But my family worked the land at home, so I know about that side of things, and Mr Shaw, who I'm going into business with, he's explained it thoroughly. It's a very interesting business, but I expect you already know how it all works?'

'Tell me.'

She watched his face as he talked about matching farmers with millers, and how the prices were worked out, and some plans Mr Shaw had to contract with farmers from further afield, once there were two of them in the business.

'It's about knowing how badly the buyer wants the grain, and how much they're prepared to pay,' he said. 'But you'd know about that already, the way you've built your own business. I don't think I've ever seen your shop when it wasn't busy.'

Ellen knew a barefaced attempt at flattery when she saw one, but all the same, he appeared to know his stuff when it came to the business, and she couldn't fault his enthusiasm. That was all very well though: how was a footman going to buy into a business like that?

'So where is the money coming from for this venture? It can't be cheap, buying in to it.'

'It's not. But it's a cracking opportunity. And the lucky thing is, Mr Shaw is keen to have me, so he's agreed I can buy in gradually, using my commission. The more I sell, the faster I build up my share, so it's a good deal for both of us.'

Durie's footsteps came clomping up the stairs, cups clattering.

'I see,' said Ellen, as she came in. 'And what does that mean for my niece? I understand you wish to marry her.'

'Aunt Ellen,' said Durie, 'there's no need—'

Malachy put up a hand.

'There's every need, Durie, your aunt's quite right to ask. I want to get myself established in the trade before we marry, Miss Proudfoot. A year should do it.'

'And you'll be staying in London? You're not expecting Durie to go and live in Ireland in a few years?'

She'd had a girl from Galway in the shop; a hard worker, but no sooner had Ellen got her up to scratch than she'd upped and sailed back across the sea, saying she was homesick.

'Not at all. London is my home now. And Durie's established here too, I wouldn't want to take her away from her work.' He grinned at Durie, who'd sat beside him, and gave her a playful nudge. 'And I doubt she'd let me anyway.'

'Good. Well, Durie, are you going to pour Malachy a cup of tea, or leave him to die of thirst?'

When they left, talking about a walk to Kensington, Ellen watched them from the window. Well, that had been unexpected. When Lucinda said he was Irish, she'd imagined someone a bit more rough and ready, with more of the silver tongue about him. He certainly had plenty of chat, but his manner was open and honest, and though she knew full well he was trying to get on the right side of her, she liked his enthusiasm about business. A young man trying to make something of himself, and if he did, he'd be a good match for Durie – better than poor George Layton, anyway. He understood how much Durie's work meant to her too; that was rare in a man. There were Lucinda's suspicions about him going to the papers, of course, but mightn't there just be a touch of jealousy there? He didn't seem the type to do something like that, and Durie was certain he hadn't. She'd keep an eye on the situation but really, he'd been quite a pleasant surprise.

Chapter 57

It was such a relief to Durie that Aunt Ellen had taken to Malachy. It just went to show, what did Lucinda know? She hadn't exactly proved herself a good judge of character before, had she? Whereas Aunt Ellen was sharp; her opinion was worth having. Not that Durie needed it, but still.

Over the next few weeks, nothing the doctors had to offer could puncture the bubble of happiness around her. Dr Candleford could mutter 'Charlatan!' at her, and 'A fool and his money' at her customers, all he liked; the customers kept coming. And when the weasel-faced one said loudly as she passed, 'If we must have women in here, can't they at least be decorative? She's enough to put a man off his coffee,' she thought of the way Malachy touched her face when he kissed her, as if it was precious to him.

The only dark spot was that Lucinda still wouldn't speak to her. Durie had written, apologising for telling Malachy about Tom but saying she was certain it wasn't him who'd given away her secret. Lucinda had replied with one brief line:

You haven't even asked him, have you?

302

Well, she hadn't, and she wasn't going to. It was ridiculous; if Malachy had recognised Lucinda that day, and seen her going into the house, he'd have said so! Lucinda obviously couldn't believe there was a soul in London who didn't know her face, but Malachy didn't go to the theatre, so why would he? And he'd suffered Aunt Ellen's questioning with such good humour, he didn't deserve to hear that another member of her family suspected him of being on the make.

Obviously, one of the theatre people had sold the story, but of course Lucinda wouldn't want to think any of them didn't worship at her feet. Quite likely she was jealous, too: who wouldn't prefer the thought of Malachy's kisses to being pawed by that old man, with his droopy jowls and slobbery lips? And now the old man didn't want her anyway, because she wasn't Tilly whatever her name was, the unsullied milk-maid. No wonder she was annoyed, but that wasn't Durie's fault, so if Lucinda wanted to sulk, she could sulk.

It was just a shame that Malachy was going to have to wait another three months to join the Corn Exchange. Mr Shaw was eager for him to start on the basis of a handshake, and not wait till his lawyers had drawn up a contract, but as Malachy said, their future was too important to take any risks. So he'd asked Aunt Ellen, did she think he should insist on it all in writing first, even if it might take a while? Aunt Ellen had said very forcefully that he should, so he'd taken her advice and asked the Philimores to extend his notice, which, good footmen being in short supply, they'd happily agreed to do. It was sensible, of course, but Durie had been so looking forward to seeing him more often than once a month. So she was delighted when he called round one morning, still in his livery, and suggested a walk to the Corn Exchange.

'I've to pick up papers for Mr Philimore in Fenchurch Street, so I thought, if you're free, why don't I show you where I'm going to make our fortune?'

It was a surprisingly elegant building, on a narrow street near Bear Quay, where the grain ships unloaded. She'd been feeling proud that he was going to introduce her to Mr Shaw, but when they got there, he said they couldn't actually go in – just like at the coffee house, the men apparently became quite unable to conduct business if a woman was present. So they peeked through the columns at the front to a big room crowded with men, all with the well-fed look of merchants. The floor was covered with drifts of grain, and a man standing nearby threw a handful onto the floor.

'That's a sample,' said Malachy. 'See, he shows that to the buyer to let him know what he'll be getting. Then he's got to throw it away, so the next buyer sees fresh grain, and not what's been made damp and dirty in his hand.'

He pointed to one of the stands, where a florid man in a fancy silk waistcoat and a wine-coloured coat with silver buttons took out a gold pocket watch and checked the time.

'That's Mr Shaw.'

'He's younger than I expected,' said Durie. 'He can't be more than thirty.'

'I know – that shows you how well you can do in this business in a short time. Did I say to you, he said I ought to get myself a smart coat like his? You've got to look prosperous, he says, if you want people to trust you with their money.'

He protested when she offered the money for a new coat, but in the end he accepted it, on condition it was added to the loan. By the time he'd walked her back to South Audley Street, they'd agreed she could add enough to buy the silver buttons to put on the coat too, and a silk waistcoat, and a gold watch like the one they'd seen Mr Shaw take out and look at.

'You're right, Durie, I ought to look the part,' he said, as she handed him the money. 'It's like your aunt says about her shop, isn't it? If you want to attract the right sort of customer, you've got to look as though you've got something they want.'

He looked worried for a moment, then said, 'But do you think we could keep this between ourselves? I don't want your aunt to think—'

'Of course,' she said. 'Besides, Aunt Ellen always says a woman should take charge of her own money. That's what I'm doing.'

Chapter 58

It was when Malachy asked her to add some more money – quite a lot more – to the loan, for the lawyers' agreement, and some sort of licence that the Corn Exchange required, that Durie begin to lie awake at night wondering. And then, on his last day off before leaving the Philimores', when they took a picnic out to Camberwell and sat on the village green in the sunshine, he said there was to be a trip up north, to meet the owners of some large mills who were interested in buying through Mr Shaw.

'He thinks it should be me who goes, since I'll be the one handling their business. I'll need to create a good impression, so he says to stay in a good standard of inn, and hire a coach to visit the mills. And I'll need to stand the millers dinner as well. I hate to ask you to lend me a bit more, but if we get this business, I'll really be on my way.'

She said yes, of course, and he planted a kiss on her forehead and said she was going to be the best wife a man could wish for.

On the long walk home, as he talked about the trip to the north, how big the mills were, and what a difference it would make to the business, she faced the facts. The man walking beside her could have his pick of London's pretty parlourmaids and shopgirls but he'd chosen her. And that was not unconnected to the fact that she had a strongbox full of money that could help him make his fortune. She'd doubted, even at the time, that he could have raised the money to buy in to the Corn Exchange from a moneylender, so for all his protestations, he must have hoped she'd make the offer. Then all these other expenses: how would he have afforded them, even if he'd been able to borrow the initial amount? And after she'd taken a hard look at the situation, what she thought was, so what? Women married men for their money all the time. How many grand houses had she visited, where the wife was pretty and vivacious, and the husband ugly, dull and rich? Sometimes you could tell they'd grown to love each other anyway, and sometimes not. Which meant that arrangement was no more or less likely to result in happiness than any other – look at George and his wife, who'd thought they were in love and ended up with nothing to say to each other. And it wasn't even as though Malachy was planning to live off her money for ever, like women who married rich men did; he just needed some to get him started.

She looked sideways at him, striding beside her, smiling as he talked about Mr Shaw trusting him with the trip. He turned, and grinned.

'Sorry,' he said, 'you know I get carried away sometimes.' He stopped, slid his arm round her waist, pulled her towards him and planted a gentle kiss on her lips. 'It's all so we can be together.'

That couldn't be faked, surely? You wouldn't kiss someone if you didn't want to, and you wouldn't look the way he looked when he said 'so we can be together'. So if part of the reason he wanted her was the strongbox under the bed, she could live with that. It was tempting to tell him she knew and didn't care, and have it out in the open. But he'd been so prickly about what other people might think of him; best it was left unsaid.

All the same, there was one thing she needed to bring up. She'd never really talked to Malachy about Tom, beyond the fact that it was Lucinda's pregnancy that had brought them to London. Besides not wanting to slip up and say anything about Lucinda, it had felt wrong, in a way she couldn't quite explain to herself, because so many of her happy memories of Tom had George in them too. But he needed to know about the other strongbox under the bed, the one with Tom's money in it.

Once you marry, he owns everything.

She'd happily share everything else she had with Malachy, but she couldn't give him that.

As they reached London Bridge, there was a stall by the roadside selling apple juice.

'Could we stop here for a minute?' said Durie. 'I want to tell you something.'

He bought them each a mug of juice, and they sat on the makeshift bench the stallholder had provided.

'This sounds very serious,' he said. 'Should I be worried?'

'No, of course not. It's just something important, that's all.'

She told him all about Tom: how she'd grown to love him in the months he'd been with them, and wished with all her heart that they hadn't had to give him up to the Foundling Hospital.

'I didn't want him to grow up not knowing if his mother loved him. You know, like I did.'

He squeezed her hand.

'But they give them a good life there, don't they?' he said. 'I've read about it in the papers. They get a better education than most children.'

'But if you saw them . . . they're like little soldiers, all the same, and surely they must wonder where their families are and why they've been left there? I want Tom to know he's got a family who loved him, even if we couldn't keep him, so I write to him once a year. He won't get the letters till he's grown-up, but at least he'll know then.'

'That's a kind thing to do.'

'There's something else. I've saved money for him to have when he's grown. Enough to set himself up, and have the life I could have given him if we'd kept him.'

He whistled when she named the amount.

'That's a lot of money.'

'That's why I wanted to tell you about it. Because I won't touch that money. I can't give it, or lend it, to you.'

'I wasn't expecting you to. I didn't even know you had it, did I?'

'I just wanted things to be clear. That money is Tom's. And I was wondering if you'd promise we'll keep it for him.'

He laughed.

'Would you like me to write a document, and sign it in blood?'

'No—'

'Then I promise.' He made the sign of the cross on his chest. 'On Mother Mary and all the saints, you have my word.'

'Thank you,' said Durie. 'I knew you'd understand.'

She was a peculiar one, thought Malachy, as he strode away after saying goodbye to Durie. Saving all that money for a child she barely knew, and wouldn't ever see again. She seemed to think he knew what she meant about not wanting him to grow up like her, but he only had the faintest recollection of her talking about her mother. Something about her dying young, was it?

At the end of the street, he looked back; of course she was still standing on the steps, watching him go. He blew her a kiss and turned the corner. Funny thing was, he'd been feeling a touch guilty earlier on: she was a weird creature but she was a good person, even good company sometimes, when she wasn't yabbering on about bones. But then when she said that, about the money for the boy, well, that changed the situation, didn't it? If she had that lot lying around for no better purpose, she'd hardly miss what he'd had off her. So there was really nothing to feel guilty about, not when no one but the aunt and the sister even knew; he was glad now that he'd insisted on that, less complicated all round. She'd be upset, for a while, but no lasting damage.

He wished, really, that she hadn't told him about that extra lot of money, because it was annoying, now, knowing it was there. Still, he was going home with plenty, and by this time next week, assuming fair winds, he'd be in sight of Dublin docks.

Chapter 59

The ten days Malachy was away seemed very long, and on the Sunday, Durie decided to walk out to Putney, to take her mind off missing him. She entertained herself on the way to the river with thinking about where they should live when they were married; perhaps Clerkenwell, one of the small houses along the high street. Not too far from the Corn Exchange for Malachy, and nicely placed for her to walk anywhere she needed to.

At Putney Bridge, she had to wait to pay at the tollbooth. The keeper was deep in conversation with the driver of a cart, about an accident that had happened on the other side. Impatient to be on her way, she was only half listening, but then the carter said, 'Young lad got his leg trapped underneath, looked like it was broken. Two fellows stopped to help them right the cart and catch the horse, but I heard the father say they came from Wapping. Long way to go in that state.'

Durie slammed her penny down on the tollbooth ledge and ran across the bridge, her boots pounding on the wooden boards. She hadn't fixed a break in a while – outside the hunting season and without ice on the ground, London's rich and fashionable did little that was dangerous enough to break a bone – and there was nothing like it, feeling the ends slide back into place and knowing it would knit back together good and straight.

The accident was only a few hundred yards from the end of the bridge, so she got there quickly. The cart had been righted and a man was hitching a jittery chestnut horse to it, while another gathered up the potatoes scattered across the road. The boy was lying at the roadside; about fifteen, white-faced and sweating, biting his lip against the pain. A man she took to be his father was crouching beside him.

'I can fix him,' she said, hitching up her skirt so she could get down on the ground. 'I'm a bonesetter.'

'I know who you are,' said the man, gesturing at her hat with its crown of bones. 'And we can't afford you. We'll take him home and get the farrier to set it.'

'Don't be stupid, that's miles and your son's in pain. I'll set it for you, no need to pay me.'

'I could give you ten shillings, that's what the farrier charges—'

'I've just said, there'll be no charge. Now, make yourself useful.' She pointed at an ash tree across the road. 'Get some branches, and give me straight sections to use as splints.'

The lad was brave – she gave him his shoe to bite on, and he only cried out once – and the break was a clean one. She had the bone set quick and neat and had ripped a strip from her skirt for bandaging by the time the father came back with the branches. In the meantime, the two men had come

over to have a look, one muttering, 'You know – that bonesetter woman, fixes up all the nobs.'

She snapped the branches into manageable lengths across
her knee, breaking off the twigs, then lashed them in two
bundles on either side of the boy's leg.

'He's young and fit, so it should heal well,' she told the
father, 'but it'll need splinting properly. Tell me where you
live and I'll come tomorrow, and bring him a crutch – he'll
need to keep his weight off it for about six weeks.'

One of the other men huffed and said, 'That'll cost ya,
mate.'

'I said we couldn't pay for this,' the father said, his face
reddening, 'and we can't pay for that neither.'

'For goodness' sake, I said there'd be no charge, didn't I?
I wouldn't be much of a bonesetter if I'd left your son in
pain. Now, give me your address, and then I'll help you lift
him into the cart.'

Setting a bone usually left her cheerful for the rest of the
day. And it had been good, fixing the boy's leg so quickly
and neatly and knowing that, because she'd happened along,
his leg would heal straight and true, with nothing more to
remind him of the experience than a story about 'that bonesetter woman'. But as she strode on past the market gardens
to Putney, she kept thinking about the father's words. How
far must it be to Wapping, eight or nine miles? Through the
narrow streets of the city, that'd be at least two hours, bumping
about in a cart with a broken leg. And he'd thought she'd let
the boy suffer that because he couldn't afford to pay her.

The knack is a gift.

She hadn't ever forgotten her father's words but there hadn't been any reason to give it away when all her customers were wealthy. That didn't mean there weren't people who might need it though, did it?

That evening, over a supper of coddled eggs and kippers, with Lucifer pacing round the table and yowling for a share, Durie told Aunt Ellen the story.

'It was the right thing to do, but let's hope the newspapers don't hear of it,' said Aunt Ellen.

'I don't suppose they will.'

'Well, good.' Aunt Ellen leaned down to feed Lucifer a piece of fish. 'You don't want people thinking you lay hands on any old person you pass in the street.'

Durie took a deep breath.

'I know that, but I was thinking, I'm going to go there tomorrow, to splint his leg properly. So I might see if any of their neighbours need treatment. That I wouldn't charge for.'

Aunt Ellen sat up so straight that Lucifer had to stand on his back legs to lick the last flakes from her fingers.

'That's really not a good idea.'

'What harm can it do?'

'You know perfectly well what harm it would do. Do you think Mrs Edwards would have wanted you touching her back if she'd known you'd come fresh from manhandling a carter's son in Wapping?'

'But even if people found out – and I don't see why they would, I doubt the penny scribblers wander round Wapping looking for gossip – I'm established now. People come to me because they know I can fix them, not because I'm the new thing that someone fashionable recommends.'

'But they don't come for ever, do they?'

'Of course not, because I fix them.'

'And what happens then? Because people might keep coming until they're better, but they're not going to recommend you to their friends, not if you're going about offering your services for free to anyone. You'll ruin everything you've worked for and your income will dwindle to nothing.'

'Father always helped people who couldn't pay him.'

'Durie, I told you, right at the beginning, London isn't Lewes. Your father had a reputation that was handed down from our father, and our grandfather. In London, you can be the name on everyone's lips today, and absolutely no one tomorrow.' She sighed. 'You're a grown woman, and I can't tell you what to do. But please, think carefully about what you might be throwing away.'

When Durie arrived next morning, the carter's wife opened the door.

'Oh,' she said. 'You've really come then?'

'I said I would. And just so we're clear, there's no charge for this visit. Or the splints. Or the crutches. Now, can I come in?'

The boy was sitting with his leg propped up on a stool, while three younger children played on the floor.

'How's the leg?' she asked.

'Hurts like stink,' he said, quite matter-of-factly.

'Joe!' said the woman.

'Well, it will do,' said Durie, handing him the crutch. 'But it'll heal well, if you use this and keep your weight off it.'

'Fred's out on a job,' said the woman. 'But he said to tell you he was sorry. In the shock of it all he didn't even think to thank you yesterday.'

'Well, as it happens I enjoy setting broken legs and I don't see as many as I'd like, so it was useful for both of us that I was passing. Now, let's get that leg splinted properly, and then you can have those branches for firewood.'

On the long walk back, she told herself she'd done the right thing. Or rather, not done the wrong thing. She'd gone to bed the night before determined to ask if the carter's family knew of anyone who might need her help, free of charge. But in the early hours she'd woken and lain there, thinking about it. If Aunt Ellen was right, and she lost her paying customers, what then? At one time there'd been enough in the strongbox to keep her going for ages, but not now; apart from Tom's money, most of it had gone to Malachy. And he was only just getting started – he might need more. She'd made her peace with the fact that her money was part of the reason they were together but it meant she couldn't risk not having any. No, for the time being at least, best to leave things as they were.

Chapter 60

The day before Malachy was due back, Durie was at the coffee house a bit early, so she could have a look at the newspapers. Unlikely they'd found out about the carter's boy, but best to check. Nothing about him, thank goodness, but in the *Mercury*, there was a story about Lucinda.

> *We hear a certain member of the Yorkshire aristocracy*
> *purchased an exquisite diamond bracelet in Bond Street this*
> *week; friends whisper that the piece is a gift for his wife, to*
> *make amends for the embarrassment caused by his connection*
> *with Miss Lucinda Ellwood. Miss Ellwood, once the darling*
> *of Drury Lane, has lately removed from an elegant apart-*
> *ment in Queen Street to smaller premises in Bow Street.*

Fashionable people were so peculiar. The duke's wife hadn't seemed bothered by her husband's 'connection' with Lucinda before, and the duke had been quite happy to flaunt it. It made Durie think of Aunt Ellen's warning again.

In London, you can be the name on everyone's lips today, and
absolutely no one tomorrow.

Lucinda's name was still on their lips, but almost overnight, the way they talked about her had changed. And even though Durie was still angry with Lucinda for suspecting Malachy, she was angry for her too, and she wished she knew who had told the newspaper about Tom, so she could give them a piece of her mind. What business did they have, spilling secrets that were nothing to do with them?

'Miss Proudfoot looks deep in thought this afternoon,' said Dr Candleford. 'No doubt dreaming up some new way to fleece unwary people of their money.'

She'd got used to their comments now and was usually quite able to ignore them.

'She ought to dream up a way to get herself a husband, and leave men's work to men,' said the weasel-faced one.

Dr Candleford snorted.

'I suspect we'll see a female physician before we see Miss Proudfoot walk down the aisle. Unless she breaks someone's legs and carries him there.'

They all laughed. She ignored them, sipping her coffee and reading the back page of the *Mercury*.

'She'd have to break his arms as well,' said one of the others. 'To stop him crawling away!'

So they were going to treat her to that routine. Ever more ludicrous remarks, each one topping the last, and the laughter getting more and more raucous until they were practically choking on their own jokes.

Sure enough, weasel face's neighbour said, 'And then he'd be begging her not to set them, so he could shirk the wedding night!'

That got them all roaring, and despite herself, Durie's

cheeks flushed hot. Jeannie came over and topped up her coffee.

'Take no notice of them,' she said quietly. 'For educated men, they sound a lot like fools.'

'As it happens,' said Durie, loudly enough for the doctors to hear, 'I am engaged to be married. To a fine man, who's worth ten of anyone on that table.'

'Hear that, gentlemen?' said Dr Candleford. 'Miss Proudfoot is taken. Do try not to show your disappointment.'

More jokes followed, but she didn't care. Just saying the words had made her feel better, because it was true, Malachy was worth ten of them and he'd chosen her.

Malachy watched from the Liverpool dock as the Dublin ship set sail at dawn. His ticket was still in his hand, and right up till they'd pulled up the gangplank, he hadn't been certain he wouldn't go. He'd been longing for home for months, longing to hear voices that sounded like his and said 'press' instead of 'cupboard', to smell clean air, rinsed by soft Irish rain, and to taste his mother's bacon and cabbage. And he'd been looking forward to seeing his brothers' faces when he showed them his stash of golden guineas. No need to say how he'd got it, they wouldn't have a clue it was six or seven times what he could have earned as a footman. He'd be the man of the hour, and it wasn't just his brothers who'd be impressed, the entire village would be too.

But now he wasn't going. Now, he was going to catch the coach back to London, and do what he'd promised. He was going to marry Durie Proudfoot.

Chapter 61

As she waited for the Newcastle coach to appear, Durie couldn't help thinking of the day she and Lucinda arrived from Lewes. The inn was a different one but the scene in the courtyard was the same: people coming and going, porters heaving bags and trunks, the ticket man in his booth yelling out final calls. What would the furious seventeen-year-old Durie have said if she'd been told how it would all turn out?

Malachy had promised to call round as soon as he arrived back, but she'd had a customer on Fleet Street that afternoon and on the spur of the moment decided to meet him. The coach wasn't due until six, but she'd only be watching the clock at home, and the inn was just round the corner. Hard to believe she knew London so well now, when you remembered that long, sweaty walk to Mayfair, having no real idea where it was or how far. The city felt like home now, and one day they'd have their own home in it. Their own family.

Church bells ringing five interrupted her thoughts and just as the ringing died away, a coach pulled in and clattered to a stop. Steam rose from the horses' flanks as the passengers climbed out, stiff after the long journey. She was idly wondering where they'd come from when the last passenger dismounted, in a russet coat. He was early!

Grabbing her cloak, she ran out to him.

'Durie! What are you doing here?'

Why didn't he look happy to see her?

'I was nearby, so I thought I'd meet you. I thought you'd be pleased.'

He smiled then and took her in his arms, planting a kiss on her forehead.

'I am. You caught me by surprise, that's all.'

'You caught me by surprise too – the ticket man said the Newcastle coach was due at six.'

'Oh, I didn't come straight from there, the roads were so bad going up, I came back another way.' He squeezed her hand. 'Well, I've got a lot to tell you. Shall we find ourselves somewhere to get a bite to eat?'

In a chop house round the corner, they ordered mutton stew and dumplings, and he told her all about how big the mills had been, and how he'd had to think on his feet for some of the questions the millers asked about the factoring business.

'But I got the contracts, from all three. They're going to bring in a lot of money.'

He reached across the table, and took her hands in his.

'There's more. Before I went, I was talking to Mr Shaw about us getting married, and he made me an offer.'

'What kind of offer?'

'You remember I told you, he wants to spend more time at his house in Chelsea, for his health? Well, he said, if I got all three contracts, we could live in his place on Thomas

Street, near the Corn Exchange, till we find ourselves some-where permanent. So what do you think? Will you do me the honour of becoming Mrs O'Neill, at your earliest conven-ience?'

What did she think? She'd never wanted to hear any words more, and yet at the same time, it was a little bit frightening and she wasn't even sure why.

'But I thought . . . didn't you want to get established first?'

'I don't need to now, do I? I've proved myself to him.' He sat back. 'Unless . . . do I still need to prove myself to you, is that it? You want me to show I can make my own fortune?'

'Of course not.' She'd upset him now, he was so prickly about money. And what was she thinking of? Of course she wanted to marry him. 'Yes. My answer is yes.'

He smiled.

'If we post the banns tomorrow, we could be married in three weeks.' He brought her hand to his lips, and kissed it softly. 'I just want us to be man and wife. As soon as possible.'

There was longing in his voice, like the longing she used to see on men's faces when they looked at Lucinda. It made her feel a bit strange, but not in a bad way.

'You're right,' she said. 'Let's not wait.'

Durie said nothing to Aunt Ellen until they were settled by the fire that evening, with cups of chocolate. Then she explained about the offer of the house, and Malachy's sugges-tion that they post the banns the very next day.

'Why does it need to be so soon?' asked Aunt Ellen. 'Margie and Richie haven't even met him, and they can't travel on those awful roads from Sussex at this time of year.'

'I know, but you like him, don't you? I'll write home tomorrow, and I thought, perhaps you could write too? If they know you approve, they won't worry. And we'll go and see them in the spring.'

'Are you certain this is what you want?'

'Yes, I am. It's like Malachy says, why wait? We have somewhere to live now, and he's already doing well for Mr Shaw. He'll get commission on all the sales to those millers.'

'And that gets him started on buying in to the business. He got himself a good deal there.' Aunt Ellen took a sip of her chocolate. 'If it's what you want, I'm happy for you. But I'll miss you, when you go.'

'I'll miss you too, Aunt Ellen.'

Aunt Ellen raised an eyebrow.

'With that handsome face around? I shouldn't think you'll give me a thought.'

Chapter 62

Aunt Ellen's approval did reassure Margie: her reply was full of felicitations, and said she and Richie looked forward to meeting Malachy in the spring. She added at the bottom, 'Ask your sister to write – we've had no news from her in months.'

No surprise there: Lucinda would hardly write and say she'd been a rich man's mistress and now she wasn't even that any more. Margie probably thought she was still on the stage every night. For the first time in her life, Durie experienced the enjoyable sensation of feeling superior to her sister, but she knew in her heart that it would make her much happier to know she and Lucinda were friends again, and have her sister by her side on her wedding day. And though she wasn't looking forward to telling Malachy who her sister was, it was ridiculous to keep the secret now, when he was about to join the family. So the week before the wedding, she walked round to Lucinda's new address. Malachy was taking her to see Mr Shaw's house that afternoon; if she told Lucinda about the wedding now, she could tell him about Lucinda then.

In distance, Bow Street wasn't far from Queen Street, where the duke had installed Lucinda before he realised she wasn't Tilly Tipworth. But in other respects, it was a long way to go. Lucinda had rooms on the first floor of a house that was small, and though not shabby, certainly nothing like her former home. A sullen-looking maid let Durie in without bothering to ask her business.

Lucinda was sitting at a little desk by the window, a small pile of what looked like bills beside her.

'This is a surprise. Come to gloat?'

'Of course not. Do we have to carry this on, Lucinda? It's so stupid.'

'Well, it was all your own fault. But all right, come on, sit down.' Lucinda smiled, moving to clear a space on a little settee that was piled with clothes. 'I suppose the Irishman's taken off, has he? You can't say I didn't warn you. How much did he get out of you, besides the money from the papers, for ruining my life?'

'How many more times? It wasn't him. And as it happens, we're getting married. Next week.'

Lucinda stopped moving, her hand still on a cushion.

'You're marrying him?'

'Yes. I came to ask if you'd come.'

'Are you actually mad? You can't seriously trust him after what he did to me?'

'Have you asked any of your so-called friends in the theatre whether it was them?'

'Have you asked him?'

'No and I'm not going to.'

'Can you tell me honestly that he hasn't asked you for money?'

Durie's face felt hot.

'Oh, Durie. How much has he had off you?'

'It's none of your business what I do with my money.' She turned to go. 'This was a stupid idea, forget I asked. You're just jealous because I've got an honest man who loves me and wants to marry me, and you haven't.'

'You've got a chancer, that's what you've got. And if you want to be left standing at the altar like a fool, you go ahead. But I won't be there to see it.'

Who cared what Lucinda thought? She shouldn't have bothered going to see her at all. Why had she even thought it was a good idea? To suggest that Malachy would jilt her! She squashed down the sudden shot of fear; Lucinda just couldn't stand the idea that her sister was happy when she wasn't, and that was the truth of it. Well, Durie wasn't going to give her or her stupid warnings another thought.

She'd agreed to meet Malachy by London Bridge, and he was already there as she walked up. He waved, but his expression was serious.

'Is something wrong?' she asked.

He took her hands in his.

'I'm so sorry, my love. I'm afraid I've got bad news about the house. It seems Mr Shaw didn't tell his wife he'd promised it to us, and she's offered it to a niece and her husband.'

It took her a second to realise what it meant.

'But then we can't marry next week.'

'Mr Shaw was very apologetic, but naturally, he can't give it to us now, not over family.'

All she could think of was Lucinda laughing when she

found out, which was stupid, because that was the least of it.

'No, of course not.'

He stroked her cheek, very softly, with one finger.

'I want to make you my wife so badly, Durie Proudfoot.'

'And I want you to. I didn't mind waiting before, but now, when it was so close . . . Couldn't we move into your lodgings, just to begin with?'

He shook his head.

'It's a room for a single man – I wouldn't even think of asking you to live there. No, there's nothing to be done . . . unless . . . no, you wouldn't want to do that.'

'What?'

'Well, do you think your aunt would let us live with her for a while? It wouldn't be long – the way Mr Shaw's talking, I'll be able to afford a proper home for us by springtime.'

'She might, there's plenty of room.'

'Then let's ask her. Because I don't want to wait a second longer than we have to.'

Chapter 63

Durie had the feeling Aunt Ellen actually quite liked the idea; certainly she agreed very readily, with the proviso that the two of them took themselves off somewhere most Sundays.

'I like my day off to myself, as you know, and my temper won't be improved by two lovebirds mooning around the place.'

The last week passed quickly, with two busy afternoons at the coffee house and, thanks to an icy spell, several sprained ankles and wrists among the citizens of Mayfair. And then – quite suddenly, it seemed – Durie and Aunt Ellen were sitting by a crackling fire, drinking tea, on the night before her wedding.

'To think you and Lucinda were only supposed to be here for a few months,' said Aunt Ellen. 'And now I'm lumbered with you permanently.'

'It won't be for long, Malachy says—'

'I'm joking, Durie. I'm happy to have you and Malachy here for as long as you need. Don't let it go to your head, but I enjoy your company.'

'And you like talking about business with Malachy, don't you?'

'I do. He's got a good head on his shoulders.'

'I wish Lucinda thought the same.'

'Well, Lucinda hasn't made the wisest choices about men herself. Perhaps she doesn't like seeing that you have.'

'I never thought I'd marry before she did. For a long time, I thought I'd never marry at all.'

Aunt Ellen looked at her sharply.

'You know, I hope, that Malachy's as lucky to have you as you are to have him?'

Durie thought of the doctors, laughing about her having to break a man's legs and carry him to the altar, and of Peter Gleeson running away when Susan Hopkiss teased him about marrying her.

'It's nice of you to say so, but you know it's not true. Malachy could have his pick of women, and he's not exactly fighting off competition for me.'

Should she tell Aunt Ellen the truth, that Malachy had his own reasons for marrying her? If anyone was going to understand that it was entirely fine, that she was just doing what men did, Aunt Ellen was, and that would quiet Lucinda's stupid voice in her head, saying, 'How much has he had off you?'

But before she could put the words together, Aunt Ellen said, 'I wouldn't encourage you to marry any man, a good one or no, just because he asked and you don't think anyone else will. That's not what you're doing, is it?'

'No, of course not.'

'Well, I'm going to tell you something I never planned to

tell you, because I think you need to know it. And I hope you'll understand, I acted for the best of reasons.' She smiled. 'A young man came looking for you at the shop. Two years ago.'

No. It couldn't be.

'What man?'

'George Layton was his name.'

This was a dream, surely? But the crackling of the fire and the ticking of the clock said it was completely real.

'What did he say?'

'He thought you'd gone back to Sussex; he gave me a letter for you. He wanted you to know his wife had died, and to ask if there was still a chance for him with you. So you see, Malachy isn't the only one who—'

'Why didn't you give it to me?'

How quiet and calm her voice sounded, when someone had turned the world to water and she couldn't find her way up for air.

'You were doing so well, you'd just got yourself established. I didn't want you getting caught up with someone who wasn't worthy of you.'

'George, not worthy of me? George understood me better than anyone else ever has. George gave me the monkey bones.'

'What?'

'The bones in my hat. George gave them to me. He believed in me when no one else did, and he gave me a monkey skeleton to practise on. And now you're telling me I could have been with him two years ago, but you just decided he wasn't good enough for me.'

'Durie, what would you be doing if you were married to

a man like that? Living in two rooms and taking in washing? You certainly wouldn't be Miss Proudfoot the bonesetter. And anyway, you're marrying Malachy now. I understand you're angry I didn't tell you, but it's worked out for the best, hasn't it?'

Had it? How on earth was she supposed to compare the two of them? Malachy, who kissed her and called her 'my love', and talked about the future he was going to make for the two of them. And George, who hadn't had a chance to do any of that, but who'd comforted her when Tom had to go, and said she was unusual, not odd, and stunk the hut out boiling up bones for her.

'What happened to the letter?'

'I burnt it.'

'So he thinks I didn't even bother to reply?'

Aunt Ellen sighed.

'I went to see him. I told him you were getting married.'

'But I wasn't, not then.'

'No, well, you are now, and—'

'What did he say, when you told him that?'

'He said to tell you he hoped you'd be happy.'

'Just that?'

'He didn't fall to the ground sobbing, if that's what you're hoping to hear. Durie, I can't believe you're being so silly about this, you're not Romeo and Juliet. And five minutes ago, you were happy to be marrying Malachy. As you should be. He's a good man, with a good future.'

Durie stood up.

'Aunt Ellen, I know you've always tried to help me. And I'm grateful for the way you helped me get established. But you had no right to do this, and I'm so angry with you that I don't even know what to say. So I'm going upstairs to be on my own, and think about what to do. I'll see you in the morning.'

She took the monkey skeleton from the wardrobe, and sat on her bed with it, running her finger over the little skull. Two whole years when she could have been with George. When he didn't belong to someone else. She'd have gone straight to him, she wouldn't even have wasted time on a reply.

She could still go to him, even now. She pictured him standing in front of Crowley's cage, a smile of disbelief spreading over his face as she walked up. 'I thought I'd lost you,' he'd say, and she'd explain what Aunt Ellen had done, and how she hadn't known he'd come looking for her. The lions would witness their first kiss; only right, since they brought them together in the first place.

She laid the skeleton across her lap and looked down at its face. She'd wired the jaw a bit too loosely, and she'd never noticed before but when you laid it down the bones settled so it looked as though it was grinning happily. Upright, the mouth was more of a grimace. Which was quite appropriate, really.

If she'd got George's letter two years ago, of course she'd have gone to him. But it wasn't two years ago, it was now, and tomorrow morning, Malachy would be waiting at the church.

She sat there, thinking over the past few months.

There's a frost fair setting up on the river. Would you fancy coming to have a look at it?

The feel of her arm on his. The look on the face of the woman at the counter, when he'd ignored her flirting and walked back to Durie.

I've thought quite a bit about what it might be like to kiss you.

His arm round her waist, as though she was light as a feather.

If I could know that we were promised to each other.

The ten days he was away, that had seemed so long.

I want to make you my wife so badly, Durie Proudfoot.

When he said those words, and looked into her eyes, the way men looked at Lucinda, she'd wanted nothing more than to be his wife. And he hadn't changed, had he? He was still the same man she'd wanted to marry then, and he'd still be the same man tomorrow. And yes, there was the business of the money, but she'd made her peace with that. He was using it to build a future for both of them, after all.

The skeleton grinned up at her; she lifted it upright, and the jaw fell into its usual grimace. If only there was time to think. If only Aunt Ellen had told her about the letter sooner. If only she'd never told her at all.

When Durie heard Aunt Ellen calling Lucifer indoors for the night, she blew out her candle and pretended to be asleep, but there was no prospect of actually sleeping. The thoughts fighting each other in her head wouldn't allow it, and in any case, she couldn't afford to. She had to decide, now, tonight, what to do. The wedding was at nine. Malachy had taken rooms somewhere near Holborn after leaving the Philimores', but she didn't know the address; there'd never been a need to ask. So if the marriage wasn't to go ahead, she would have to catch him outside the church and tell him. And if she made that choice, she'd have to make it without knowing whether George still thought of her, or had simply given her up as lost when he thought she was engaged. Whether, even, she could trust her memories of that time; it was nearly five years ago, she'd been seventeen, and unhappy. Perhaps it was just a romantic dream that wouldn't survive everyday life. Then she looked at the monkey skeleton, pale in the moonlight, and knew it wasn't. But nor was Malachy.

Hours passed, marked by the bells of St George's, the church where Malachy would be waiting for her at nine, and sleep slid further away. At three, she went downstairs. In the parlour, the fire was banked and the embers still glowed. She sat on the floor, her arms around her knees, leaned into its warmth and tried, again, to decide what to do.

The stairs creaked: Aunt Ellen in her nightgown, a shawl round her shoulders, and her hair in two long plaits. Lucifer padded in behind her and stared hard at Durie; the hearth was usually his place.

'I couldn't sleep either,' said Aunt Ellen. 'I'm sorry, Durie. I thought it was for the best. I still do. But I should have let you decide for yourself.'

'I don't know what to do,' said Durie. 'I've thought and thought and I still don't know.'

Aunt Ellen sat in the chair, pulling her shawl around her.

'You know what I think. I've already said, Malachy's worthy of you, I don't think this other fellow is, and for all you know, you could be risking losing a good man with a good future, only to find out that the other one isn't interested. But none of that convinced you.'

Lucifer jumped onto Aunt Ellen's knee, padded a half circle round and fixed Durie with cold green eyes.

'So I'm going to say this,' Aunt Ellen went on. 'Imagine I hadn't told you about the letter. Imagine you went to bed last night, dreaming of your wedding day. And then when you got to the church, Malachy wasn't there. Imagine that he jilted you.'

Durie had imagined that, thanks to Lucinda.

'Can you really do that to Malachy?' asked Aunt Ellen.

The clock ticked. An ember shifted in the grate. Lucifer yawned.

'No,' said Durie. 'No, I can't.'

Chapter 64

Before they left the house, Aunt Ellen looked Durie up and down and smiled.

'That dress suits you, you should wear green more often.' Then she caught sight of her feet. 'You're not wearing those boots, surely?'

The new dress was nothing fancy, but for once she'd not asked whether the fabric was hard-wearing, but chosen purely on the colour, a rich dark green that wouldn't have matched anyone's eyes, but did seem to make her brown ones look more brown, in quite a nice way. Aunt Ellen had come with her to the shops, and taken the opportunity to persuade her to buy shoes: 'Something with a little heel would so improve your posture.' And she had, brown kid ones with silver buckles, but at the last minute, she'd taken them off, thrown them across the room and put on her sturdy boots instead. She was wobbly enough inside, she didn't need to be wobbly on her feet as well.

'The shoes pinched,' she said. 'Shall we go? I don't want to keep Malachy waiting.'

As she reached for her cloak, Aunt Ellen put her hand on her arm.

'You made the right choice,' she said. 'He's a good man.'

'I know,' said Durie.

She did, of course she did.

She'd thought he might wear his new coat with the silver buttons for the wedding, but he was standing outside the church in his familiar russet one. And he was alone, though he'd said he'd asked a fellow servant from the Philimore house to be their witness, along with Aunt Ellen. But he smiled his handsome smile as they walked up, and gestured at the blue sky.

'Haven't we a fine day for a wedding? Robert couldn't get away after all, but there's a woman in the church, cleaning the brasses. She'll do it for us.'

He held out his arm.

'Shall we?'

She nodded and they walked into the church to become man and wife.

When they came out it was raining. Margie always said it was unlucky to see raindrops on your wedding day; Durie didn't usually listen to nonsense about things being lucky or unlucky, but the thought gave her a little shiver.

Don't be stupid. It's November. Of course it's raining.

Aunt Ellen had insisted on standing them a wedding breakfast at the shop, and when they got there, it was, as usual, full of gossiping women, the feathers and flowers on their hats dancing as they wittered on to each other. Aunt Ellen bustled Durie and Malachy to a table near the window, set with a basket of hot rolls and a pot of hot chocolate, then tapped a fork on a cup and said, 'May I have your attention? My niece, Endurance, who many of you know as Miss Proudfoot the bonesetter, has this morning been married to this gentleman, Mr Malachy O'Neill. Please join me in wishing them every happiness, and I hope you'll all take a slice of the wedding cake with us.'

Everyone clapped, a woman who Durie had treated for a stiff knee called out 'Hurrah!' and from behind the counter, Aunt Ellen produced a large square cake covered in white icing.

'Well, Mrs O'Neill,' said Malachy, pouring chocolate for both of them and then raising his cup, 'here's to us.'

Durie raised hers in return, took a sip, and then another. The sweet chocolate settled her stomach. She looked round at the smiling faces, and glanced down at the ring glinting on her finger. It was done. She was married. He had turned up, she had turned up, all these people were happy for them, and they were going to be happy together. And when she got home, she was going to put the monkey skeleton in a drawer, make a wish that George Layton was happy too, and then put him out of her mind.

Being as there were no wedding guests to entertain, they parted company after the breakfast. Malachy had some important millers to see, and Durie had arranged to visit two new customers. The first had a simple sprained wrist that only needed splinting, the second a very stiff back that took a good hour to get loosened up. The customer, the wife of a ship owner, was a talker, yammering on about the weather, some gossip she'd heard about the Prime Minister's wife, and the shocking price of coal, and for once, Durie listened to it, as a welcome distraction from thoughts of what was yet to come that day. That in a few hours, she would climb the stairs with Malachy, close the door of the room that was now theirs, and learn the secrets of the marriage bed.

Though her only glimpse of what was inside a man's breeches remained the unedifying sight of the rector's private parts, she'd long ago interrogated Lucinda about precisely what she'd done with Tom's erstwhile father, so she knew what would happen when she and Malachy were alone that night. She also knew, thanks again to Lucinda, that although it sounded horrible, if the man knew what to do, it was delightful. Something about the way Malachy touched her suggested he would know what to do, but all the same, the thought made her feel quite peculiar and rather anxious. Because what if, when it came to it, when she was before him in her nightgown . . . what if he was disappointed?

It was beginning to get dark as she walked home through the rain; a stiff breeze had blown up too, and when a sudden gust sent dust swirling and lifted bits of rubbish into the air, she had to grab at her hat. As she did, one of the monkey bones, a small one, fell to the ground. She bent down, but the street was slick with watery mud and her cold fingers couldn't grasp it. A carriage passed, sending up spray and driving rivulets of water across the street. She snatched at the bone, then stopped and let the water sweep it away.

You're married to Malachy now.

When she got home he was sitting in the parlour, chatting to Aunt Ellen. With the curtains drawn, the lamps lit and Lucifer dozing by the fire, the picture was cosy and ordinary and yet at the same time very strange. She took off her hat and cloak, conscious of her bedraggled appearance.

'Well, if it isn't Mrs O'Neill,' said Malachy, with a smile that made her stomach flip. 'Take this seat by the fire, you look frozen.'

'I'm constantly telling her to hail a chair in weather like this, but you know what she's like,' said Aunt Ellen.

'I do indeed,' said Malachy, with a conspiratorial wink.

'I like walking,' said Durie. 'And it's good for the spine.'

She didn't add that she avoided taking chairs because once, near the stand on Piccadilly, a surly-looking chair man had looked her up and down and muttered, 'Walk on by, miss, walk on by.'

'I was just telling Malachy,' said Aunt Ellen, 'I took three orders for wedding cakes after people tasted yours. Lady Walsham enquired after the price too, and I know she's very friendly with the Duchess of Bolton, whose eldest gets married this summer'.

'Perhaps we should get married every week,' said Malachy, and winked at Durie.

He seemed so easy and comfortable, and Aunt Ellen the same, that Durie's nerves began to settle. Until, after a cosy supper of coddled eggs and buttered toast, Aunt Ellen stood. 'An early night for me, I think.' Her cheeks were pink – Durie had never seen that happen before – as she nodded at the sideboard. 'I don't usually encourage strong drink in the house, but there's a bottle of brandy in there, should you wish to drink to your health before you . . . retire.'

She closed the parlour door behind her, and they looked at each other for a moment. Durie's stomach fluttered.

'Well,' said Malachy, 'it would seem rude not to.'

He poured them each a small glass.

'To our health,' he said, raising his glass to hers.

Durie had never tasted brandy before. She took a good mouthful; on her tongue it was warm and honeyed, but the fire when she swallowed made her cough and splutter.

'Steady there, Mrs O'Neill,' said Malachy, patting her back. 'Take it slowly.'

She sipped at the glass in the hope it might help quell the fluttering. Malachy drank his quite fast, then poured another, and a third. He was telling her a story about someone getting very drunk on the strong spirits they made at home in Ireland; the brandy was making her feel warm and slightly dizzy, and she watched his mouth move, remembering him kissing her hand and saying he wanted them to be man and wife as soon as possible. He swallowed the last drops from his glass.

'Another for you, Mrs O'Neill?'

She shook her head. Best to get on with it now, before the nerves started up again. Suddenly unable to meet his eye, she looked at the clock and said, 'We should probably go up.'

'Ah, it's early yet, my love. And your aunt has surprisingly good taste in brandy. Go on, have another.'

She shook her head.

'All right,' he said.

They'd go up now, surely?

But he poured another glass and raised it to her again.

'You won't mind if I do, then. As we say in Ireland, *sláinte*.'

Durie did not discover the secrets of the marriage bed that night. When the brandy bottle was empty, her new husband stumbled upstairs and before she could follow came the sound of him using the pot. Not wanting to embarrass him, she made a performance of checking the front door was locked before she followed him upstairs, only to find him lying on his back on top of the quilt, still fully dressed and fast asleep. He grunted and turned on his side. There seemed nothing for it but to undress and get into the bed.

He was an easier bedmate than her sister, lying perfectly still and only occasionally snoring, whereas Lucinda was forever tossing and turning and her snores could wake the saints. But even so, Durie couldn't sleep. Not just because it was very strange indeed to have a man sleeping beside her, but because she didn't know what to make of the situation. Weren't men supposed to be desperate to get under a woman's skirts? Back when Lucinda had designs on the son of her employers, she'd said he pursued her around the house, lying in wait in case of a chance for a fumble in a cupboard. But that was Lucinda, wasn't it? Not her. She looked at Malachy. His shirt had fallen open and in the grey moonlight slanting through a chink in the curtain, he looked like one of the statues in the museum. She lifted the coverlet and looked down at herself in the new nightgown she'd bought. The fine linen couldn't conceal the fact that his body and hers could have belonged to two completely different types of animal; the comparison that sprang to mind was a thoroughbred horse and a shabby old donkey.

She touched the ring on her finger.

He married me, didn't he?

He probably wasn't the first husband to get drunk on his wedding night. It was strong, that brandy; perhaps he wasn't used to it. And come to think of it, hadn't she taken quite a long time locking up? He might have been waiting for her, and then the brandy got the better of him. She turned over, and counted sheep, trying not to think about donkeys and horses.

In the morning, she woke to the sound of splashes in the pot and kept her eyes firmly closed, trying not to wrinkle her nose at the smell. Who knew that human beings were like lions? Crowley's den always stank worse than the lionesses' did. You probably got used to it.

She opened her eyes a tiny bit; he was in his nightshirt. Did he wake in the night and get under the quilt with her? He must have seen her eyelids flicker, because he said, 'Good morning, Mrs O'Neill. It's a chilly one out here. How about I get back into that bed and you warm me up?'

So of course she thought the thing she'd expected to happen the previous night was going to happen then, and after the thoughts that plagued her through the early hours, she was mightily relieved. But after a good deal of very pleasant cuddling and kissing, he pulled away and said, 'I was thinking, we should avoid making a child right away.' He kissed her lightly on her forehead. 'I want to be able to support my family. So give me three months, to prove to you I can succeed. Then we'll make all the babies you want.'

He was a very convincing man, Malachy O'Neill. And Durie was so relieved he had an honourable reason for not wanting to bed her that she actually thought better of him for it, even if she was disappointed at having to wait so long to discover what all the fuss was about. So they got up, and started their married life together with a breakfast of hot rolls and tea, taken with Aunt Ellen, who said rather pointedly that she was glad they enjoyed the brandy.

Then, it being Sunday, the two of them went for a stroll in St James's Park. Lots of people were walking dogs, and they talked about getting a puppy, when they moved into their own home. Durie wanted a spaniel, but Malachy favoured a Pomeranian, and after a good-natured squabble, they agreed to get both. They ate apple tarts by the lake, and watched some children playing with a kite. When it got stuck in a tree, Malachy rescued it; their nursemaid gave him a smile, but he just tipped his hat to her and walked back to Durie, and at that moment she thought she was probably the happiest woman in the world.

A week later, he was gone.

Chapter 65

That first week, they'd settled so easily into life together. Durie had customers to see and Malachy went off each morning at nine. In the evening, they took supper with Aunt Ellen; he'd ask how business had been in the shop, and Aunt Ellen would happily chat about who'd been in and what was selling and what wasn't, her usual quiet read forgotten.

At night, after a kiss and a cuddle, Durie and Malachy lay spooned against each other. It was rather overheating when you'd got used to sleeping alone, but Durie didn't move away until he was fast asleep. And she was almost getting used to the smell of the pot in the morning, though she saved her own ablutions till he went downstairs.

At the coffee house that Tuesday, she was unpacking her bag when Dr Candleford said loudly, 'One pities the poor fellow of course – imagine waking next to that in the morning.'

'Imagine trying to mount it in the night!' said weasel face, to guffaws round the table.

How did they know she was married?

In a very poor Irish accent, Dr Candleford said, 'Not tonight, dear, I have a headache!'

They loved that one, laughing their heads off. Weasel face slapped the table and repeated, hardly able to speak for laughing, 'I have a headache!'

No worse than anything they'd said before, but it found its way through her defences like a little dart of poison. Malachy's reasoning made perfect sense, of course it did, but in truth it was still galling to know she was insufficiently tempting to make him change his mind. A man wouldn't be able to share a bed with Lucinda for three nights and remain happy with a kiss and a cuddle, would he? Her cheeks felt hot at the thought of how the doctors would laugh if they knew the truth, that she was three days married and still untouched.

When Jeannie came over with her coffee, and offered her congratulations, Durie asked, 'How does everyone know?'

Jeannie nodded at the table where the penny scribbler sat. He raised his dish of coffee to them.

'It was in the *Mercury*, and the *Gazette*.'

'But we didn't tell them.'

Jeannie shrugged.

'Someone did.'

She picked up a copy of the *Mercury* from another table, flicked through and handed it to Durie, open at page seven.

Our felicitations to Miss Proudfoot the bonesetter, married last week to Mr Malachy O'Neill, at St George's, Mayfair. The happy couple were seen after the ceremony at Ellen's on Brook Street, where a wedding cake was shared with customers, including Lady Walsham, who was heard to say it was the best fruit cake she had tasted.

The question was answered when she got home that evening. Malachy and Aunt Ellen were chatting on either side of the fire, a copy of the *Mercury* on Aunt Ellen's lap.

'Have you seen it? What a clever husband you have!'

Malachy smiled.

'I wanted all of London to know our good news. And if it brings more orders for wedding cakes, so much the better.'

'You should have written a line about your own business too,' said Aunt Ellen. 'You never know who might be reading.'

'Ah, there'll be time enough for that,' said Malachy. 'I wanted to show my gratitude for the way you've welcomed me into your home. If it wasn't for you, we might have had to wait quite a while to be married.' He smiled at Durie. 'And I'm very happy that we didn't.'

As she joined them by the fire, Durie suddenly thought who else would read the story. She smiled to herself.

Well, Lucinda, do you still think he's a chancer?

At the end of that first week, their second Sunday as man and wife was as pleasant as the first: wrapped up warm, they walked out to Bethnal Green to take the air, had some further debate on the matter of dogs, then came home and dined very cosily on mutton chops with Aunt Ellen.

So on the Monday, when Durie got home and found he wasn't there, she was disappointed, but not concerned.

'He said he was seeing a miller with a large order today,' she told Aunt Ellen. 'That must be what's keeping him.'

They were just debating whether to eat supper or wait, when Betsy answered a knock and brought in a letter for Durie. Thinking it was from a customer asking for a visit,

Durie was still talking to Aunt Ellen about whether they should just save Malachy some cold cuts, when the first words caught her eye.

Dear Durie,

    By the time you read this, I'll be far away, and you may already know what I've taken with me. You'll be angry, and you've a right to be, but I wanted to explain myself, so you understand.

'What is it?' said Aunt Ellen. 'Durie, what's happened?'

I'm not a bad man, but I'm a poor one, and I saw a chance to take from someone who has plenty, and go home to Ireland to look after my family. I thought I could get a good bit of money from you and then go, without tangling you up in a marriage. And I would have, if you hadn't told me about the money saved for your nephew. That money is enough to set up all my brothers at home with a start in life, and you had it sitting there, waiting for a boy you barely know, whose future is already taken care of.

    I sail back to Ireland from Liverpool the day after tomorrow, and I promise you won't ever hear of me again. So in seven years you'll be free to marry, and I hope you will. As for the money I took as a loan, you've said yourself, you earn more than you know what to do with, and you'll soon make up the loss.

    You'll be glad now we didn't make a child. I did right by you in that at least, if nothing else.

    Malachy O'Neill

She handed the letter to Aunt Ellen, and walked upstairs, so weighed down with sadness and humiliation that she had to haul on the banister to climb the final step.

And there it was: a clean square in the dust under the bed, where Tom's strongbox used to be. She'd never told Malachy where it was, but he'd have found it easily; most people think under the bed is the safest place, don't they? It probably is, if the person it needs guarding from isn't the one in the bed with you.

She sat down heavily as her aunt appeared, still holding the letter.

'I don't understand,' said Aunt Ellen.

'It's quite simple. He's taken almost every penny I had. I lied to you, Aunt Ellen, I did give him the money to buy in to the Corn Exchange, and more on top. A lot more.'

'Oh, Durie—'

'I knew he wanted my money, but I thought he wanted me as well. I've been so stupid.'

Aunt Ellen sat beside her, folding and refolding the letter.

'Lucinda was right,' said Durie. 'He was a chancer.'

'He was more than that! He was a thief!'

Durie shook her head.

'I gave him most of it willingly. We called it a loan, but I never expected it back. But I wouldn't give him Tom's money, so he had to marry me to get it. You warned me, didn't you? You told me, when you marry, your husband owns everything.'

'I should have seen what he was up to,' said Aunt Ellen. 'He had me fooled completely.'

'You didn't know the full story. I did, and he still fooled me. Or maybe I fooled myself.'

They sat in silence for a minute. Lucifer padded in, looked at them both and then, for the first time ever, jumped onto Durie's knee and rubbed his face on her arm. It was only then that she started to cry.

Chapter 66

When Durie woke the next morning, her eyes were still red and scratchy. The previous evening, Aunt Ellen had encouraged her to let the tears fall, sitting beside her and rubbing her back.

'I'm not a crier either,' she said. 'But I've heard people say it helps.'

It hadn't though. Standing to get dressed, in the cold light of day, she felt a hundred years old, and the hours ahead were impossible to face. No appointments that morning, thank goodness, but she was due at the coffee house that afternoon, and the thought of the doctors made her eyes prickle again. The risk of crying in front of them was not to be countenanced. She got back into bed and pulled the covers over her head.

She must have drifted back into sleep, and the knock on her bedroom door wove itself into her dream: Malachy was knocking on the front door, he was back and it was all a mistake.

'Come on,' said Aunt Ellen, and the dream slipped away. 'Come down and have some breakfast.'

Durie sat up.

'I need to send a message to the coffee house,' she said. 'I can't go there today.'

'All right. We'll tell them you have a head cold. Now, wash your face, get dressed, and come downstairs and eat. It'll make you feel better.'

'I very much doubt that.'

'Well, do it anyway.'

Despite Aunt Ellen's instruction to go out for a walk and 'not waste the day moping over that scoundrel', when her aunt left for the shop, Durie took up Malachy's letter and read it again.

He was right, about the money for the so-called loan. She had no use for it, and the loss of it wasn't important. It certainly hadn't been worth as much to her as it apparently was to him. But to take Tom's money, when he knew what it meant to her and he'd looked her in the eye and promised . . . that was how she knew what she'd really lost, and couldn't get back.

She couldn't get back the happiness of knowing he wanted to be with her when he could have his pick of women. She couldn't get back the feeling of a warm body that wanted to lie beside hers in the night, or the sound of him saying 'Mrs O'Neill', as though he was proud to have her as his wife. She couldn't get any of that back, because it hadn't really existed. He didn't exist, the Malachy O'Neill who'd given her his arm because the pavements were slippery, and kissed her by the side of the Islington road and asked her to promise herself to him. He never had. And what an idiot she'd been, believing he did.

All those months . . . had he realised slowly that she was worth tapping, or was it planned from the start? That first morning, when he said he was out on an errand and happened to be walking near the house, was he lying even then?

Of course he was.

Such elaborate lies. The details about the Corn Exchange – where had he got all that from? He'd clearly never been inside the place. Then it came to her: all those evenings spent standing in the Philimores' dining room while they entertained guests. The man he'd pointed out when he took her to see the Corn Exchange might or might not be called Mr Shaw, but she'd put money on him or someone like him having sat at that table. Probably bored the company senseless but he'd have had one avid listener.

Suddenly cold, she fetched her shabby old cloak and wrapped it round her, ignoring the new one she'd bought so she didn't shame him when they were out together. Everywhere she looked, another reminder of her stupidity: the sugar bowl, bought because he liked his tea sweet; the table where they'd eaten breakfast together and talked about the future; the ring, still shiny on her finger. It didn't belong there, but if she took it off, people might notice and what was she going to say then?

Just a few nights before, he'd sat right where she was sitting now, thanking Aunt Ellen for welcoming him into her home, and saying how glad he was they hadn't had to wait to get married. How could you do that, sit there and smile, and lie and lie, and never once let the act slip? Was there nothing real inside him at all? He should have been on the stage, he was a better actor than any she'd seen in Lucinda's plays. But then, was he really? Or was it her who wanted to believe what he said so badly, she closed her eyes to all the signs?

When Aunt Ellen came home, Durie didn't bother pretending she'd been for a walk.

'Right,' said Aunt Ellen. 'Well, you've had a day of moping, and perhaps you needed it, but any more won't help. The best thing you can do now is get back to work. You can leave the coffee house and those blasted doctors till next week, but get back to your other customers tomorrow.'

'I can't face telling people.'

'Then don't. It's no one else's business.'

'If only he hadn't put that stupid notice in the *Mercury*. Everyone knows we were married, when they needn't have done. What am I supposed to say if people congratulate me?'

'I've been wondering why he did that, but he did, and there's nothing to be done about it. So if people congratulate you, you smile, say thank you and change the subject. Sooner or later it will have to come out, but it doesn't have to be now.'

It took all her willpower to step outside the front door next morning, but Aunt Ellen was probably right, working would distract her. And it did: her first customer was a man she hadn't seen before, with a swollen ankle, and while she was asking him what the pain was like and how it happened, she could push thoughts of Malachy away.

The second was a regular, Mrs Baker, an elderly widow with a habit of wittering on about her three grandchildren, evidently all child geniuses, while Durie worked on her shoulder. Normally she let the chatter wash over her, but that day she made the effort to listen, even ask the odd question, so she could keep her own thoughts quiet. She was all right until, as she was strapping the shoulder, Mrs Baker said, 'I think marriage has mellowed you, Mrs O'Neill. You used to be so stern and silent, and here you are, talking away.' She winked. 'You'll have little ones of your own soon, and see what a joy they are.'

Durie dropped the strapping, and it unravelled across the floor. She picked it up, but her hands seemed to have forgotten what to do with it. As she knotted the ends, it was already coming loose. She should have redone it, but instead she scrabbled her things together, bid Mrs Baker a hasty goodbye and ran, actually ran, to the front door.

A roundabout route home avoided streets they'd walked down together, but she couldn't get Mrs Baker's words out of her head, nor her stupid reaction to them. All very well Aunt Ellen saying it was nobody else's business but people made your business their business. How was she going to do her work, knowing that at any moment it might happen again, and she'd fall to pieces?

Impossible to go on with that hanging over her. When she got home, without even taking off her cloak, she found pen and ink, sat down and started to write.

Chapter 67

When she opened the door to the coffee shop the following Tuesday, one of the lawyers looked up, and nudged the man beside him. He smirked and nudged another. As she walked to her corner, conversation dwindled to murmurs and sniggers. She caught the words 'took every penny' and 'gone back to Ireland', and then Dr Candleford called out, 'So you've lost your husband and your money, Mrs O'Neill. What a shame.'

She steeled herself to keep her voice light.

'Thank you for your sympathy, Doctor, but I've lost nothing of value. The husband was no good to anyone, and the money was a fair price to get rid of him.'

'I daresay he's happy with the bargain too.'

'I daresay he is.'

Out of the corner of her eye she glimpsed the penny scribbler, writing furiously. Couldn't be helped, but she wouldn't be giving him anything else.

Jeannie came over with a dish of coffee.

'Are you all right? I'm sorry about . . . what happened.'

'Don't be. As I told the doctors, I'm well rid of him.' She took a sip of the coffee, and attempted a breezy tone. 'Should be a busy afternoon. This damp cold always stiffens the old ones up.'

'She should have sent her husband out in it then,' said Dr Candleford. 'Might have had half a chance of keeping him.'

You'd have thought it was the funniest thing anyone had ever said. As the place dissolved into whoops and guffaws, Durie busied herself unpacking her bag, hoping to hide her flaming cheeks, but the laughing went on and on and on. Even when it began to subside, Dr Candleford wasn't going to let his moment go. He banged the table and repeated, 'Should have sent her husband out in it!' and they were off again, rocking back in their chairs, wiping tears from their eyes.

'Ignore them,' said Jeannie. 'They're idiots.'

'I'm well aware of that. They don't bother me.'

When her first customer arrived, she braced herself for a comment, but either he hadn't heard the story, or was too polite to mention it. But he was certainly fully apprised of the situation by the time she'd finished manipulating his neck, thanks to Dr Candleford reading, loudly, from the *Mercury*, to an acquaintance who'd just come in. The letter she'd written had contained just the bare facts, that Malachy had defaulted on a loan, taken her savings and was believed to be heading back to Ireland, but of course they'd embellished it.

'"Mr O'Neill skipped aboard the Dublin boat,"' read Dr Candleford, '"and was heard to say his pockets were full of money."'

'Good luck to him,' said weasel face, 'but I couldn't name the amount that would make me go' – he picked up his pipe and jabbed it lewdly upwards – 'where that poor man had to go.' To a chorus of sniggers, he added, 'And I don't mean Ireland.'

On and on it went, all afternoon: she tried not to listen, but their words cut through and the laughter was so loud that people coming in peered around, curious to know what was going on. And when weasel face mimicked her, saying, '"As it happens, I am engaged to be married. To a fine man, who's worth ten of anyone on that table,"' it was like being stuck with a pin, remembering how happy she'd felt to say those words.

Halfway through the afternoon, Jeannie came over with fresh coffee.

'Thought you might need this.' She sat beside Durie, and said quietly, 'Is it true that he took all your money? Because me and Jake were talking – you bring in a lot of extra custom these days, so if you wanted, we could take our arrangement down to, say, five per cent.'

Durie could take the doctors being nasty, she'd steeled herself for that. But the unexpected kindness made her eyes prickle again.

You can't cry in front of them.

'No need,' she said, the effort to keep back the infuriating tears making it come out more stiffly than she intended.

Jeannie shrugged and stood.

'Suit yourself, but the offer's there.'

Just before six, Durie's final customer left, and she could pack her bag and go, ignoring the hail of parting comments. As she trudged up Holborn Hill, setting her face against a biting wind, a hawker was selling copies of the *Mercury* on the corner of Bishopsgate. A smartly dressed man in a snow-white wig handed over a coin and walked away with a copy; another one who could smirk at her humiliation. Well, let him. Aunt Ellen had tried to dissuade her from sending the letter, but she'd stood firm. She didn't like knowing it was there in black and white for people all over the city to see, of course she didn't – but better than waiting for people to find out, and never knowing when a well-meaning comment like Mrs Baker's might catch her unawares. She'd have to endure a few more weeks of ribaldry from the doctors, there was no way out of that, but if she didn't rise to it, surely they'd settle back into merely laughing at her hat, insulting her face and calling her a quack, all of which seemed quite bearable now.

'It's better this way,' she'd said to Aunt Ellen. 'Anyone who cares can laugh at me now, all at once, and then they'll move on to someone else and leave me alone.'

And she really thought that was what would happen.

Chapter 68

Unfortunately for Durie, the report in the *Mercury* coincided with one of those rare periods in London life when nothing much was happening; no countesses running off with their dancing masters, no noteworthy murders and even reports of lost dogs were thin on the ground. Short of news, several London papers repeated the story, but added new and entirely fictitious details. She read in the *Weekly Miscellany* that, as well as her money, Malachy had taken a necklace of pearls (which she'd never possessed and wouldn't miss if she had), while the *Chronicle* said he'd run off in the dead of night and she'd woken in the morning 'raging to find the bed empty beside her and swearing to find the miscreant'. And the *Flying Post* claimed she'd pursued him to Wales, in a bid to stop him setting sail for Ireland, and was seen banging on the front door of an inn near Holyhead as he was escaping out of the back window. She was very tempted to write and say she wouldn't pursue Malachy O'Neill across the road, let alone to Wales, but that would only give them more to play with.

'Better to keep a dignified silence, and wait for the whole episode to become old news,' said Aunt Ellen.

But it didn't. A bored London found the story highly entertaining; as she walked to the coffee house the day after the *Flying Post* came out, a messenger boy grinned at her from across the road, jerked a thumb and yelled out, 'Looking for your husband? He went that way.' As she walked between appointments, passers-by nudged each other and sniggered, and one morning when she stopped to buy an apple from a hawker, he smirked and said, 'Sure you can afford it, darlin'?'

Not everyone was nasty. Quite often, she'd see one woman nudge another, and hear a whispered 'Poor thing, only married a week' or 'Absolute scoundrel, should be horsewhipped'. But the pity was no easier to stomach than the mocking.

On Aunt Ellen's advice, and after a brief fight with herself, she took the monkey bones out of her hat, to make herself less recognisable, but it made no difference; still she heard the whispers, saw the looks, never knew when someone might yell 'Found your husband yet?' from across the road. And one morning, as she passed the print shops in the shadow of St Paul's, she caught sight, in one of the windows, of the reason why. She stopped, not wanting to see but not able to walk on. Alongside drawings of the Prime Minister slipping on a banana skin and the King tucking a sack of money under his throne was a coloured print with the words 'The Bonesetter Woman's Revenge' across the top. The figure in the picture was marching along a road, a crutch held high as though ready to hit someone, past a signpost that said 'To Wales'. As well as the hat, the artist had captured her tattered cloak, her lumpy, uncorseted waist, her big old boots, even her unwomanly gait. And though the features were unkindly exaggerated, the face was unmistakably hers.

For a moment, she couldn't catch her breath. You couldn't do a drawing like that from a description; he must have watched her as she went unknowingly about her business. She pulled her cloak tight around her, feeling, ridiculously, as though she was naked. How could someone make their living from humiliating people they didn't even know? Surely you could only bring yourself to do it if you could look at them and not see a person at all, just the butt of a joke. So that was what she was to the artist, if you could call him that.

A man passing by glanced at the window and instinctively she moved to block the picture from his sight, realising even as she did how pointless that was. It was a print, not a painting; they could have made any number of them. Those prints of Lucinda, when she'd got herself painted as Tilly Tipworth: people had bought them in their hundreds and hung them in their houses. Were people actually paying money for this one, so they could take it home and laugh at her?

Hot anger rose through her and before she could think twice, she'd pushed open the shop door. A tall man with piggy eyes and a face like uncooked dough stood behind the counter, engrossed in neatening the edges of a print with a blade, while towards the back, a lanky boy was hanging prints on the wall. Durie banged the door behind her so hard that they both jumped and the man nicked his finger. He swore and glared up at her.

'Could have had my finger off!'

'Who gave you permission to sell prints of me?'

Recognition dawned on their faces. The boy's eyes widened, and the man smirked, making dimples in the dough.

'Good, aren't they? Been very popular this week.'

'But I didn't agree to it. The artist just watched me, without asking.'

'How else was he supposed to get a likeness?' He pointed at one of the prints on the wall. 'Do you suppose His Majesty sat for that one? If people want it, we print it.'

'Well, I want you to stop selling the ones of me.'

'And I want to go home and find my wife's been replaced by a twenty-year-old with a tiny waist and big bubbies, but I won't be getting what I want and neither will you.' A bubble of blood appeared from the cut on his finger; he sucked it, then said, 'Of course, you could always buy them all.'

'How many do you have?'

'Hundred or so. Give you them for sixpence each.'

Two pounds ten shillings. Worth it to get them out of that window.

The finger was still bleeding; he sucked it again, then picked up a stack from under the counter, and held them out.

'Call it two and five if you like.'

Only the glimpse of a smirk passing between them saved her.

You idiot. Walk out with those and they'll print another hundred.

'Keep them,' she said. 'And I hope your finger goes putrid and drops off.'

Aunt Ellen sighed as she handed Durie the *Mercury* two evenings later.

The eccentric behaviour of London's female bonesetter continues to entertain. Patrons at Johnson's Print Emporium witnessed Mrs O'Neill – formerly Miss Proudfoot – haggling over the purchase of one hundred prints of herself. On failing to agree an acceptable price, she expressed the wish that the proprietor, Mr Johnson, might die of a putrid finger, and slammed the door hard enough to make the glass rattle. Mr Johnson confirms that a stock of the prints, entitled 'The Bonesetter Woman's Revenge', remains available, priced at sixpence each.

'I slammed the door on the way in, not the way out, and I only wished his finger would drop off,' said Durie.

'Oh, Durie,' said Aunt Ellen. 'When will you learn?'

Chapter 69

In the weeks after Malachy left, Durie pictured him sometimes, arriving back in his village, his pockets filled with shiny
golden guineas. What did he tell his family about how he
came by them? Not the truth, that was for sure. Perhaps
another of the Philimores' guests had furnished him with a
story he could use. He'd sit at his mother's kitchen table, blue
eyes shining, telling them how he'd seen a business opportunity and jumped in and made his fortune overnight. All
of them looking at him adoringly, believing every word, just
like she had.

It was three weeks before she discovered none of that had
happened. Four paragraphs, near the bottom of page four in
the *Weekly Miscellany*, and she'd have missed them but for
the date catching her eye as she was about to turn the page.

All souls were lost when the Pride of Galway *was sunk off
the coast of Ireland two weeks ago, in a raging storm. The
ship was headed for Dublin, having sailed from Liverpool
on 7 November.*

There was more, about how storms in the Irish Sea had claimed two other boats that month, and what freight had been lost, but only one phrase mattered.

All souls were lost.

He was at the bottom of the sea, her money with him, and it had all been for nothing. She tried to feel sorry; no one deserved such a horrible death. But she hadn't known the Malachy O'Neill who drowned that day any better than she knew any of the other passengers on that ship, and she couldn't bring herself to care that he was dead. She told Aunt Ellen, but no one else: it would only add spice to the story and there was enough of that already.

You'd have thought Malachy's death would mean at least one of his promises would come true, that she'd never hear from him again. But he couldn't even keep that one. After a month, bills started arriving, addressed to Durie. He might not have graced the Corn Exchange during their single week of married life, but he had been busy. On one day alone, he'd purchased a coat and breeches from a tailor on Cheapside, a pair of shoes ('finest cow leather') from a cobbler two doors up and a silk waistcoat round the corner; other sprees had taken place along the Strand and in the streets around Covent Garden. A little here, a little there, never too much in a single establishment.

'I thought as much,' said Aunt Ellen. 'Remember the announcement?'

I wanted all of London to know our good news.

Of course he did, because then he could put his purchases in his wife's name; everyone knew she was good for the credit.

Aunt Ellen insisted on paying the bills, since Durie couldn't.

'Those shopkeepers gave him credit in good faith, and I won't see them go unpaid.'

'I'll pay you back as soon as I can.'

Aunt Ellen shook her head.

'There's no need. I'm not blameless in this, Durie, I fell for his nonsense too, when I should have seen him for what he was and protected you.'

She hesitated.

'And I did worse than that, didn't I? If I'd told you about George Layton's letter, you'd never have married Malachy. I thought I was saving you from an unsuitable husband, but he can't have been worse than that scoundrel.'

Durie didn't answer. She didn't want even to think about George now, other than to hope, very hard but probably in vain, that he didn't read the papers, and so wouldn't know what a fool she'd been.

15 February 1763

Dear Tom,

Another year gone, and nearly five since you left us. I'm writing this in the room I used to share with your mother, where you slept in a crib beside our bed. When I think of you – which is often – I picture you as you were then, with tufty hair like a baby bird. It's hard to imagine the boy you must be now; your grandfather was tall and I wonder if you are too.

I always thought that if you had been able to grow up with us, your family, I might have been the kind of aunt you could come to for wise advice. However, I have one of those, and it turns out she isn't as wise as both of us thought. No, that's not really fair: she was taken in by someone who was very good at taking people in, and I can't criticise, because so was I. It's a sorry story, and one I won't share with you, but I will just say that my aunty advice to you is, be very careful who you trust in life, because it's really surprising just how much lying a person can do.

I don't know if I'll send this letter, Tom. I've read it again and it seems very cheerless. I wouldn't like you to become a cynical person who trusts no one, and really, who am I to give you advice anyway?

Yours,
Aunt Durie

Chapter 70

Durie could have put up with it all, the nudges and the sniggers and even the thought of people handing over money for those prints. She could have put up with sitting in the coffee house, trying to do her work while the doctors speculated loudly about where Malachy might be, what he was spending her money on, and what horrors might have been revealed in the bedroom to prompt his departure (the version of events that had him fleeing in the middle of the night had turned out to have the widest appeal and was generally accepted as correct). Her customers never joined in, and at first she was touched by their loyalty but then the truth dawned; they weren't going to risk a laugh when she had her big, strong hands on a painful part of their bodies. It didn't mean they wouldn't recount the afternoon's entertainment to their wives and their friends and enjoy a good laugh then.

She could have put up with all that, even though some days, it laid her so low she had to give herself a stiff talking to before she could step outside the front door. Because she thought it would pass; like Aunt Ellen said, if she kept her head down and didn't present the papers with any more material, people would lose interest. And eventually there was a week where none of them wrote anything about her, and she thought, at last, now it'll fizzle out and be over.

She left it another week, then bought a selection of the papers, just to check. Her spirits rose as she turned the pages of the *Mercury*, and then the *Gazette*, her eyes scraping the text for the familiar shape of her own name and finding it nowhere. Hearing Betsy open the front door to Aunt Ellen, she was about to set aside the *Chronicle* for later, but when Aunt Ellen began berating Betsy about the front step being grubby, she opened the paper anyway.

It was on page four.

We hear of a strange encounter with the female bonesetter Mrs O'Neill, lately deserted by her husband of one week. Attending on a lady in Henrietta Mews who was troubled with a painful knee, she seemed distracted, muttering to herself, and attempted to treat the left knee. On being reminded that the pain was in the right, the famously short-tempered practitioner flew into a rage and said that she well knew right from left and anyone who said she didn't was a liar. On completing the treatment on the correct knee, she apologised to the lady and said there would be no charge as she was not in full fettle that day.

Aunt Ellen bustled in, still complaining about the step. She stopped short when she saw Durie's face.

'What now?'

Durie handed her the paper.

'I don't have a customer in Henrietta Mews. I think it's the doctors. They tried to take my work away before, and I beat them, didn't I? And now Malachy's given them the chance to get their own back.'

All evening, they discussed what to do, but without coming to any conclusion. This time Durie didn't need Aunt Ellen to tell her that confronting the doctors at the coffee house, with the penny scribbler's quill at the ready, was only going to make it all worse, though Aunt Ellen said it anyway.

'If you so much as raise your voice in there tomorrow, you'll be falling into their trap, and half of London will read about it.'

So she gritted her teeth, got on with her work and did her best to block out the doctors' comments. As she left, Dr Candleford asked if she was 'in full fettle', to which she answered politely that she was. His open irritation at the thought that she might not have read about the fictitious encounter in Henrietta Mews was the only pleasure of the afternoon.

The next attack came the following week: a letter in the *Mercury*.

I wish to warn customers of the female bonesetter Mrs O'Neill that they should no longer expect the customary relief from her ministrations. As Miss Proudfoot, she has successfully attended on my wife for a troublesome backache, but since her marriage and subsequent troubles, she seems quite to have lost her skills, which may or may not be attributable to the taint of brandy on her breath. After an hour's manipulation

*my poor wife's back remains as painful as ever, while I am
lighter a guinea.*

   Isaac Carrell, Bishopsgate

Passing the doctors' table that afternoon, she saw, just in time,
the weasel sticking out his foot to trip her. Stepping to one
side to avoid it, she stumbled slightly.

'Whoa ho,' he said, 'looks like the brandy bottle's been
opened already.'

Amid the laughter, Dr Candleford said loudly, 'I pity her
customers – doubt she can even see straight.'

She was a second away from picking up his dish of coffee
and tipping it over his head, and then doing the same for
the weasel. All that stopped her was a movement glimpsed
out of the corner of her eye; the scribbler, sitting up, all ears.

You are not taking my work away from me.

Forcing a smile, she said, 'You gentlemen will have your
jokes. But I'm afraid I can't stand here chatting, I'm expecting
a busy afternoon.'

She hadn't given them what they wanted, but she knew
now, they wouldn't stop trying.

The week after, three more letters appeared, in the *Mercury*,
the *Flying Post* and the *Chronicle*, all from fictitious customers,
variously complaining that she had failed to ease a stiff elbow,
turned up for an appointment 'even more slovenly in appearance than usual, and unsteady on her feet', and frightened
the correspondent's sixteen-year-old-daughter with a rant
about faithless men and a warning against marriage. Again,
she pretended not to have seen the letters, parried the doctors

with polite indifference. There was a certain satisfaction in seeing how it annoyed them, but it cost her all her self-control and left her exhausted by the end of the day. Trudging home, she caught sight of her reflection in a shop window, head down and shoulders hunched. She used to stroll away from the coffee house with her hands tired but her heart happy, knowing she'd done good work. She'd done good work that day too, but it was hard to take pleasure in it when every muscle in your body ached from the strain of gritting your teeth, holding your tongue and pretending you didn't care.

Still she clung to the hope that, if she didn't rise to it, they would stop.

Chapter 71

Later she would wonder if the final blow had been planned all along, or the doctors had just got bored with trying to provoke her into losing her temper and confirming the picture they'd painted. Not that it made any difference.

This time, they made sure she couldn't pretend she hadn't seen it. As Durie came downstairs that morning, Betsy was closing the door.

'Messenger brought this for you.' She handed up a copy of the *Mercury* as she passed the stairs. 'Didn't say who sent it.' It was on the front page.

As physicians, we have watched with concern recent warnings about the conduct of a well-known female bonesetter, variously accused of drunkenness, irrational and aggressive behaviour and incompetence in the art – for it is certainly no science – that she claims to practise. We have long held that there is no place for quacks or mountebanks of any stamp in our modern city, but that a female of this persuasion should dupe so many, for so long, is doubly regrettable. As recent events show, a woman's tender emotions may easily outweigh her judgement and, once knocked off balance by affairs of the heart, she becomes a danger to herself and others. We implore those afflicted with conditions of the spine and skeleton to avoid putting themselves in harm's way, to seek instead the advice of a recognised medical practitioner, and to allow this lady the leisure required to ease a troubled mind.

She sat down hard on the stairs. Her bag tipped; a jar of salve rolled out, bounced down the steps and smashed on the hall floor, filling the air with the scent of rosemary. Who'd have thought a smell could mock you?

The noise brought Betsy running back up from the kitchen. 'What is it? What's happened?'

Durie read the words again. The letter was signed by Dr Candleford and ten others; she didn't know the names but she could picture their smug faces and hear their pompous voices.

People were going to read this and they were going to think she was mad and drunk and pathetic. Because people listened to doctors, didn't they? They listened to doctors even when the doctors told them to do stupid things like resting a bad back or curing a stiff shoulder by binding their arm, and now they were going to listen to doctors telling them that because of Malachy O'Neill, she'd fallen to pieces and couldn't do her work any more.

'Are you all right?' asked Betsy, stooping to pick up the shards of glass.

'No,' she said. 'I don't think I am.'

* * *

Durie's face told Ellen that whatever was in the newspaper she was clutching was worse than what had gone before. It had been a busy morning in the shop, and she'd just taken the chance to have a quick sit-down in the kitchen and tell the pastry cooks about some new ideas she'd got from Monsieur Laurent's window, when Durie came thumping down the area steps and crashed open the door.

'Look what they're saying,' she said, holding out the paper with a shaking hand. Wisps of hair were plastered to her sweaty brow, and her face was red; she must have run all the way. 'Aunt Ellen, what am I going to do?'

Ellen had seen Durie angry, more than once. But now there was fear in her eyes, and she'd never known Durie to be truly afraid of anything. She ushered her into the little storeroom where she usually sat to do the accounts, and shut the door.

'Why are they doing this?' said Durie, pacing backwards and forwards. 'I've done what you said, I've kept my head down, and they still won't leave me alone!'

She waved her arm and a basket of spoons clattered to the floor.

'Sorry.'

She knelt and picked them up.

'Same reason it's always been,' said Ellen. 'They can't stand competition from a woman. It's just that now they've got something new to use against you.'

'Well, I wish I was a man, so I could go round there and punch their stupid faces.'

Ellen rather wished she could do that herself. All Durie had ever done was work hard and be good at what she did, and yet between Malachy O'Neill and that set of bullies, they'd turned her from a happy, confident young woman making her own way in the world into the one she saw having to steel herself just to leave the house.

'I know you won't like this,' she said, 'but I think it's time to give up the coffee house.'

'But that's letting them win.'

'Up to a point, yes. But I've seen you when you come home from there, Durie. You're tired and you're crushed and I can't remember the last time I saw you smile. And sooner or later – probably sooner – you're going to give them the outburst they want, you know you are. Can you honestly say you can go there tomorrow and not say a word about this?'

Durie looked up at the ceiling, drew in a big breath, and sighed.

'No.'

'And if you do, you know they'll make the most of it. So let them have their stupid victory. You've got plenty of customers without putting yourself through that twice a week, and perhaps, if you're not under their noses, they'll leave you alone.'

It was certainly worth a try. But in truth, Ellen didn't think it was likely to work. This wasn't like the rivalry between her and Monsieur Laurent, where they both enjoyed the competition, and secretly admired each other's skills. The doctors wanted Durie off their patch, and she was very much afraid that didn't just mean the coffee house.

Durie sent a message to Jeannie, and the reply came in the morning.

We're both sorry it worked out like this. I'll miss you, and to be clear, because I know what you'll think, not the money, you. You made me laugh and it was nice to have another woman about the place. If you ever want to come back, you'd be welcome.

PS: I spilled Dr Candleford's coffee in his lap this morning, my hand must have slipped. It was good and hot.

Chapter 72

At first, it looked as though it had worked; no more false stories, no more letters from the doctors. The curious looks and the smirks hadn't stopped, and she still got the odd sniggering 'Looking for your husband?', but she could live with that, especially without two afternoons a week of the doctors to add to it. She tried not to think about how pleased they must be to have got rid of her.

And the dwindling number of messages asking her to call at fashionable addresses was nothing to worry about, was it? Things were always quieter once spring was on the way. No one was slipping over on icy cobbles; milder weather eased stiff joints; people were just busier and might not have time to make an appointment. She was still seeing her regular customers, ones whose ailments couldn't be fixed but could be eased whenever they became particularly troublesome. And the dozen or so new ones who'd started treatment before the whole saga began had continued until she pronounced them fixed.

But where once new enquiries came at the rate of a dozen a week, they dribbled to half that, then half again, until one Monday, she came home to find the tray on the hall table, where Betsy stacked her messages, empty. It was empty the next day too, and the one after. One enquiry on the Thursday, a sprained wrist, attended to the same day since she had no other appointments. Nothing on the Friday.

She mentioned it, quite casually, at breakfast. Aunt Ellen would say it was just a quiet week, probably. Nothing to worry about.

But Aunt Ellen didn't say that.

'I was afraid of this,' she said. 'It was damaging, that letter they sent.'

The words hit Durie like a splash of cold water when you weren't expecting it.

'Well, they meant it to be, didn't they?' she said. 'And it was bound to put some people off. But there are plenty who know me, people I've fixed. They know I can do what I say I can do.'

Aunt Ellen poured herself a second cup of tea and took a sip.

'Durie, I'm afraid that's not the problem.'

'What is, then?'

'They may know how good you are at what you do. But they won't recommend you to their friends, and risk making themselves look stupid if their friends believe what they've read in the papers.'

'But that's ridiculous—'

'Don't forget, people reading that letter, and what came before it, don't know why the doctors are doing this – they'll take it at face value.'

Durie knew the letter by heart now.

As physicians, we have watched with concern.
 A danger to herself and others.
 Allow this lady the leisure required to ease a troubled mind.

Responsible doctors, warning the public for their own good. Even expressing concern for her. They'd been very clever.

'You really think people will stop recommending me?'

Aunt Ellen sighed.

'I spoke to Mrs Edwards today. I thought perhaps, since she was the one who got you your start, and she's always spoken so highly of how you cured her back problem, she might put a good word around for you. She said she couldn't help.'

Aunt Ellen's face told Durie that wasn't all.

'You might as well tell me what else she said. It won't help not to know.'

'She said people were saying the business with Malachy cast doubt on your judgement, and they didn't think it was quite the thing to associate with a deserted wife.'

'It's not catching!'

'And that a lot of people believe what they've been reading about you.'

'But you told her it wasn't true?'

'Of course I did. But she won't go against the grain. People don't.'

'But I can't lose my work!'

'Well, you still have your regulars, who depend on you. And you know, it doesn't matter if you don't earn much for a while. You have a home here, and I was thinking, I could give you an allowance.'

Oh. This was serious, now.

'You always say a woman should be independent. Make her own money.'

'And you did,' said Aunt Ellen. 'I'm proud of what you did, how successful you were.'

Did. Were.

'But for a woman to hold her own in business, she has to persuade men she isn't a threat. It's their world, and if they decide they can't tolerate us in it, we don't stand a chance.'

'You compete with Monsieur Laurent.'

'I compete with him, but I don't challenge him. I make sure he knows there's room for both of us.'

'But there's room for me and the doctors! I never tried to take their customers – if someone needed a physician, I told them so.'

'You also told people that doctors had given them the wrong advice.'

'But they had!'

Durie slapped the table in frustration; her hand clipped the side of her cup, spilling tea across the tablecloth. As they mopped it up with napkins, Aunt Ellen said, 'Sometimes Monsieur Laurent's cakes are stale. I don't tell people that.'

'It's different though. People aren't going to be left in pain because they eat a stale cake, are they?'

Aunt Ellen sighed.

'No. And I'm not saying you were wrong. But you picked

a fight you couldn't win, because men won't stand for us winning. It's not fair and it's not right, but it's the way it is, and it will never change.'

Durie dabbed up the last of the tea, but it had left a stain right across the tablecloth. She looked down at her big, clumsy hands that didn't know how to do anything else but fix people, and remembered the days of ragged stitching and hats tumbling to the floor.

They've taken my work away.

'Aunt Ellen, if I can't fix people, I'm just . . . I don't fit anywhere.'

Her aunt hesitated for a moment, then said, 'Don't think I want this, because you know I like having you here. But there's your brother's offer to consider.'

Go home, with her tail between her legs. Ask, actually have to ask, if she could be Richie's assistant. And then spend her days with him telling her what to do and how to do it.

'So I have to let him win too?'

'I wish I had a better idea, but I don't. As I've said, I'd be very happy if you'd stay here, keep up your regular customers, maybe help me a bit with the accounts if that makes you feel better about taking an allowance. Or you can swallow your pride and work with Richie. But there's no need to make a hasty decision. You can take your time to think about it, and decide what's best.'

'Or least worst.'

'Yes, or that.'

Chapter 73

In the week that followed, Durie had three appointments, all regular customers. She took the long way to each of them, and the long way back, and by that means, she could spin out an hour's work to fill most of a morning. Better than having to suffer Richie telling her what to do, and she'd earned three guineas for it, more than enough for her needs and certainly more than she'd get in Lewes. And if she had to, she could wait it out till autumn came. The people who needed her to keep coming because they had stiff knees or elbows or shoulders always felt it more when the weather was cold and damp.

But at night, she couldn't sleep. Her body wasn't tired, and her mind didn't know what to do with itself. When there were new customers coming every week, she'd doze off thinking about what might be the cause of this one's pain, or how she could better ease that one's stiffness. Now, if she lay awake in the darkness, her thoughts went round in circles:

I should have listened to Aunt Ellen when she told me not to aggravate the doctors.

*But I couldn't let people take their advice when it was
wrong, could I?*

Why didn't I just watch my tongue?

I didn't do anything wrong!

I let them win. I let them take my work away.

On Friday she woke bleary-eyed and headachy, an empty day
stretching ahead. Fearful of another sleepless night, after
Aunt Ellen left she decided on a long walk; perhaps a tired
body would overpower her unquiet mind.

She'd taken to avoiding busier streets; in London there
was always a back route you could take, through little alleyways and courts that were dark and dank, but weren't full of
people who might have bought a print of you and hung it
on their wall to laugh at. Somehow though, she missed her
way in the back streets behind the Strand, and came out on
Drury Lane, opposite a theatre. A man on a stepladder was
pasting up the bill for the next show, and as she stopped to
get her bearings, he climbed down.

She was dreaming, surely? She had to blink to check. But
the name of the play was still the same.

Love Earns Its Reward

Or

The Bonesetter and the Irishman

Underneath were listed the roles, and the actors playing them.
She didn't recognise the first two names. But the third one
was very familiar.

FRANCES QUINN

Moll Crunchem the bonesetter: Roxana Worthington
Seamus O'Leary: Will Collyer
Nora Nolan: Lucinda Ellwood

Chapter 74

She had to hide. She doubled back down the dark little alley and pressed her back against the wall of a house where the windows were shuttered. Her chest was tight and she had to breathe deeply, a dozen or more times, before it eased. Even then, she couldn't bring herself to move.

Someone had taken her humiliation and made entertainment out of it. It was going to be raked up all over again, in the papers, and in the street. And her own sister was taking part in it.

How could they? How could she?

Shock gave way to anger; she was hot with it. There'd be a song, wouldn't there? When Lucinda played Tilly Tipworth, her final song, 'My Love Was True', was everywhere: all that summer, you heard flower sellers singing snatches of it and messenger boys whistling it. And jokes: you didn't use a name like Moll Crunchem unless you wanted to get people laughing.

It was one thing for the doctors to mock her, and for people in the street to snigger. But Lucinda . . . no, that was too much. Well, she couldn't stop her, but before Lucinda stepped onto that stage, she was going to hear exactly what her sister thought of her.

When the same sullen maid showed Durie in, Lucinda was reclining on a chaise, flicking through a yellowed copy of the *Lady's Magazine*; a pile of others lay by her feet, the top one open at a picture of her as Tilly Tipworth.

'You cow,' said Durie.

'Well, that's a nice greeting.' Lucinda sat up, and made a shooing movement at the maid. 'We won't be wanting tea, Mary. Close the door after you.'

'How could you, Lucinda?'

Lucinda rolled her eyes.

'I suppose this is about *Love Earns Its Reward*?'

'Yes it is! Are you really so desperate for attention that you'd be in a play that mocks your own sister? That takes the most humiliating thing that's ever happened to me and makes a joke of it?'

'I'm not desperate for attention, I'm desperate to make a living, and it's your fault I need to! If you hadn't blabbed to your so-called husband, so he could blab to the newspapers, I'd still be living in Queen Street on ninety pounds a year, so don't come over all sanctimonious with me.'

Durie opened her mouth to say it wasn't Malachy and then closed it again. Because of course it was. Another contribution to the fund he took back to Ireland.

'It's not as though I didn't warn you,' said Lucinda. 'So if you look ridiculous, you've only yourself to blame.'

'I'm your sister. Doesn't that mean anything to you at all?'

Lucinda sighed.

'I didn't take the role because it was you, did I? I'd have done it just the same if it had been some other woman daft enough to be taken in like that. And if I hadn't, someone else would have.'

Of course; she'd forgotten how Lucinda could always justify her behaviour to herself. It struck her then that her sister was very like Malachy in that. No point in saying anything more. At the door, she turned.

'I don't want this play to happen at all,' she said. 'But if you really think it makes no difference to me whether you're in it or not, then you are more stupid than I would ever have believed possible.'

For a second, Lucinda looked as though she'd been smacked, but it was only a second. As Durie closed the door, she shouted, 'I take it you don't want a ticket then?'

After that the decision was easy. Aunt Ellen came to see her off; as they waited in the courtyard of the inn for the horses to be hitched and the luggage stowed, she said, 'You can always come back, you know that, don't you? If it doesn't work out with Richie, you come back and we'll figure something out.'

'I know. I'll miss you, Aunt Ellen.'

'And I'll miss you. Very much.'

There was only one other passenger for the first stage of the trip, an elderly lady who fell asleep shortly after they crossed London Bridge, leaving Durie alone with her thoughts. They'd be surprised to see her, when she got home. She hadn't written: people would be talking about the stupid play soon, she had to get away before that started. Besides, she couldn't bring herself to write to Richie and ask if she could come back and be his assistant; he'd probably make her wait for an answer, just to get his own back. She'd say it was just a visit and then, in a few days, talk to him about staying for good.

What would her father have made of it all? She'd read his last letter again, before leaving.

Your mother would have been very proud of you, and so am I.

They wouldn't be now. But perhaps they wouldn't think it so much of a failure if she was at least returning home to help Richie keep the work in the family. The prospect was still a humiliating one, but the alternative was impossible: staying in London, becoming a figure of fun again; being reminded, every time she left the house, of how stupid she'd been, and this time, not even having her work to make up for it. At least if she went home, she'd still be fixing people.

Chapter 75

How strange it was, being back in the house without her father there. His coat still hung behind the door, and his shoes were under the sideboard, where Margie always put them, tutting at his untidiness, after he'd sat by the fire and kicked them off. As though he might walk into the room at any moment, and yet you couldn't look at Margie's thin, drawn face and sad eyes without remembering that he never would.

'I couldn't bear to move them,' Margie said. 'I know it's silly, I know he's gone, but I still like seeing them there.'

She'd cried when Durie walked in, late that afternoon. Happy tears, she said, but they came so readily that the other kind couldn't be far away. Richie was out on a job over towards Brighton, and wouldn't be back till late – 'I think there's a young lady over there,' said Margie, 'but he's keeping me in the dark.' So tea was made, fruit cake cut, and they'd sat in the garden, in the dappled shade of the apple tree, just the two of them, enjoying the summer sunshine.

As a blackbird sang from high up in the branches, and a lone bumblebee buzzed around the honeysuckle that scrambled over the back wall of the house, they talked about Durie's father, about all the humdrum things that make up a person: the way he sliced butter onto his bread as though it was cheese; the tune he always hummed when he was shaving; his attachment to one old shirt that Margie had mended so many times it was more thread than fabric.

'This is so nice,' said Margie. 'Nobody else mentions him any more, not even Richie. He thinks it'll upset me, but I like talking about your father, it brings him back for a minute or two.'

'I had a friend, in London,' said Durie. 'His daughter died, very young, and he said the same, that people got embarrassed if he talked about her.'

'It's not badly meant, but it makes you feel even more lonely.'

Margie poured them both some more tea and handed Durie her cup.

'I've been sitting here, going on, when you've been left alone too, and I haven't even asked about your troubles.'

Durie shook her head.

'It's not the same. You loved father. I didn't love Malachy O'Neill. I loved someone who didn't exist, and I'm sorry that I was so stupid but I'm not sorry he left. I'm not even sorry he's dead. That's all there is to say.'

It wasn't, of course, but telling Margie what had happened since would bring up the question of her working with Richie and she wasn't ready for that yet. To change the subject, she said, 'I meant to say, Aunt Ellen sends her regards.'

'She's a good woman, your aunt. That's one good thing that came out of Lucinda's trouble, that your father was reconciled with her before the end. They never should have left it so long, but she was stubborn, and so was he. But it gave me a bad conscience to think it was on account of me they'd fallen out – she told you the story, I expect?'

Durie started to say Aunt Ellen had, but Margie told it again anyway, how Aunt Ellen thought her father disrespectful to her mother, in marrying again so soon.

'But there he was, you a baby and Lucinda only little, what was he supposed to do? And let me tell you, I was in no doubt – I came a very poor second to your mother in his eyes. Well, anyone would have – half the lads in town were in love with her, she had a face you just wanted to look at, like your sister has. And she was sweet-natured with it.'

Margie knew her?

How could it be that they hadn't known that?

Margie smiled wistfully.

'He came to love me, in his way. And a better husband I couldn't have wished for. But when he married me, he wasn't forgetting your mother, he was just trying to take care of you.'

Durie's heart was hammering so hard she could feel it in her ears.

'I didn't realise you knew her,' she said carefully, not wanting all the questions to spill out.

'Of course I did! Knew her all my life, danced at their wedding, wept at her burying. You've forgotten what Lewes is like, living in that big city, full of strangers. I thought to myself, that time we came, how odd it must be, never seeing a familiar face and . . .'

As Margie rambled on, Durie tried to put the most

important question into words, in case there might only be a chance to ask one before Margie's smile was replaced with the 'We don't talk about this' look she remembered so well.

'Did my mother see me?' she asked.

Margie looked puzzled.

'See you? What do you mean?'

'I know she died giving birth to me. Because I was too big, and I wore her out. But did she see me, before she died?'

'Durie, love, your mother didn't die giving birth to you. Who on earth told you that? She died of childbed fever, twelve days after you were born.'

The words were such a shock, and then such a relief, that tears came and Durie couldn't stop them. Margie took her hands.

'You really thought that, all this time?'

Durie nodded.

'Oh, Durie. I wish I'd known. We didn't talk about her, did we, ever? Your father didn't like to, because it upset him so much, and I'll tell you the truth, it made me so jealous to see that, I was glad he didn't. But if we'd known you'd got such a terrible idea in your head, we'd have told you.'

'Tell me now then.'

'Well, it was a quick labouring, much quicker than with your sister, that's often the way with second babies, but then you were such a tiny little scrap, the midwife thought you were early. I remember she said, this one should have waited a bit longer—'

'I was small?'

'You were tiny! For the first few days, we weren't sure you'd live. You didn't want to suck, and that's always a bad sign. But the third day, you got the hang of it. I remember Elizabeth sitting up in bed, with you in her arms, and saying to me, "Look at her, Margie, did you ever see such a strong face on a baby? She's a fighter, this one – she's going to take on the world." That's why she named you Endurance, because you didn't give up.'

All those years, she'd thought her father had given her that name because of the suffering she'd caused her mother.

But she named me. For myself. Because she thought I was strong, and a fighter.

There was another question Durie wanted to ask, only she didn't trust her voice to speak. But Margie answered it without her needing to.

'She loved you so much, it shone out of her. That's how I try to remember her, how she was that day. It was the next morning she was taken bad – that's often the way with childbed fever.'

She squeezed Durie's hands, then let them go and sat back.

'We should have told you all this before, and I'm sorry we didn't.'

They sat in silence for a few minutes, watching the bee buzzing in and out of the honeysuckle blossoms. In the warmth of the sun, the scent drifted across; in later years, Durie would always smile at the smell of honeysuckle.

Margie sighed.

'There's something else you need to know as well,' she said, 'and I'm worried you'll hate me for it, but I'm going to tell you anyway. It was because of me your father didn't take you as his assistant.'

'I don't understand.'

'Oh, I don't say he loved the idea, not at first. He thought bonesetting was a man's job, you know that. But he saw you had the knack, and he was coming round to it.'

'So why . . . ?'

'I asked him to take Richie. To prove he loved my son as much as he loved your mother's daughters.'

And to prove he loved you as much as he did my mother.

Poor Margie.

'You've every right to be angry with me,' Margie went on, 'but didn't it work out for the best? Your father was so proud of you, making a success of it up there in London. And you proved your mother right, didn't you? You took on the world.'

Lying in her old bed that night, Durie was bone-tired from the long journey but the thoughts whirling round in her head chased sleep away. She couldn't be angry with Margie and she'd told her so, before she succumbed to a tearful hug – Margie's tears now, not hers – and promised never to tell Richie he hadn't won fair and square.

The revelation made her feel less prickly about her brother's offer and when he arrived home late that evening, their greeting was friendly. If he'd been annoyed at her reply to his letter, he wasn't showing it; perhaps he was relieved she wasn't bringing it up either. Richie had never been one to look for a fight. He even asked her opinion about a customer with a backache that nothing seemed to ease. Perhaps working with him wouldn't be as bad as she feared? Perhaps, tomorrow, she should tell him she'd take up his offer.

But what would her mother think if she saw her now? Saw that she'd turned tail and run. Given up.

She loved you so much, it shone out of her.

Well, if her mother loved her, she wouldn't want her to go back to all that, surely? To people smirking at you in the street, and laughing about your husband running away because he couldn't stand to bed you, and buying pictures that made you look ugly and mad, so they could laugh at them. And then your own sister not just joining in with the mockery but using it to revive her career. A mother who loved you wouldn't want that for her daughter.

Chapter 76

After a very nearly sleepless night, in the morning she offered to fetch the water; the walk might wake her up. Richie looked up from preparing his bag.

'I'm pretty good at carrying the water now,' he said.

'I didn't mean—'

He winked.

'I'm joking. Come on, we'll fetch it together.'

As they strolled along the High Street, their buckets occasionally clanging together, people nodded to him, respectfully, like they used to do with her father. She didn't miss his sideways look to see if she'd noticed.

She said, 'This is how I first saw him work, you know. We were fetching water, and a woman came running up, saying her husband had hurt his shoulder. I brought him his bag, and stayed to watch.'

'You were so keen to do it, I couldn't understand it back then.'

'You like it now though?'

He nodded.

'Father was right, it's in our blood. I wouldn't want to do anything else.'

'Aunt Ellen says a person's very lucky if they can make a living from something they enjoy.'

'Well, it's you I've got to thank for my luck.'

'Me?'

'It was you being so good at it that made me want to get better. And it was only when I got better that I began to like it.'

At the pump, he took her bucket and set it underneath. As he worked the handle, he said, without looking at her, 'You were right, you know, about me asking you to be my assistant. I wasn't thinking straight – Father died so suddenly, and at that time he was still doing most of the work. You know what it's like once the cold weather comes, I was called all over the place. And Mother was in a state, I didn't like leaving her, but I didn't want to let him down by not managing it all. So I was a bit desperate and I wrote that letter without thinking what I was saying.'

Why hadn't she thought of that?

'I should have realised. I should have come back to help.'

He moved the full bucket aside, and slid his own under the pump.

'Well, I managed, and it was probably good for me. I don't know that he'd ever have let me take on much while he was alive. He trusted you more than he did me.'

Durie reached over for her bucket, so he wouldn't see her face when she told the lie.

'He chose you, not me. And people here respect you now, like they did him.'

'I hope so,' he said, and in his face she caught a glimpse of the little brother who used to try and impress his big sisters. 'I try my best.'

The second bucket was full. She turned to go.

'Wait,' he said. 'I just wanted to say, if you ever get tired of living in the city, there's custom enough for us to work as partners. If you wanted to.'

If she was going to stay, now was the time to say it. She looked back down the High Street. A handful of people going about their business; a single cart rumbling past in one direction, the Brighton coach just visible in the distance heading the other way. No hawkers yelling their wares at the tops of their voices. No fog of coal dust in the air. No one selling newspapers. No theatre.

She could do her work in peace here. The widowed Mrs O'Neill, daughter of the bonesetter, come back to work with her brother. Margie had told people when she married, but they didn't know the rest and they didn't need to. A fresh start.

But she called you Endurance because you didn't give up.

'Thanks,' she said. 'Maybe one day I will. But I have things to do in London first.'

When Durie left a week later, Margie came to see her off.

'It's been so nice having you here,' she said, flapping a handkerchief. 'Oh, look at me, tears again! I'll put you off coming back.'

'I'll visit more often, I promise.'

Durie took a deep breath, because she wasn't sure if her own voice might wobble and she didn't want to set Margie off properly and have to leave her crying when the coachman yelled everyone aboard.

'Thank you for telling me about my mother,' she said.

'I just wish we'd told you earlier,' said Margie. 'She was proud of you then, and she'd be proud of you now. And so am I.'

The coachman shouted for the stragglers, and there was only time for a quick goodbye. As the coach pulled away, Durie thought how lucky she'd been to have two mothers who'd loved her.

Chapter 77

Aunt Ellen's mouth formed a perfect O when she came home to find Durie sitting in the parlour, and then broke into a smile.

'You're back. To stay?'

'If Lucifer will let me. I see he's taken possession of my bed.'

'He's warming it for you, I expect. He's a clever cat, he knew you'd be back. I only hoped you would.'

A bit of an awkward moment then, as Durie thought perhaps they ought to hug, and it looked like Aunt Ellen might be thinking the same, but they didn't, and the moment passed.

'Well,' said Aunt Ellen, sitting at the table, 'what changed your mind?'

'My mother,' said Durie.

She started to tell about the conversation with Margie, but of course none of it was news to Aunt Ellen.

'Why didn't you ask me about your mother? I had no idea you didn't know how she died.'

'Because I thought I did know. If you'd spent your whole

life thinking it was your fault your mother died, you wouldn't ask about it either. But anyway, the important thing Margie said was that my mother was proud of me for being strong, and not giving up. So I'm not giving up, I'm back and I'm going to do my work here in London.'

'I'm pleased you want to. But it won't be easy to get your customers back.'

Durie shook her head.

'I did a lot of thinking in Lewes. Aunt Ellen, you know I'm grateful for everything you did for me – getting me talked about, getting all the fashionable people to recommend me to their friends. I couldn't have got started here without you.'

'But?'

'But I'm not selling jam tarts. The knack is a gift, and it's not right that only people who can pay me a guinea a time get the benefit of it. So I'm going to work like my father did – charging enough to make a living, but fixing people who can't pay as well. There's plenty of need, I saw it in Wapping and that can't be the only place.'

'What about your old customers?'

'I think the regulars will come back – they stuck with me through all the nonsense, didn't they? And if anyone else with a big house and a smart carriage wants to pay me a guinea a time and doesn't mind being touched by the same hands that have treated a docker or a shrimp seller, they know where to find me. But I won't be chasing the people who dropped me like I was poison because my husband deserted me.'

'Well, that should appease the doctors, at least.'

'I hope so. But if it doesn't, they won't have the same

influence over the people I'll be fixing now. Whatever else they do, they won't be able to take my work away again.'

'You have been doing a lot of thinking.'

'I know you won't approve, and I won't make a lot of money, but I don't need a lot. I really only wanted it to give Tom a better start in life, and maybe it's better for him to make his own money too.'

'I'm hardly in a position to disapprove. I've always tried to give you good advice, but I haven't shown the best of judgement lately, have I?'

'Malachy wasn't your fault.'

'But me falling for his act didn't help. Anyway, the point is, you're right. You know better than I do how to use your gift. So, when do you intend to start?'

'Tomorrow. I'll go to Wapping, get that carter's wife to put the word about for me.'

'You don't think you should wait a bit?' said Aunt Ellen. 'Lucinda's play starts tomorrow. Wouldn't it be better to keep your head down till it's over and done with?'

'I tried keeping my head down before. And I'm not doing it any more. So tomorrow evening, how about we go to the theatre?'

Chapter 78

The carter's wife answered the door with one of the smaller children grizzling in her arms.

'Oh,' she said. 'We meant to bring the crutch back, but—'

'I haven't come for that,' said Durie. 'I need your help. Can I come in?'

They sat at the small table in the corner, two of the children playing on the floor, the other fixing Durie with a hard stare from his mother's lap, as she explained her plans.

'So you'll charge people the same as the farrier does now?' said the woman.

'If they break a bone, yes, or put a joint out. But I can help people with other problems as well – sore joints, for example.'

'Plenty of those round here. All the dockers have stiff shoulders, for a start.'

'If I were to say I'll come here once a month, and visit people in their homes, would you tell your neighbours? People here don't know me personally, so—'

'They all know what you did for Joe. And we'll always be grateful to you for it, so you leave that to me, I'll put the word around.'

'Thank you. I'll leave you a list of my prices, they're reasonable, but if anyone can't pay, tell them to come anyway.'

The woman laughed.

'What if they all say they can't pay?'

She'd asked her father the same thing, all those years ago.

'I'll worry about that if it happens,' she said.

The first night of a new play was always popular, and there was quite a crowd strolling up the Strand towards the theatre that evening. The whispers and sniggers started as soon as it became obvious they were heading there too.

'Are you sure about this?' said Aunt Ellen. 'We don't have to go in.'

'We do.'

Inside, a woman said to her companion, in a not very quiet whisper, 'Fancy her coming to see it.'

Durie glanced behind; as the voice suggested, ordinary folk, respectable but not rich. She took a deep breath, turned and handed them one of the cards she'd had printed that morning, listing her new prices.

'Enjoy the show, ladies. I've heard it's very comical.'

The women tittered, but they took the card, and Durie handed more to the gawpers around them. Exactly as she'd hoped, they were all ordinary-looking too: the fashionable set didn't turn up early, they sent their servants to keep their seats.

Their tickets were for a box beside the stage, but with an hour still to go, people were milling about, greeting acquaintances and queuing for fruit and bonbons.

'You go up now,' she said to Aunt Ellen, 'and get us seats

at the front. I want to hand out some more cards before it
starts.'

She worked her way round the theatre, smiling and offering
a card whenever she heard a whispered 'Is that her?'

A man reached for one.

'Bad back,' he said. 'They say you can work wonders.'

'I can. That's how I got rich enough to land a thieving
husband.'

Behind her people laughed, and someone said, 'Good for
her.'

When they lit the candles on the stage, Durie went up and
stood in the shadows at the back of the box. Her heart was
pounding and for a second, she considered just slipping into
her seat beside Aunt Ellen.

You're a fighter, remember?

The orchestra was playing now, a merry, vaguely Irish-
sounding tune, and as the strains of that faded away, Lucinda
came on, barefoot and dressed in rags. As she began a mawkish
little ballad about being a poor girl whose lover was off on
a boat to England, people stopped chatting and eating and
fiddling with their fans, and every face looked at her.

Durie waited until she got to a bit about how much she
missed him – you could hear tears in her voice, she really
was very good – before slowly and noisily jostling her way
to the front of the box, knocking three people half out of
their seats as she passed. They were right beside one of the
great lanterns, so she was easy to see, and the buzz of conversation as people in the box realised who she was caught the
attention of those down below. By the time she reached the

front, there were as many faces looking up at her as at Lucinda. Lucinda kept her poise and didn't follow their gaze, but if you were looking for it, there was a flicker of irritation in her eyes.

Ignoring Aunt Ellen's quizzical look, Durie stood by her seat for a full minute – she counted the seconds – fiddling with her hat as though she was having trouble taking it off. Then, taking care to make it look accidental, she fumbled and tossed it over the edge of the box. That turned more faces her way, and as she held up her hands in a gesture of resignation and took her seat, laughter bubbled up as those who hadn't already realised who she was heard it from a neighbour.

That was when Lucinda glanced up to see what they were looking at. The mixture of recognition and surprise flashed across her face for just a second before she went back to being the lovelorn maid. But Durie saw it, and she saw that Lucinda knew she'd seen it.

'Well,' said Aunt Ellen, as Lucinda made her exit and a troupe of unnecessary Irish maidens began a dance, 'it wasn't just your work you've been plotting and planning about, was it? That was naughty, but I can't say she doesn't deserve it.' She peered down at the seats below. 'And with any luck, we've seen the last of that blasted hat.'

To give the audience a pretty couple to sigh over, Lucinda's part had been shoehorned in – the poor but loving maiden whose arms Seamus had been torn from when he was forced to seek his fortune in London. And far from being drawn in by his promises of love, Moll Crunchem pursued him, until his simple Irish head was turned and he agreed to marry her. Well, Durie hadn't expected flattery and, if anything, Moll was less of a fool than she'd been. Aunt Ellen tutted at every ridiculous new turn in the story, and more than once, Durie felt her aunt's anxious eyes on her, but she made sure she laughed with the rest, and when Seamus sailed back to Ireland, clutching improbably heavy sacks of Moll's money, no one cheered louder than her.

Put that in your newspapers.

Then it was time for Lucinda's last song, a ballad bemoaning her lost love and asking why he'd been so long away. She hit every note, but she had a distracted air, and once or twice her eyes flicked towards their box, though she didn't look at Durie directly. The audience noticed; where before they'd fallen silent when she sang, this time there was muttering, and people nudged each other. Lucinda could see that, of course, and in the second verse she faltered and seemed to forget her words. At that point a messenger brought the news that Seamus was on his way home, and she gathered herself up well enough to belt out the rest, but Durie had got what she wanted by then.

They didn't talk much on the way home. Durie had expected to feel triumphant, and she had, while they were inside the theatre. Lucinda intended that play to make her the public's darling again, but as the audience spilled down the stairs from the boxes, laughing and joking, no one was talking about her. The newspapers wouldn't be either. How furious she must have been, back there behind the stage.

But as soon as they were outside in the cool evening air, the triumph slipped away and Durie felt as if she'd just walked a hundred miles. It was exhausting, pretending. How did Malachy do it so well, for so long? Her face ached from the fake smiles, and her body was stiff from the effort of holding her head high and looking as though she hadn't a care in the world. And for what? She'd got her own back on Lucinda, but she'd a hundred times rather Lucinda had shown her some loyalty and said no to the play in the first place.

Was it entirely Lucinda's fault though? It was Malachy who told the newspapers about Tom, she couldn't doubt that now. And though it was pure chance he'd spotted Lucinda coming to the house that day, if she hadn't told him about Tom, it wouldn't have mattered. Lucinda wouldn't have lost her duke, and perhaps it really was true that that was why she'd said yes to the play.

'You're very quiet,' said Aunt Ellen. 'Penny for your thoughts?'

'I was thinking,' said Durie, 'how much I miss her.'

Chapter 79

The *Mercury*'s report was the first she read, and it said exactly what she'd hoped.

> *At the New Playhouse this week, patrons were entertained to see a certain female bonesetter attending a performance of* Love Earns Its Reward, Or The Bonesetter and the Irishman. *The lady laughed heartily at the story of Moll Crunchem and her Irish husband, and when the Irishman returned to his true love in Ireland taking Moll's fortune with him, she was heard to say that Ireland was welcome to any number of useless husbands, and for her part, she was glad to be rid of one, whatever the price.*

No mention of Lucinda. Over the next few days, other papers picked up the story, and though none of the words quoted had actually left Durie's mouth, the gist was the same, that she was in perfectly good humour, not mad, drunk or hysterical with grief, and glad to be rid of Malachy. One or two mentioned Lucinda's return to the theatre, but the play itself was entirely overshadowed by the entertainment off stage.

That Friday evening, as they sat reading in the parlour, Betsy opened the door to a knock. Hearing Lucinda's voice, Durie looked up, expecting Aunt Ellen to be as surprised as she was. But Aunt Ellen said, 'I asked her to come. You two need to make this up.'

Lucinda looked surprised to see Durie too; Aunt Ellen must have said she'd be out.

'Well,' she said, without so much as a hello, 'that was a fine performance you gave the other night. I had no idea you could act so well.'

'Nor did I,' said Durie. 'But then I had no idea you were so disloyal, so we've both learned something, haven't we?'

'Stop it,' said Aunt Ellen. 'Lucinda, sit down. I didn't ask you here for the pair of you to fight like silly children. You've both behaved badly, and you both had your reasons. Can you agree to that at least?'

'Yes,' said Durie.

Lucinda pursed her lips, then said, 'She's got to admit it was the Irishman who talked to the papers about me.'

'Yes,' said Durie. 'I'm sure it was. And I'm sorry. But I didn't tell him on purpose, and I didn't know he'd find out who you were.'

'I know that,' said Lucinda. 'I just wanted you to say it. And all right, I'm sorry about the play. I should have said no to it.'

'Well, that's a start,' said Aunt Ellen. 'Now, stubbornness runs in this family, and because of it, I lost your father for too many years. If it hadn't been for Lucinda's trouble, I wouldn't even know you two now, and that would have been a terrible loss to me. Though I hope it won't swell your heads to hear it.'

Lucinda looked at Durie and gave a little roll of her eyes, and Durie bit back a smile.

'So I want you to promise that you'll remember something for me. And it's this: you are stronger together. All women are. You've both seen enough of men, surely, to know you can't count on them. So make sure you can count on each other.'

'I promise,' said Durie.

'Lucinda?' said Aunt Ellen.

'As it happens,' said Lucinda, 'I was thinking that anyway. And I've got an idea.'

Chapter 80

The result of Lucinda's idea appeared in the *Mercury* three days later.

The story of Mrs O'Neill the bonesetter's visit to Love Earns Its Reward *at the New Playhouse took a curious turn in recent days, when we learned she is the sister of none other than Miss Lucinda Ellwood, star of the play which — whisper it — bears a certain similarity to Mrs O'Neill's own recent marital troubles. An acquaintance of the sisters revealed that Mrs O'Neill was secretly delighted with Miss Ellwood's performance, but declined to divulge which parts of the play were a true rendition of her story, saying the audience should find the clues for themselves. During her visit, Mrs O'Neill took the opportunity of acquainting patrons with her new working arrangements, offering bonesetting services and manipulation to customers in their own homes, at moderate prices. Customers in straitened circumstances may even be attended free of charge, at Mrs O'Neill's discretion.*

'You're not as daft as you look,' said Durie, as she and Lucinda read it together. 'They've said everything we wanted them to.'

'Well, it was you that gave me the idea, with your antics at the play. You made them look where you wanted them to look, and that's what we're going to do now. They think they've found out a juicy little titbit – they don't know it's us that fed it to them. Your friend Jeannie did a good job.'

Durie wasn't sure if she could really call Jeannie a friend, but it had a nice sound to it. It had come as quite a surprise, how pleased Jeannie was to see her when she'd called in to the coffee house early one morning. They'd taken a dish of coffee together and Jeannie had almost fallen off her chair when Durie told her Lucinda Ellwood was her sister. She'd readily agreed to disclose the 'secret' to the penny scribbler.

'They got their fun out of you,' she said. 'Let's see if you can get some fun out of them.'

Perhaps Durie might call in again, if she was passing early in the morning, to say thanks. It had been nice, chatting to Jeannie, and she wouldn't mind doing it again.

Over the following week, the story was copied by half a dozen of the London papers.

'Time for the next stage,' said Lucinda.

On Friday evening, they hired an open chaise pulled by two chestnut ponies, with a driver, to go to the Marylebone pleasure gardens. Lucinda was dressed in blue, with a lace-edged cap not unlike the one she'd worn as Tilly Tipworth, and Durie had bought a new hat, in a bold shade of green, to which she'd attached the monkey bones, making sure, on

Lucinda's instructions, that they were easy to see. That was the point of it all, of course, but still, it came as a shock when passers-by were looking and pointing even before they'd left Mayfair. Lucinda smiled and waved.

'I know you don't like this,' she said to Durie, 'but trust me. And for goodness' sake, smile.'

Durie didn't like it, not at all, and she liked it even less when they turned onto Marylebone Lane, where their driver had to fall in behind all the carriages heading in the same direction. People were strolling along too, and as the chaise slowed to walking pace, their words floated up.

'Look, that's them!'

'Sisters, can you believe it?'

She didn't know where to look, or how to have her face, and then when a frisky horse up ahead brought the whole parade to a halt, an elderly couple actually stopped and stared in at them.

'Look, it's that bonesetter woman,' the man said.

When that turned other heads towards them, she took a deep breath.

You're a fighter, remember?

'Yes, that's me,' she said, with what she hoped was a smile, though it felt like a grimace. She leaned out and handed the man a card. 'Next time that knee gets stiff, here's where to find me.'

She'd only seen him walk a few steps, but both their faces told her she was right. As the chaise moved off, the woman called out, 'I'll see he does!'

Lucinda grinned at Durie.

'See?' she said. 'You can do it.'

By the time they arrived, she'd managed a few waves, and when she heard a woman say 'took all her money and went back to Ireland', she called out, 'Yes, and Ireland's welcome to him!'

To her surprise, it raised a little cheer among the people walking by.

'Told you,' said Lucinda. 'That's what I saw when you did your little caper at the theatre – you made them look at you differently. They're not laughing at you now, they're laughing with you.'

At the gardens, they strolled, arm in arm, along the avenues of sycamore trees. Durie still had to force herself to smile when people stared, but Lucinda, of course, was in her element: waving and twinkling, calling a hello to perfect strangers and singing little snatches of songs from the play, just quietly as though she was singing to herself and had no idea anyone was listening, let alone that they were turning to look and walking off whistling the tune.

When music drifted over from the bandstand, they joined the edge of the crowd. After a few lively tunes, the master of ceremonies, an oily-looking character in a very tight crimson coat, stepped forward.

'Please welcome this evening's guest, Miss Maria Morton,' he said.

A young woman with red hair and an ample bosom imperfectly contained in a lilac dress launched into a popular folk song, encouraging the audience to sing along.

'Right,' said Lucinda. 'Here we go.'

She tapped the woman in front on the shoulder. The woman turned, making a slight gap in the crowd; Lucinda gave a big smile and said, in the voice that carried all the way to the back of the theatre without her ever seeming to raise it, 'Excuse me . . . thank you, so kind,' and dragged Durie through to stand in front of the woman. They stood there until the song ended, heads turning towards them all the while, then Lucinda repeated the process three times more, until they were by the stage and there couldn't be a person there who didn't know it – including poor Miss Morton, who was looking distinctly irritated.

Lucinda whispered in Durie's ear, 'Learned that from you too.'

The audience were singing along now, and Lucinda joined in. Quietly at first but then, quite as though she'd got carried away by the music and couldn't help herself, her voice soared above the others, her pure, clear tones making Miss Morton's sound flat. When the song finished, she put her hand to her mouth apologetically, and blushed very convincingly. Had she taught herself to do that at will too now, like the crying?

'You have no shame,' Durie whispered.

'I haven't finished yet,' Lucinda replied. 'Wait here.'

The master of ceremonies smiled as Lucinda walked towards him. While Miss Morton did her best to win back her audience with a spirited rendition of 'The Dashing White Sergeant', Durie watched Lucinda whisper in his ear and get a nod in response. Even before the applause had finished, he bounded up the steps to the bandstand.

'Thank you, Miss Morton. And now, a surprise and a treat – Miss Lucinda Ellwood has agreed to sing for us!'

Lucinda stepped lightly up onto the stage – blushing again! 'Only one song,' she said, wagging her finger, 'because I'm really just here for a jolly evening with my sister, Mrs O'Neill, the famous bonesetter.'

She really was incorrigible. And at the same time, quite marvellous.

'This song is from my new play, *Love Earns Its Reward*. If you want to see it, do hurry – tickets are selling very fast.'

Chapter 81

The play ran to full houses for weeks. Between the people who'd watched Lucinda steal the show from Miss Morton, the ones who'd read the original revelation and were looking for clues about the real story of Durie and Malachy, and the ones who saw the report of their visit to the gardens, it seemed there was barely a person in London who hadn't bought a ticket. And before the run was halfway through, Lucinda had negotiated a doubling of her fee – 'I said to them, do you think we'd be selling this many if you had anyone else playing Nora?' – and been promised the lead role in the next two productions.

Gleefully reporting the conversation to Durie and Aunt Ellen afterwards, she said, 'And from now on, I'm going to be like you, Aunt Ellen, and avoid men completely.' She dashed a hand to her chest, and struck a pose, mock-dramatic. 'My only love will be the stage.'

'I'll believe that when I see it,' said Aunt Ellen.

'Maybe I won't avoid them completely. But you were right. I'm lucky I can earn my own living, and my audiences have been more faithful to me than men have. I was daft to give it up and I won't be doing that again.'

Durie, meanwhile, found five customers waiting for her when she made the first of her monthly visits to Wapping, all willing to pay the moderate fees listed on her cards. And requests were landing on the hall table again from new customers, working people who could never have afforded a guinea a time. One, a cobbler with a sore shoulder caused by stooping over his work, told her:

'I'll be honest with you, Mrs O'Neill, I wouldn't have entertained the idea of a female bonesetter before. But my wife said to me, she was good enough for the nobs, she's good enough for us.'

So Aunt Ellen had been right, in the end, even if it hadn't worked out quite the way she'd expected.

A few weeks before Tom's sixth birthday, Durie sat in her room, sharpening a quill, paper by her side, and thought about what to write to him. So much about the year gone by she had no wish to remember, and certainly no wish to tell him about. Dear Tom, after I was made a fool of by a man I thought loved me and lost all the money I saved for you, I become the laughing stock of London, and my customers deserted me. And yet, though every word of it would be true, now it was like someone else's story.

The monkey skeleton lay on the nightstand – earlier, she'd been trying to work out what might help all the dockers' stiff shoulders – and the loose jaw bones fell into the look of a smile, just as they had the night before her wedding. That she'd chosen the wrong man that night was obvious, but could she really say, now, that she wished she'd never married Malachy? She picked the skeleton up, and its familiar grimace replaced the smile. You could look at it in two ways, couldn't you? All she'd lost: the husband, who was no loss at all, and the money and the wealthy customers, neither of which she missed. Or all she'd gained. Finding out the truth about her birth and her name, and learning that her father hadn't really chosen Richie at all. Actually getting Lucinda's respect for the business at *Love Earns Its Reward*, and coming to respect her sister in return; that performance at the pleasure gardens still made her laugh when she thought of it. And finally getting to do her work the way she always should have, the way her father had, and his father before him. Aunt Ellen had meant well, but Durie wasn't selling jam tarts, she was fixing people, and that was a gift you were supposed to share with whoever needed it.

There was really only one thing worth having that she'd lost by marrying Malachy. But perhaps it didn't have to stay lost. She set the pen and paper aside; before she wrote to Tom, there was something else she needed to do.

Chapter 82

The price had gone up to eightpence. She paid with shaking hands, and followed the crowd across the moat. A young lad was yelling 'I'm going to see the lions!', dancing round and round in his excitement, and a tiny part of her mind was doing likewise, but most of it was saying, wait and see, it's been a long time. We might have nothing to say to each other. It might just be a silly romantic dream, straight from one of Lucinda's plays. Or – how had she not realised this? – it might be horribly awkward. Because what did you say to someone, when the last time you met, they'd told you they loved you, and you'd said the same, and then you hadn't spoken again for five years? Nice weather we're having, do you still love me? And that was if he wanted to talk to her at all, when as far as he knew, she hadn't even bothered to answer his letter.

She'd asked Aunt Ellen to try and remember what he'd said in it. It was a long time ago, of course, but one phrase, Aunt Ellen said, had stuck in her mind: 'I never stopped thinking about you.' She could almost hear him saying it, and it was quite a thing to say. But since then he'd have read, or heard, about her humiliation. Could he think of her the same way after that? What if, when he set eyes on her again, all he saw was the half-crazy woman in that horrible print? He must have seen it, everyone had. Maybe it would be better not to know, to remember the time they'd had and be happy with that.

I could still turn back, I don't have to go in.

The pungent smell of meat and wee and dung hit her, and nothing sends you back in time like a smell, does it? A Sunday morning, waking up happy to be seeing him. The weight of Tom in her arms, his contented gurgling on the long walk there. Standing by Crowley's cage, watching for George to walk up; his smile as he caught sight of them.

Her footsteps slowed; the dancing boy's mother tutted as the family walked round her. If I don't go in, he'll remember me the way I was, and it won't be spoiled. I've got my work, I don't need anything more, do I?

She called you Endurance because you didn't give up.

From inside came a great roar. Crowley, surely? The little boy turned round.

'We're going to see the lions,' he said.

Durie reached up and touched one of the bones in her hat, for luck.

'So am I,' she said.

'You look scared,' said the boy. 'I'm not.'

'I'm very scared. But I'm going in anyway.'

Best to go straight to the hut and knock. He might not even be there, might have had a final falling out with the Keeper of the Lions and be working somewhere else entirely. Better to find out now than dawdle around for nothing. She walked up to the hut, raised her hand to knock, but then didn't. She'd just have a walk round first, see the animals. Calm the churning in her stomach.

The hyenas were still there, and the tufty-eared wildcats, but not the tiger; a green-eyed wolf paced her old den. And there was the snow-white owl that always used to calm Tom. She watched it for a few minutes but no, her stomach was turning somersaults now.

She'd go and see the lions, then she'd knock on the door of the hut. The crowds in front of the lionesses' dens and Edward's were three or four deep, she couldn't see past them, but there was Crowley, curled up at the back of his, tail twitching, watched only by the family she'd seen at the gate. As she walked over, the father lifted the boy, who yelled 'Wake up!' and threw a stone into the den.

'Hey,' came a shout that made her heart jump – if a heart was able to jump, that is. 'You stop that right now!'

George strode across to the den. He looked exactly the same.

The little boy's father said, 'We were only trying to wake it up.'

'Well, don't,' said George.

Durie walked up behind them and stood watching as he stooped to speak to the boy.

'Do you think you'd like it if someone threw stones at you while you were sleeping?'

The boy shook his head.

'Well, he doesn't like it either. So why don't you go and see the other animals and come back when he's woken up?'

The kind of man who stands up for his lions. With eyes the colour of hazelnuts.

As they walked away, George turned. His face broke into a smile. So that was a good start.

'I've got a lot to tell you,' said Durie. 'And I'm quite nervous about it. So I'm just going to say it all, all right?'

'All right by me,' he said.

She told him about Aunt Ellen burning the letter, and her only knowing about it the night before her wedding. As she was talking, Crowley strolled to the front of his den, for all the world as though he wanted to hear the story.

'She shouldn't have done it but she thought it was for the best. And you'll know, I expect, what happened then.'

'I saw what was in the papers.'

'Did it make you think badly of me?'

'Durie, nothing on this earth could make me think badly of you.'

'Good. Because Aunt Ellen told me you said in the letter you'd never stopped thinking about me. And I never stopped thinking about you. So I wanted to see if you were still . . . thinking about me.'

'I never stopped thinking about you, and I never stopped loving you.'

At that moment, Crowley threw back his head and gave a great roar.

'I think,' said George, 'he's trying to tell us something.'

He lifted her chin and kissed her, gently at first and then not gently at all, and she didn't want to think of Malachy at that moment, but when you've only been kissed by two people, it's hard not to make comparisons. And what she thought was, now I know what it feels like to be kissed by someone who loves me, yours were a very poor imitation. It was like coming home; how could she have thought it ever would be awkward?

He took her hands, looked her up and down and smiled. His smile still made crinkles round his eyes.

'You look just the same,' he said.

'So do you.'

'I like the hat. Are they . . .'

'The monkey bones you gave me, yes.'

'I thought they must be, when I read about it. Made me very happy, that did, and proud. And then I saw you once, must have been three years ago, walking along Tower Street. You had that hat on and you looked as though you were on your way to take on the world.'

Well, she was, wasn't she? And she might not always have won, but she hadn't given up.

'Another thing I've got to tell you,' she said, 'is the story of how I got my name . . .'

Dear Tom,

Another year passed, and with it your sixth birthday. I've told you before how I took you to the Tower menagerie to see the animals, but I don't suppose you'll remember our friend George, who used to carry you around and tell you about them. He remembers you though, and sends his love. We didn't see each other for a long time, George and I, but now we do, a lot. My stepmother Margie always used to say there was someone for everyone, and it turns out she was right.

I wonder what sort of boy you're growing into. Your mother has a wonderful singing voice, perhaps you have that too. She has lots of talents, actually: she's funny, she's cleverer than you'd think, and she knows how to make people like her. That's a very useful thing; I hope you have it too. I've only ever had one talent, but I've learned that's enough, if you use it in the right way.

It will be years before you read this letter, Tom, but when you do, I hope you're as lucky and happy in your life as I am in mine.

Yours,
Aunt Durie

From the *Mercury*, 11 February 1780

In hopes that this letter will reach the eyes of my aunt Durie, surname unknown. You know me as Tom, your nephew given up to the Foundling Hospital on 19 October 1758. If you would be willing, I would very much like to make your acquaintance. Please be assured, I am well-established in life and do not seek to make any claim on you. I simply wish to thank you for the care you gave me as an infant, and the letters you sent me every year, which are among my most precious possessions. I may be contacted at my business premises.

Joseph Phelps
Apothecary
10, Tower Street

Author's Note

All the characters in this book are fictitious, but Endurance and Lucinda Proudfoot were inspired by real people, both of whom I found in the *Oxford Dictionary of National Biography*, an incredible collection of mini-biographies of almost 54,000 people who lived in Britain over the centuries and in some way made their mark (if you're curious, you can access it online with membership of most local libraries). Endurance is loosely based on Sally Mapp, a bonesetter who became famous in eighteenth-century England. She learned bone-setting from her father in their native Wiltshire but after a falling out between them, left home and set up a practice in Epsom, Surrey – even then the town was a centre for horse racing, and tumbles from horses presumably gave Sally some of her customers. She became so successful and well-known that she began travelling to London twice a week, holding consultations in the Grecian Coffee House. Her success upset the medical fraternity who denounced her in the press as a quack, and she features in an engraving by Hogarth which depicts her as such.

There are a number of contemporary newspaper reports

of Sally curing long-standing injuries or deformities in one go, which to modern medical experts sounds unlikely, but we've no way of knowing whether she really was exceptionally skilled, or exactly what techniques she might have used. We do know though that she must have been strong – even with today's muscle relaxants and strong painkillers, it takes a certain amount of strength to set a broken bone or fix (in medical terms, reduce) a dislocation, and it must have taken a lot more when those aids weren't available. It's assumed that that's the reason why, in the absence of a specialist bonesetter, the job was often done by the local farrier, and very rarely by women.

Sally was, sadly, very unlucky both in love and, in the end, in life. Despite being warned off by her friends, she married a footman, who left her after a week, taking a hundred guineas of her money with him. By now known as Crazy Sally for her eccentric ways and short temper, she turned to drink, and eventually died so poor that she had to be buried by the parish.

When I was researching Sally, I found a couple of sources that said her sister was Lavinia Fenton, one of the most famous actresses in Georgian England. She became best known for her role as Polly Peachum in John Gay's *The Beggar's Opera*, which made her, in modern terms, a star – pictures of her sold like hot cakes, and songs and poems were written to her. She caught the eye of the Duke of Bolton, retired from acting to become his mistress and had three sons with him. When his wife died, the pair of them shocked English society by getting married; Lavinia became the Duchess of Bolton and never went back to the stage. It's unclear whether she and Sally Mapp actually were sisters – most sources about Lavinia say she was from London, so I'm inclined to think probably not – but the idea that they might have been was too good a gift for a novelist to ignore.

Acknowledgements

When you write historical fiction, you often need to find out weird little bits of information, and what I discovered while writing this book is that however niche the question, someone on Twitter knows the answer. So my first lot of thanks go to people I've never met: to @aliciakerfoot for helping me find out what kind of shoes an eighteenth-century boy might wear; @bcdonnelly and @ScribblerJB for confirming that the horrid little brat Gregory Philimore could have opened the carriage door from outside; and @travels_along, @Helen_Fields, @jackiesreading, @JonCG, @DianeSetterfie1, @JillCucchi, @CarolineGolds63, @Scott_McArthur and a surprisingly large number of other people who offered suggestions as to how George might turn the deceased monkey into a skeleton. What a weird afternoon on Twitter that was.

As always, thanks to my brilliant writing buddies, Kate Clarke and Lucy Smallwood Barker, who brainstormed ideas, hauled me out of plot holes, read and commented on any number of drafts, gave me the idea for the monkey bones (Kate) and talked me out of adding a daft and unnecessary extra bit of plot at the end (Lucy). Thank you too to my friend Katie Bishop, for telling me about the Tower menagerie – George wouldn't be George without his lions.

A massive thank you to the D20 Authors, for moral support, emergency plot clinics and all the laughs on our Friday Zooms, which have been the highlight of the week through three lockdowns and beyond. The D20s began as a Facebook group of authors who share the weird experience of having launched our first novels into a pandemic, and we've gone on to support each other through our second and for some, third and even fourth books. We've become good friends, even though at the time of writing this most of us have yet to meet, and though I'm obviously biased, I feel I should mention that my D20 mates have produced some seriously good books – follow us on Twitter as @TheD20Authors and you won't go short of great reads.

Thank you to Drs Ben and Philippa Singer and osteopath Amy Thornton, who helped me figure out exactly how Durie and her father might have set about mending bones and fixing dislocations, and what the accompanying sound effects might have been. Any mistakes or tweaks of the facts to serve the story are, of course, down to me. While I'm on the subject of fixing people, not many people get the chance to thank NHS staff in as public a way as this, but given what this story is about, I'm invoking author's privileges to say thank you to the doctors, nurses, orthotists, physios and podiatrists who have, at various times, fixed me, especially Mr William Bartlett at the Whittington Hospital, Mr Shelain Patel at the Royal National Orthopaedic Hospital, Dr Matilde Laura and Professor Mary Reilly at the National Hospital for Neurology and Neurosurgery, and the fantastic teams who work with them (and apologies for the fact that doctors really don't come out of this story very well – different times!).

Thank you to my amazing and inspirational agent, Alice Lutyens, for sound advice, great ideas, her own inimitable brand of cheerleading and the all-caps emails that always make me laugh. I'm too old to say you rock, but you do.

I'm very lucky to have a super-talented editor, Clare Hey, who this time freaked me out with a set of editorial notes that basically amounted to 'Change everything' but was, as always, entirely correct. Editor's notes will always feel a bit like having your homework marked but it helps a lot when you like and respect the teacher as much as I do. Clare – thank you for helping me turn this one round. Thanks too to the team at Simon & Schuster: Judith Long in editorial, Hannah Paget for marketing, Jess Barratt for publicity and the often unsung heroes, the sales team, who get the books into shops, and especially my near neighbour in Hove, Rich Hawton. And to my sharp-eyed and wise but never nitpicky copy editor, Susan Opie, who I can completely trust to spot when a character has been pregnant for thirteen months or daffodils are blooming in July.

This is my second novel, and writing it has been quite a different experience to writing the first one, which, like most debut authors, I'd basically had my entire life to think about. It's harder when there's a deadline, and there's a lot of second guessing yourself. Is it too similar to the first one – or too different? Was the first one a fluke, and you just won't be able to do it a second time? One of the things that kept me going on those days when a scene wouldn't work or a character flatly refused to come to life was seeing Tweets from perfect strangers saying they'd read my first novel, *The Smallest Man*, and liked it. I don't know if people realise how much that means to an author – especially a new one – but I can tell you, it's a lot. So thanks go to them too, and also to Jo Finney and the members of the Good Housekeeping Book Room on Facebook, who had *The Smallest Man* as their Book of the Month and said some lovely things about it. I was also lucky enough to get the book reviewed by some of the best book bloggers around, who do such an incredible job of bringing books and readers together, all in their own time and just for the love of books – thank you.

Finally, a huge thank you to my amazing and very long-suffering husband, Mike Jeffree, for looking after me during the three-month-long part of writing this book when I was mostly horizontal after a foot operation; for doing more than your fair share of cat litter tray duty; and for always knowing when to put the kettle on.

About the Author

Frances Quinn grew up in London and read English at King's College, Cambridge, realising too late that the course would require more than lying around reading novels for three years. After snatching a degree from the jaws of laziness, she became a journalist, writing for magazines including *Prima*, *Good Housekeeping*, *She*, *Woman's Weekly* and *Ideal Home*, and later branched out into copywriting, producing words for everything from Waitrose pizza packaging to the EasyJet in-flight brochure.

She lives in Brighton, with her husband and three Tonkinese cats.

THE
SMALLEST MAN

My name is Nat Davy. Perhaps you've heard of me? There
was a time when people up and down the land knew my
name, though they only ever knew half the story.

The year of 1625, it was, when a single shilling changed
my life. That shilling got me taken off to London, where
they hid me in a pie, of all things, so I could be given
as a gift to the new queen of England.

They called me the queen's dwarf, but I was more than that.
I was her friend, when she had no one else, and later on,
when the people of England turned against their king,
it was me who saved her life. When they turned the
world upside down, I was there, right at the heart
of it, and this is my story.

AVAILABLE IN PAPERBACK AND EBOOK NOW